ALSO BY JAMES BRUNO

PERMANENT INTERESTS

CHASM

TRIBE

A NOVEL BY

JAMES
BRUNO

TRIBE, a novel by James Bruno

First Edition, July 2011

Copyright © 2011 James Bruno

Author Services by Pedernales Publishing, LLC.
www.pedernalespublishing.com

Bittersweet House Press
4477 Ridge Rd.
Cazenovia, NY 13035

ISBN: 978-0-9837642-0-5

Printed in the United States of America

To my daughters, Lara and Annika, and to the daughters of all loving fathers.

Acknowledgements

I thank doctors Steven Cunion, USN (ret.) and Cynthia Jones, and Oliver Brown for educating me on Batten Disease and stem cell therapy. I also thank budding Brit Arabist Tom Parker for his fascinating observations into Yemeni society. I am indebted to my wife, Tosca, who often calls herself a "writer's widow," for putting up with my extended absences, mental as well as physical, to enable me to write. Finally, I extend heartfelt thanks to my friends and colleagues in the intelligence community, who choose to remain anonymous, for their insights into espionage tradecraft, thus, lending added authenticity to my story.

TRIBE

FOREWORD

In 1998, the Taliban concluded an agreement with the American oil exploration firm Unocal to build a thousand-mile pipeline to transport natural gas from Turmenistan across Afghanistan to Pakistan and India, culminating at the Arabian Sea. Civil war in Afghanistan, however, scotched the plan. Pipelines have also been envisioned to tap into Caspian Sea oil reserves estimated at twenty-five percent of the world's total and valued at some $25 trillion at today's prices. The region's natural gas reserves are also vast. Afghanistan lies at the crossroads of this veritable sea of energy.

In the 19th century, Afghanistan was at the center of the so-called "Great Game" in which Imperial Russia and the British Empire competed for power. Its geographical position as a potential transit route for oil and natural gas pipelines makes Afghanistan extremely important in today's Great Game by energy powers to obtain control over these precious resources. Today's players are the United States, Russia and China. This story presents a plausible scenario linking competition for Central Asian petroleum resources with peace in Afghanistan. Those age-old drivers of statecraft, power and money, drive the plot.

As a former official of the Federal government with top secret clearances, I am required to submit for security review to the U.S. Department of State all of my writings prior to publication. This review process has resulted in redactions and text modifications to TRIBE in order to protect what government reviewers deemed sensitive information. These modifications do not, however, impact the integrity and authenticity of this work. It is my aim to present readers with as authentic insights as I can into the workings of our national security apparatus without violating mandated safeguards on classified information. I do not, however, submit to gratuitous censorship. The clearance process is one of negotiation between author and official reviewers in which I have the readers' interests and enjoyment at heart. Given my training and experiences, my novels possess a sense of realism rarely matched in the political thriller genre.

These people play for keeps.

Henry Kissinger

Trust a snake before a harlot, and a harlot before a Pathan...Most true is it in the Great Game, for it is by means of women that all plans come to ruin and we lie out in the dawning with our throats cut.

Rudyard Kipling
Kim

PROLOGUE

The girl lies still. Her ice-blue eyes stare off at some far place. Barely a blink. Unusually, the room is engulfed in shadows, softened by the institutional lighting. The girl breathes slowly. Her lungs take in air as if it were a luxury rather than a necessity. As if she might stop and it wouldn't be a big deal.

The girl's mother stands near her, hand at her mouth, stifling weeping. The girl's father is on the opposite side of the bed. Arms crossed, he is thinking, pondering. Foreign faces, reflecting the universal expression of parental concern. The expression that says, No, not my child. Not this one. Not this one.

The sound of sirens punctures the taut cover of tension around this room with sterile, chemical-laced air. But the ice-blue eyes remain fixed and the elders stay deep into their emotions. The chain of family holds fast, impervious to outside influences.

Drip, drip, drip. The slightly off-color liquid courses from the hanging IV bag through the tube and into the girl's still right arm. Both arms are positioned slightly outward, almost crucifixion-style.

A nurse slips in, her rubber-soled shoes squeaking on the polished gray linoleum. She scans the IV, feels the girl's forehead and bends to look into the crystalline eyes. "How'ya feeling, honey?" she says in a loud whisper.

The eyes shift a fraction toward the nurse, yet betray no emotion. The eyes of a veteran of bad things. Eyes familiar and yet wary.

"It's time for her topamax," the nurse says. Any seizures since last time?"

The parents shake their heads.

"Good," the nurse says.

The girl takes the medicine.

"Atta girl."

"Please miss," the mother says in heavily accented English. "Can we bring her cake?"

"Cake?"

"It's her birthday," the father adds. "She will be thirteen tomorrow. We want to celebrate her birthday."

"Oh, how wonderful," the nurse says. "I don't think there'll be a problem with that. And, hopefully, we can give her a nice birthday present in the form of an early release."

The parents smile wanly. They know they'll be back.

CHAPTER ONE
ISLAMABAD, PAKISTAN

I used to fly into Islamabad in the dead of night, in black C-130s, the U.S. Air Force insignia miniaturized so that only eagles and Clark Kent could make them out. The Paks wanted it that way. The idea was to keep the American government's role in supporting the Afghan *mujahidin* as invisible as possible. After all, our cargoes were lethal. Yet, Allah forbid, should one crash or be shot down with by an SA-7 or, worse, one of our own Stingers, we could claim the marked aircraft was not on a spy mission. Another kind of plausible deniability. Covert guile. Cold War.

Now, CIA personnel fly into the Pakistani capital on commercial aircraft in bright daylight, irrespective of whether we're under cover or not. Islamabad International Airport is like a tiny patch of unblemished skin on the otherwise pocked face of an impoverished country. Modern, spiffy, efficient. Much like Islamabad itself, an artificial new city which belies the hand-to-mouth existence of 172 million people.

I pass quickly through immigration and customs with my black diplomatic passport in hand – in my real name. Two people await me past the customs posts: a white face and a brown one. The former is a junior officer from Islamabad station; the latter a Pak intel agent whose excessive efforts to make himself inconspicuous have the opposite effect. His task is to follow me.

"Larry O'Connor," the junior officer says as he offers his hand. This blond, clean-cut, horn-rim-spectacled generation-Y-er looks like he just stepped out of the Harvard MBA program – except that Harvard MBAs shun the CIA. He has been here a while, judging by his combination Indiana Jones bush jacket and caftan trousers.

After, "How was your flight?" "The weather is hell here now," the usual banter, Larry's face darkens. "It's hard to operate in this place, do anything here," he says with a gesture toward the pick-up with two armed Pak guards that leads our vehicle, itself a fully armored Toyota Landcruiser with inch-thick bullet-proof windows. Pakistan is a dangerous place for U.S. officials, the targets of Islamist assassins. "Fifty percent danger pay helps, but it's still tough. It's hard to have a life much less do your job," he adds. The rest remains unstated but looms in the air like a foul gas. Since the rise in Islamist terrorism, eight American diplomatic staff have been ambushed, gunned down or bombed in cold blood in this country.

With that, no shop talk. Opsec – operational security – requires us to save business for the "skiff," or Secure Conferencing Facility at the embassy, commonly referred to by laymen as the "bubble."

Larry begins to speak, then swallows whatever it was he was about to say.

"Yeah?" I ask.

He looks at the back of the head of our Pakistani driver and ponders a moment. "Hey, Ahmed, plug in the cd, will ya?" The driver obliges. *Guns and Roses* fills the air. Just loud enough not to assault the senses.

"I mean, you're a legend out here. They, the Pushtuns, talk about you in awe. 'When is Harry returning?' 'God is great and so is Harry.' 'In his last life, Harry was a Pushtun.' You're the Lawrence of the Afghans."

I smile. "The Pushtuns have a saying: 'Trust your family and God.' If you win their trust, they are friends for life."

"The station," he says under his breath. "They're all jealous of you. Half have a positive jealousy. They want to emulate you. The rest, well, they're frustrated little geeks. They see you as a threat."

We pull into the high-walled, heavily guarded embassy compound. A local guard opens the hood while another passes a mirror on a long stick underneath the chassis. They're checking for hidden explosives. A U.S. Marine checks our ID's. There is good reason for the heavy security, apart from the present danger. In 1979, a mob stormed the compound and burned it down. It was subsequently quickly rebuilt, down to the last detail, based on the original blueprint.

It is a handsome structure, as American embassies go. A red-brick façade gives it a Federalist air, while broad windows and metal beams lend a modern touch. We pass another checkpoint, a bullet-proof booth manned by two Marines in fatigues. One presses a button and salutes smartly. The heavy metal door buzzes. Larry uses both arms to pull it open. Female staff sometimes need a lending male hand to budge this portal to American power.

I haven't been inside the place in years. The faces, of course, have changed, but otherwise the embassy has altered little. I feel at home.

We get off the elevator and face another vault-like door, this one with an electric push-button cipher lock. Larry quickly presses the five-digit combination and this door too buzzes open. Islamabad station lies before us. Nothing mysterious about it. Just a bunch of small offices, cubicles, fluorescent lights and computer terminals. Bureaucrats and their helpers flit about with papers in their hands. Others slump in front of their terminals, laboring over intel reports, ash and trash, letters to their insurance companies, whatever.

Larry guides me to the only sizable office amid the warrens, that of the chief of station, Kyle Handley.

Handley gets up from behind his desk and shakes hands. He has a direct, penetrating stare, his way of checking you out, to see if you have the guts to stare him right back. One of the many tricks of the control freak. His huge hand clamps down on the visitor's like a vise. Another trick. If Handley didn't open his mouth, one would peg him for a Bavarian butcher. Big, beefy, cheeky, ruddy-faced. Two pounds of sirloin, please.

"Good to see you again," he says flatly.

"Likewise," I lie.

"How's it feel to be back in your old stomping grounds?"

"This time I'm not stomping."

"Good," Handley says without missing a beat.

On a wall is a painting displaying a small horde of victorious Central Asian warriors huddled around a table bellowing at a scribe with quill pen on parchment. A small plaque says, *The Zaparozhnye Cossacks Draft a Reply to the Turkish Sultan -- Ilya Repin.*

"Diplomacy. The way it used to be practiced," Handley says with a chuckle. "At least in this part of the world."

I nod and smile.

On Handley's desk is another plaque: *Happiness is to Slaughter All Thy Enemies and to Hear the Wails and Lamentations of Their Women and Children -- Attila the Hun.*

Handley the barbarian. A real cut-up. The kind of guy who gives the Agency a good name. The fact of the matter is, Handley's reputation within the Agency is not far off the mark reflected in these gews-gaws of adolescent humor. "Handley takes no prisoners." "Handley machine-guns the survivors," are some of the refrains that infuse his corridor reputation.

"Since you're not stomping, the next flight back is exactly eighteen hours from now."

Save the diplomatic obliqueness for the State guys. "Can't complete an op at 30,000 feet," I say. "Look, let's cut the crap. TALISMAN is locked and loaded. We have a 24-hour window to pull the trigger and send al-Qaeda in Afghanistan to hell in a billion pieces."

Handley is leaning back in his chair, hands clasped behind his beefy neck, tie loose. He exhibits a smug cat-ate-the-canary look on his fat face.

"Oh! You haven't heard?"

"Heard what?"

"TALISMAN's been canceled."

"What do you mean, 'canceled'?"

"Canceled, as in your mission is ended. As in, get your ass back on the next plane out of here." He hands me a document.

It's a cable from headquarters.

CENTRAL INTELLIGENCE AGENCY
S E C R E T 301515Z AUG STAFF
CITE DIRECTOR 517911
TO: IMMEDIATE ISLAMABAD
WNINTEL RYBAT
SUBJECT: TERMINATION OF OPERATION TALISMAN
REF: DIRECTOR 419577

1. ALL OPS RE OPERATION TALISMAN ARE HEREBY SHUT DOWN.

2. OPSOFF BRENNAN TO RETURN TO HEADQUARTERS ASAP.

3. NO FILE. ALL SECRET

I don't believe it. I read it again. "All ops re Operation TALISMAN are hereby shut down." Clear as the cloudless Punjabi sky. A year of intensive preparations for a covert

mission aimed at knocking al-Qaeda in Afghanistan out of
the box. Tortuous negotiations and coordination with testy,
fight-happy Pushtun tribes helped along by a steady stream
of C-notes and hard-to-procure black market weaponry,
down the drain. A small army of ops officers like myself
dismissed and dispersed. Zawahiri and other al-Qaeda
leaders lurk in these parts. And the pressure is lifted with
nine words through the ether. TALISMAN is shut down. I
just don't believe it.

I look up at Handley. "What's this all about?" I demand.

He sports a smug grin. "This is Kipling country. 'Ours is
not to reason why. Ours is but to do and die.' Now, you've
got seventeen hours and thirty-seven minutes till your flight
departs."

He leans forward in his chair.

"Let's understand each other," he says. "Till that time,
everything you do, you do it within the confines of this
embassy. And I will be kept informed of everything you
do. You talk to the political counselor, I wanna know. Go
call on some Pak officials? Out of the question. Take a ride
outside the capital? I'll have your head. Need to take a piss?
You have my permission to do so without my approval –
within the confines of this embassy. Do we understand each
other?"

"Gee, now let me get this straight. When I wake up in
the morning, do I rush in a taxi from my hotel to piss in the
embassy loo or directly on your desk just to prove that I'm
following the ground rules?"

The Ox belies his size and rushes nimbly at me as if I
were holding a red cape. Before I can comprehend what's
happening he's in my face, all red and blubbery. I can smell
the aftermath of a garlicky South Asian lunch on his breath.

"Listen you wise-ass fucker. I run this station. All spies
here obey the station chief. You included. Otherwise, I'll see

to it that your boney ass is on the next Pak ballistic missile out of this rotten place. Do we understand each other, mister?"

I feel as if my face were just exposed to Pakistan's latest nuclear explosion. The radiation fall-out from his curried breath alone leaves me semi-paralyzed.

"No problem, chief," I answer. "You're the boss."

Handley leans back. The cold, dark eyes are again boring in on me. "You know, Brennan. I don't trust you. Your reputation here bears that out. But I respect you. You've got balls and balls are hard to find among our post-cold war, affirmative actioned, Congress-scrutinized crowd. Just play by my rules. Get my drift?"

"I think we understand each other," I say enigmatically.

"Good," Handley replies.

Being Irish has never done me any good in the follow orders department. I'm convinced the ancient Hibernians were a lost Pushtun tribe. Or maybe it's the other way around. I go in search of TALISMAN. The four-hour ride to the Khyber Pass is not bad. The road is smooth, well-maintained, a costly affair for a dirt-poor country. It is a strategic road, a military superhighway to enable the Paks to move troops and equipment rapidly in response to conflicts erupting on their volatile western border.

The small van breezes along the stretch at a rapid clip, occasionally steering suddenly clear of an ox cart, flock of chickens or playing kids. After a couple of hours, we come to Peshawar, the last sizable town before one reaches the Afghan border. This indeed is Kipling country, an unruly place little changed in many ways since the heady days of the British Raj. Pushtun women navigate dusty streets peering through the narrow slits of cotton body-bag *burkahs*, fierce, bearded tribal males troop by with weapons slung over their shoulders. These arms are not of Victoria's era, however. They are a limitless array of Russian, Chinese, East European, British and even some American guns, grenades and sidearms. At the insistence of the Paks, the heavier stuff – rocket launchers and mortars – are checked at the gate of the Khyber Pass. These modern tools of war and the ubiquitous white Toyota landcruisers and pickup trucks, in contrast to the ancient walled setting, mark the time as the turn of this century and not the last.

The smelter-like atmosphere exudes a punishing heat and white light which takes one's mind temporarily off the odors of ox dung, pungent spices and stale sweat that is a hallmark of the subcontinent. My head swims, not from the assault on my senses, but from a jarring resurfacing of memories that such sensations trigger. Of war, intrigue, fear, death and love.

My companion and guide on this journey is Haji Rakhman, an old friend. He is a learned man, younger than myself, a graduate of Peshawar's Islamia College. Haji is not his first name. It means someone who has done the *haj*, the pilgrimage to the holy city of Mecca which all Muslims are supposed to undertake at least once in their lifetime. It is an appellation of honor. In the '80s, Rakhman and I collaborated on collecting intelligence on Soviet troop deployments to enable the Afghan mujahidin to target their enemy more effectively. I, armed with satellite photographs and signals intercepts; he, with eyewitness accounts and the occasional defector. Together we strove mightily to expand Russia's hell.

"But, Harry. I do not understand why you must hide from your own people," says the balding, bearded Rakhman. He gawks at me and laughs. "You are dressed like an Afghan, but you walk like Ricky Martin."

I am seized with an attack of self-consciousness. I look down on my sheer *salwar kameez* outfit and leather boots.

Looks okay to me. I straighten the cloth *lungee* turban binding my head.

"I'm out of practice, I guess. It's been a while, let's face it."

"But you still shoot as straight as an eagle's gaze, I am sure." He hands me a Marine-issue Beretta M9 pistol. It is the same gun I used to pack in my heyday here, preferring it over the CIA's adoptive handgun, the Browning "King of Nines" 9mm. Rakhman has carefully stowed the thing for me all these years. I take it, try out the grip and trigger, then stuff it inside my belt. I place my hand on Rakhman's shoulder and smile. "You forget nothing," I say.

"As we Afghans say, 'Forget your enemies, but never your friends.'"

From the van it is a short distance to the small *Qissa Khwami* Tea House chosen in advance as our rendezvous point with Engineer Bashir. The title "Engineer" connotes great learnedness among the semi-literate Afghans, whether or not a person actually has an engineering background.

"You Afghans do not monopolize treachery, my friend," I say.

"Hah!" exclaims Haji Rakhman. "Explain no further. We Afghans understand such things. We just don't expect you Americans to be quite as…complicated as ourselves. After all, we are a tribal people."

The tea house is dark and smoky. Klatsches of men hover around short tables, their low rumble of conversation rolls through the place like a distant thunderstorm. A storyteller in a far corner regales a small crowd with tales of ancient valor and noble tragedy. Women are not to be seen in this establishment, in custom with the sexual apartheid of the Afghans.

He stands before me with arms outstretched, wider around the girth and grayer at the temples from when I'd last seen Bashir over a dozen years before. He lets out a bellow of a laugh.

"Ahh! My American commander. You bless us again with your presence." We embrace and press cheek to cheek in the Afghan manner.

"It is Allah's will," I reply.

"Maybe yes, maybe no. But you are still an infidel," Bashir admonishes.

He gestures me to sit. He pours green tea into three small glasses.

As he does this, he nods toward the street. "And I see you do not come alone."

I look out and see a heavy-set man loitering across the street. His street clothes, short, uncovered hair and mustache sans beard mark him as a Pakistani operative.

A knot tightens in my stomach. "ISI?" The Interservices Intelligence Directorate is Pakistan's spy agency.

"Who else?" says Bashir with a shrug.

"Shit."

"Do not blame yourself, my friend. They follow me. They probably don't know who you are. Then again, we knew the instant you arrived in this country. Which means so did ISI."

"The station tipped them off."

"Your agency. They are scoundrels. And there is more, much more. Taliban know no limits to their evil. They mouth the Koran, but they are not Muslims. They slaughter whole villages, women and children. They poison wells. Now they grow opium. They learned from the Soviets."

"Show me."

Bashir exchanges a look with Haji Rakhman. He sips his tea and ponders. In the distance, a muezzin's call to prayer wafts on the winds, a sinuous harkening to eternity.

"Who am I helping," Bashir asks. "The CIA or Mr. Harry Brennan?"

"As you say, we are also a complicated people."

"I will help you, Harry. Only you."

As we leave the tea house, in the corner of my eye I spot a male fast approaching from the rear. I pull my Beretta, spin around and aim point-blank at his face.

"Whoa! I'm one of the good guys!" His hands are in the air.

"Shit, O'Connor!" I retract the gun and reholster it inside my garb. "Keep on approaching men around here like that and you won't live to see your next promotion."

"Uh, right. Guess you got a point there," he replies.

O'Connor is also in full Aghan dress, choosing a handsome *chapan* coat and round *pakol* hat. Blond stubble adorns his face.

"How'd you know I was here?! That pig-face Handley sent you! So, the station's taken to tailing its own people..."

He waves both hands in front of his chest as if to deflect my verbal onslaught. "Chill. Will ya'?"

I stop and listen.

"So, there's these two Irishmen in Afghanistan for the first time, and their captain promises them twenty bucks for every Taliban they kill. Pat lays down to rest, and Mick takes up the watch. Pat hasn't rested long when he's awakened by Mick shouting, 'They're comin!'

'Who's comin'?' shouts Pat.

'The Taliban,' replies Mick.

'How many are there?'

'Gotta be at least two thousand.'

'Begorrah,' shouts Pat, jumping up and grabbing his rifle, 'Our fortune's made!'"

Silence. I stare at him speechless.

O'Connor smiles sheepishly.

"Let me get this. Two micks go off to Afghanistan to fight and..."

"We're a wild, fight-crazed race," O'Connor says. "I want in. You're going through with Talisman, aren't you? I can help."

"Handley doesn't know you're here then?"

"Hell no. Nobody knows."

I place my arm around the young man's shoulders and pull him a few paces away from earshot of others.

"O'Connor…"

"Larry."

"OK, Larry. Yes, the Irish can be a wild, fight-crazed race, suicidal even. But just because I commit professional suicide, doesn't mean you should too. If Handley knows…"

"Screw Handley," retorts O'Connor. "I don't care. I didn't become a spy just to sit behind a desk and process reports. I've been here six months and Handley treats me like I was his *chai wallah*, his tea boy. And this canceling of Talisman is wrong, it's immoral. We'll lose a generation of Afghans if we betray them like this."

I pause and ponder his earnest face. His eyes show a steely determination. I know that the only thing to deter him would be physical force.

"In for a dime, in for a dollar," I say.

"*'Pe harakat ke barakat dey.'* Pushtu saying. 'In movement there is blessing.' Let's go!"

We enter Afghanistan plum, smack through the Khyber Pass, typical of the boldness of Bashir. He and three men in the pickup and myself; I in Afghan garb, my beard coming well along, and ever vigilant not to strut like Ricky Martin. We pass ourselves off as traders. The checkpoints on both sides of the border are notoriously cursory. When they were in control, the Taliban borderguards used to search for music cassettes. Reams of recording tape waved at the top of poles like banners greeting the condemned at the gates of hell. Music was outlawed in Afghanistan, as was television and virtually all other manner of entertainment; the rules were enforced by humorless, born-again Islamic hillbillies. Ruled as a one-party theocratic state, Taliban-ruled Afghanistan exceeded the early New England Puritans in religious fervor and moral oppression – until American cruise missiles and strategic bombers blew them out of power in early 2002.

It takes a day to reach Jalalabad on the cratered road and another to arrive at the capital, Kabul. We make it through the many additional warlord-controlled checkpoints. Bashir greases the way with small payments.

In the '80's, I'd done my part to kick the Soviet occupiers of Afghanistan in the ass and then some, but I'd never been to Kabul. It was merely a name in intelligence and news reports, the seat of power of Moscow's puppet government, but otherwise an abstraction in my distracted mind.

Kabul is part urban wasteland of bombed-out neighborhoods, gutted infrastructure and masses of displaced people living hand-to-mouth, and part boom-town.

We stay overnight with contacts of Bashir. Next morning before dawn, we head out with two more escorts northward to the Panjshir.

The dust and heat take their toll on me. Bashir sees this.

"Not much longer," he says.

I look forward to the five times each day that we stop so that our troupe can get out, lay their prayer rugs on the ground and pray toward Mecca. Fresh air, a piss and an opportunity to stretch.

We arrive in the town of Golbahar, at the entrance of the Panjshir Valley. The resurgent Taliban have returned here. Their fighters, most appear to be barely into their teens, are everywhere. Golbahar is a city under occupation.

"When we lost this part of the Panjshir, they went at our people with a vengeance," Bashir says. "Here we split up so we do not draw attention to ourselves."

We are hidden with more members of Bashir's network during the day. Bashir, a young underling named Yunis and O'Connor and I head out at sundown on mules in a northeasterly direction. Haji Rakhman and the others leave at different times in the same direction, all to link up again at Ruka.

The reach of any authority ends here. Jamiat-e-Islami fighters, loyal to Commander Mohammad Rahim, appear out of the hills. They rejoice upon seeing Bashir; many embraces and greetings. Every living being totes a gun, a rocket launcher, a mortar, ammunition, the whole array of lethality for guerrilla combat. We sit with a local chieftain for tea. Ibrahim is pushing seventy, if a day. He is a robust man, his hair and beard dyed henna-orange.

"Ibrahim was the town chief of Paghmani," Bashir says. "Now Paghmani is no more." He repeats this in Pushtu. Ibrahim nods gravely and rattles off his own commentary.

"He says Taliban rounded up the people after we were defeated in battle and slaughtered them. Everyone. They buried them in mass graves. They then turned their houses over to the Arabs."

"Arabs? Where?"

"We show you, commander Harry. Come."

Outside of Ruka we link up with Rakhman and the others. We are now two dozen men meandering the serpentine paths of the hills on the south side of the valley. We pass through three deserted hamlets. Each had been vacated in the past several months, ghost towns now. Those inhabitants who managed to escape the brutal fury of the Taliban fled to Kabul or Pakistan.

We set up camp several miles from Paghmani. Scouts are sent out to survey. Additional fighters of Bashir are massing on the opposite ridge over Paghmani. Bashir instructs them to stay low and take no action until ordered to do so.

"What's going on?" I ask.

"Operation TALISMAN," Bashir replies.

"Everything's in place?" I say.

"We will proceed with the operation, upon your command," he says. "Come."

Scouts take us to an overlook, concealed by brush and rock outcroppings. Bashir is handed binoculars. After exchanges with his men, he hands them to me.

"Look," he says.

I view the erstwhile town of Paghmani, nestled in a depression. Among the mud houses and simple wood structures, I see men, only men, working, drilling, carrying out daily chores. Many are armed. Small, dirt bunkers encircle the settlement. The barrels of heavy machine guns and mortars jut through sand bags.

Bashir points to two long wooden buildings with metal roofs.

"You see those? They are their schools."

"But I see no kids."

Bashir pats me on the back and laughs. "These are schools not for children, my friend."

I look at him.

"Yes. They are schools of terror."

"Al-Qaeda."

Bashir nods. "So, Harry. These are the Arabs we were told to find and destroy. They train here. To kill you." He pokes his index finger into my sternum. "Al-Zawahiri is here. Or, at least his men."

"Ayman al-Zawahiri? Successor to Osama bin-Laden?"

"The very same."

I stare at Bashir.

"You see Taliban troops over there?" He points to the far ridge.

I nod. "They're there to provide security for the Arabs."

"Yes. Now your agency, your CIA, with the Pakistanis, tasked us to do destroy them. I was meant to be here, to crush the Arabs and to fight the Taliban," Bashir says almost too loudly for comfort. "And now they tell us to leave them alone. Why?"

"I don't know," I reply.

"So, what do we do, Harry? Let them be, or kill them?"

TALISMAN was exceedingly well planned, supported with superb intelligence. It would also reflect well on the U.S. and its Pakistani and Afghan allies. So, why do they call it off, with no explanation?

"We're locked and loaded. Let's pull the trigger now," urges O'Connor.

"Harry, we need to act now! Our moment will be lost. We must fight or run! So, what do we do, Harry? What do we do?"

I look down into the valley. My country's worst enemy. The same folks who brought us 9/11. Osama bin-Laden's own. They'll strike us again. No doubt about it. Do I salute and follow orders which make no sense? Or pull the trigger now, as O'Connor says? It's a no-brainer.

"Let's do it!," I say.

Bashir smiles. He barks a command into his radio.

A distant explosion thunders. We all turn.

Bashir brings the binoculars to his eyes. "See, Harry. Look."

There are more explosions, the thump of mortar rounds, small arms fire breaks out. Below I witness the Arabs running in all directions like rabbits. Bashir's fighters have deployed in an arc around the encampment and are firing freely. Clearly caught by surprise, the Arabs don't stand a chance, surrounded in their own little Dien Bien Phu. Other fighters trap the Taliban men and easily annihilate them on the ridge.

It takes Bashir's troops less than an hour to complete their operation. We watch as they stream down to Paghmani, the lead squad with the red, black and green flag of Afghanistan unfurled in the breeze. More small arms fire as the last Arab hold-outs fight to the death. Bashir's troops mop up. We see them kicking bodies and plugging fallen Arabs in the head either to finish them off or to make sure they're dead.

"Hooray!" Rakhman shouts, arms extended. "*Allahu akbar!*" God is great!

Over lunch of flat bread and dried meat, we discuss what we just witnessed.

I furrow my eyebrows as I try to piece it all together.

"TALISMAN was meant to knock a big blow against al-Qaeda and to check the Taliban. Bin-Laden's followers and the Taliban are blood brothers. For over a decade, the U.S. has been attacking al-Qaeda camps inside Afghanistan, first with cruise missiles, later with air and ground assets, especially drones. Al-Qaeda clandestinely install themselves at this location. We learn about it and spend months setting up TALISMAN to annihilate them not only here but throughout Afghanistan. Then, with no explanation, Washington calls it off. I shake my head. "I don't get it. Why?"

"Exactly," says Bashir. "Our side gets sold out to Taliban in the process." He looks at me with the face of a man betrayed.

"It wasn't me, Bashir. You must believe me," I say.

"I know, Harry."

"Who then?"

Bashir shrugs. "If I knew this, Harry, I would now be president of Afghanistan." He lets out a deep breath of resignation.

"Hm. A deal. A fix is in. The truth will come out," I say.

"*Inshallah*," says Bashir with a gesture skyward. If God wills it.

Our journey back is uneventful. The breathtaking, snow-capped peaks of the Hindu Kush loom over us like gods in repose, reminding that beauty can exist next to tragedy in a blood-soaked land like Afghanistan. The rushing, frigid waters of the Kabul River inspire awe for nature's grandeur. We forget for some moments the pain, sadness and betrayal that afflict this land. We bathe, enjoy a picnic. AK's always at the ready, however, keep us close to reality.

Bashir's fighters split off and return to their villages. The pickup with Rakhman and three others also peels off; they stay in Jalalabad for a day. Our pickup with Bashir, a driver, a bodyguard in the back, O'Connor and myself continues on back toward the border. It's been a week since I sneaked out of Islamabad in direct contravention of Handley's orders. I ponder this. Having to confront that pig-knuckle face and nitro-glycerin temper adds to the nausea I feel from day-after-day of bad Afghan trail food.

We fuel up and eat in Torkham, a dusty, hardscrabble town only thirty-five miles from the Pak frontier. Bashir spots agents surveilling us outside the little restaurant.

"Paks," he spits. "They miss nothing here. We'd better go now." Bashir wipes his mouth with the back of his hand and rises. The bodyguard picks up on Bashir's body language and releases the lock on his AK. We tumble out into the street and jump into the pickup.

We race through the arid, rolling landscape between Torkham and the border. The land is desolate. Shards of rusting steel jut out of the cracked earth in places along the way, mute reminders of the mayhem of war. The traffic on both sides of the pocked road picks up the closer we get to the pass. The surrounding terrain narrows into a passage, in places broad as a mile, in others as tight as fifty feet. Inside the cab, the air is tense and still. My stomach continues to grumble, crying out for pepto-bismol. Bile gushes up into

my mouth in between gastric belches. My supply of Lomotil
has run out, but I don't want to interrupt our journey with
too many pit stops. I struggle with my digestive system.
Down boy, easy now. Not much longer to go.

We reach a narrowing of the pass which turns sharply to
the right. We see a makeshift checkpoint where a couple of
disheveled soldiers are checking papers in what appears to be
another shakedown operation to exact "tolls" from travelers.

Bashir mutters something in Pushtu which I sense is best
left untranslated. I notice the guard in the rear unlatching
the safety on his AK-47. I discreetly reach into my belt and
follow suit with my M9, confident that I will not lose my
manhood over a jarring bump in the road because of an
overly sensitive double-action trigger.

We wait as the soldiers carry on vociferous negotiations
with the drivers ahead of us. Bashir takes out a leather pouch
and removes several pink Pakistani rupee notes. It is now
our turn.

One of the soldiers, a semi-toothless bloke with one
wandering eye and the odor of countless bathless days, sticks
his head in and looks around. He's talking to me. My heart
pounds. Bashir answers in my stead. The smelly man again
rattles off something directed at me and orders Bashir to shut
up. I can act deaf and dumb, reveal myself as a foreigner, or
shoot this fellow in the head and hope for the best.

Ahead of us the road is empty. The gap between us
and the vehicles to our rear lengthens as two more soldiers,
heretofore not visible, order them to back up.

Bashir's eyes catch what's happening. "When I say three,
we kill them," he says with the matter-of-factness of a
weather reporter.

Funny thing about life-threatening circumstances. One's
mind – or mine, at least – becomes more lucid and rational
than under normal situations; as if one's brain is always

half checked-out except when confronted with survival, whereupon every gram of one's senses gets mobilized to keep one alive. People talk about events moving in slow motion when facing, say, an aircraft plunging noseward toward the earth, or a mugger blasting them at short-range. Having had my share of life-endangering experiences, I attribute this sensation to the mind's collecting every detail. The brain is in overdrive, studying the immediate environment, every scintilla of experience, and analyzing it all in electron-fast motion, looking, searching, screaming for a way out.

The hideous man is still addressing me, only now he's shouting. Spit spews from his lips and gloms onto his beard. His eyes are bloodshot. He smells of rotting food and body odor. His teeth are yellowed and broken. My mind registers no shock as his brains splatter the inside of our windshield. Bashir's Makarov is a mere three inches from the soldier's head. I see the man's eyes, including the wandering one, roll back into his head. I see him fall back, his arms extended, his beat-up rifle falling to the earth.

I pull my M9 out reflexively. I look back to the sounds of automatic fire. The bodyguard has his AK shouldered and is firing away at the soldier in front of us. The man catches several rounds in the legs and drops, screaming.

The other "soldiers," now clearly revealed as Taliban, have taken positions behind rock outcroppings and are blasting at us. Our driver has swung his own Uzi from under the seat and is having at them from behind the left door. A series of rounds from automatic fire rips through the center of the pickup's hood, the windshield, into the seat and up into the back window. Bashir and I look at each other. Neither is injured.

"Out! Now!" he yells. And rolls onto the dusty road. He slams another clip into his gun and shoots, taking careful aim and time between rounds, to my astonishment. Bashir has survived by being cooler than the rest.

The driver jumps into a ditch. As he lifts himself up and signals us to follow him, he catches a bullet in his shoulder. He flies back, his Uzi drops. Bashir and the guard follow and take positions several yards apart. I'm on their heels. I spot a head popping up from the rocky peak above us. I aim and shoot. The head rises. I shoot again, at his chest. The man remains standing, but gapes desperately at the cloudless sky. He drops to his knees and falls forward down the promontory. His still body comes to an abrupt halt close enough to me to see his lifeless eyes staring at me, the mute admonishment of the dead.

A projectile slams into our pickup. The B-40 round explodes, igniting a secondary explosion from the vehicle's gas tank. We duck. Shards of metal and glass cut through the air. I hear a man's scream, but cannot ascertain whether it's one of theirs or ours.

The pop-pop-pop of automatic fire intensifies. We hear the roar of large engines. Racing down the road in our direction is a Soviet-made APC loaded with troops. Its 7.62mm top-mounted gun is blasting at us. The closer it gets, the deadlier the aim.

Our driver has recovered himself and is again firing his Uzi with one hand. The guard carefully picks off the enemy with short reports from his weapon, sign of a highly trained professional fighter. Bashir and I train our sights on those enemy who manage to reach close range. Off to the right, I see O'Connor fearlessly – recklessly – standing, his left hand steadying his right wrist, as he fires his pistol in deliberate, well-aimed shots. But we're running out of ammo. We know it. We also know the end of this nightmare is nigh. My "rational" mind manages to ponder whether I'll be written up in American newspapers ("CIA Agent Slain in Afghanistan") or whether I'll simply be unaccounted for; for the Agency, this is probably the more desirable outcome. Maybe, just maybe, they'll chisel a single black star in the CIA's main lobby alongside the eighty-seven other officers who lost their lives in the line of duty. It occurs to me, I'm not in the line of duty. I'm a renegade bucking orders here. Got to stay alive. Got to stay alive for my kid.

A sharp pain punctures my side. I drop. My mind races. Yes, the nightmare is coming to an end. Or will it? What if they take me alive? What sport their torturers would make of an American spy. Or Taliban and al-Qaeda propagandists. The sorts of revenge they could take are limited only by the imagination.

I feel myself losing consciousness. I struggle to get up, but my head is swirling. I keep a grip on my M9. That I won't let go. Stay alive...for...for...I shake my head to stave off the encircling darkness. I see my cohorts through a fading blur, firing madly away at their attackers. The darkness takes over.

CHAPTER TWO

"Die asshole!"

I open my eyes, blink. White permeates everything. Fluorescent white lights. White walls. White bed sheets.

"I hope you die. If you live, I'll kill your career, at least."

The foul breath and sirloin face bring back a bad memory into my aching head. Handley.

"You hear me, shithead?"

"Not if I can help it," I say. A ham hock fist comes straight at me like a ground-to-air missile. It stops inches from my face, restrained in the nick of time by both of Larry O'Connor's arms. The young man is flush red as he strains to physically hold back this raging bull.

"Sir. The man's a hospital patient. He's one of us. You can't do this, Larry stammers through strained breathing.

"Yah." Handley about-faces, goes over to the window, his back to me, hunched over with knuckles planted squarely on the sill instead of in my face. He takes several deep breaths.

After two silent, tense minutes, Handley speaks. His voice is eerily calm. "You know, I enlisted in the Army at eighteen, spent ten years there. Two tours in Vietnam. Joined the Agency when the nuclear holocaust clock was two minutes to midnight. We played ultra-hardball with the Soviets in the field. People sometimes ask if I ever killed anybody." Handley rubs his nose vigorously.

"You know what? Not only have I never killed a non-combatant, I never even laid a hand on another human being. Not since high school anyway."

While this overweight Hamlet carries on with his soliloquy, I do a systems check on my body. How long had I been out? How damaged am I? And this clown is threatening a hospital patient with bodily harm, imprecating him with death. I move my left leg, then my right. They work. Next, my arms. Ditto. Gingerly, I run one hand along my chest, down my abdomen. Meantime, my head feels like Desert Storm was just fought in it. I continue my manual check. Whew! Vital parts seem intact. Then I feel it, fresh stitches, followed by a sharp pain as I touch the wound. I wince.

I turn to O'Connor, ignoring Hamhead, and say, "What happened to me?"

Without missing a beat, answering me as if we had just turned up for happy hour at Hooter's after a hard day of selling computer software, O'Connor says, "You took one in the side. Missed your kidney by a millimeter, the surgeon said. It was small caliber. Knocked you off balance. You landed on your noggin, struck you unconscious."

Handley turns on his heel. "Shut up, O'Connor. What do you think this is? *E.R?* And you can take your career, or what's left of it, up your sorry ass. You think Pakistan is a pile of shit? For your insubordination, I'll see to it that you end up in a place that makes this one look like the Riviera. Now get outta here."

The younger man shuffles out of the room.

"I don't take temperature through the rectum, nurse," I quip jocularly at Handley, but he doesn't seem to appreciate the humor.

He returns to my bed and thrusts one fat index finger toward the bridge of my nose. "Maybe not a thermometer, pal. But be prepared to take your career and your whole sorry future up your ass. 'Cause that's what's going to happen. I'll see to it personally."

Handley struggles to contain his rage. "You disobeyed my explicit instructions not to leave Islamabad. Not only that, but you illegally enter Afghanistan, hook up with armed rabble there and then get yourself inconveniently wounded after executing an op headquarters canceled. Are you out of your fucking mind?!" He takes a deep breath, and in a calm voice laced with satisfaction, says, "That kind of insubordination verges on criminal. You're finished, Brennan. Kaput. I'm seeing to that. We've reported every last detail to headquarters."

"Oh, did you include the part about how this station yanked the rug from under our allies, unilaterally torpedoed TALISMAN, which saves al-Qaeda and the Taliban?"

Handley ignores this. "You've got three days to heal. Then we're putting you on the next flight back to D.C. I'm firing off a cable recommending a strong reprimand and dismissal." He nods in the direction of a thin Pakistani man standing outside my door. "Meantime, at my personal request, our good friends at ISI have assigned people to cover you twenty-four-hours a day." With one beefy hand, he taps my wound, causing me to cry out. "For your own protection, Gunga Din. Ha!"

I take a deep breath as the pain subsides. "Does this mean we're finished?" I ask in mock remorse.

"It means *you're* finished, Brennan."

"Who put those cruds up to ambushing me? Just try and get me fired! Who did it, Handley?" I shout as he storms out the door.

After three days, I'm far from healed. Nevertheless, I'm unceremoniously escorted to the airport by two embassy security officers, who stand on the tarmac watching the aircraft until the doors are secured. Just to make sure I don't get any wild ideas like slithering out of the plane and hooking back up with *mujahidin* for a bumpy 200-mile jeep-cum-donkey ride over cratered roads in bombed-out Afghanistan with a leaking stitched-up wound over my right kidney.

The Karachi-to-Frankfurt flight is a long one. Ten hours of monotony. Sleep in coach is not an option for a six-foot-two-inch post-operative trouble-maker with lots on his mind. And good Muslims that they are, Pakistan International Airlines serves no booze.

My mind turns the mental reel back; back to the ambush. Back to Paghmani, our successful elimination of an Arab terrorist camp in defiance of strict orders; back to Peshawar, the ISI agents surveilling us; back to what made me decide to return; back to Handley. To my now very conflicted emotions.

I arrive in Frankfurt with no answers and still no sleep. I catch my connecting flight to the U.S. and face another agonizing and restless journey. It's as much a journey of my soul as of physical distance. I desperately need to anchor myself in something meaningful, something normal, something that is me. At JFK, I pass up the last leg, to Dulles Airport. Instead, I amble over to a commuter airline in time to catch that day's flight to Burlington.

I haven't seen my daughter in five months. The ease of phone and email contact has kept us close to each other, but only by long distance. I breathe deeply of the rich northern summer air that whips through the rental car. The drive to Middlebury over open, rural roads is invigorating and liberating. The bursts of red, yellow and brown fall foliage make the Green Mountains look like they are on fire. Neat, pristine villages dot a landscape dominated by forest, dairy farms and pastureland. I recall how delighted I was that Laurie chose Vermont for her university studies: safe, peaceful, bucolic. Such a contrast with her dad's habitats of congested Washington and steamy third world pits.

I arrive in my rental car at Middlebury's rolling campus. The sky is a vast clean slate of pure blue. Young people loll under the trees; some make music, others smooch. Many simply read. Yet more chat it up, books in hand.

I park and walk to her dorm. Kids I've never met say "Hi" as they exit the building on their way to class. Room 312. I tap on the half-ajar door. "Yeah?" comes the response. I push the door open and pop my head in. Laurie is seated at her desk poring over one of those huge hardback tomes one finds only in law and medical schools.

She looks up, her jaw slackens, eyes widen in surprise. "Daddy!"

"The one and only," I say. I hold my arms wide.

The heavy book falls out of Laurie's lap as she rushes into my arms. I wince from my wound.

"Dad, what is it?" she asks with concern.

"I'll tell you later. Let's find someplace nice where we can talk."

We go to a café, get some hot designer coffee in real china cups and warm succulent pastries. I tell her that I changed flights on a last-minute whim just to see her.

I sit and take her in. At nineteen, she is all woman now. Her eyes sparkle like her mother's. In fact, with her wavy lustrous red hair, green eyes and unblemished beauty, she looks like Kate when we first met.

"You look so grown up."

Laurie's face flushes. "Dad. I *am* grown up."

"Where did the years go?"

She reaches and places her hand over mine. "Happens to the best of us, Pop." She asks about my job, about Washington.

"Either I'm getting too old for it, or too tired of it."

Laurie studies my face. "Of what? All the bullshit?"

"Young lady. You watch your mouth! What did I raise here? Bluebeard's daughter?"

"Oh, Dad. Don't be so retro."

"Don't be so conformist. Just because—"

"I know. I know. 'Just because everybody else is jumping off Golden Gate Bridge doesn't mean I have to," she recites in a sing-song fashion, while bobbing her head side-to-side. "Okay, okay. So work suck—I mean work's getting you down. Do you have like, a life and stuff?"

"If you mean, do I have other pursuits, uh, nope."

Laurie lowers her eyes, toys with her empty cup with both hands. "Mom. Mom confided in me that she misses you." She lifts her gaze, a hopeful gaze, square at my face.

I smile. Let a moment pass. "So, how is your mother?"

"Barking up the wrong tree, huh?"

I nod.

"She's doing real well. Her graphic design company is going gangbusters. She calls too. But she doesn't have time to come see me either." Laurie crooks her mouth and shrugs. "She's dating a guy named Mel. Mel? Like, yoo-hoo! Only dorks and greaseballs are named *Mel*." She looks at me again, this time with a smile of resignation. "And you?"

"I should be asking you these questions. You always had a knack for turning the tables on your decrepit old dad."

"Well?"

"If you mean, am I 'seeing somebody?' How can I when I'm working my butt off to pay for all of this?" I make an encompassing gesture of the campus.

"Ha. Ha," she retorts. "You spooks are all so *inscrutable*."

I lean forward on my elbows. "And nosy. So, tell me how it's going so far."

Laurie relates a story of a pretty typical coed. Good and bad professors. "Yucky" cafeteria food. Boys who are "geeks." College is "awesome." Friendships forged for life.

"I'm glad you're here," she says. "I want to tell you something."

Alarm bells sound in my brain. She's marrying. She's pregnant. She's joining a cult.

"I've decided what career I want. I want to work for the CIA. Follow in your footsteps."

I look at her with the hard eyes of a disapproving parent. She's just told me something as disturbing as my initial panicked thoughts.

"Well?"

"No, baby. No."

"What do you mean, 'No'?"

"I mean what I say. You can't."

"Dad, I'm an adult now remember? I make my own choices. I want to work in intelligence. I liked living overseas. I liked the secrets we had to keep. I liked the kind of people you worked with. It's just, like, so *cool.*"

"Listen to me." I lean forward. "I feel buried alive. There's no cause. But more important, there's no integrity. You find yourself answerable to pea-brained zeroes, people who couldn't get a job cleaning toilets at the bus station on the outside. People who'll act like your friend one minute and think nothing of disemboweling you the next to steal your thunder, to get them a promotion. It's the Land of the Living Dead. Some good people, yes. Otherwise, gutless nullities."

Laurie recoils. She ponders this. "That bad, huh?"

"Sorry if I laid it on a little thick. It's just that...I'd prefer to see you steer clear of government. You're much too smart, too talented."

"And do what? Be a bond trader?"

"Good money in that."

"That's the point, Dad. Bust my hump to make rich people richer? Where's the honor in that? I can see my tombstone now: 'She died with the most toys.' Like, huh?! I want to live my life serving humanity, pursuing ideals. Having adventure."

A single chuckle emits through a wan smile on my face. "What then?"

"We've got three years to continue this discussion, young lady."

An armistice ensues. I again take her in. Late adolescence is falling away like the fuzz on a growing duckling. She's stronger, more self-assured, smarter. I know she'll be completely on her own in a few short years. I can counsel but I won't be able to instruct. Laurie idly observes swallows swirling in the autumn sky. She then turns to me.

"Dad?"

"Yes, sweetie?"

Laurie reaches out with both arms. We embrace.

CHAPTER THREE
LANGLEY, VIRGINIA

Entering CIA headquarters is not as difficult as most people think. A guardhouse with opaque windows at the entrance of Dolly Madison Parkway merely monitors traffic at the stoplight where most of Langley's 11,000 commuters enter in the morning and exit later in the day. It was put there fifteen years ago after a mad Pakistani immigrant blithely popped four employees with a semiautomatic during rush hour. After four decades of existence, the Agency decided to announce what the world already knew and installed a simple reflective white-on-green sign, "CIA Headquarters, Next Right." Fifty yards down a speed-bump-riven entrance way, one is directed right for visitor check-in or left for employees entry. I veer left, flash my ID at the vehicle gate and head along a long loop past the original headquarters building, an off-white seven-floor structure set amidst a sylvan rolling landscape that could pass for a college campus. I circle the new headquarters building, similarly designed as the original, but with a façade of puky-green windows. What outsiders don't realize is that they are faux windows, lined with a system to counter electronic penetration from "hostile intelligence" services. God's great sun doesn't show itself within this inner sanctum of American spydom. My 1958 MG roadster fits neatly in an inner space of the lower parking deck of the south lot, a mere five minutes' walk to the office. Such are the perks that over two decades of federal service get you.

The lobby of the new building – employees simply call them the "new" and "old" buildings – is filled with natural brightness via skylights. Lining the walls are mementoes of the history and successes of American espionage – photos of "Wild Bill" Donovan, who headed the CIA's predecessor, the OSS; samples of KGB bugs uncovered by American agents during the cold war; a photo display of the U-2 spy plane. I swipe my ID through a card-reader and push through the turnstile. Past this point lies a hermetically sealed inner world of secretive bureaucrats who labor intensely in office cubicles swathed in ice-white fluorescence. Only the push-button combination locks on office doors, ubiquitous safes and occasional special access control units in corridors distinguish this place from a zillion other unremarkable office warrens of insurance companies, state agencies or computer conglomerates. This includes the workers, mostly sporting department store suits and shopping mall haircuts. Serious, sexless, sober people with a passion not to stand out.

I return fast greetings to passing colleagues as I wend my way to the elevator and up to the fifth floor, home of D/NCS/SAD – Director, National Clandestine Service, Special Activities Division.

"Well, look who the cat dragged in," says Harriet Friedman, a Bette Midler look-alike who, in the guise of an "executive assistant," ferociously guards the portal to the den of one William Hanscom Croswell, Special Activities Division director.

"Am I late?"

"Are you ever on time?" she says with a hint of exasperation in her voice.

I shrug.

"The Op Center is all geared up. And *he* is waiting."

Harriet points to *his* office, then reverts to idly scanning routine this-and-that paperwork which has a habit of replicating itself like a new life form on bureaucrats' desks if not triaged regularly.

I strut into the office without knocking. Croswell sits erect at a GSA-furnished pseudo-Scandinavian desk, poring over the morning's take of intel reports, office budgets, taskers and nitnoy bullshit.

"TALISMAN's 'shut down'?!" I demand. "What the hell is—"

"Sit down," he commands without lifting his gaze.

Croswell is the coolest of the cool at an institution that requires ice-water in the veins of its operations officers. He resembles Heinrich Himmler's better-looking brother sans heinie haircut, but replete with rimless glasses that magnify zinc-gray pupils.

He looks up. Croswell has a robotic smile. One would not describe his thin-lipped, sharp-nosed, impassive face as simpatico. "You've failed," he says. This paragon of the cold-blooded professional also never wastes time on life's inanities, such as greetings.

My first instinct tells me that this is a stab at humor, but it is quickly overcome by the realization that Croswell is incapable of humor.

"Say what?!"

"It's a roll-up. Your operation. Total fiasco."

"*My* operation."

"You're in charge, Brennan. And TALISMAN is finished. Total botch. We had to end it." He hands me a sheaf of papers.

They're SIGINT – signals intelligence – reports. Stuff picked up by satellites and spy planes. The juicy intel that the public gets wind of only when scandals break out over covert action ops.

The first one is headed ULTRA - TOP SECRET - NOFORN. Titled, "Operation TALISMAN: Collapse of Jamiat 4th Army Corps," it gives highlights of radio traffic between Engineer Bashir Khalili and his field commanders.

"Hold positions at all costs!" Bashir implores one Ali. "We know they are short of munitions."

"They are coming at us like locusts," Ali responds. "They knew we were coming. They knew!"

"Use the B-40s!" commands Bashir. "Use your rockets!"

"Oh, my commander. They are all gone. It is too late. Allah is Great."

The report indicates, "Radio silence."

The next exchange is between Engineer Bashir and field commander Haji Azim.

"Goshtam is located fifty kilometers east. You have nothing to worry about. Stay alert."

"No, Engineer Bashir. They are here already. They come at us from the east and the north..."

The text indicates, "Radio interference - likely from explosion."

Bashir loses contact. He shouts into his radio, "Are you there, Azim?! Are you there?"

"...heavy artillery. And mortars. It is through for us, it is..."

I look up. Croswell's face is stone. His eyes say, *it's yours. You'll take the fall.*

The other reports are raw intelligence on battle losses. There are satellite photos showing burning buildings and destroyed vehicles. Little white arrows point to "Opposition force units" and "LOCs - Goshtam Forces." In the acronymania of government, LOCs stands for Lines of Communications – routes along which supplies and troops travel. The little arrows show Bashir's enemy has LOCs coming at him like lances at his heart.

"Stunned, are we, Brennan?" Croswell says none too helpfully. "The Op Center is waiting for us. The Director will be there. You'll have some explaining to do."

"Shit rolls downhill. Some things never change. Who pulled the rug out on TALISMAN, and why? And Bashir betrayed. You won't get away with it. I'll see to it."

"I'll remind you to watch yourself, Brennan. You've been treading on thin ice for some time now. And your little renegade Rambo foray was not exactly 'career enhancing.'"

I stare at this man. I wonder now as I have every day for the past twenty years how is it that they allow such little men to play God with other people's lives. Middle-class, suburban super-functionaries who shop for grass-seed on Sunday and smuggle rocket-propelled grenade launchers to tribals on Monday.

"Bashir is good. The best," I say.

"Correction. Bashir *was* the best. Actually, I've always questioned his asset-worthiness. And State's been on our backs about his human rights abuses." Croswell removes his glasses, huffs vapor on them and wipes them with a crisp, fresh white hanky. Without his eyeglasses, Croswell appears even more non-descript, if that were possible. "Human rights is serious business, Brennan. Yet another stain on your fitness report."

I feel a hot red flash surge into my face. I hold myself back. Take a deep breath. Look to my right, at an aluminum-framed poster extolling the "Leipzig Musikfest 1993." CIA's office art becomes dated quickly.

"That's bullshit. Bashir is terror incarnate to the Taliban and al-Qaeda. He has the highest body count."

"He had the ears to prove it," Croswell shoots back.

"That's not true. Al Jazeera made up that story. Bashir hit them where it really hurt. We helped him, and we got our bang for the buck. And..." I stop myself dead in my verbal tracks.

"Yes, and?" Croswell asks.

"He could be trusted. He saved my life."

Croswell nods, but the shitty little Himmler grin does not signal agreement.

"Mazar-e-Sharif," he says.

"What about it?"

"You weren't supposed to be there in the first place. Such a hot-shot, weren't you, Brennan? Intelligence Medal of Merit, commendations out the wazoo. Fast-tracker. First into Afghanistan in'02 with Jawbreaker. And then there's a little problem of Osama getting away at Tora Bora." Croswell shakes his head and tsk-tsks. "The fast track turns into a brick wall."

"Like I said, shit rolls downhill." What I keep myself from adding is that the last thing he ever won was a gold star in his third-grade spelling bee, and the only reason he reached the senior ranks is because he kissed all the right asses as a Washington REMF – rear echelon mother – never mind.

The cold war lives, between this drone and myself, but we're stuck with each other. A silent cease-fire ensues.

Finally, Croswell looks at his watch and then me. "You're basically not a bad officer, Brennan. Aggressive. But you've got to watch yourself. Learn from the rest of us. Anyway, you're being reassigned. To training, to be precise. Until these charges of insubordination and human rights abuses can be investigated."

I remain silent.

"Right. Off to the Op Center then." He says this as if he were Lord Kitchener on his way to Khartoum to conquer the natives. "Diversity" notwithstanding, the rank-and-file white-male oligarchy that run our foreign affairs are shameless Anglophiles, about as relevant to twenty-first century America as spats and monocles.

We rise simultaneously, but with our eyes locked onto the face of the other, like two gunfighters. We read the other's mind as well: How can I destroy this man?

The CIA has few friends, and in a friendless institution of cynical manipulators, success is measured by body count.

CHAPTER FOUR

CIA's Operations Center is a whiz-bang place, full of so many state-of-the-art bells and whistles that the technically-challenged such as myself just look wide-eyed and let out a long, hollow whistle, like an Iowa farmer gazing at two-thousand acres of record-high corn. "Hoo-wee. Don't that beat all!"

A couple dozen people sit at terminals and other fancy devices. These monitor the "traffic" – reports from the CIA's 120-plus stations worldwide, intercepts from listening posts, diplomatic dispatches from U.S. embassies, military situation reports, press reports and so on. Their job is to see to it that the Director of Central Intelligence, or DCI, other senior officials and the White House are alerted to new crises, kept abreast of current ones, and are just generally kept informed about the important doings in the world. It is the 24-hour awake brain to the eyes and ears of America's far-flung overseas information-collecting empire. All of this multi-million dollar gadgetry is helped along by the fastest, least secret and most efficient information-gatherer ever known to man. TV monitors beam CNN from overhead.

There are several compartments within the Op Center, including secure video-conferencing to enable people from various agencies as well as from stations and embassies to talk about the most sensitive matters in real time. Off to the side is a small, secure auditorium. Himmler-Croswell and I sit down, he in the front row where the Director is likely to seat himself, and I am safely removed in the next-to-last row. Technicians scurry around making final checks. Eight or nine other people sit in small clusters engaged in idle conversation, their voices creating a low-frequency buzz. I spot a cute redhead who I vaguely recall having met in OTS, the Office of Technical Services, whose job it is to create and improve the tools of the spy trade, ranging from listening bugs to tiny transmitters to concealable cameras. I flash a beaming smile. She nods and turns away. She doesn't look back. She needs to maintain her cover, no doubt.

The doors swing open. The small crowd rises, I as an afterthought. A phalanx of a half-dozen people walks in, led by a smiling sixtyish gentleman with a florid complexion and dark, barely graying hair. This is Carl E. Kinneard, known informally as The Warden. A Texas attorney and judge, he turned that state's abysmal penitentiary system from an archipelago of overcrowded, rioting gulags into a smoothly functioning prison network that doled out equal measures of order and rehabilitation. In the wake of yet more scandals at the Agency, the President yanked him out of the Attorney General's job to head the equally overcrowded and riotous intelligence community as both Director of National Intelligence and DCI. Equal doses of punishment and rehabilitation did wonders there as well.

On Kinneard's heels is a well-decked out woman in her mid-thirties who looks about as much a government denizen as I do a Jehovah's Witness door-pounder. With a Watergate hairdo and Dolce & Gabbana ensemble, this fine-featured blonde with regal bearing is clearly an outsider, most likely a charter member of America's ruling class.

Beside her and so close on The Warden's footsteps that he's in danger of tripping the boss is a stocky middle-aged man in blue pin-striped suit, wearing those big horn-rimmed glasses favored by attorneys and other high-powered parasites. By his cloying, twitching attentiveness, I conclude immediately that I dislike him and all that he stands for, whatever it may be.

The others in the king's wake are the pilot fish, those ever-hungry aides, special assistants, deputies and directors who swim alongside the big fish in hopes of catching a few morsels of recognition and respect. These are the modern-day equivalents of spittoon-bearers and fan-wavers.

The small group take their seats at a long birchwood table in front, Kinneard in the center. Altar of the gods.

Kinneard scans the room sporting a benign smile and, with a slight nod, says, "Good morning ladies and gentleman. Please sit down." He introduces the blonde and the twitcher as members of the President's Intelligence Oversight Board, a sort of independent citizen's committee to investigate and report to the President on intelligence matters. "Ms. Camilla Harrington Loomis and Mr. Robert Norfolk join us today. They are to be given access to everything we have on this matter."

Kinneard slips on his demi-frame reading glasses and peruses the file placed before him. After two excruciating minutes that seem like two hours, the DNI removes his specs, looks at one of the pilot fish on his right and says, "Okay, let's get on with it." The flunky ricochets the signal to Croswell.

Who said 'Nothing focuses the mind better than being hanged'? You wouldn't know it from Croswell, who rises and skips up the few steps to the platform as if he were the favored finalist on a quiz show.

"Operation TALISMAN, Mr. Director. Small in scale, modest in its objectives, low-budgeted, high in risk. As you know, it folded over the past week. It was a gamble in a high-stakes game and, frankly, we lost." He shoots a direct gaze at me. "As we assess the after-action reports from Islamabad, it is increasingly clear that we bet on the wrong horse. The Jamiat-i-Islami, who are now loosely part of Hamid Karzai's government in Kabul, is a fractured band of scoundrels and opportunists. They did themselves in. A treacherous lot who are their own worst enemy." Croswell the Crisp stands smugly, ready to take the heat.

"Maybe you haven't heard. The CIA doesn't back scoundrels any more, Mr. Croswell. Where did we go wrong?" demands the Warden.

"Bad intel, to be candid, Mr. Director."

Kinneard's floridness turns to scarlet, his jugulars throb. He gnaws on the end of one of the reading glass bows. "Cut to the quick, Mr. Croswell. I haven't got all day and I don't read minds."

Oh, goody. Indeed a hanging, I think.

"We ordered this op canceled. But it went through anyway. Our ops officer in charge of agent recruitment can tell you better, I think." Croswell is gesturing for me to come front and center. "This is Harry Brennan, Mr. Director. He was in charge of TALISMAN. He knows the Afghans like his own family. Worked with them during the Soviet occupation. On the basis of his expertise, we gave Mr. Brennan a virtual free hand on this operation until we ordered it shut down."

The eyes of the gods all bore in on me like the rifles of a firing squad. I don't believe what is happening. Croswell passed the buck so deftly that he managed to stick it up my rectum without my feeling it. Croswell bounds down the steps as briskly as he climbed them. With his trademark mass murderer's grin, he raises his eyebrows at me like, 'get yourself out of this one, smartass.'

I see the shit rolling downward in my direction turning into an avalanche of Himalayan proportions. I rise and shuffle up to the platform. My hanging. I don't help my case by stumbling at the top step, nor by the ancient plaid sports jacket, a Christmas present of yore from Mom, and polyester tie I threw on indifferently this morning.

I collect my thoughts, but not fast enough for the DNI.

"Brennan. So, you're the guy who recruited the Jamiat, is that it? And you disobeyed orders, went through with it and got shot out there?" He looks at his watch. Now I have a better appreciation of why Texas's death row backlog got cleared up lickety-split while the Warden was in charge.

"Sir. Ahem." I stand there all alone swathed in incandescent spotlights. A crazy thought punctures my mind. I'm in final Jeopardy, haven't a clue to the breaker answer to which I must fashion a question: "corona borealis." But it's not real Jeopardy. It's a Twilight Zone play on it. Rod Serling is smirking in the shadows....

"Mr. Brennan?" Kinneard's leaning forward on his elbows.

"Right. I mean, no. Not exactly, that is." I'm dissembling and I know it. I spot Croswell with his arms crossed and sporting the biggest Cheshire grin this side of the Potomac. That sight stiffens my spine. "Er, yes I got injured. As for Jamiat, without their fighters, it would've taken two more years to force the Soviets to quit Afghanistan."

"Great, officer Brennan. If I want history lessons, I'll call in some academics. Answer me two things: (a) what was the mission, and (b) why did you, er, the Agency, decide to back this particular horse?" He turns on Croswell. "And I want you to advise me on how far up the chain this...this Operation TALISMAN was scrubbed and approved. The Washington *Post* has the full story, unsurprisingly. CNN is comparing Bashir's destruction to the fiasco we suffered supporting the Kurds covertly against Saddam. I have to brief the President. And frankly, gentlemen, I'm currently at a loss as to what to tell them. 'The Jamiat are their own worst enemy' just won't cut it. This kind of blowback we just don't need."

Croswell loses his smugness. I'm hoping he'll next lose his lunch.

"The mission was to check the Taliban and crush al-Qaeda," I interject, making a fast play for the defensive high ground. The Jamiat are not only effective and trustworthy fighters, they have also been friends of the U.S. Their military commander, Mohammad Rahim, is one of Karzai's senior advisors. But without much outside support and with Pak intelligence covertly undergirding the Taliban, the Jamiat has been marginalized. I decide to launch a pre-emptive attack on Croswell. I look straight at him and answer the question posed to him. "TALISMAN was approved by the D/NCS, the DDCI, you sir, as well as the President in a finding issued last year. It was thoroughly scrubbed by the Covert Action Review Group." I hold my breath.

Kinneard sits there, the mental wheels are in high gear. "Okay then. What went wrong?"

"Bashir was sold out…"

"Nonsense," states Croswell, now on his feet.

"Let him finish," Kinneard commands. Croswell slumps back into his seat.

"I've reviewed the raw intel over and over. Rahim's Fourth Corps' internal security was sound – unlike that of the Kurds fighting Saddam in Iraq. They held onto strategic strongholds they'd been fortifying for years. They had spies inside the Taliban. Their commanders knew their territory intimately – in contrast to Taliban commanders, most of them religious students in soldier's garb. We helped on the logistics side – support equipment and ammunition."

"Sold out how?" asks Kinneard.

"I don't know. If I were to bet my paycheck, however, I'd lay it on the ISI."

The society blonde shakes her head and whispers in Kinneard's ear. "Use English, Mr. Brennan," Kinneard says.

"The Inter-Services Intelligence Directorate. Pakistan's secret service."

"Okay. Why then?"

"The Paks always favored the Islamic fundamentalists. I think they were glad to finally rid themselves of the Jamiat, who are anything but. The Paks seek 'strategic depth' in Afghanistan as a means of countering Indian power and influence. They want to keep the Afghans under their wing and they do it by favoring the Pushtuns, who dominate the Taliban. This is why it took so long to find and kill Osama bin-Laden. The Pakistani leaders were playing us while allowing him to hide out in their country so as not to further rile the Pushtuns, who revered bin-Laden."

"But aren't the Paks shooting themselves in the foot?" asks Norfolk in a whiny voice.

"I believe the Taliban tarantula will end up biting the Paks. They're playing a dangerous game," I answer.

"You're in no position to predict what Pakistan's policies will result in," Croswell snaps.

Kinneard looks exasperated. He signals Croswell once again to keep his trap shut.

"Well, it seems to me that we can expect diplomatic problems with Pakistan," Ms. Loomis says with the profundity of a Sioux City cheerleader. Everybody politely ignores her.

"Mr. Director, Bashir was done in by leaked intelligence. Detailed intelligence handed to Taliban on a silver plate. But TALISMAN worked. We completely wiped out an important al-Qaeda base."

"That's unverified," Croswell blurts. The Covert Action Staff is putting together a working group to investigate. We're on top of this. Ops officer Brennan here disobeyed orders, went into Afghanistan and launched TALISMAN anyway. He faces disciplinary action…"

Kinneard rubs his face with both palms. "Yah. Okay. Investigate. It appears, however, TALISMAN did indeed achieve its objective. But Taliban's subsequent crushing of our ally Bashir is another story. Makes us look stupid. And this Administration will have to go full throttle in damage control to explain."

Norfolk raises a pen upward like a student seeking to ask a question. "But, can we say that northern Afghanistan is now more or less pacified?"

"Yes," Croswell answers quickly. "Fighting is essentially ended in that part of the country."

"I would suggest that we undertake a mission to Islamabad to enter with the Paks in constructive engagement, offering a basket of carrots and sticks to encourage them to go after the Taliban on their own territory. Show them that it is in their interests," Norfolk chimes in. I can't decide whether Norfolk was one of my college professors or if he's fishing for a bigger role for himself.

"We need focus groups to flesh this out," offers the society bimbo. She then whispers something to Kinneard, to which he nods. I like to think she's offering him oral sex in the parking lot after the meeting, but I quickly dismiss this as highly unlikely. Washington power players are too image conscious.

Ever the judge, Kinneard looks down at me over his reading glasses. "Brennan. You've disobeyed orders."

"Yes sir. I did," I reply helplessly.

He points at me with his pen. "We don't cotton to freelancers in this business. Do you understand?"

"I do."

"But you're right. Your operation paid off even though the Afghan commander on the ground then got his ass kicked. But so did al-Qaeda. That's what we want. But I advise you, Mr. Brennan, to mind your p's and q's from now on if you want a future in this outfit."

"I understand sir," I say.

"Good. Thank you people," Kinneard says with finality. He again looks at his watch. The pilot fish rise, keen to the fine signals that their host is about to move on. Kinneard and his entourage are out the door. Croswell and I avoid eye contact and exit separately.

CHAPTER FIVE

On October 5, 1993, Vince Colletta and I bugged out of Somalia together. Young and foot-loose, we had nothing to lose – except our lives. It's the kind of friendship, tempered by danger and time, that doesn't drift away. As junior CIA field officers one step ahead of a horde of murderous militiamen, we realized then that our relationship would end only in death.

In an organization in which trust is a luxury of fools, Vince and I confide everything to each other, our ambitions, the loves of our lives, our imminent divorces. Vince is one of those people who always seems to be plugged in, knows lots of things about lots of people. He trades information like a Moroccan bazaar merchant trades gems, exchanging lesser quality stuff for better quality stuff. A nosy son of a bitch, some might say. But it's served him well in fast promotions and good jobs. I drop by to see my buddy in his spacious office in the Directorate for Policy and Planning, one of those catch-all offices that has carte blanche to poke into anything in the name of the DCI.

He looks up at me through a cloud of blue smoke with his feet propped up on his desk.

I cough and wave smoke from my face. "Jesus. It smells like burning skunk shit in here!"

"Vintage skunk shit." Vince proudly displays a box of Cuban cigars the size and color of turds from a large-size skunk.

"Maybe you haven't heard. It's against the law to smoke in a government building," I respond.

"It's not the first time the CIA has broken the law." Vince blows rings at the ceiling.

"You're in trouble," he says.

I begin to express surprise, but then know better and check myself. "I won't ask how you know, but what you know."

"Scuttlebutt is that you blew TALISMAN. Twenty-five million of the taxpayers' misappropriated bucks down an Afghan sewer."

"Who's saying it?"

"Oh. Everybody."

"It's not true."

"I know. But somebody on the seventh floor is putting it out."

"Croswell," I say.

"One of the usual suspects, as usual," he says.

Vince stubs out his cigar and sits up, layers of an enriched belly protrude over a Navajo belt. He fixes his eyes on me. The *Post* is running its story on 'the CIA's TALISMAN fiasco' tomorrow. Focus is on how your CIA-funded buddy, Bashir, fell on his face and got wiped out. Nothing about two-hundred al-Qaeda pukes buying it. Yet another case of the Agency not knowing its ass from its elbow. Like I said, word is filtering down from above that one Harry Brennan screwed up big time."

"You know better than anybody that one ops officer doesn't an operation build nor destroy…"

Vince raises a hand for me to calm down. "They need a fall guy. And you're it."

"You've got to be shitting me."

"Wish I were. It's the Washington blame game. Can't fault the Pres – even though he signed off on it and was briefed regularly. Can't blame the DNI-DCI. He approves covert actions, doesn't manage them. Can't allow the American people to lose faith in their leaders. Ollie North took the fall for Iran-Contra. That sourpuss broad ambassador – what's her face? – got nailed for being 'too soft' toward Saddam. The list goes on. Look, these guys plan character assassinations better than they ever did the real thing. It comes naturally to them."

"So, my name will be in print. My cover will be blown. I'm re-assigned to training. Accused of human rights violations. Where's that leave me job-wise longer term? Working in the mailroom?"

"I doubt your name will be leaked, not unless this gets way out of control and some pains-in-the-asses on the Hill want to glom onto TALISMAN to go after the President."

I look at Vince with a scrunched brow. "How do you know this?"

"I don't 'know this.' It's the Washington blame game. They want an internal scapegoat, and that's you. Chances are, in the extreme scenario, if it came, they'd try to sacrifice you publicly out of desperation, but it'd be a long shot. The DCI would have to take a fall as well. Maybe the National Security Adviser too. But then there's Ollie and what's her face. They got publicly hanged to save two presidents. I think the Republicans are better at this 'let's make the careerocrats take the heat.' They're more treacherous. The Democrats get too conscience-stricken and commit suicide or write a book."

"So then, it's not the mailroom for me?"

"Bashir's fall is an embarrassment, but it's small potatoes. I wouldn't worry. About losing my job, that is." Vince suddenly loses his concentration and braces both temples with his fingertips.

"You okay?" I ask. I start from my chair.

Vince shakes his head as if throwing off fatigue and smiles. "Of course I am," he says unconvincingly. "Where were we?"

"Small potatoes," I say.

"Yeah. Your career will stay more or less intact because Kinneard saved your ass, but your reputation is another thing."

"You mean I'll be seen as a screw-up."

"On the contrary. As a hero. You got to run a real paramilitary operation. You know how many people get that opportunity? They're all jealous, failure or not. *You*, Harry Brennan, got to play cowboys and Indians for real while all the rest of us nerds got to shuffle more paper."

"You keep losing me, Vince. I 'blew' TALISMAN, our overlords throw me to the wolves, but I'm envied, and that's not good? Who's on first?"

Vince wags an admonishing finger at me. "Beware the long knives. They, that is, all the little pukes up to Croswell's level, will be going after your scalp simply because you stand out and they don't. *You* get to play with the big boys, and they get to worry about how they're going to get their kids into the gifted program."

"Vince, sometimes I think you were born a few hundred years late and a continent off. You belong in a Venetian court."

"Yeah, well. The real clincher is this. We're reaching out to the Taliban. Wanna make some kind of a deal."

"A deal?! So, that's why TALISMAN was canceled abruptly."

"Yeah. Offering carrots and sticks and all that bullshit."

"Norfolk."

"Right. He's about to be named Special Envoy. He'll be sent out to meet secretly with the Taliban cruds, Paks, even to Russia and one or two of the 'Stans.' He'd better pack

lomotil. How'd you know it was Norfolk? I just heard from
the NSC. Maybe ten people know about this."

"Call me Nostradamus," I say.

"My ass. Anyway. Here's the real clincher. Hold onto
your seat. Croswell's been promoted."

"They closed Auschwitz years ago."

Vince ignores my sick humor. "He's Director of the
National Clandestine Service."

Every muscle in my body freezes. I can't believe what
I've just heard. Croswell is given one of the most prestigious
and sought-after jobs in American intelligence – head of
HUMINT – human intelligence, actual spies on the ground,
old fashioned espionage.

Vince reaches in his desk and pulls out a bottle of Jim
Beam, pours two glasses. I take mine, but can only take a sip.
At 9:00 am, I fear chucking up.

"Croswell's the biggest screw-up in the agency," I say.
"And he has all the imagination of a sea slug."

"Never stopped anyone in this business," Vince says. "In
fact, it helps. Birds of a feather screw up together. It's The
Culture. The Ol' Boys still rule this place. They suck up to
each other and help each other. It never changes."

I go to Vince's window overlooking the rolling,
landscaped CIA grounds, called the "campus" by insiders.
I stare into a time tunnel. "Remember how exciting it used
to be?"

"We were young."

"Times were different."

"Times change."

"But we had a cause."

"My God. You don't want the Soviet Union back."

"Nah. Those last days in Mogadishu," I say. "Remember
how we felt we were perched on the edge of a sharp knife?
It was all coming to an end, but there we were, in tenth gear,

trying to salvage…something. It was a lost cause, and maybe we didn't believe in it, but we did believe in ourselves."

"A mortar round almost ended it for the both of us, cause or no cause," Vince says.

"Yeah, but the juices were flowing. Same thing in Kuwait. Saddam's troops are at the embassy gates. There we are frantically stuffing the shredders. I still remember. You were telling a dirty joke. And I was laughing. We must've been nuts."

"Like I said, young. We weren't laughing for four months after that as virtual hostages of Saddam. But, you're right. We believed in ourselves."

"Do you believe now?" I ask. "I don't. The pygmies have taken over. Our tribe lost."

"Harry, why don't you leave?"

"Ah. Tried it once. Remember? Two years on the outside. Security work is a booming business, but…. I'd rather whore myself for the public good, believe it or not, than for the bottom line. Then again, Kate puts the Somali warlords and Iraqis combined to shame in her drive for alimony payments. And Laurie just entered Middlebury."

"It's the juice, Harry. You're in it for the juice. Age doesn't temper that."

"Maybe." I let out a weak laugh. "*We're* in it for the juice. Right buddy?"

Vince looks up at me with a sadness in his face. He then stares into his empty glass. "Not me. Not anymore."

"Come on. You aren't giving up now, are you? Don't let the pygmies drive you down."

"Naw. It's not them. I can deal with the Croswells." Vince's eyes remain on his empty tumbler.

I turn away from the window and face him. "Vince, what is it?"

"The verdict's in. I'm no longer in remission."

I stare silently at him.

"The doctors prescribed 'aggressive therapy.' I said, no thanks."

"No. Vince—"

He raises a hand for me to stop and flashes a wan smile. "It's my last great adventure, buddy. Let me handle it my way."

I drive for hours. I drive aimlessly around the Virginia suburbs. Driving for me is an elixir in times of trouble. My mind is forced to focus on other things, on the road, the people, the countryside. But I still need comfort. I give in and seek it one of those anonymous watering holes that caters to salesmen and the local insurance crowd who thrive in the exurbs. Each year these devour more and more of the capital's outer reaches, homogenizing farmland and small villages into sprawling strip malls and housing tracts.

It's late and no one's in the place except a forlorn bartender and one honey-skinned waitress. The latter greets me and asks if I want to eat or sit at the bar. I look at her sparkling black eyes and I decide that I'd like to eat something.

I glance at the laminated menu featuring a handful of forgettable items. "First a beer. What's the special?"

"Corn bif and cobbage," she replies.

I make a face.

She giggles. "You don' like corn bif and cobbage, eh?"

"Me and most other Irishmen, actually."

"How 'bout cheeckin freecasee on toas?"

"Uh, how about the mushroom burger with fries?" I fold the menu and hand it back.

"Oh, sorry. No moshrooms."

I look irritated. "No mushrooms."

She giggles again and toys with her pencil playfully. Strands of straight, long, black hair loosely tied in the back float freely from their barrette harness. The girl is in her twenties and has a freshness about her that I find infectious. I start laughing with her.

The girl looks furtively from side-to-side. "I tell you what. You look to me like a jalapeño man. Me and my friends eat jalapeños with our dinner. How 'bout I put some on your burger?"

"Deal."

"Deal?" She looks perplexed.

"Yeah. Um. *De acuerdo.*"

"*Ah, sí!* Deal." She runs off to get the beer. She's back in a minute and a half and sets the frosted mug before me, then off to the kitchen.

I take a long, deep gulp. The ice-cold cataract flows cleanly into my stomach, leaving a pleasantly burning sensation. After another swallow, my brain begins to mellow. I think about Croswell. I tell myself he's one in a cast of thousands of grasping nonentities with teflon-coated consciences. If he suddenly got run over by a car of my make and year, for the sake of argument, a clone would simply take his place.

I ponder my being made the 'fall-guy' for a successful op that's been depicted as a failure and my blood begins to boil along with my beer-inflamed stomach. I feel helpless. The more so when I think of life without Vince.

I move onto the peace-in-our-time initiative toward the Taliban and I'm stumped. A small horde of zealots right out of the middle ages, who banish women behind doors, who stone adulterers, amputate the limbs of thieves, sponsor terrorism. Why reach out to a bunch of maniacs, al-Qaeda's best friends?

My jalapeño burger arrives. The girl carefully sets it in front of me, then straightens out my silverware in a fussy manner, more special attention than the average customer gets. She pauses and smiles. I smile back.

"So. You taste it. Tell me how you like it," she says teasingly.

I bite in. As I chew, my face flushes and I choke. I grab for the beer.

The girl looks panicked and slaps me on the back. "What's wrong? Has it gone down the wrong throat?"

"Pipe," I gasp. I finish the beer and hold out the mug desperately for another fill. "I thought you said jalapeño, not hell's pain."

She giggles again. This annoys me.

"That's what bothers me about you people. Fresh off the boat and you think you own the place."

She furrows her brow and lets off with a burst of machine-gun fire Spanish that I take as not wishing me a happy day. She then pulls out a wallet and opens it in front of my face. "You see this? It's my green card. I am legal. And besides, we come here by airplane, not boat." She looks indignant, like a small girl who's being picked on by the boys.

I take her in. Five-feet-six inches of hell-bent beauty. I sense a person with limitless passion. I want to know more.

I laugh uncontrollably. At first, she's confused, then joins in. The sadsack bartender looks over. "What's so funny?" he shouts. "This place is a graveyard tonight. What's so funny?"

This makes us both laugh more.

I extend my right hand. "Harry Brennan."

She reciprocates. "Roni Castillo." Her hand is warm and small, and moist. I don't let loose.

"What time do you knock off?"

"Eleven. That's when they close on week days."

"Got plans?"

"No."

"Can we continue this after eleven?"

"No."

She reads the disappointment on my face. "I don't know you."

"I told you. My name's Harry Brennan."

She lets out a long breath of impatience. "Yes. I know your name, but I don't know *you*."

"You can start right after work."

"Where I come from, we have rules. Not like here."

"An old fashioned girl."

"I am from El Salvador, señor."

"Okay. I meant no offense. My intentions were at least partly honorable." I ask for the bill.

She does some quick calculating and hands it to me.

"Keep the change." I get up.

As I reach for the door, she sidles up and holds out another piece of paper. "This is my phone number. Call me. But not during the day. I am studying. Call me on the weekend."

Our eyes lock. I desperately want to kiss this young woman. I tell myself it's the beer, on top of a bad day. We both smile. I take the paper and stuff it into my pocket.

CHAPTER SIX

SOUTHERN VIRGINIA

The classroom has fifteen students, all in their 20's or early 30's, paying rapt attention as I lecture them on "The Art of Countersurveillance." I start with the textbook rendition of how to spot a pursuer, how to detect "handoffs," how to circle dead drops, how to shake a follower, feints and sleights.

This is CT, or the Career Trainee program at CIA training grounds, located in the rolling, green pasturelands and wooded knolls in the tidewater area of Virginia. This is the newest batch of trainees. Over the next nine months, they will be taught how to recruit and run agents, surveillance and countersurveillance, reporting, weapons use, counterterrorism, how to maintain cover and all the other tricks of the spy trade. There are no road signs to herald the location of "The Farm," as it is known colloquially. Yet every Billy and Joe-Bob in the county can direct you there.

It's a great and fun place to learn how to be a spy. It's also a convenient way station for those sent into bureaucratic exile, such as myself. Frankly, I had no problem with this manner of sweeping me under the rug. I needed the break and I find the clean, uncrowded countryside of southeastern tidewater Virginia invigorating.

A woman raises her hand. "How do you shake surveillance if you're not of the dominant race of the local society." She's black.

I mull that one over. "In Cambodia, I was a six-foot-two-inch white male with reddish-brown hair that fell over my ears in a country where the average male is five-five, dark-complexioned and has short, straight black hair."

"So, you stayed in your office," a male trainee quips.

"No. Not exactly. You play the invisible man. Do your business at night, at safe houses, after going through detection procedures you're learning here, of course. You use cut-outs. Espionage is the fine art of the oblique. If you practice your craft properly, your adversary either will not spot a thing, or he won't know what he saw."

The young woman seems reassured with this answer.

We break up. I head for my office. I've been seeing Roni Castillo and expect her call any time now to tell me whether she will come down for the weekend. It's a big moral dilemma for her. What will her family think? What would she expect to do with me? Such anxieties seem quaint and archaic in post-'50's America. But they give me a deeper appreciation for Roni as a person.

The phone chirps and I grab it. A man's voice says, "Hello." My heart sinks. "Is this Harry Brennan?" he asks.

"Yup."

"I'm Jeffrey Wilder of the Washington *Post*. Please don't hang up."

"How'd you get my number?"

"That's not important. I just want to tell you something. That's all. If you wish to comment, that's your business, but I'm not planning on citing your name. So don't worry."

"Okay, shoot."

"Our South Asia correspondent just came out of Afghanistan. The Jamiat took him in and out. He has ghastly photos of slain villagers. Men, women, children, all massacred. If you want, I can send them to you."

"Massacred? Where? How?"

"Not far from Mazar. Goshtam ul-Haq's Uzbek fighters apparently were given orders to "teach Bashir's people a lesson they will never forget.' It looks like some kind of nerve agent was used. We're getting soil and tissue samples tested."

I have a sudden urge to go to the bathroom.

"Mr. Brennan? Can you give me any insight? Any reaction? Does the CIA know this yet? Somebody's singled out Bashir Khalili's faction for destruction. Who, Mr. Brennan?"

"Wha'? Uh, look, uh, give me your number. Yes, I want those photos. Leave copies with Vince Colletta." It was Vince who put this guy on to me, I conclude. I hang up.

Before all this can sink in, the phone rings again. This time, it's Roni.

"Harry. It's me, Roni."

"And?" I say tensely.

"Is it okay if I come to see you this weekend?"

The nausea brought on by the first call is instantly replaced with other basic feelings.

"Of course."

Roni pulls up in a red Mustang. Her tan legs are the first part of her to extend out the door. Roni is wearing a white shift that ends well above her knees and a snug blouse that gives full justice to a young woman who the good Lord endowed more generously than the average female. Profiled in the Indian summer sunshine, Roni Castillo looks absolutely luscious.

She pecks me on the cheek.

I throw her bags into the trunk of my non-descript Agency vehicle and we head into the hills. Liberating breezes fill the opened-window car as it picks up speed. I turn off onto a narrow, country road. Roni reaches back to undo her hair, then tosses her head back and fills her lungs with the country air. Her hair flies on the breezes.

"I love the countryside," she says. "I feel so free."

Maybe it's her youth, but Roni's breathless enthusiasm is like an electric spark. I ask myself if this is part of mid-life perturbations on my part. But I leave that thought aside and simply take every moment as it comes.

I pull onto a dirt path that leads into a secluded meadow on a wooded hill. We get out and fetch the picnic basket from the back seat. I spread a blanket on the ground and take out an assortment of deli goodies. With a big smile, I present bottle of wine and a bouquet of country flowers.

"Aahh! How sweet!" Roni gushes. I get another peck on the cheek.

I open the wine. "Gewürztraminer '05. Just the thing with a light meal outdoors on a beautiful day with a lovely woman."

After a few minutes of eating and small talk, Roni asks, "Harry, what exactly is it that you do?"

"I told you before. I work for the State Department."

"Doing what?"

"Diplomacy."

"In Virginia?"

"Have some more pâté.

"I find you to be a mysterious man."

"It only seems that way. And you? What do you want to do after you get your accounting degree at George Mason?"

"See the world. I will share a secret with you, Harry."

"Ah. The mysterious Veronica Maria Dolores Castillo de Noval reveals herself at last!"

"Ha. Ha. My secret is that I hate accounting."

"Then why are you studying it?"

"My father told me to."

"Oh, well. Now that explains it. If your father told you go jump in the lake, would you do it?"

"Probably. This is the way we Salvadoreños are. Family is everything. I will tell you another secret, you man of many secrets. I lied to my family. I told them I was going to visit a girlfriend at UVA."

"I see." The more I know this woman, the more I take her seriously.

"I wanted to be with you this weekend. Very much." Her eyes are wide. Her black hair falls seductively over her face.

I lean over and touch her cheek with my lips. She responds by finding my lips with hers. A long, languorous kiss. We fall back onto the blanket. The wetness of her tongue sends a flash straight through me. A warm breeze laps our entwined bodies like tropical waters.

Her breasts are pliant under my touch and she lets out a primal moan from deep inside. We rise to our knees and kiss tenderly. Roni leans back. She lowers her gaze demurely and removes her blouse. She reaches behind and releases a snap. A golden glow from the pre-autumn sun illuminates her skin. Roni reaches out and caresses my chest. Soon we are naked.

Our bodies move in eerily natural synchronization. As the pace quickens, an ecstatic tension builds. Our excitement is enhanced in the glory of open nature and a vaulting deep blue sky.

It doesn't get better than this and it has been a very long time since I've felt so fulfilled.

After class on Monday morning I find a message on my desk: "Call Vince."

"Hello buddy. You're being reassigned," Vince says in his trademark exuberant bluntness, betraying not a hint that his body is being destroyed from within.

"What are you talking about?"

"I've rescued you from the collective farm. You're sprung from that place. Get your ass back up here."

"What's the job?"

"Russians. Back to the juice. Can't tell you more than that."

I'm too stunned to believe this news and wonder if maybe Vince's cancer hasn't already gotten the best of him.

"Hey, Harry. You there?"

"Is this a bad joke, or what?"

"Serious as a heart attack. I know what you're thinking. That asshole Croswell. Look. You get back to doing what you like best *and* you have a chance to get back at the son of a bitch. I leave the modalities up to your twisted imagination."

I think about this. Back to agent running. Back to Roni. And a chance to trip up Croswell.

"Croswell calls the shots. No way he'll have me."

"Don't worry. You won't be working for him. Anyway, this is a directed assignment straight from the office of the DCI. I managed to persuade some friends here that you got a bum rap from TALISMAN and deserved better. So, you can leave the gulag and come back home."

"I don't know, Vince. Just when I was polishing up my fly fishing skills."

"Fuck the fish and get your butt up here. And, before you ask, I got those pictures. Devastating."

"Why Vince. Why me?"

"Somebody's got to have a conscience in this outfit… and be around long enough to do something about it."

CHAPTER SEVEN
LANGLEY, VIRGINIA

The Domestic Resources Branch and the Foreign Resources Branch of the NCS shop are sort of like the Pugsley and Wednesday of the Agency. Weird little stepchildren who don't quite fit in. The DRB's job is to try to coax Americans – usually sympathetic businessmen or academics – to fill the CIA in on what they pick up in their travels overseas. It's fairly above board and the citizens are not asked to spy per se. The FRB, on the other hand, targets foreigners within the United States for recruitment. In practice, they focus most of their attention on foreign diplomats assigned to embassies who may be intelligence officers. FRB concentrates to a large degree on Russians and Chinese.

Vince wangled a job for me in FRB's elite CI-60 team, formerly CI-11 – CI standing for counterintelligence. A single successful recruitment of a Russian intel officer is like placing first on American Idol. Your career is made for life. My track record in quality agent recruitment went in my favor.

CI-60 is a creature of Operation ROUNDUP, having previously been called COURTSHIP.

I report to ROUNDUP's cover officer, who occupies a cubby hole in the bowels of the new building at Langley. Prescott L. Kaiser manufactures lies. His task is to create new identities for ops officers and to help maintain them in the face of hostile foreign agents, pesky hotel reservations clerks and aggressive busybodies of every stripe.

"O-kay," he says in a nasal twang. "Here's cover sheet number one. Study it carefully. Your name is Ronald P. Ginsburg. You are an executive with Aurora National Transmissions, Inc. You have a wife and three children in Winnetka, Illinois. Here're your VISA and MASTERCARD cards, driver's license, social security card, health club membership. Sign for them here."

Kaiser broadcasts Nerd, with a capital N, with his brylcreamed hair, coke bottle horn-rimmed glasses and pens neatly arranged in the front pocket of his Wal-Mart shirt.

"Cover number two. Your name is Melord H. Peckwood, a systems analyst with the National Oceanic and Atmospheric Administration. You are homosexual and you collect ships in bottles. Sign here.

"Finally, cover number thr-e-e." He drawls this out like a quiz show host presenting a contestant with a third impossible option. "Nelson R. O'Meara, energy analyst at DI, of this agency. This is your soft cover for when you have to deal your own kind."

"My 'own kind'? Like vampires?"

Kaiser looks up. He obviously doesn't get the joke. "No. In case you have to deal with our own people but undercover. You get a dip passport for this one. Sign here."

"Why do I need all these covers? You're making me gay? And what do I know about oceans and atmosphere or transmissions?"

"ROUNDUP requires multiple covers. You're operating in the U.S., sometimes abroad. Can't leave too many fingerprints. Got to cover your tracks. Those are the rules. Sign here."

My grandmother used to say, "Never argue with a fool. People won't know the difference." I sign. Kaiser dumps

large envelopes on me, stamped TOP SECRET, containing
cover stories and assorted phony ID's and credit cards.

Croswell bolts out of his desk chair and comes toward
me with an extended hand and broad, insincere smile. You'd
think I was his long lost twin. He places an unwelcome arm
on my shoulder and directs me to sit down.

Croswell's new digs are more plush than his last office.
Large, with sofa, chairs and lamps on end tables and his own
toilet, those seemingly minor trappings that, in the peculiar
culture of government bureaucrats, define status.

"Harry, let's not engage in pretensions. We've had run-
ins in the past. But the past is the past. Welcome aboard."

I scrutinize my right hand. Yep, my fingers are all there.

"We've recruited you for ROUNDUP for good reason.
Your recruitment record is tops."

I remain silent.

"You'll be working with a nine-member team. Five FBI
special agents and four of our own, all cherry-picked for
their recruitment skills. CI-60 gets the first cut of resources.
No red tape. It's an ops officer's dream assignment."

I put on one of those patronizing grins that tells the
person to whom it is directed that I owe him neither respect
nor obeisance.

I sense that Croswell reads my body language as clearly
as a spring day. But he bravely moves on.

"As you know, the Russians remain among our top
targets, just as we are theirs. The cold war may be over,
but the spying goes on. The names are different. SVR has
replaced KGB essentially in name only. You're assigned to
Sergei Maximovich Nemsky, whom we believe to be the
SVR officer responsible for technology. He has lots of
friends in Silicon Valley. It's not difficult to figure out what
he's after."

I don't pick up the thread. "You said, 'We've recruited you.' Let's cut through the pretensions after all. The DCI assigned me to CI-60. And ROUNDUP straddles domestic as well as foreign. Now that we understand each other...."

Croswell smiles with an air of resignation. He absentmindedly brushes lint from a pant leg.

"Harry, I've often thought that your singlemindedness was both your boon and your bane. Okay. I didn't ask for you and I don't direct ROUNDUP, but I do have a big say in what CI-60 does and who they go after. And since we're cutting the crap, I can appreciate that you felt you were set up on TALISMAN. That wasn't my intention...."

"Never mind," I interject. "Let's just not get in each other's way from here on in. How's that?"

Croswell's face freezes. Behind the hard eyes, the wheels are turning. He says nothing. This isn't the end of it.

The CI-60 team operates out of a front corporation in a glass and concrete office building just off the beltway in Tyson's Corners, Virginia. Brass letters on beige masonry announce the Allied Services Group. A lone female receptionist greets visitors in a posh, teak-paneled receiving area adorned with Persian rugs, glass-top tables and tasteful, understated artwork on the walls. Only the team members may enter the inner offices, which comprise six small rooms with desks and cabinets and a communications vault. A compact common area with a conference table occupies the core.

Real people have no business with Allied Services Group. Should some dumb soul stray into the place, the receptionist would turn him away with some story and a smile.

Ray Frasini is the FBI Special Agent in Charge, or SAC. He's my boss. Son of a cop and as straight an arrow as the FBI can muster, Ray never loses his sense of mission nor of being in charge. He is vintage FBI: clean-cut, erect, five-feet-nine inches of sleek muscle, the body of a wrestler. He puts down a hefty box of FBI gadgetry as if it were a packet of popsicles.

Ray asks me to sit down at the conference table rather than in his office. The other CI-60 officers, six men and a woman, move around briskly yet casually, in loosened ties and, in the woman's case, stocking feet. A Redskins poster shares wall space with a grinning Alfred E. Newman and a cunning W.C. Fields, white top hat tipped as he's scrutinizing what obviously is less than an ideal poker hand. McDonald's bags and remnants of boxed Chinese take-out litter the place. I instinctively like this lair of American spydom and its denizens.

Ray hands over the file on Nemsky. "He's low-profile and smooth. Takes no chances and abides his time. A true pro. Married with one child – a thirteen-year old daughter. The kid has some kind of neurological disease; needs regular medical attention. Nemsky is devoted to her, spends gads of time away from work to attend to her needs. Problem is, it's expensive. We're not sure how he pays for it. We know the embassy is basically broke half the time, always bugging Moscow for more funds for everything from official entertainment to the light bills. We doubt he's raiding the embassy's cookie jar, since it's usually empty anyway, and he's getting nothing from us. Yet."

I examine the photos. Nemsky is 45, balding, a face in the crowd, but an open, disarming face, boyish. His wife, Irina, is a puckish blonde with the deepset blue eyes and high cheekbones of a fashion magazine cover girl. The passport photo of the daughter, Anya, displays the face of an emaciated waif staring blankly into nowhere. She has dark circles under her eyes and a sepulchral pallor. This picture jolts me; I can't put it down.

"Nemsky and missus have a thing for American culture, especially jazz and modern literature. They frequent jazz clubs and poetry readings at universities and what not. SIGINT picks up lots of bitching and moaning about Russia turning backward, Moscow gives stupid instructions, their kid has no future much less hope for effective treatment back home, how can they live in Washington on next to nothing, blah, blah, blah. He's prime for recruitment. That's why your NCS and our Intelligence Division turned him over to us. He's yours. You pitch him successfully, we run him; if he jilts you, we send him back to ID."

I retreat to my cubicle to become acquainted with the Nemskys, to try to get to know their likes and dislikes, habits, foibles. Before I even set eyes on him in person I want to know Mr. Nemsky as well as a devoted groupie does a pop star. Back to the juice.

CHAPTER EIGHT
WASHINGTON, DC

In the espionage game one stalks one's quarry like a wolf tracks a buck. You sniff and smell, circle around, follow the trail of your prey, trying to maneuver yourself into the ideal position from which to leap and grab at his jugulars. Perversely, this hunt aspect of the business is what drew me to becoming a spy and it is what keeps me in the game.

The grazing lands of the spy are the limitless diplomatic cocktail parties and receptions where herds of migrating emissaries flock to watering holes of bordeaux, chardonnays and campari sodas, where klatsches of foreign intel officers stop to feed on smoked salmon on rye, Swedish meatballs and spring rolls. This is my natural habitat, where I belong.

The Pakistani ambassador has invited over two-hundred of his dearest associates for a cocktail in honor of his country's energy minister, who is on an official visit. Nuclear testing notwithstanding, business does go on, after all. NCS has wangled an invitation for me as a State Department official. I choose to discard the cockamamie covers the evil twit Kaiser has invented for me and simply represent myself in my own name as an aid official at State.

I roam around the crowd, ginger ale in hand, smile plastered on my face, looking for Nemsky. Fully armed with a dossier that includes details on his hobbies, drinking habits, past assignments, money problems, hang-ups, culinary predilections and tastes in music and literature, I will seek a "chance" encounter. From small talk, I will escalate the conversation to U.S.-Russian relations, jazz, health care, or whatever else might grab his fancy and hold him. A good ops officer then manages to get a target to exchange cards and to agree to a follow-on meeting. This would lead to yet another. Next thing you know, you're a friend of the family, you worm your way into his life and constantly, constantly seek the hook, the opening to make your pitch. It's more than a game, it's an art form. Pitching an intel officer, however, requires infinitely greater care and persistence than a common functionary. He is wise to the professional spy, being one himself, and thereby is equipped with defensive measures. Or, in a truly dangerous twist on things, he will seek to outmaneuver you and snag you as an agent for his country's service. The thrusts, counterthrusts, traps and treacheries of this métier require the skills of a Gary Kasparov and Bobby Fischer to be very good at it.

A diminutive, olive-complexioned man, standing awkwardly alone with a drink in his hand, lumbers over to me and stiffly offers his hand. "Hello. My name is Zani," he says. I politely shake hands and attempt to move back onto the hunting trail.

"I am counselor at Albanian embassy," he says.

"Yes. Pleasure." I continue to scan the banquet room for Nemsky.

"And you?" He attempts a congenial smile which ends up looking like a swinish leer. A small blizzard of dandruff covers the shoulders of his black suit.

"Uh, my name is Brennan. State Department." I make a feint to the left to get around this troll, but he blocks me.

"Oh, really? What office do you work?"

"Energy."

"Ah. Very interesting. You know, we may have oil in Albania."

Silence.

"But political situation is so bad. You know, the communists ruined our country."

"Oh, yeah? How long have you been a diplomat?"

"Well, twenty-four years, but I had always difficulties with them because they knew I did not like communism. Furthermore, if you look at the history of my country…"

Before we get into the ancient Illyrians, I intercept a South Asian man whom I assume is Pakistani.

"Hi. Name's Brennan. You with the embassy?"

"Yes. My name is—"

"You know Zani?" I gesture toward the troll.

"I don't believe—"

"Zani, meet Mr., uh?"

"Khan."

"Indeed." The two shake hands. I slip away.

I quicken my pace. The predator who doesn't feed, after all, goes hungry. At the same time, I become the teflon-coated guest, giving the slip to any more Zanis.

At the makeshift bar I spot him. He's taller than I had envisioned, but there's the same open, youthful face. He looks more like a summer camp counselor than an intelligence officer. Time's awastin'. I go in for the kill.

"Vodka on the rocks, please," I tell the bartender.

Nemsky looks up. *"Govorii po Ruskii?"* he asks.

"N'ye khorosho," I reply. I don't speak Russian very well.

"I see you drinking vodka. I thought perhaps you were one of us."

"Us?" For a flash of a second, I think he's on to my cover.

"Slavs."

I laugh. He doesn't. A careful grin punctuates his face. His eyes study me.

"Brennan's my name," I say a bit too eagerly.

"I see."

"Er, State Department."

"I see."

If Croswell's cold-blooded, this guy's positively cryogenic. "You are?"

"Nemsky," he says simply.

My heart starts sinking. This guy's obviously built his own Berlin Wall around himself. Cautiousness verging on the impenetrable. I pause to collect myself. I sip my vodka. Nemsky sips his orange juice. Some Slav. He looks around the room, turns and gives a polite farewell nod.

"Um. I fund research...into...diseases."

Nemsky pauses. "Is that so? Then you must be with AID."

"Right."

"But you said State Department."

Great. I get the Grand Inquisitor. "Right. USAID is a part of State."

"Hm. Not quite." Nemsky's face is a billboard of doubt. He shows me his back.

"At the moment, we're looking into funding research into wasting diseases, neurological disease."

Nemsky stops in his tracks. He looks back at me. The hook.

"I enjoyed your presentation," a female face calls. I ignore it as I frantically search my brain for the next lie.

"I said I enjoyed your presentation the other day," she persists. I look to my right. It's the blonde society broad, Camilla Loomis. The predator instinct in me suddenly turns to flight.

"You stood up for yourself. I like that. It was so obvious what Mr. Croswell was up to. And you showed him!"

I crack an anemic smile. How can I shake this dingbat? Nemsky will dart out for sure.

"Afghanistan. What a sorry place," she continues. "Frankly, I never thought that anybody could influence events there. What with all that tribal business going on. And..."

I don't believe my ears. This poster girl of patronage, whose knowledge of foreign affairs probably begins and ends in her boudoir, is proceeding to blow my cover.

Nemsky's ears perk up. He has a bemused smile.

"...just because we could get the Russians out doesn't mean we can get the bloody Taliban out...."

I clear my throat. "Mrs. Loomis, may I introduce Mr. Nemsky," I say in a voice two decibels louder than normal.

Loomis takes a breath and offers her hand as if she were being introduced to Prince Charles. The rose gloss on her smiling lips bends light in the direction of the opposite sex like an imploding galaxy. Nemsky gallantly does one of those *küss die hand* numbers one sees only in old Claude Rains movies.

Nemsky looks me in the eye. "So, Mr. Brennan, about your work on, uh, diseases for AID, or was it the State Department? And you, Ms. Loomis?"

I'm tongue-tied.

"I'm a member on the President's Intelligence Oversight Board," she says proudly. She sees the look of utter horror on my reddened face. It finally dawns on Camilla Loomis that maybe, just maybe, she let a virtual pride of cats out of a black bag. She shuts up, looks like she just swallowed a goldfish.

"How interesting," Nemsky continues. "Call me Sergei. I am with the Russian embassy." Another, last, polite nod. Nemsky is gone.

I am left holding the bag with Mrs. Loomis. She looks embarrassed. I look embarrassed and enraged. A minute of silent shock ensues. I contemplate two things: my blown cover and whether I shall murder Mrs. Loomis or merely deck her.

She takes my hand. "Come Mr. Brennan, I want you to meet some people." She leads me toward a group of men in the middle of the reception hall. This, by appearances, is the radioactive core that gives power to this particular Washington gathering. Cardin-clad, Gucci-shod, self-important men in various stages of middle age and older stand in a small circle exchanging views on subject matter that is well above my pay grade.

In the middle, standing straight and high, the graphite rod in this power circle, is a six-foot-three, good-looking man with a thick head of gray-brown hair whom I recognize immediately as Senator John Dodge.

Dodge is holding forth on China policy. Is "comprehensive engagement" the best way to deal with Beijing, or should Washington judiciously apply a "basket of carrots and sticks"? "Why, only a fool would think we could brow-beat a nation of over a billion people to do things our way," he answers his own rhetorical question.

"That translates into two-hundred-odd fools in the lower house alone!" snaps a silver-haired gent with a bourbon in one hand and a stylish cane in the other.

The group guffaws. Their heads turn as if on command as Mrs. Loomis comes sailing into their midst like a sleek, blonde cutter. The Washington ritual of polite kisses on both cheeks greets her. In Peoria this happens only in living room video screenings of *Dangerous Liaisons*. She is welcomed like Cleopatra. There is a certain staginess about all of this as if they were performing before a camera.

"Cammy, you're always a sight for sore eyes," declares Robert Norfolk in an unctuous tone as he takes each of her hands in his and she offers her cheek.

"Not to mention empty political coffers," says the silver-haired one. This is hearty humor for all. Belly laughs all around.

Meanwhile, I'm apparently dogshit. Something that lurks below and is to be avoided for I am neither acknowledged nor greeted. Such is the fate of the Washington unknown.

"Gentlemen, may I introduce Mr....uh..."

"Brennan. Harry Brennan." I shake hands all around. Perfunctory smiles.

"Yes. Robert, you remember Mr. Brennan. At the briefing."

"Ah yes, good presentation Brennan," he says a tad patronizingly. He turns back to the senator like, "Where were we before dogshit here loped in?"

"Briefing?" says a small dark man with clever black eyes. He sizes me up.

"At the" – before I can stop her, Camilla finishes, "CIA. Mr. Brennan gave a marvelous briefing on Afghanistan."

Suddenly, I'm dogshit no more. All eyes come back to me. I think, what purpose would it serve to slay Camilla Loomis on the spot now other than out of pure revenge? She's blown my cover to Russian intelligence and a group of strangers within a matter of minutes. With my cover flushed down the tubes also goes what was left of my career. I look like Daffy Duck caught red-handed.

"Ah. So, Afghanistan," says the dark man, whom Camilla identifies as Jamsheed Mansoori, the Pak ambassador.

"Uh, maybe I should be going," I say.

"Don't be silly, Harry." She has one arm looped in mine as if we were sweethearts at the prom. "Tell them what you told us, about that one group being sold out by the other one and how we stood by and did nothing."

I recall that the District of Columbia does not have capital punishment. I weigh the pros and cons of a life sentence without parole at Lorton in return for shattering Loomis's larynx with fatal results.

The silver fox fumbles inside his jacket and pulls out his business card. Blair W. Evans. Partner, Cairns, Blumenthal &

Evans. It hits me. Dean of the Washington power brokers: ex-congressman, former Secretary of the Navy, ambassador to Moscow, adviser to Presidents. Mr. Establishment.

"Tell us about Afghanistan, Mr. Brennan," he says. "Will it be pacified?" There's that word again.

"A 'pacified Afghanistan' is an oxymoron," I reply.

More guffaws all around.

"I read the *Post*'s story on the CIA's role. They called it 'the greatest intelligence covert action failure since the Kurds' rebellion in Iraq collapsed in 1996,'" Mansoori says. He's maybe eighteen inches from my face, which makes me feel uncomfortable, especially since he's apparently gulped down a kilogram of smoked salmon.

"You know that I cannot comment on such things," I reply, seeking desperately for an opportunity to escape.

"But you are with the CIA," Mansoori presses.

I look at my watch. "Well, it's getting close to my bedtime," I say. With Nemsky onto my cover and me stuck with these effete assholes, my reason for being at this place at this time has evaporated. But Loomis has an arm-lock on me. She won't release. The only way I can flee is indeed to deck her. But she looks up at me with these incredibly deep blue eyes set in a vulnerable face, the expression that all females seem to acquire from birth to capture a man, and which advanced coquettes use to seduce them. I stay put.

"Tell me, friend, is the old Northern Alliance truly finished? The Taliban appears to be returning with a vengeance," Norfolk says, as he holds his bent forefinger pensively to pursed lips and balances an elbow in the palm of his other hand.

"Like Mike Tyson," I answer. A wave of perplexity hits each in the face like a custard pie. "The boxer. He was down for the count more times than you can shake a glove at, but he kept coming back." I can see that they and I talk on different wavelengths. Restrained, not-quite-comprehending chuckles titter around.

"So, these warlords who say they back Karzai will come roaring back like lions!" Mansoori snickers. "They've been finished for years. Only you, the CIA, kept them going. Then, after the Soviets quit, pfft, the CIA quits Jamiat. Bye, Bye Bashir." He snorts, catches each of the others face-to-face like a bouncing jack-in-the-box. "The fact is, my dear boy, those people are not and never were representative of Afghan society. We know the Afghans much better than you."

"And I suppose the Taliban is?" I shoot back. "Your intel service put them in power. And by most accounts, you're still supporting them. But, believe me, those scrappy Afghans which you Paks know oh-so-well, are going to turn right around and bite you in the ass so hard, all of your brand-new toy nukes will be as useless as a bar of soap in Karachi."

A cloud of shock covers the little man's face. He looks at me speechless. Then a rolling-thunder belly laugh seizes him. He slaps his knee. The others join in. "You know something, Mr. CIA? I like you. You tell it like it is. Why aren't there more like you?" He smacks me on the shoulder. I think these are the thickest-skinned peckers I've ever met.

Loomis presses her hand on mine. "This will be the subject at my Issues Night. You must come, Mr. Brennan."

CHAPTER NINE

My best suit set me back $275 at Sym's discount store. My shoes run the gamut from Bostonians to Hushpuppies. I get my hair cut at Sal's Barber Shop for ten bucks. My idea of a gourmet meal is fried clams at the Eastern Shore. I actually like California rosés. And Woody Allen turns me cold. So, what am I doing at Camilla Loomis's swank Georgetown home, one of those Federalist affairs – red brick and clean white doric trim – rubbing elbows with the capital's elite, fitting in about as well as a bottle of Heinz in a sun-dried tomato world? I'm unable to answer my own question. I just show up. Maybe it's Afghanistan, or rubbing elbows with the capital's power elite, or maybe it's Camilla's décolletage, which is absolutely stunning in a sleek, black Versace cocktail dress slit along each leg.

She sidles up to me as I enter, breaking off a tête-à-tête with a TV news anchor whose nip 'n' tuck-taut face and dyed hair are not betrayed on the screen as they are in real life.

"This is my CIA man," she gushes before assorted guests.

I pull her aside. "Madame, do *not* identify me as being with the CIA! For a member of the President's Intelligence Oversight Commission, you sure don't understand much about intelligence."

She smiles coyly. Beguilingly. Mischievously. "What's wrong, lover boy. Can't stand the heat?" She flips a golden tress behind an ear and struts away to greet Undersecretary so-and-so and his carefully coiffed wife.

I grab a glass from a passing waiter. I sip it and wince. "What is this?"

"A kir, sir."

"A what?"

"Kir. A chardonnay laced with crème de cassis."

"Is that so?" I abandon the drink on a credenza.

I turn and find myself smack in the middle of a group of distinguished-looking women all fighting a noble and ongoing battle against age, with varying degrees of success.

"Let's ask him," says one. "We're trying to settle an argument. "My friends here maintain that *Wings of a Dove* – the movie? – is a faithful adaptation of the Jamesian themes of the soullessness of elite society. I posit that the man's love of painting a world external to private states of mind is the central message. What do you think?"

I ponder this. Finally, I say, "Was Bruce Willis in that one?"

"Er, no."

"I missed it then."

Camilla stands at the head of the large banquet room and is clapping her hands. She calls on everyone to take a seat in some three-dozen simple chairs whose backs are covered in white linen. The seats face a huge fireplace whose white mantel sports an ancient clock and eighteenth-century silver pieces, above which hangs an oil depicting hunters amid a sylvan landscape off in merry old somewhere or other. In front of the fireplace is a small linen-covered table with a pewter pitcher of ice water and several glasses.

"Friends. Thank you all for coming this evening." The overhead chandelier casts a sparkling light on Camilla that makes her hair more golden, her skin more fair and her figure-hugging dress more inviting. "This is the third Issues Night sponsored by Americans for the New Millennium and I promise you a fascinating evening of discussion on a topic much in the news and bound to impact on our country's political and economic future."

Liveried busboys make the rounds holding trays of brandy and liqueurs.

"And lest the refreshments make you too warm and fuzzy, just a reminder. Americans for the New Millennium is a political action committee. Your contributions are indeed welcome. And this PAC is dedicating this evening to one of our party's most vibrant and innovative figures – Senator John Dodge."

The statuesque senator with blow-dried hair waves one hand modestly.

"But first, a special treat. A mainstay of our party whose untiring efforts over many years have contributed to a better America. Jared Byron Loomis." She extends her arms as if introducing an act on American Idol.

A wheelchair is rolled into the room. In it is a shell of an old man, whose contorted face reflects the ravages of a stroke-racked brain. He sits hunched forward, unmoving except for his dark eyes, which dart in all directions, taking in what's around him. The body may be inert, but the mind appears to be on full charge.

The gathered powerful and mighty stand and give this pillar of the old Establishment a respectful ovation. Cammy bends over and gives him a peck on the cheek, then flashes her pearly whites.

"Jared has always stood for change. Jared has devoted his entire life toward building a stronger America. He wants me to tell you that he's glad you're all here and that he wants us to bring about the change that will make America stronger."

More applause.

"Old codger bilked more people out of their savings than any robber baron of the past." A tall, balding man in his thirties says this while clapping.

He stands to my right. I look over at him, not sure who he's talking to.

He gives me a side glance, grins slightly. "Jason Mariner." He extends his right hand. We shake. "Cammy gets more mileage out of men than a Toyota Prius gets out of a tank of gas."

"You know her that well, huh?" I say.

"Work for her."

"As what?"

"Chief of staff." He gives me his card.

"I'm—"

"The CIA guy."

"Yeah. The whole world knows by now. But it just so happens that about 16,000 people work for the Agency. So, I'm *a* CIA guy. Not *the* CIA guy."

"Twenty-two thousand. Sixteen-thousand is what they're always dishing out publicly. I say *the* CIA guy because Cammy likes you. In her terms, you are *the*, not *a*."

Cammy signals everyone to settle down. She gives a gushing introduction to Dodge, who sits up front, taking in the praise with a genteel smile. A decorated Gulf War vet, she says, who bravely fought for veterans upon his return. He was an angry young man then. Now he's an angry man, but he has a positive anger because all that needs to be done to bring America into the twenty-first century isn't being done.

Dodge rises and faces the group. After acknowledging all the "distinguished guests," he pours fulsome praise on Mrs. Loomis, "who combines the empathy of an Eleanor Roosevelt with the grace of a Jacqueline Kennedy."

"Not to mention the sex drive and cunning of a Madame Bovary," snipes Mariner through one side of his mouth while maintaining a false smile.

Dodge softens the troops up with a dollop of humor, an acerbic quip about how some people hold that sex and politics don't mix, but without sex there would be no politicians and without politicians there would be a lot less sex, but maybe it would be better sex. Har-dee-har-har. Without notes, he then launches into this night's theme: oil.

"People thought that after the '70s oil crisis, all was fixed. America, the petrol addict, got hooked again on cheap imported oil. Well, the last twenty years have been a mere respite. Mark my words. With China and India on tap, we're already seeing the demand skyrocket. All it will take is another Mideast crisis, and our goose will be cooked again. Develop new forms of energy? Yes. Conserve? You bet. But the name of the game if we are to ensure our national security in the near term is diversification."

"Hold on to your wallet, here it comes," whispers the irrepressible Mariner.

"Picture, if you will, a veritable ocean of oil – and natural gas – which the United States, and other industrialized nations, can tap over a period of decades. An ocean of energy not in the Middle East, not subject to the vagaries and treacheries of Middle East politics. Controlled by nations not gripped by Muslim fundamentalism, countries who are eager for American friendship and investment. Newly freed nations from a hundred years of big power domination. I am talking, ladies and gentlemen, about the four new nations bordering the Caspian Sea. Kazakhstan, Turkmenistan, Georgia and Azerbaijan are sitting on reserves estimated at 200 billion barrels. This is a quarter of the earth's oil reserves. At today's prices, this would be worth *twenty-five trillion* dollars." Here Dodge, the master stumper, pauses for dramatic effect. Let it all sink in.

You could hear a platinum card drop. These people understand money.

"Think about it," Dodge continues. "Whoever controls that oil is going to have a big say in how the world is run in this new century. At the beginning of the last century it was whoever controlled the high seas that had the upper hand strategically. Then it was Britain. Energy, ladies and gentlemen, is what makes the world go around. If we, as the only superpower, cede control over oil to the Russians, the Chinese or to future Saddams, we're in big trouble."

Three-dozen graying heads bob in unison. Dodge is preaching their religion: power and money. In the Ebenezer Baptist church one mile and a world due east from Georgetown, they fall out of the pews waving and praising the Lord during a stirring sermon. In this particular temple, the worshipers nod solemnly as their brains are crunching the numbers and devising plots on how to out climb the others up the political ladder. Dodge's personal tailor will have to equip his coattails with handles, judging by the reaction from this crowd.

I turn to Mariner. "Well, Jason, where do we go from here?"

"The White House, my dear man. No way from here but up." He points an index finger furtively skyward. And again, that sly grin. This man knows on which side his own bread is buttered, cynicism notwithstanding, I conclude.

Polite applause breaks out. Dodge has finished. He soaks in the adulation with a wry smile and an aw-shucks manner. I notice more women sidle up to him than men. He parries their questions with the deftness of a champion fencer. Upright, handsome, charming, bright. A magical elixir to the opposite sex.

Cammy is doing the p.r. thing, posing for group photos with fat-cat contributors and contributors-to-be. Her starburst smile and devilish eyes make love to the lens. Her worshippers are of the male variety. The Washington mating game. An anthropologist's delight.

Mariner has left to chat it up with a bevy of abandoned wives. A round of those cheek kisses again, followed by light banter and giggles. I see such skill in ingratiating oneself with women only among professional gigolos and gay men. I conclude Mariner is of the latter category. The charm is laid on thick, the sex is absent.

Robert Norfolk glides into this gathering. He moves with a nimbleness that belies his size. More kissy-cheeks, followed by a swell of laughter. The women clearly adore this man, who is neither handsome nor fit. Maybe it's his hundred-fifty dollar haircut, navy Brooks Brothers suit, Patek Philippe wristwatch and custom-made English shoes.

"It's power."

I turn. It's Mariner again. He's retreated in face of Norfolk's advance.

"I know what you're thinking. 'What's he got that I don't?'"

"No. Only what's he got, period."

"Like I said, power. And in a town where bullshit talks big time, Robert is king of Mount Bullshit."

I burst out laughing. Mariner laughs with me. Cammy spots us guffawing and makes a bee-line for us. She sports a questioning look on her face as she loops an arm through each of our elbows.

"And what are two of the handsomest men here finding so funny?" she asks.

"Just b.s-ing, is all," Mariner tries to say with a straight face.

I shake again with laughter.

Cammy grabs my arm and leads me in the direction of Norfolk, who has now been joined by the ever present Blair Evans, Dodge and none-other-than intelligence czar Kinneard. They're shaking Norfolk's hand heartily.

"Ah, Brennan!" exclaims Evans in an octogenarian's crackled voice. "Congratulate Norfolk here. You may be working with him. Or for him, may be more like it."

"Hello Brennan." Norfolk takes my hand in a firm handshake. "Look forward to working with the Agency."

"Hard beat, though. Those guys make death row inmates look tame," Kinneard chimes in. "We have Brennan on another beat now. But don't ask him about it. We've got to keep *some* secrets."

They go all atwitter with laughter. I can barely muster a half-smile. I look at Camilla with a question-mark on my face.

"The President has just named Robert Special Envoy for Central Asia," she says, with both hands wrapped affectionately around Norfolk's upper arm. "He's going to make it all happen."

"Make what happen?" I ask.

"Forge a new Alliance for Freedom," Norfolk quickly informs me in his nasally, Ivy League inflection. "The President wants me to weave a tapestry of relations with those nations to bring them closer to us, to promote democracy and human rights, and to settle ongoing disputes."

"What? Armenians and Azeris?" I ask.

"Yes," Norfolk answers firmly. "And region-wide."

"What will Moscow think of this?" I ask again.

"Leave that to those above your pay grade, Mr. Brennan." Kinneard pulls rank and puts me in my place simultaneously. He gives me that official grin that says "you're dismissed, private."

I leave these toads to revel in each other's ego-glow. Indeed above my pay grade. I grab a whisky-and-soda from a passing server and down it. I ask myself what I'm doing here. I should be bowling, watching the fights on ESPN, changing the oil in my car. This is not my crowd and I don't belong here. These people lose or win more money in the stock market in a day than I make in a year. And they speak a different language, one of privilege, power, prestige.

Like Harvey the Rabbit, Mariner floats up to me again. He looks me up and down, takes a gulp of Coke.

"Hmm. Heard the news, eh?"

"Yeah. And I don't get it. First of all, isn't Norfolk a card-carrying Democrat? I mean, he's here tonight, for this John Dodge love-fest."

"The Senate leadership pushed the White House. In the interest of bipartisanship. The position and Norfolk are both throwaways. Oh, and besides, the Democrats caved on Anwar. It was: 'Okay, let's rape Alaska; in turn, we get to forge links with the oil commissars of Central Asia.' Read: 'Big bucks from Big Oil in the form of political contributions. And it's both parties. Watch your step! The logs are rolling faster and faster.'"

I wince. "Okay. And what about this 'We're going to build an Alliance for Freedom' with the likes of Kyrgyzstan, Azerbaijan and those other shit-eating countries? Democracy and human rights? They don't even know how to elect a town mayor. Most are one-man satrapies, Soviet states by a different name. Besides, who cares?"

"He does." Mariner points to an unassuming little man in a dapper suit lurking in the corner, trying successfully to look inconspicuous.

I shake my head.

"Frank DeFalco. CEO of First Eagle Petroleum."

I run this through my mental computer. "Oil."

"See? The CIA isn't as dumb as people like to think. What did they tell you over there? All that democracy and human rights mumbo-jumbo. Right?" Mariner swigs down the remainder of his Coke. "Naw. Just plain greed. That's all. It's in their collective character, like the need for fresh blood is to wolves. One sniff and they're circling around the victim in a pack."

"That's why TALISMAN was shit-canned," I let slip.

"What?"

"Uh. Never mind."

"Cammy told me she needs to see you. In her study. Second floor. First door on the right." Mariner keeps a straight face, but there is a twinkle in his eye.

"What about?"

"I'm just the messenger." He raises his empty glass and throws me a wink, then struts off.

The same indefinable force that motivated me to come here in the first place pulls me to Camilla Loomis's lair and, like one of Nosferatu's victims, I slink up the curving stairwell with measured steps.

At the top, I tap on the door. Nothing. I knock louder.

"Yes. Come in."

With a combination of fear and anticipation, I crack open the door. The room is semi-lit. I stick my head in; my body, however, remains in the hallway.

At the far end of the room, I see her, back turned, glass in hand. She's looking out the window. She turns her head. An amused smile unfurls across her face. Only the desk lamp illuminates the room. The light reflected from below accentuates her black-satin-draped figure, the blond strands tumbling loose around her ears and neck, the glint of her eyes.

"You're welcome to enter. I promise I won't eat you up." Giggles flow easily from her, like water in a brook. She makes me feel silly, a little boy again. I struggle to re-find my manhood.

"Drink?" she asks, saluting me with her scotch-on-the-rocks.

I nod.

She pours an aged malt into a cut-crystal tumbler.

"Ice?"

"No."

"You like it up."

"Up?"

"Straight up." She hands me my drink, stirs the ice in hers with a forefinger, slowly, in languorous circles. She sucks the liquid off her finger.

"So, what do you think?" she asks.

"Of what?"

"All this." She waves a hand in an encompassing motion.

"Not my crowd, I'm afraid."

"I'm not surprised." She saunters by me, sipping from her glass. "You're the strong, silent type, a straight-shooter. A...cross between Clint Eastwood and Gary Cooper. That's why I like you." Cammy turns suddenly, her face inches from mine. She looks up with teasing eyes and a challenging grin.

I meet the challenge with my eyes. "What's going on here?" I say.

"You mean *here*?" She points to the floor.

"No. I mean downstairs. Norfolk, Evans. That crowd."

"Oh. The usual Beltway games. Everybody's scratching each other's back. She speaks rapidly and dismissively, betraying her disinterest in this matter.

"More?" She holds the decanter out.

I ignore her offer. "I get badgered about whether Afghanistan can be pacified," I say in a mocking voice.

She shrugs and pours for herself.

"And tonight, I learn that Robert Norfolk, that pillar of earnestness and self-effacement, has finagled himself the job of opening Central Asia to 'democracy and human rights.' A nice fat sinecure with a fancy title and a line to the White House."

Camilla sidles up to me and touches her shoulder against mine. She looks up expectantly.

I'm trying to stay on track. "What are you people all about anyway?"

"This is what we're about." Camilla drops her glass. She presses her body against mine; her hands expertly take mine and place them squarely on her buttocks. She plants a long, warm kiss, her tongue burrows into my mouth. I let it happen, I knew it would happen, wanted it to. I reciprocate. We stand in the middle of Jared Loomis's musty study, flesh against flesh, hungrily taking each other in. I picture the old man slumped in his bed next door, knowing what's going on but frozen in his own useless body, but then banish this thought. Cammy's thigh is inching its way up my inner legs, to my groin. Our breathing becomes heavier.

My hands grasp behind Cammy's thighs. I jack her up, her legs lock around my middle. I place her on Jared's desk. Our lips are still locked. My mouth eagerly takes in the pliant flesh of her neck, down to her shoulder. I feel her hand pulling my shirt out, reach inside, press against my chest. I feel dizzy. Things are moving so fast between this woman and myself. Out of control. Primal. Hormones at full charge.

Her low-cut dress slips down, revealing full white orbs and abs like rippled beach sand.

"I want you, Harry. I want you," Cammy says hoarsely. Those expert hands undo my belt, pull down my zipper.

I pull back and look into her eyes. Those fiery irises send bolts into me. Challenging eyes, wild, like those of some beast unconstrained by conscience. I search those eyes deeply. Images flash through my mind. But these are not erotic thoughts. Scores of dead villagers, sprawled on the spot of their last living moment; dead kids with the open lifeless eyes of statues; dead women clutching the tiny corpses to their breasts in a last futile effort to protect them from the lethal gas; dead men with the tools of their trade still clasped in their rigid hands.

I stiffen; the proceedings come to a grinding halt. Cammy senses this and looks up questioningly.

"What is it? Did I do something? Come. Come to me. Now."

I turn away, button up and zip.

Cammy approaches, places her hand gently on my shoulder. "Please tell me. Is it me? Ever since we met at that briefing, I detected a spark between us. There's something. I thought we both felt it."

I look at her. Her blue eyes are all sympathy and questioning. "I don't belong here. These friends of yours…"

"They're powerful people. They can do wonders for a civil servant's career."

I shake my head. "But there's something more. Something wrong."

"Wrong?"

"It's just too neat, too coincidental."

Cammy shakes her head.

"TALISMAN is summarily canceled. Jamiat is sold out. Playing footsie with the Taliban. Norfolk is the anointed one. Blair Evans is happier than a pig in shit. I'm sidelined."

"You're sounding paranoid. You CIA types tend to get that way," Cammy says.

I turn on my heel, grab her by the shoulders. "What the hell do you know about me or my profession? You come lah-de-dahing in, a complete novice, pretty as you please with your big bucks, big name and big connections. Well, let's play spymaster today. That should be fun! Maybe I'll buy me an ambassadorship tomorrow. That'll be just peachy!"

Her open hand comes at me faster than a bullet, smacking me hard on one cheek. Instinctively, I cover the stinging area with my own palm. I glare back.

Cammy's face morphs from sheer rage to remorse. "I…I'm sorry. I didn't—"

"Who's Frank DeFalco?"

Cammy goes rigid, goose bumps crawl across her flesh. She feigns ignorance with an unconvincing shrug.

"Oil man? You invited him here. Little guy? He figures in the picture. How?"

"Frank? Why he's another contributor. Likes to hobnob with the Washington set. Comes to a lot of these functions."

"He fits in with Evans and Norfolk and those other vultures."

"Why, I don't know what you're talking about."

"I intend to find out. When I do, I'll let you know."

"Harry, stay. Please."

I'm out the door.

I haven't seen Roni in almost two weeks. Having been hobnobbing with the silver spoon set, I've neglected her. She's hurt and shows it with silence during a forgettable pasta dinner not far from my place. I pay the bill and we depart. We walk slowly in the direction of my house. Roni stares at the sidewalk. I take her hand. She pulls back.

"Roni. I'm sorry I didn't call. It's just that…my work… it's been extremely busy for me."

She sees right through me. "You could have called. You didn't even return my calls."

"I wasn't at my office."

"You don't work there anymore?"

"Of course I do. But I had to be away."

"Your secretary would not even tell me where you were."

"Well, she's protecting my privacy. You know how it is."

"When they answer the phone at your office, they say, 'Hello' only"

"Why, sure—"

"I called the State Department to ask them to track you down. They said they have no record of a Harry Brennan."

"Well, they never have their act together—"

"They answer the phone, 'Department of State, how may I help you?'"

"Different office—"

"Harry, the phone prefix of your office is completely different from the State Department's. I read them your number. They said it was not the State Department's."

We reach my apartment door. We both hesitate.

"Come in?" I say with a cocked grin and eyes that seek forgiveness.

Roni looks at me deeply, dead serious. "Okay," she whispers. I open the door. With arms crossed and head bowed, she walks in.

I don't switch on any lights, but move to the sofa and beckon her in the dark. Roni sits beside me. I kiss her lips, but she doesn't respond. I sit back, run my hands through my hair.

"Roni. There are things about my work I can't tell you about. Or anybody, for that matter."

"You work for the CIA, don't you?"

Roni never ceases to amaze me with her razor-sharp perceptiveness.

"My job requires secrecy. That's all I can tell you."

"Who is Camilla Loomis?"

This hits me like a rocket. I start to say something, but the words don't come out.

"You mentioned her to me before." She reaches into her purse and pulls out a page of newspaper, carefully folded. She unfolds it. It's the Style section. She points to a photograph. It's Cammy at her Georgetown house. The fundraiser. A few short feet to the side is yours truly.

"Mrs. Loomis happens to be on a government commission which I have to deal with."

"Harry. Don't lie to me any more. I know what you do for a living. And my woman's intuition tells me there's somebody else. I put two and two together. It adds up to Camilla Loomis and you." Tears run down Roni's cheeks. "I think we should—"

I touch her lips with my fingers. "Sshh. Listen to me. I work for Uncle Sam and am proud to do so. I add two and two and I get Harry Brennan and…you. I kiss her softly on the forehead. The tears continue to stream down. She sobs softly. "Do you hear me?" She nods. Our lips come together. We then cuddle in each other's arms, say nothing.

"Please trust me, Roni," I say softly. "I can't tell you much about my work. Just be patient. That's all I ask."

Roni's sobs erupt into powerful weeping.

CHAPTER TEN

"I said get a conscience, not get yourself killed," Vince says agitatedly as he paces back and forth. He's lost weight and appears pallid. There's a slight tremor in his hand gestures. "Jesus Christ, Harry, you must have a death wish. I always knew you did."

"Somebody definitely wanted me dead. And I don't need to play ten little Indians to guess who."

"How do you know that? You insert yourself into the most lawless place on earth, play like you're Captain Marvel, then get your ass shot out. And you come waltzing back in here as if you'd just returned from a fishing trip."

"I did. You put me on to it."

Vince plops down into his desk chair, exhausted from the pacing and agitation. "Yeah, well."

"Why? So that I'd get my ass shot out?"

Vince waves a hand dismissively. "You need to know. It was your op and the bastards pulled out the rug. You ought to know."

"Is there more I should know, Vince?"

He looks at me warily. "Go to hell."

"Just returned from there."

Vince breaks out into a hoarse laughter. It turns into a dry cackle and gets out of control as phlegm gurgles upward and out his mouth. I rush over to steady him. He shrugs me off as he wipes his mouth with a tissue.

"Aw. I'm all right."

I look at him silently, trying hard not to reveal pity.

"Ahh. The chemo's tearing my guts inside out. But I'm licking it," he says unconvincingly.

He pulls a diet Coke out from a little office fridge. He offers me one. I take it. I look around. No more Jim Beam, no more Monte Cristos.

"I know what you're thinking, pal. Yeah, for the first time in my life, I'm following doctor's orders." He pops the can and takes a deep swig. He tips it toward me. "Now look. You've used up all nine of your lives. I'm taking the heat for your little misadventure in Afghanistan. I signed your orders, after all. Told them you were doing some passive recon, gather some facts, got a little carried away, that Handley is the world's biggest horse's ass, which they all know anyway. Now, you've got to keep a lid on. Return to CI-60. Lots of challenge in that. Forget TALISMAN. It's over. Finished."

"What do you mean, 'finished'? Hundreds of people were gassed after the weasels in this fudge factory pulled the plug. No explanations. No apologies. Nothing."

"Worse has happened. It's the nature of our business."

I hold back. It's clear that Vince is not a well man. I thank him and draw our meeting to a close.

Ray Frasini welcomes me back without any questions. In the spy game, one's occasional extended absence is accepted as a matter of course. A covert professional life means one's whole life becomes a Chinese puzzle where boxes within boxes govern one's existence. Headquarters may yank an ops officer off a current assignment briefly to deal with some unfinished business from a previous assignment. I once was plucked out of Bangkok to meet an agent I had run earlier in Switzerland, thence to Hong Kong to troubleshoot a covert op that threatened to fall apart. In the space of days I had

three different passports bearing three different names. I
literally had an identity crisis when, jetlagged, I inadvertently
signed into my Hong Kong hotel under the alias I had used in
Switzerland, prompting some fast shuffling and embarrassed
explanation.

Ray hands me Nemsky's file, which the staff has
assiduously kept updated. "Mostly intercepts. Mickey Mouse
stuff. He and everybody else in that embassy is constantly
nagging Moscow to cough up back pay. I don't understand
why we can't buy off the whole lot of them for the equivalent
of a down payment on a house in Chevy Chase," Ray says.

I open the folder. On top is an intercepted fax from the
Russian foreign ministry to Nemsky asking him to attend a
public air show out at Dulles on the weekend. No further
explanation.

"Yeah. They may be bankrupt, but, in some ways, they're
on automatic pilot. Go after our technology, especially
aviation. It fits with his cover as a commercial officer.
Public show. Lots of free handouts. But, not least, lots of
useful people to get acquainted with – engineers, company
reps, pilots and crew. You name it. These affairs are usually
swamped by foreign intel officers. CI loves the air shows. All
they need to do is to track who attends from the embassies
and the guess is good they're intel."

I leaf through the dossier. Another fax intercept catches
my eye. It's from the Mayo Clinic. It's long. It's written not by a
doctor but an administrator, one Harvey S. Barnes. He provides
a detailed readout on tests done on Nemsky's daughter. It
confirms that she has "Batten-Mayou-Spielmeyer," a disease
of the central nervous system of children that is always fatal.
Rarely does a child live past age fifteen. Gene splicing research
has offered a glimmer of hope, but it's still experimental.
There are several more paragraphs with medical jargon
and technical details that are lost on anyone not possessing

a medical degree. The letter ends in a bureaucratic fashion befitting an administrator. The treatment is prohibitively costly, there is a long waiting list topped with patients with more advanced forms of the disease. Do keep us informed of your daughter's condition, blah, blah, blah.

I put the folder down. I think of Laurie. So vibrant. For her the world is an oyster on the half shell, or, more pertinently, a double-cheese pizza with the works. Limitless opportunities and adventures await her. I look down again at the photo of the sepulchral thirteen-year old Anya and shake my head.

"What is it?" Ray asks.

I break out of my contemplation.

"Nemsky's daughter," I say. "On a human level, I feel for Nemsky and his wife."

"The daughter, huh?" Frasini says.

"Yeah. She's got a terminal illness. Here she is in the Land of Cutting Edge Medicine and they can't help her. At least not without a huge investment."

Frasini angles his neck to take a look at Anya's picture. "Gee, yeah. Tough." He scratches his head. A bulb turns on. "You know? There's the hook. Pitch him on that. Offer him the best medical care known to man. We can make it happen. 'Give us the secrets or your girl dies," says Frasini. He then frowns at his own dark humor. "Seriously, though. We could arrange things. Pay for the medical treatment. At least we'd be in control of our own payments – and it'd be for a good cause," he adds as an afterthought.

"Hm."

"Oh, I almost forgot, Harry. Bill Croswell wants to see you urgently."

He takes me by surprise. "Croswell?"

"Yeah, you know. The man with the sunglow heart. Everybody's Friend Croswell. That one."

"Fuck 'em."

"No, buddy. He owns us now. You're the fuckee now."

"What do you mean?"

"Some big bureaucratic power play. Per the DNI. The Russia Division directs us on Russian recruitment. And the NCS boss directs them. Get the picture?"

"Shit."

"Is he in?" I ask.

"Yes, but he's off to the branch staff meeting."

"Oh, I'm sure he'll want to see me." I brush past Harriet, who makes a vain gesture for me to halt, then smiles the resigned smile of a middle-aged spinster with a long crush on a naughty male.

Croswell's standing behind his desk, organizing stuff to take to his meeting. As he lays eyes on me, a shit-eating smirk emerges on his pale face.

"Well, well, well. Look what the cat dragged in. Long time no see, eh Brennan?"

"Not long enough."

"Tsk, tsk, Brennan. That's no way to greet your new boss."

"I report to Ray Frasini," I retort.

"Yes. Frasini belongs to the FBI. *You*, Brennan, belong to the CIA, and that's me."

"Let's cut through the bullshit."

"Let's indeed. So, how's Mr. Nemsky coming along?" he asks.

"Mr. Nemsky sleeps a lot," I lie. I don't want Croswell interfering in this case, so I paint a picture of a worthless asset target, hoping he'll then get off my back.

Obersturmbannführer Croswell holds his gaze on me with the demi-grin of a mildly bemused tyrant about to murder.

"Sleeps a lot," he repeats.

"Yeah. He goes home, argues with the little woman, guzzles a half-liter of Stoli and crashes. Up the next morning at the crack of eight-fifteen, tumbles into his car bypassing breakfast or even a good morning to his daughter and flies like a bat out of hell to the embassy. He punches the clock, careful not to work a nanosecond of overtime, grabs a quick double José Cuervo at Red's Bar and Grill in Arlington, careful not to talk to anybody, then speeds off back home just in time for a repeat battle with the wife, eats dinner and crashes again."

"I see," says Croswell. I see flashes of ice daggers from his steely eyes.

The phone rings. "Right. I'll be heading out," he tells Harriet through the speaker phone and promptly cuts her off.

"Nemsky's ready. Need I remind you, Brennan, that he's a promising access agent. A recruitment link to bigger fish. A solid hard target. We need hard target recruitments, Brennan."

"The guy's still a developmental," I say.

"For crying out loud. He's been a developmental for two years. He'll be transferred out of here by the time you get around to pitching him." Croswell says this, as he says everything, in the same even, steady voice. I imagine him ordering a Big Mac in the same tone. Or ordering a coup d'etat.

"It'd have to be a cold pitch. I don't think he's ready."

"Nemsky's been scrubbed. We gave you the green light months ago." Croswell is referring to the Asset Validation System – AVS – an assessment requirement instituted in the '90s to ensure case officers were not recruiting worthless assets.

"AVS is a joke."

"Brennan, I don't have time for this." Croswell rises and methodically places documents into a black leather satchel. "I have the impression that you view the entire agency as a 'joke.' Cold pitch Nemsky if you have to. But I want one Russian on this agency's payroll and pronto."

The unspoken haunts Croswell as it does the entire agency. Aldrich Ames sold the few good Russian agents we had for a song. Then came Robert Hanssen, of the FBI. As hard as hard assets get, one-by-one these men got dragged off to a firing squad or prison, leaving the CIA with no eyes or ears in the Kremlin, the intelligence agencies or military. In the aftermath, the pressure has been on to make up the loss, through agent recruitment.

"Nemsky's been spotted and assessed. Now it's your job to develop and recruit him. If you don't, I'll get an officer who will. We see eye-to-eye on this, don't we, Brennan?" Croswell lingers in the doorway with his gaze on me, to drive his message home. He turns and struts off to the staff meeting of the National Clandestine Service.

CHAPTER ELEVEN

I return to the art of stalking. In this I have ambivalent feelings. Agent recruiting has always been my professional pride and a source of adrenaline-driven excitement. A predator am I in my natural habitat. And yet. And yet, I am nagged by a feeling of unfinished business from TALISMAN. And I ponder Nemsky and his daughter.

I put these thoughts behind me. This time, I opt for a hunting ground considerably less posh than the diplomatic reception circuit. The Safeway supermarket on upper Wisconsin Ave., a short hike from the Russian embassy, attracts quite a number of its staff for grocery shopping. A couple of them have been caught shoplifting in recent years, such is the plight of the post-Soviet diplomat. CI-60 has observed Nemsky buying there regularly, particularly on Friday evenings. Nemsky tends to linger. Perhaps he just relishes being among such a cornucopia. He purchases judiciously, as one would expect of a man with a modest paycheck. No doubt, were he a West European diplomat, he would join the crowds of the stylishly affluent at the decidedly upscale Whole Foods a few blocks further down.

The pressure to recruit being what it is, Croswell's shop has laid on a significant budget, one cleared right at the top. I'm authorized to offer Nemsky one million dollars in cold hard cash, to be deposited in an overseas bank account of his choice. I am instructed to consult headquarters should

Nemsky demand more. The sky's the limit. Alternatively, any amount of this can be directed toward medical treatment for Anya, which the Agency can arrange with the Mayo Clinic or other top medical institution. In return, Mr. Nemsky must sell his soul. He would have to divulge the mother lode of secrets he no doubt possesses between his ears, including SVR officers operating in the U.S., the inner workings of that spy agency, Moscow's intelligence targets, means and methods of spying, the names of American agents on their payroll and a whole host of other juicy tidbits that would benefit our national security and diminish their own.

Nemsky would also have to be vetted to ensure he wasn't a double agent – pretending to spy for us, but actually a plant of Moscow's aimed at ascertaining our own intel interests and at inserting disinformation into the spokes of our wheels. The spy game indeed is a wilderness of mirrors in which the glass panes may be crystal clear, yet misleading.

At 6:00 pm, Friday, I join the crowds of government commuters, lobbyists, students, retired folks and Georgetown denizens to paw over piles of produce, poke at mounds of plastic-wrapped meat and puzzle over which brand of low-fat muesli to drop into my little steel shopping cart.

I stroll up one aisle and down another. Finally, I spot Nemsky in the produce section, bent over a small sea of fresh tropical fruit. Mangoes, kiwis, guavas, coconuts, some designer fruit I've never seen before. This is obviously a pleasant experience for him, judging by the blissful look on his face. He then makes a long shrug as if to an impossible love and reaches for a bunch of bananas.

I work my way very gradually toward him, nonchalantly tossing things into my cart. I'm not paying attention to the purchases. I eye the mangoes, take one and study it, sniff it, then set it back in the bin. Nemsky sees this and seems curious.

"Not very good, and way too expensive," I say.

"Really?" says Nemsky.

"Yeah. I almost never buy mangoes here."

"Oh?"

"Well, first of all, they're from Jamaica, or somewhere else in the Caribbean."

"Yes, of course. They're obviously not from New Jersey," he says with a wry smile.

"The Caribbean mango is stringy and has a medicinal taste to it. The Southeast Asian mango, on the other hand, is succulent, sweet and rich in flavor."

"I see. You are an expert on mangoes," he says. He tips his head and begins to walk away.

"Well, I've lived in Southeast Asia," I say perhaps a bit too quickly.

Nemsky eyes me closely. A flicker of recognition crosses his face. "We have met. You are the…the aid man from the State Department. Or something like that. Yes?"

"Oh, yeah. The Pak reception."

A moment of awkward silence ensues.

I offer my hand. "Brennan's my name. Harry Brennan."

Nemsky hesitates a second, then reciprocates with a less than enthusiastic handshake. I panic inside. I'm too aggressive, I tell myself. I'm spooking him. He's as intimately familiar with the art and craft of recruitment as I am, antennae strung tight for the smallest, obliquest sign of an approach from an adversary's intelligence service.

As I see his eyes narrow on me, I make a split decision to cut out all the bullshit, end the minuet and simply cold-pitch him, as Croswell demanded.

"Look. You obviously know who I am. I know who you are. It's clear these two meetings aren't by chance. I'll lay it out to you cut and dry. I'm authorized to offer you one million dollars to switch sides. That's one million United

States dollars which we can deposit in an account of your choice – preferably overseas – no strings attached other than your working for us from now on."

Nemsky exhibits no reaction. He just looks at me. The wheels are no doubt whirling in his mind, but whether he's tempted or turned off, I have no way of telling from the man's trademark poker face.

Meanwhile, my heart is racing, I've broken out into a sweat and I can barely think straight. I feel like the geek who's asked the prom queen out on a date.

A grotesquely fat, bearded man inserts himself between us as he reaches to rummage through a mound of discounted loose bananas. He stinks of old sweat and cheap booze. I place my hand on Nemsky's shoulder to steer him toward the underfrequented designer lettuce section. We pause in front of a sorry scattering of wilting arugula.

Nemsky puts his thumb and forefinger under his chin as he ponders what I've said. "Let us say for the sake of argument that I am indeed who you think I am. Why would I do such a thing?"

This throws me off guard. 'For the thrill of it,' I want to throw back at him sarcastically. But I restrain myself. "A million bucks is a lot of money, especially when it's tax-free. Also, what do you owe to your present system? To Putin? The Soviet Union is dead. Your country is run by corrupt oligarchs and the gangster set. What is there left to believe in?"

"Money is everything to you Americans," he replies. "The Walkers. Aldrich Ames. They also believed in nothing. Except money. And they are Americans. Do you think I am like them?"

I have no retort. He's turned the tables on me.

Nemsky picks up an arugula. "This vegetable. It is exotic, yet decaying, falling apart. Much like Russia was. I love this vegetable, yet I cannot afford to buy it. I love Russia, yet I cannot alone save it. I love my country, my friend, and do you know why?"

I give a slight shake of my head.

"Because it is my blood and my soul. What I could never understand is why Americans sell their country – their blood and soul – for a few 'bucks.' Tell your people this: Sergei Maximovich Nemsky is not for sale."

I now know how the geek feels when turned down by the prom queen. But we stand there. He looks at me foursquare in the face. I glower back. Nemsky not only throws a million bucks back at me as if it were soiled toilet paper, but he questions the integrity not only of myself but of the entire American nation. The guy's either nuts or has more balls than the whole Marine Corps. And this pisses me off. I reach for the last card up my now tattered sleeve.

"And Anya?"

Nemsky blinks fast and I see him recoil internally as if catching both barrels of a twelve-gauge shotgun. He breaks his gaze, lowers his eyes to the floor. He raises them again at me. There is hurt in those watery orbs.

"My friend, my daughter is everything to me. And to my wife. And you know her condition, or you would not be here attempting to purchase me like some expensive trinket on a shop shelf."

I nod. "We can offer the best medical treatment. Free."

I read the emotions play out on Nemsky's normally unreadable face. His eyes well and flit; his jaw muscles tighten and his lips press inward. A reddish hue infuses his boyish face. He seems, ever so briefly, to have lost his emotional anchoring. He then looks up and at me, with contemplative eyes. "Hm. Maybe we can stay in touch." Abruptly, Nemsky turns and walks toward the exit. He then stops and returns.

"I will tell you this, since you work, or was it worked, on Afghanistan," he says in a low, but determined voice. "Your leadership has concocted a scheme, a grand and stupid scheme, to make inroads in Central Asia, at my government's expense. You should know and check it out. Next time we can discuss it —and perhaps other possibilities."

At this, Nemsky puts down his half-filled basket and walks out into the night.

CHAPTER TWELVE

It's Columbus Day weekend. I take government holidays seriously. Always have. I shut myself in and chill out. I decline invitations from pals to watch the playoffs. I need to think. I watch a slew of old movies on Nickelodeon. William Powell, Virginia Mayo, Bogart, Ginger Rogers, Cary Grant, Gary Cooper, Lana Turner, Jimmy Stewart parade in and shuffle off my Sony 27-inch screen. My mind is half in and half-tuned out, however. I survive on frozen pizza, cokes and apples.

Nemsky referred to "a grand and stupid scheme" by Washington. In Central Asia. Aimed against Moscow. I place that fragment of insight like a template onto what has gone before – TALISMAN's betrayal, the ambush on Bashir and me on our way out of Afghanistan. And I keep coming up with the same thing: nothing.

Adding to my lack of lucidity is a depression whose black wings have enveloped me and swept me into the nether reaches of my conscience. A voice deep inside tells me: "You offered money for a dying girl's life." I replay over and over again my last encounter with Nemsky. I see his welling eyes; I hear the choke in his voice at the mention of his daughter, Anya. I think to myself, *Have I really gone that low? And for what? Where does one draw the line? Is there a line?* I think of Laurie. What if Nemsky offered me a million dollars to save her life in return for my selling myself to Moscow? I've done many a strange thing in the service of my country, but never this. Croswell, for whom I have no respect and Ray Frasini, for whom I do, both egged me on to bring the dying Anya into the equation. Was their prime concern their country, or their careers? Pitiless merchants in a market of souls.

Surely, as a fully inducted member of one of the most secretive conclaves there is, I should be able to find out about a "grand scheme" concocted by my government, especially one targeting an area of the world in which I specialize. But the funny thing about the CIA, which outsiders rarely comprehend, is that, as an organization, it is as balkanized as the former Yugoslavia. "Compartmented" is the bureaucratic term. All intelligence information is compartmented, protected by codewords, keys to kingdoms. An official working on, say, Poland, would not be privy to intel on Surinam, much less any covert operations or agent networks, and vice-versa. Furthermore, an analyst whose job it is to scrutinize the Russian economy would be walled off from in-depth information on the Russian space program. There are compartments within compartments. So many that even the Director of Central Intelligence can't be aware of but the broadest parameters of most programs. Rather than futilely attempt to scale these Berlin walls on information, I go to a source that is not so much of the system, but rather above it, one who has spilt one or two beans already in my very presence: Norfolk.

In fact, he comes to me. I receive a fancy, gilt-edged invitation card requesting the honor of my presence at the swearing-in ceremony of Robert Stephen Norfolk, the President's Special Envoy for Central Asia. Mariner calls me to nail down my attendance. I have little doubt Cammy put him up to it. I accept.

As a government worker, I receive somewhat less security scrutiny by the uniformed Secret Service at the northeast

gate of the White House than the hoi polloi. I show my
cover State Department ID. They take down the data, then
I join the line to pass through the metal detector. We are
led to the Rose Garden. About a hundred-fifty of Norfolk's
dearest friends and associates and lackeys of the former
mill around sipping iced tea and munching on watercress
sandwiches served by liveried staff. I fall into the lackey class.
I've taken care to wear my best dark suit and a new somber
silk tie. I actually feel I fit in more or less with these people
who are dressed to the nines, perfectly coiffed and trying
their mightiest not to look too awestruck at being feted at
the White House.

At the White House, time is the next most precious
commodity after pecking order. The efficient executive
mansion staff begin the formal proceedings ten minutes
after the allotted hour. We are motioned to take seats in rows
of folding chairs facing a podium and mike set up on the
grass.

The President appears through the French doors of
the West Wing. He goes through his paces. First the formal
welcome, followed by the earthy quip with a twang, then the
effusive praise and c.v. rendition of Robert Norfolk – "a man
whose commitment to bringing about peace is paralleled only
by his extraordinary abilities." As special envoy, his mission
will be a daunting one of building partnerships among the
Central Asian nations and bonding them closer to us. Then
comes the real clincher – the vast untapped oil reserves
which "have the potential for bringing untold prosperity to
those nations."

Norfolk stands humbly at the side of the Chief Executive,
basking in the glow of public adulation. As the President
finishes, Norfolk steps up to the podium and delivers a
speech that is more of the same. His theme is, "Whatever
I can do to advance the interests of my country, I will do.

However I can serve in advancing peace and prosperity in the framework of democracy, I will make it my cause." And on it goes, sorry stabs at copycatting JFK-eloquence, a popular game in the nation's capital for the past four decades.

I'm in the last row, along with a couple dozen other extras, last-minute add-ons to the invitation list to fill in for worthies who couldn't make it.

In the front row, a blonde female head turns and catches my eye. It's Cammy. Our eyes meet only an instant. She radiates a French Lieutenant's Woman kind of aura. Sad. Mysterious. Beguiling. Was that a smile, or a wistful look, or merely a chance visual encounter?

The speechifying is over. The President zips back into the Executive Mansion via the Cabinet Room. The attendees rise and mingle. The multitudes crowd around Norfolk to congratulate him. I'm not sure what to do, so I do nothing. Just stand awkwardly searching vainly for an iced tea. The servers have retreated, no doubt the first of several signals that the party's over. Except for the traffic lights, all signals in Washington are oblique.

Cammy wends her way toward me, oblivious of the rest of the high and mighty in her midst. Unusual for her.

"Hi, handsome," she says, looking up at me.

"You never know who you're gonna run into at the White House," I reply.

"Keeping busy?"

"Yep. I'm catching spies these days. Or, at least trying to. And you?"

"Oh, same old same old. Throwing parties and playing politics."

"What're you doing deep behind enemy lines?" I ask, gesturing at the White House, currently Republican.

"Bipartisan event," she replies. "It's the administration's way to get Congress to buy off on this Central Asia thing."

"How's Dodge doing?"

Cammy casts an eye over each shoulder to ensure the enemy isn't tuning in, then leans into me. "Oh, he'll be the next President. No doubt about it. God knows the preparations for the *pre*-campaigns start earlier and earlier. Fundraising and coalitions are *everything*. Even now we're gaining key contacts in New Hampshire and he just happens to be in Iowa next month to co-chair a cancer conference and—"

She throws her face up to the sky.

"Here I go again. Sorry."

"I asked the question."

"Yes. You did." A sweet laugh pours out from her like a melody. "Listen. About that night. I'm sorry. I went too fast. It's just that, I find you, so – magnetic. In every sense. How does it feel to have that kind of an influence over women?"

"I don't. And no apologies are necessary."

"Friends then?" She holds both hands out, palms up. I place mine in them and welcome her warm grasp.

"Friends."

Norfolk comes lumbering over. They exchange the ritual two-cheek kiss. She echoes her congrats and "how so proud we all are."

Norfolk has on the appropriate dark blue suit, off-white French cuff shirt with American-flag cuff links, silk socks and a white hanky popping jauntily out of his breast pocket.

As I shake his hand, he places the other on my shoulder. "Hello, Brennan, my friend. You're just the man I want to see. We face a great task. A great task. And to fulfill the mission entrusted in me by the President, I'll need expertise. I want you, Brennan, to work for me."

He places his arm around both my shoulders and steers me off to a corner of the garden. Suddenly, I'm a confidant.

"It's like this, my friend," he continues in his nasally voice, now a bit hushed to conceal from others the great mysteries he is about to share with me. His eyes, however, aren't much on me, but are shifting constantly surveilling the crowd, catching the eye of Senator So-and-So and flashing a latex smile, or giving a wave and a wink to an investment banker. He appears to have multiple split attention disorder. Norfolk's got more wheels turning than a Swiss watch.

"I'm putting together a team and I mean a top-notch team. The best there is. And I want you on that team. How about it, my friend?"

If he says "my friend" one more time, I'll throttle him with his hundred dollar Milano necktie. He sees my face covered with doubt.

"This an historic opportunity. A chance to make a difference, Brennan. I've got people from State, DOD, the military. I need someone from the CIA, someone with area expertise. Can I count you in?"

His attention is now commanded by a pair of long female legs attached to the body of a shapely young blonde.

"Shari! Darling! My, but you're a sight for sore eyes."

He's broken off and attached himself to this woman faster than spit to gum. I shrug and wander toward the exit, but stop dead in my tracks.

I go back to Norfolk and with the subtlety of a vise-grip, pull him by his arm away from the blonde. He looks flustered and confused. Norfolk is the kind of guy who jerks people around, not the other way around.

"What's this job entail? What do you want me to do exactly?"

Norfolk straightens his tie and pulls at his jacket.

"Yeah, well. When you want to get someone's attention, you know how to do it, eh Brennan?"

"You're the one who approached me."

"Right. Well. I want someone who'll get me the straight scoop, all the intel I'll need. But he also needs to be plugged in, be able to tell me who's doing what to whom at the Agency, why they're doing it and who they'll likely go after next. I need a guy who will do my bidding there." Norfolk again throws his arm around me, but this time firmly, with the vaguely menacing manner that the Godfather would use. "And above all, my friend, above all, I demand loyalty." He points his index finger at me and looks me straight in the eye, again like Don Corleone.

"And why should I work for you? After all, I have an assignment."

"Because I reward those who perform well. Look at my track record." He sweeps a hand in an arc directed at the crowd, now beginning to break up and leave the scene. "Any number of these people, the younger ones, owe their position to me. I placed them and I boosted their careers – like Apollo."

"I see," I answer neutrally.

"You can hitch your wagon to me, or you can stay in the slow lane, Brennan. From what I hear, your career's in the crapper anyway. Troublemaker, they say. But, you know what? I like troublemakers. Takes one to know one." A naughty grin. A pause. "Tell you what. If you want, I'll fix it so you can continue what you're doing now – spy catching, right? – part-time so that you'll have a fallback in case things don't work out with me. Deal?"

I mull it over.

"Deal." We shake hands.

A pair of female hands land on my shoulders and deftly turn me around. Cammy kisses me on a cheek, her warm lips lingering a moment longer than customary. "Welcome to the team, Harry."

CHAPTER THIRTEEN

They give me one of those high-fallutin' titles that everyone outside the Capital Beltway finds incomprehensible and amusing: Special Assistant to the President's Special Envoy, in Charge of Intelligence Support. I work side-by-side with Principal Deputy Assistant Secretaries, Assistant Deputy Directors, Joint Task Force Commanders, Brigadier Generals-Promotable, Vice Admirals-Lower Grade, Senior Staff Aides to Under Secretaries, and on it goes like a chain reaction in a cancerous alphabet. If titles were money, fully half of Washingtonians would be multimillionaires.

With the fancy title comes a snazzy office in the Eisenhower Executive Office Building, the sprawling French Second Empire-architectural add-on adjacent to the White House on the west side. My office has a 12-foot ceiling embellished with turn-of-the-19th-century molding, an old oak desk and, the ultimate hallmark of having arrived, two windows, overlooking the Ellipse no less. I have a secretary dedicated solely to me, Marilyn, and a junior aide, Warrant Officer Hicks. I'm given a parking space between the EEOB and the West Wing. To go from being a nobody to a somebody is a Washington epiphany.

My job is to gather all the intel for Central Asia, glean that which is timely and useful and to pick out those items of particular import to pass on to Norfolk. In addition, I brief him daily on trends and events. Conversely, I get to tell intelligence agencies what they need to target for information gathering and when we need it. This could entail tasking a lowly analyst with preparing a report on oil exploration to instructing the National Reconnaissance Office to reposition a satellite in order to gain a better view of events on the ground.

My first morning on the job I sit at my desk poring over stacks of forms I must fill out to process myself in. Marilyn will do what she can, but I see hours of my time wasted on this favorite wheel-spinning game of the administrative bureaucrat. I have the clearances already as well as an updated physical from the CIA. But, like every other government organization, the White House has its own way of doing things, its own devices for tying crew to its mast.

The phone calls start pouring in. Marilyn the miracle worker triages them, forwarding the truly important ones, taking messages on the rest. She zips into my office: "You are being summoned by Ambassador Norfolk."

Norfolk's office is down the hall from my own. Word is the President's National Security Advisor exiles all foreign policy denizens to the EEOB, permitting only herself to occupy an office in the West Wing of the White House, a mere heartbeat and a half from the Chief Executive. Proximity to the President is to the White House groupie what good rays and the perfect wave are to the surfer: everything. Restrict access and you have the beach to yourself. Rule number one of the Washington Pecking Order game.

I walk into the ante-office of the new special envoy and, behold! – the delicious legs, number ten body and brilliantly golden tresses of the fair Shari. Shari's model's face has the 'come jump me' daringness of the expert tease. I don't know what Shari's true role is in Norfolk's life, but her effect on men coming to see the boss is one of getting the former to leave their guns at the saloon door – disarming, not to mention distracting. As far as female federal workers are concerned, she is a crown jewel in a vast field of rubble.

Shari rises in all her Yves Saint-Laurent glory, not the customary garb of the GS-9 Washington secretary. Blond strands falling invitingly over her forehead, Shari offers her hand. "Hi. We haven't actually met. I'm Ambassador Norfolk's executive assistant." She says this, as she does everything apparently, in a Jackie O. breathlessness.

"Glad to meet you. I'm his lordship's chief disciple and alternate boinker of blonde bombshells who have gotten their jobs with fancy titles under dubious circumstances," I want to say, but stick with a simple, "Harry Brennan."

Out of the shadows appears Jason Mariner with a stack of files under his arm. "Howdy. I'm helping them set up," he says. "On loan from Cammy."

I don't bring myself to ask how a private citizen gets routine access to the White House much less a security clearance, which I assume he has. Rule number two of the D.C. power elite: the rules apply only to those who don't count.

I'm ushered into a sprawling office featuring a sitting area at one end and a huge oak desk at the other. White House decorators have lovingly maintained the turn-of-century ornateness of these offices, while also allowing for functionality. Cherry wainscoting and electrified gas lamps, along with painting reproductions of the American West adorn the walls. The Executive Mansion's other trademark color, blue, marks the carpet and high back chairs. Measured power embedded in history is the overall theme.

Norfolk has his feet propped on one end of his desk and his hand clutching a phone receiver at the other. He sports a striped, cuff-linked shirt with red tie and yuppie suspenders to hold up pants around a bulging girth. The jacket of his cream suit hangs neatly on a wooden coat rack in the corner.

"Now look. We need those UN resolutions pronto. Got to

get some political momentum geared up early in the General Assembly's session," he drones on into the phone. "Are you with me on this? Good." He abruptly hangs up.

"Ah. Brennan, my man." He gestures at the couch and plops his stocky frame into one of the chairs opposite and crosses his legs. "You don't mind if Jason joins us?"

I nod, knowing I have no real choice in the matter, but I like Jason because he fills in the missing pieces when I'm all puzzled out. Jason strolls in, the sumptuous Shari in tow with three cups of steaming coffee.

"I'm glad you're on the team, Brennan. Real glad." Norfolk opens a box of Macanudos on the coffee table, pulls out one of the bronze torpedoes and proceeds to lop an end off with a cigar-cutter. "You're a key person on the team. Big responsibilities. The intel community needs to be harnessed for the effort." His eyes follow Shari's ass as she sashays out the office. Norfolk mouths the cigar caressingly with his lips. A man with an oral fixation. My worst fear of noxious blue fumes engulfing us all goes by the wayside as Norfolk merely plays with his oversized coffin nail.

"You can't smoke on Federal premises any more," he says pointedly. "Good rule. My doctor approves."

Mariner chuckles obligingly.

"So, here's the picture, Brennan. We have a monumental task before us. We've got these new countries out there. They need our help. Post-communist ex-colonies of the Soviet Union which happen to be situated very strategically between Russia, China, Iran and the Indian subcontinent. We've got to exert American influence, get a strategic toehold before the barbarian hordes start rushing in again," says Norfolk, conveniently overlooking the fact that history's barbarians were spawned from this very region.

Norfolk points his cigar at a wall map of Central Asia. "Look at it. Throughout the centuries, these countries were overrun by Tamerlane, Attila, Alexander the Great, Genghis Khan, Peter the Great, the Ottomans, finally the Bolshies. They never had a chance. Now they do."

"And of course, there's the oil," I chime in.

"I'm glad you mentioned that," Norfolk says, pointing with the cigar, as if I just happened to spout something about today's weather. "Two-hundred million barrels – at least. Rivals Saudi Arabia. It needs to be exploited wisely. And American companies are going to do it. Democratization, free markets, oil. These are big stakes."

In this holy trinity, something tells me that oil is the Father, democracy is the Son and the free market is the Holy Spirit that drives the rest.

Norfolk gets up and goes to a window. He contemplates the view a moment, then gestures out, Macanudo in hand. "See that?"

"Uh, yeah."

"What do you see?"

"The Washington Monument, the Ellipse, Constitution Avenue."

"Yes, and more, Brennan." He does a quick turn. His eyes narrow, hone in on me straight on, all meaningfulness. A pregnant pause. "History." Norfolk mouths this as if it were a revelation straight from God. "What we have here is an opportunity to alter – to *make* – history. A unique opportunity, Brennan. At this point, Norfolk is on his feet, pacing before the map, fingering his cigar like a baton. He's animated, but his mind is off in some other dimension.

"Ever read Mahan?" he asks.

"Alfred Thayer Mahan?" I ask.

"Precisely. One of the modern era's greatest strategic thinkers. An American at that. He said, whoever controls the Heartland will dominate the world "— the Heartland being the Eurasian landmass."

"Mackinder."

"Hm?"

"Sir Halford Mackinder. British. He's the formulator of the Heartland theory. He actually contradicted Mahan, who advocated sea power as key to strategic superiority."

Norfolk looks annoyed, then waves a hand dismissively. "Anyway, we're not going to let Russia back in. And we've got to keep China in her box, not to mention the Ayatollahs in Iran. And I'm going to do it. Not since Churchill was called to save his people and democratic societies has such a monumental challenge gone out looking for a leader. The right leader." He slams one fist into a palm.

I double check the coffee for any traces of illegal substances. This guy equates himself with Churchill? He's breached the line from politically acceptable egomania over to the messianic.

Before he starts dropping names like, say, Jesus Christ or Leonardo DiCaprio, I interject a question.

"Is there a National Security Presidential Directive on our policy?"

"Huh?" I break Norfolk out of his trance.

"An NSPD. Something official that lays out exactly what our policy is. Chopped on by the President."

Norfolk comes back down to earth, rudely plucked from his dreamland by the suggestion of reality.

"Uh. It's being worked out, Brennan," he says quickly. "In the meantime, I'm in charge of making the policy," he says, ignoring minor details like the Constitution and the fact that there are a sitting President and Secretary of State who do just that.

I leave my inaugural meeting with Sir Winston Norfolk prepared to launch myself into the Great Quest to Bring Democracy to Benighted Central Asia.

I first task the CIA with pulling reports on the political stability of governments in Azerbaijan and Armenia as well as on the endless tensions between the two countries. I receive post haste slickly packaged analyses from headquarters and spot reports from our stations in those countries. A picture of oil-rich autocratic Azerbaijan versus oil-deprived, but politically influential Armenia is apparent. The U.S. conducts a constant tightrope policy of currying the petroplenty Azeris while placating the wily Armenians, who have strong lobbies in the U.S. and other countries.

Next, I ask CIA and State to produce background and policy papers on the so-called "'Stans" – Kazakhstan, Uzbekistan, Turkmenistan, Kyrgyzstan. Again, oil prevails. The Kazakhs got it. Lots of it. Largely unexploited. The others have little to none. The Kazakhs and their strongman leader are our friends.

Finally, I make the same tasking for Afghanistan. The picture is a familiar one to me: a resurgent Taliban, grinding and worsening poverty, a weak central government, a country where progress is defined by achieving a life expectancy of 45. The polished analysis from the agency's Directorate of Intelligence describes recent gains made by Taliban against the government. A slick, multicolored foldout map has arrows showing recent offensives and an expanding green, representing Taliban, covering four-fifths of the country.

There is little in the Afghan materials that I don't already know. I go back to the agency and ask for raw data on TALISMAN and Arab terrorists. The answer on the former is "Access Denied – Codeword." On the latter, I get the usual sketchy intel reports on probable al-Qaeda sanctuaries along Pakistan's northwest frontier and their networks abroad.

I call the Directorate of Intelligence's senior analyst and demand information on TALISMAN. That's an operations matter, he tells me and refers me to the National Clandestine

Service side of the house. I then call the ops officer in charge of Afghanistan by secure line. She tells me her hands are tied and passes me on to the one and only Croswell.

"Well, well, well. So Mr. Brennan has gone to the big league," intones Croswell with the smugness of a jealous little man. "A White House job doesn't translate into the right to know everything under God's sun. But in this case, you know it all anyway, don't you Brennan? It was your operation. In any case, the files are under embargo pending a review."

"What review?"

"The routine review done on all failed operations. Now let me ask you this, Brennan. When can we expect Mr. Nemsky to be on our payroll? You're now with Norfolk, so I guess we'll just take you off CI-60."

"Norfolk wants me to stay on that case," I say.

"Does he now? Let me remind you, Brennan, that your next fitness report comes up very soon. Let me remind you further that the promotion boards value agent recruitment more highly than yet another detail assignment outside the agency, White House or otherwise. And recruitment of hard targets like Russians counts the most. Conversely, failure to even break the ice with an assigned hard target, one who has been deemed recruitable, will consign an officer to the bureaucratic junkyard, followed by early retirement – if they're lucky." The causticness in Croswell's voice makes it clear that this is his desired outcome and that he'd do his utmost to make it happen.

"Hey, Croswell. Can I tell you something?"

Pause. Cat's got Croswell's tongue.

"Go to hell!"

"Brennan, you don't talk to me like that. I demand an—"

I hang up.

CHAPTER FOURTEEN

Observing Norfolk in action is like taking in a Nureyev of politics, a veritable Dr. Caligari of behind-the-scenes deal-making. He is at the throats of those below him and at the feet of those above. He exercises the subtle force of a sledgehammer to get his way, never takes prisoners and frequently machineguns the survivors of his bureaucratic battles. He uses people, big and small, like tissue. The bottom line with Norfolk is that he sticks with those who are useful to him, discards those who are not. The very bottom line is Norfolk, Norfolk, Norfolk.

As he ties together networks, the workload increases commensurately. I find myself working longer days and weeks. I prepare policy papers, set up interagency meetings, manage crises. People of all ranks come to me for guidance. I sit in on meetings with the President and Vice President. As Norfolk's star rises, the sycophants and climbers stream out of the woodwork. They cultivate me as a surrogate of the boss, hoping for support to advance their silly little careers. It's the Washington mutual masturbation game.

It's Friday night. I'm buried in paperwork. I'm exhausted. The clock says 9:00. A guy from the commo unit rushes in.

"This NIACT immediate just came in," says the young man, handing me a two-page cable from embassy Islamabad, slugged for immediate action day or night. Its subject line reads: "Taliban Makes Peace Feeler to USG." I scan it quickly. "Taliban representatives approached base chief in Peshawar Friday. They want to make peace with the Karzai government and Washington. The key phrase in this message reads: "The unified people of Afghanistan will no longer tolerate on its territory the presence of revolutionary elements who engage in violence against other governments and peoples." They want a meeting.

I read it again, word for word this time. I rush out of my office into the corridor and one door down to Norfolk's. Unusually for him on a Friday night, he has no social engagements and is also working late. Shari's desk is empty and there is no duty secretary. She must be in the can, I surmise.

Norfolk's door is closed. I tap, then open it. I crane my head around to Norfolk's desk. He's not there, though the desk lamp is on and papers are strewn about. From the back of the expansive office I hear sounds, like someone in pain. I go to the small rear room where file cabinets and safes are kept. I yank the door open.

Inside I am confronted with a stripped-down Shari straddling Norfolk who is holding onto a two-door safe like a bronco buster, his pants jacked down to his ankles. Just as my embarrassed face appears, they are screaming in climax like a couple of super-charged ferrets.

I quickly close the door and race out of the place. Back in my office, I plop into my desk chair, stare out the window and mutter, "Oh my God."

Fifteen minutes later, my phone rings. It's a breathless Shari. "Could you come and see Ambassador Norfolk now please?" she gushes ever so sweetly.

"Sure. Be right over."

As I re-enter the office suite, a red-faced, tousle-haired Shari is reapplying her lipstick using a compact mirror. She smiles and gestures for me to enter Norfolk's office.

The boss is back in his seat, poring over the stack of papers on his desk. His hair is matted wet, either from perspiration or a quick wash. Otherwise, it's as if he hadn't left his seat for hours.

"Burning the late-night oil again, eh, Brennan?" he says, as if I had simply caught him picking his nose rather than banging his secretary.

"Uh, yeah. Thought I'd clear the decks before the weekend."

"Noble effort. What's up?"

I show him the cable.

He reads it, then pounds the desk with one fist. "This could be it. This is the breakthrough we need. We need to act on this immediately.

"I'll call State."

"No. Let them call me. I want us to get a leg up on this. Those bozos at State will only fuck it up. They'll want to convene an interagency meeting, water the whole thing down to the point you wouldn't want to wash your dishes in it. Then the underemployed ego trippers over there will try to steal the action." He carefully reads the cable one more time. "Yeah. And SECDEF is with me on this one."

Norfolk is leaning back in his chair, tapping his front teeth with the eraser side of a pencil. The wheels are spinning so fast that I expect to see smoke coming from his ears. It seems that getting his rocks off while on the job focuses Norfolk's mind like nothing else.

"Brennan, now's the time for you to use those contact networks of yours to open some doors for me out there. Pass the message to the Taliban that I want to meet with them, to parley. When the State pukes finally get off their collective lard-asses and call, instruct them to send a cable back to Islamabad telling Ambassador what's-her-face to cool it, not do anything till she's heard back from us. Then think up a bunch of 'scenarios', 'options', position papers for them to do to keep them busy and out of our hair."

The malevolent smile on Norfolk's face clearly indicates he is enjoying all of this skullduggery.

When deception is central to one's life, as it with intelligence officers, pulling the wool over the eyes of others in the name of policy becomes second nature, easy. I call Assistant Secretary of State for South Asia, Nancy Bassette, and convey the "White House's" marching orders. Take no action. Instruct our ambassador in Pakistan to stand by.

"Are you sure this is what we want to do?" she asks.

"We need time to analyze and assess," I respond. "There are too many risks. Not something we should dive into."

"There's also the risk that we'll miss a unique opportunity. Our pressures have obviously worked. They're now willing to close down terrorist operations on their soil."

"We agree they need to be tested, but first let's study the possibilities. We want State to put together a series of options papers outlining the choices that lie before us, accompanied by in-depth analyses."

I hear Bassette pick up a pencil and begin to take notes. "Uh-huh. OK."

"In addition, we need an assortment of carefully thought-out scenarios showing the upsides and downsides of the various options."

"I see. Yes."

"Finally, do a position paper for the President's consideration with appropriate policy recommendations."

"Right. This is going to take a while. The clearance process alone will be time-consuming."

"I understand. Take your time. We want something with a lot of thought behind it, no slap-dash products. And we're in no hurry to curry the Taliban. And this is very close-hold. So, let's limit the people working on it to the absolute minimum."

End of conversation. Bassette proceeds to mobilize a small army of her diplomats and analysts to crash on a bunch of make-work exercises just to keep them all out of Norfolk's hair. I lean back and ponder how many man hours and how much of the taxpayers' money is being squandered on this officially mandated wild goose chase.

I rack my brain for the right channel through which to reach the Taliban – unofficially. The obvious springs to mind.

Jalal Parviz, Professor Emeritus of Near Eastern Studies at the University of California at Berkeley, is one of those characters who works assiduously at ensuring that not only are both sides of his bread buttered, but the edges and ends as well. Born in Isfahan, Iran around the time the CIA engineered the ouster of Mohammad Mosadeq in the early '50's, Parviz is the son of a politically connected and ambitious merchant father. Dad ingratiated himself with the Shah, while helping the Islamic militants on the side. He raised funds for mosque-building under the Ayatollah Khomeini. Meanwhile, the government steered business deals to him, thus further enriching the family. Likewise, Parviz junior has acted as informal advisor to new moderates in Tehran, while having also served on the State Department's policy planning staff. He got quick tenure in academia by first becoming a star at the Rand Corporation, a Pentagon-funded think tank. During the Soviet occupation of Afghanistan, he befriended numerous Afghan resistance figures, particularly the Dari-speakers, closest ethnically and linguistically to the Iranians. He's written respected books on both countries.

Oh. And then there's the key detail of dad and son both having been paid assets of the CIA over many years.

I decide a few days in San Francisco are necessary. Away from the power games of Washington. I need some down time to recalibrate and relax. I check not into the Holiday Inn downtown, the abode of choice of federal functionaries visiting the Golden Gate city on business, but into a funky B&B on California Street.

I meet Jalal at a leafy bar in Little Italy. Tall, with a full head of slightly graying hair and always sporting a fashionable suit and an assertive manner, Jal passes more for a Silicon Valley businessman than a university professor. We embrace, Persian style.

"*Salaam*," I greet him.

"*Salaam eleikhem*," he responds warmly.

A good Muslim more in spirit than in practice, Jal orders a scotch, straight up. I make that two.

"It must be important what brings you here," he says with a twinkle in his eye.

I bow my head slightly. "In a word, yes."

"Bashir must be pissed," he says.

"What do you know?"

"I know this. The CIA pulled the rug out from him. Many in his group are bitter. That was your operation, I assume. But it went ahead anyway. How did Bashir pull it off?"

I never play games with Jal, whose sources are solid and who can be trusted to keep confidentialities. "It made no sense. Here's a big al-Qaeda camp. We're perfectly positioned to annihilate them after months of careful planning. And then headquarters orders the op shut down. With no explanation." I recount my secret trip inside Afghanistan, bucking orders, going through with TALISMAN and the subsequent ambush. "Does it make any sense to you?"

"Holy shit. The ambush. Your own people were out to do you in," he says.

"I don't know. I assume it was the Paks. Maybe the Taliban itself. Could've been anybody."

"No. It was your superiors," he says with finality.

"How can you be so damn sure?"

"The Taliban are not that competent. They don't even know who you are. The Paks wouldn't try to pull off such a thing unilaterally; not after those fatal terrorist shootings of embassy people over the last several years. The Paks probably orchestrated the hit against you, but your own agency set it up."

"Then, in that case, I think I know who."

"And you're in danger all the time, anywhere."

"Naw. I don't think so. They wanted to get me out of there, and teach me a lesson. I was getting too close to something."

Jal cocks his head and raises an eyebrow. "Like what?"

"The CIA went into cahoots with the Paks to sell out Bashir. After expending lots of resources using his organization to destabilize the Taliban. Suddenly, there's a sea change. They make a decision they need the Taliban, and Bashir's outfit is in the way. So, I might add, am I."

"Of course. It's as plain as the nose on my face." Jal points at his own prodigious schnozz, in a display of his self-deprecating humor.

"And?"

"Bashir was useful so long as Washington wanted to destabilize the Taliban. The Paks finally went along because they began to fear Taliban's power. In particular, some of the more radical among the Taliban have been making noises about uniting all Pushtuns into a single Islamic bloc controlled by the Afghans. Such a scenario would lead to the break-up of Pakistan."

"Are you speculating or do you know something?" I ask.

"I know something."

"But how—"

Jal holds up one hand. "Let me continue."

I raise my palms in a sign that I cede the floor.

"So, then, all of a sudden, the picture changes. Jamiat is out. Taliban is in. Why?"

"A Russian told me there is a 'grand and stupid scheme' by the U.S. government aimed against the strategic interests of Moscow in the region."

"Funny. My contacts in Tehran tell me the same thing. Only that it's aimed against *them*. They believe the United States is seeking to further contain Iran by signing up more allies; in this case, even vile ones like the Taliban."

"So what is it?" I ask.

"Your guess is as good as mine," Jal says. "But one thing is sure. It is something which ties the Paks and the Americans together. 'Mutual shared interests,' as we political scientists call it."

"Well, Norfolk, Dodge and others keep blathering on about oil," I say.

Jal points an index finger at me. "Sounds good to me."

"So, the price of oil has doubled over the past twelve months. But why Afghanistan? And what's with the Taliban?"

"Exactly," Jal says. "And why so secret? In the past, whenever the U.S. needed to diversify its oil import sources, there was no secret about it. No need to be. Business, government, academia, think tanks, the media, all engaged in public analysis and promotion of a variety of ideas. Even I offered my two cents back in the '80's when people last gave this matter some serious thought."

"On the subject of the Taliban, Jal, I need to pass a message to them."

Jal looks at me as if I were losing my mind.

"Don't be shocked."

"Why?"

"They want to meet with us. We're willing, but need to keep it under wraps for the time being. Between you and your dad, you've got inroads into everybody in that part of the world."

Jal rubs his chin. "Yes. I know some people. I helped to broker some prisoner exchanges. All the parties know me, some even trust me." Jal laughs. "But let me get this straight. First, we're racking our brains trying to figure out what the Agency is doing by colluding with the Paks to betray the good Afghans and sidling up to the Taliban. Now you're asking me to put you in touch with them. My head's beginning to spin, Harry."

"Norfolk's tasking. He wants to do it behind everybody's back. To 'bring peace among the fighting factions.' But it's obviously much more than that. Let's follow the trail."

Jal nods deeply. "I'll do it."

CHAPTER FIFTEEN

I catch a flight back to D.C. I go straight from the airport to the office. It's just before quitting time, at least for people in the normal work world. As I enter my office, there's Marilyn, looking dejected and nervous.

"Hi," I say.

"Hi," she answers in a barely audible voice.

I stop in my tracks. "Is something wrong?"

"There's been some changes around here."

"What changes?"

"He's fired everybody. Except me and you. Gunny. Ms. Cummings, the commo guys, everybody. Yesterday he did it."

"What?"

She shrugs, then listlessly tidies her desk and picks up her purse. "See you tomorrow."

I go to Norfolk's office. A decidedly disoriented but pleasant redheaded woman greets me.

"Uh, hi. And you are...?"

"Shannon," she says.

Shannon has the looks and demeanor of a stripper trying to go legit. Big boobs, frizzed hair, too much makeup.

"Let me guess. You're filling in for Shari?" I ask.

"Uh. No. Shari no longer works here," she says, then looks absently down at her long, crimson fingernails. End of discussion.

"I see."

I let myself into Norfolk's office. As usual, he's working not one, but two, phones. Feet crossed on the desk. He gestures for me to have a seat. As he juggles two conversations, he's devouring a Big Mac. Between bites and bursts of conversation, he dumps clusters of ice into his mouth from a jumbo-size cup, now devoid of coke. He grinds the ice with the grating sound of a cement mixer. His desk looks as if Ronald McDonald just had an anxiety attack at it. It's strewn with burger wrappers, cardboard containers, itinerant fries and used-up ketchup packets.

"Now look, Mike," he says unctuously into one receiver, "You've got to get me a seat at the President's dinner on Friday.... What? I don't care if it's for the Finnish-American community. My great grandfather was a Finn."

He switches receivers. Lowers his voice. "Friday night? Can do? Uh, huh. So the separation is official finally?"

Big Mac sauce oozes down his arm as he chomps down again. Back to Mike.

"His name was Larsen. Came from Goteborg...Say what? It's in Sweden? So, who gives a fuck, Mike? Close enough for government work, isn't it? Hey, Mike, I'm relying on you. You can make it happen, Mike...No, there's no 'Mrs. Norfolk.' I ditched the last one six months ago.... Way to go, Mike! Anytime you wanna change duties, you call me, hear, buddy? And, hey, are those 'Skins something, or what? I can get tickets. Call me in the fall." He hangs up on Mike.

Lowered voice again. "So, April, darling. Can do? Mm hmm, yeah...You know I do, babes. Deal?...Great. Luv ya." He finally hangs up.

He looks at his watch. "Oh, shit. I'm already late for SECDEF. You know what sticklers for time those DOD types are. He cranes his neck toward the door.

"Hey, Shannon?" he shouts. "Call over. Tell 'em my car got stuck in rush hour traffic on Memorial Bridge. Be there lickety split."

Before I can get a word in edgewise, Norfolk has stood up and is reaching for his suit jacket with one hand, wiping his mouth with the Mickey D's take-out bag with the other.

"So, Brennan. We lined up to go to Pakistan? When? I want this top secret. You hear me, Brennan?" He's pulled out a comb and is bending to see his reflection in the glass of a picture on his ego wall. He runs the comb through his hair a couple of times.

Before he reaches the door, I stiff-arm him. "Whoa!"

Norfolk raises his eyebrows. "Brennan? Whatever it is, it can wait."

I stand my ground. "What's happened here? Where's our staff?"

"Need new blood. LBJ wanted all his people to belong to the 'Can Do Club,' or they were out the door. "Our people just didn't cut it. So, they're out." He pulls out a small bottle of breathalyzer and sprays twice in his mouth.

"Gee. Shari sure seemed able to do all kinds of things. Can Do was her middle name."

"I've got no time for jokes, Brennan. Don't sweat it. We're the White House. We can get anybody we want. We'll have replacements tomorrow. Piece of cake. Let's talk Pakistan when I get back."

Norfolk is out the door.

Jal's contacts pan out. With barely a couple of hours to brief up Norfolk, we're on a black C-141 out of Andrews headed for Islamabad. The aircraft is noisy, very noisy. We sit in rigid seats thrown into the aircraft on a pallet. The crew hand out boxes containing yogurt, a banana, a plastic-wrapped sandwich of indeterminate contents, juice and a small bag of chips. They also distribute hearing protectors to shut out the roar of the engines.

I hand over to Norfolk a short briefing book that Marilyn and I slapped together. In it are recent CIA and State Department analyses, some bio and talking points that have been used with NATO governments on Afghanistan.

"You sure nobody knows about this trip?" Norfolk shouts.

"Yes. Only the National Security Advisor, who presumably has informed the President and the Chief of Staff. And, of course, some Air Force people, whose plane this is."

"State?"

"No. At least, I've gotten no wind that they know anything."

Norfolk smirks. He actually rubs his hands together like some evil wizard. "Just wait till they do. This is like when Kissinger went to China in '72. It'll knock their socks off."

"The Taliban ran a terrorist state. China wasn't," I remind Norfolk.

He waves a hand dismissively. "Don't delude yourself. Besides, Bill Richardson went out there to Kabul in '98. Tried to get them to mend fences. Didn't work. We can say I'm picking up from that."

I slump into my seat. *Right, buddy. Let's not delude ourselves.*

After overnighting in Islamabad, we head out in a small ISI and CIA-organized convoy for Waziristan. Formally a part of Pakistan, Waziristan belongs to the Federally Administered Tribal Area, a catch-all label for a hodge-podge of fiercely independent tribes who owe obeisance to no country. This is Taliban territory. It is also reputed to be the safehaven of Osama's successor, Ayman al-Zawahiri and al-Qaeda's new operations chief, Saif al-Adel, both Egyptian.

As we enter South Waziristan, we are met by armed men, agents of that region's defacto ruler and Taliban stalwart, Hakitullah Mehsud, who took over after his brother, Baitullah, was ejected from this planet by a well-targeted Hellfire missile from a U.S. drone aircraft in late 2009. They take the lead in their pick-up and we head for the hills along winding, dirt roads. We approach the area bordering Afghanistan, mountains loom ahead.

As we enter a settlement of mud-brick houses, a middle-aged man steps forward. He beams a wide smile and, in mellifluous British English, identifies himself as Abdullah al-Hakim, of the Foreign Ministry of the Islamic State of Afghanistan, the Taliban's official name for the country when they held power. He makes quick introductions with his two sidekicks, Mullah Masoom Ahmad and Mullah Syed Akhund. These are young, grave, wary. Al-Hakim mumbles something about their being from the "Central *Shura*", or council. All are bearded, in conformance with Taliban dictate, and wear the flat *pakol* hat in lieu of the Taliban's trademark black turban.

Al-Hakim takes us into the largest of the mud houses and beckons us to have a seat on colorful carpets covering the floor. He tries his best to put us at ease, regaling us with tales of his student days at the engineering faculty of Manchester University.

"You know, one day, I and my friends bought a lamb. In commemoration of *Eid al-Fitr*, we took the lamb out to the countryside. There, in the middle of a meadow, we slit the lamb's throat, in accordance with *halal*. Well, unbeknownst to us, some little children were playing in a wooded area nearby. As we cut that lamb's throat, we heard screaming from the woods. The little children were horrified. This made us very embarrassed."

Ha, ha, ha. A Taliban George Carlin.

"How was the lamb?" I ask.

Al-Hakim brings his fingertips to his lips in a gesture of delectability. "Succulent. We feasted well that day."

Placards in Pushtu and Dari hang on the walls. I draw on my rusty Dari to decipher one of them.

> *God is Great!*
> *The Afghan Nation is Great!*
> *God Grant the Taliban Strength and Victory!*

Norfolk is uncharacteristically silent. He seems deep in thought.

We are brought into a room devoid of decor. On a low chair sits a squat man with a white *lungee* turban and gray *salwar kameez*. His gaunt face betrays no emotion. A black eye patch covers one eye; his good eye is cobra-like, fixed on the quarry facing him. Al-Hakim takes a seat to Omar's right. The others sit in chairs opposite from Norfolk and myself. An old servant enters and pours green tea into small glasses.

Mullah Mohammad Omar, *Amir ul-Momineen* – Leader of the Faithful – the Taliban's chief, sits in silence, motionless. He stares at us for an uncomfortable length of time. That single stony eye bores in on us as if attempting to read the soul buried within the flesh. He is checking us out carefully, as one would expect from a coldly calculating killer.

Finally, a faint smile cracks across lips covered by a full black beard. He speaks in a low voice, rattling off greetings, which are interpreted by al-Hakim. He says he feels honored by the presence of two Americans. The Americans did so much years ago to help the Afghan people to rid themselves of the godless Soviet occupiers and their nonbelieving Afghan henchmen. Afghanistan's chaotic political circumstances after ten years of combating the foreign occupiers have resulted in more struggle and suffering of the people. A groundswell of popular support for the virtuous Taliban, rooted in an urgent yearning for peace, swept them into power – until America attacked them. Now the people fervently wish to rebuild an Islamic society. But old adversaries, those bent on holding power for power's sake, refused to join the *ulema* and continue to wage a futile war against the children of Mohammad. The Taliban therefore asks the United States to use all of its persuasive powers to get the misguided opponents of the Taliban in Kabul to foreswear further combat against their Islamic brethren and to join the peaceful rebuilding of the country.

"There is blessing in action," he declares. He raises his hands, arms bent, palms facing the ceiling. He lifts his gaze as well. "Heaven will help the Afghan nation if the Afghan people help themselves."

Omar lowers arms and eye, cracks a thin smile and gestures for his guests to drink the tea.

We all raise the glasses to our lips. It is bitter, this tea. It brings back memories for me. Exciting days that bound so many together in a common and just cause: evicting the Soviets from Afghanistan. And, in those days, the adrenaline flowed more than the tea.

Now it's Norfolk's turn. He's the only person in the room dressed in a Western suit, a pale seersucker with elegant silk tie and shirt and Bruno Magli shoes. Sweat from this corpulent man drenches the armpits, mid-back and collar, largely defeating the purpose of his polished ensemble. I had changed into a *salwar kameez* on the plane. It feels great.

I study the faces of the humorless young mullahs. They eye Norfolk as a *Kush* mountain lion would an injured lamb. They search for weakness, these young men, weaned on war, imbued with the fervor of true faith.

Norfolk goes at them with guns blazing.

"Thank you for receiving us. But our time here is short, so let me speak frankly."

Norfolk digs into a small bowl of pistachios as if his life depended on them. Like a shucking machine, he peels off the shells and stuffs the contents into his mouth, while at the same time talking, not missing a beat.

"Yes, times have changed. Yes, the Afghan people certainly desire peace. We were ready to recognize your government years ago just after the Taliban seized power. But you blew it."

Al-Hakim pauses in translation. He leans over to Norfolk. "Please, I don't understand this 'blew it.' This is American slang, is it not?"

"You wrecked any opportunities," Norfolk clarifies. "You harbor al-Qaeda, attackers of my country. Your human rights record is abysmal. You lock women up. You torture prisoners. You kill perceived opponents en masse. I can go on and on. After 9/11, we had to attack to knock out al-Qaeda's base here."

Omar stirs. He sips his tea. "This is no longer a problem. Brother Ayman has joined Brother Osama in embracing martyrdom."

Norfolk swallows his next point. It takes a moment for him to register this last remark.

"Could you clarify your last statement?"

Omar sports a cat-that-swallowed-the-canary smile. He nods at one of the young mullahs, who quietly exits the room. A moment later, the twin doors to the greeting chamber open. Two servants wheel in a gurney. On it is a simple, wooden box, about the length of a man. The men maneuver it directly in front of us. I can't help but think what I don't want to think. A rush of dizziness passes through my head. Norfolk is no longer feeding his face with pistachios. Omar nods again.

One of the men places both hands beneath the lid and flings it open. Inside the box are the remains of a man, gaunt, twisted, brutalized. Flies immediately converge onto the decomposing corpse. Norfolk turns away in disgust. I wince and gaze at the ceiling. I lower my eyes again. I force myself to look at the face of a dark, tall, bearded man, eyes frozen open in death, mouth agape. The dead man looks as if he were caught by surprise in his last moment of life, caught by the lethal blow to the head by a confidant. The face, frozen in terror, seems to be familiar. Yet, the violence done to the man, compounded by accelerating decay, make recognition all the more difficult. Is it the face of the world's most wanted terrorist, Ayman al-Zawahiri?

The eyes of the mullahs turn expectantly to Norfolk. All Norfolk can muster is a puzzled expression and upturned hands, like, "What gives?"

Mullah Omar again flashes his shit-eater's grin. "When a man is perplexed, God is beneficent," he says through al-Hakim.

"What the fuck's that supposed to mean?" Norfolk demands. The stench emanating from the crude coffin permeates the stifling room. Norfolk is green around the gills. He takes out his handkerchief and holds it to his nose.

Omar nods at the festering corpse. "Brother Ayman," he says.

Norfolk and I crane our heads back at the corpse.

"After you killed Osama, Brother Ayman was the biggest dividing point between us, no?" asks Omar.

A servant lifts a bowl of pistachios up to Norfolk. The President's Special Envoy looks as if he is ready to puke.

"Alas, we are ready to join with our Afghan brothers into a unified government," Omar continues, his arms extended outward. "In turn, we ask that you use all the powers at your vast disposal to persuade Engineer Bashir and all others who currently refuse to embrace peace, to lay down their arms and join the *ulema*."

"This is going too fast," Norfolk says. "First of all, how can we be sure that the stiff is who you say it is? Looks like any raghead, er, Afghan, to me."

Al-Hakim leaves out the colorful language in his translation.

Omar raises an index finger and nods. Good point. Almost forgot. He again signals one of the factotums. The latter runs out of the chamber and returns seconds later, this time bearing a small polished wooden box, one made for jewelry or other finery. Like Igor out of a Frankenstein movie, the flunky shuffles dutifully over to our table. Upon a second gesture from Mullah Omar, he sticks it directly under our noses and snaps the lid open. Inside, on a bed of blood-stained velvet are two hands, severed jaggedly from the wrists that once bore them.

Norfolk yanks his silk handkerchief from his nose to his mouth and barfs into it. I plop back in my chair and place my fingertips against my brow. "Oh, holy Jesus."

"He is an honorable holy man of The Book," Omar rejoins. It takes me a minute to realize the bastard is trying to be nice by reminding us that Jesus Christ is paid homage by Muslims, though he is not recognized as a prophet, the sole domain of Mohammad.

"They are yours," Omar says magnanimously. "Take the hands. Keep them with those of Che Guevara. The body, however, must remain. Brother Ayman was a Muslim and therefore must be buried as a Muslim. Not buried at sea."

"That's good, 'cause U.S. customs might have a problem with us trying to take Brother Ayman into the country in his current state," I say. Gallows humor somehow seems to fit the occasion.

Guffaws around the table, except from Norfolk and me.

They realize Norfolk has had enough. Omar orders the various body parts be removed from the room. In their place are placed vases of cut flowers.

Norfolk leans forward, elbows on knees, color returning to his face. "This is what I'm prepared to offer. Peace and our support for your entering a coalition government in return for your foreswearing harboring terrorists and an end to hostilities against Coalition troops."

Omar listens carefully. He nods once. "Our Afghan mujahidin fight for Allah against our internal enemies. Our Arab brothers will go. Except those who carry out strictly religious or humanitarian endeavors." Omar places his right palm over his heart in a gesture of a sincere pledge.

Norfolk takes this in with a nod of understanding. "I will take this message to Washington for consideration. This may take some time."

"And all foreign soldiers must be removed from Afghanistan," Omar adds.

"If Afghanistan is peaceful and provides no safehaven to terrorists, there will be no need to retain troops here," Norfolk replies.

Omar is all ears.

"We'll engage the other Afghan factions in a dialogue to encourage them to seek national reconciliation with the Taliban, of course."

"Our hearts are always open to join all of our brethren back into the *ulema*," says Omar with the magnanimity of a true blue statesman. "Mohammad – peace be upon Him – teaches that forgiveness is the essence of God," he adds with the empty sincerity of a K-Mart evangelist.

Omar orders more tea be poured. "Afghanistan is a destitute country. Ten years of occupation by the northern oppressors, followed by two additional decades of internal strife have laid our country to waste. We need help to rebuild Afghanistan."

"We are prepared to get the U.N. to expand its assistance effort and the World Bank, IMF and other financial institutions to fund infrastructure projects to reconstruct your country."

"With peace it will be safe to construct oil pipelines through Afghanistan," Omar says. He's more in our face on this point. His single eye comes to life. His expression is challenging rather than querying. "They told us it is certain. The oil people. Such a project will bring such benefits to us."

Norfolk nods. "Provided all the other conditions are met, I see no reason not to give the green light for the oil companies to operate here. No terrorists, halt attacks against our troops, roll back opium production. The oil and gas deals will more than compensate for the drugs. And you finally get peace and legitimacy."

Omar ponders this, then nods.

The other mullahs all smile and relax.

I am struck by the perfunctoriness of this whole exchange between Norfolk and Omar. Something hollow and scripted about it. Like two scam artists rehearsing a schtick, just going through the motions, confirming something that has already been agreed.

CHAPTER SIXTEEN

I grab a taxi at Andrews and head home. I'm too jet-lagged and mush-brained to think clearly about the escapades in Afghanistan. My mind, that part which is still functioning, focuses on one thing: get out of the clothes I've had on for an entire day and jump into the shower. I nod off. The driver has to shake me upon arrival at my home, a pre-WWII brick townhouse with the original slate roof. All housing built before the war was honest stuff, stolid and reliable -- foursquare American. I regularly congratulate myself for having the presence of mind to buy one of these fortresses of coziness, tiny closets, sticking windows and all, in contrast to the post-ranch house claptraps with their flimsy walls and plasticized attempts to emulate Federalist, Tudor or Georgian architecture that saturate the suburbs.

I drop my bags in the foyer, drag myself upstairs and collapse on the bed before I can carry out action items one and two. On my stomach, I drop off into deep slumber before my conscience can protest. Sleep envelopes me like warm waves of a tropical sea, the dream world parts its curtains onto the stage of mysterious fantasy. The somnolent play that takes shape is in the wide-open meadows of my boyhood. The sun shines brightly onto an unending sea of green pasture and woodlands. I romp onto this bucolic stage, the fresh breeze of springtime caressing my boy's face.

The ringing of the phone tears me out of this warm and fuzzy world back into the cold reality of consciousness. Do I answer it, or ignore it?

I can't ignore it. It won't ignore me. Shit. I raise my leaden head and lunge for the phone with a Frankenstein-like motion of one arm. "Yeah?" I rub my fatigued eyes, trying to focus.

"Mr. Brennan?"

"One and the same."

"We gotta meet."

"'We gotta meet,'" I mock. "My mother always taught me to steer clear of strangers. Call later, okay, pal?"

"Wait. Don't put the fuckin' phone down!"

I groan and shake my head. "OK. This better be good. You've got thirty seconds."

"This is Frank DeFalco, Brennan. I think you know who I am." His accent is distinctly New York. He says 'I *tink.*'

A light goes on in my head. Cammy's party. The oil guy. Keeps a low profile. Makes Cammy's flesh crawl.

"Like I said, we gotta meet."

"Yeah, sure." Sleep can wait. What I do for my country.

I grab a large coffee at Starbuck's before embarking on the forty-mile drive to Baltimore. I know that the coffee, on an empty stomach, will only induce gas and make me piss a lot. But I need to stay awake and drugs are out of the question. Frank insists on treating me for dinner at his favorite place in Little Italy, Vesuvio, on south High Street.

"'Best veal in the city.' Who said that?" he asks with a stifled snort.

Now with a half-finished martini under my belt, on top of the coffee and added to my sleeplessness, and my mind on the verge of hallucination, I shrug.

"Sollozzo."

My face registers a blank. This induces mild irritation in DeFalco.

He jerks a hand at me. "The Turk. You know. Come on! Don't you go to the movies?"

"Uh, yeah."

"You really don't know, do yah?" Frank falls back in his seat. Another hand gesture, a dismissive one. You cavun'. "Aahh."

"Turk, huh? Um. *Lawrence of Arabia*?"

Frank turns his head out of disgust and waves a hand as if swatting a fly. "Didn't you see *The Godfather*? I thought everybody has seen it."

Amid the fuzz balls in my head, I am lucid enough to wonder why I agreed to drive all the way out here to meet with this character.

He halts a young waiter in his tracks. Twirls an index finger downward in a circular motion. "Two more martinis."

I cover my glass with my palm. "I've had it."

Frank nods at the young man with a look of reassurance. "Two more." He leans forward and hunches over on his elbows. He fixes his eyes on mine. He has a face in the crowd, 50's, balding, small dark eyes, a prominent nose, but altogether nothing that would register in one's mind after a chance meeting. "You know the actor who played Sollozzo?"

Almost beyond caring at this point, I shake my head.

"Al Lettieri." He slaps the table, then points at his own head. "Hah! How's that for memory? For detail? You know what else? I can name all the two and three star generals on both sides in the Civil War."

The martinis arrive. Frank takes a gulp. We order. I get the vitello alla matriciana. Frank gets the gnocchi alla carbonara. No veal. I wonder about this.

"Yeah. Call me superstitious. Sollozzo got his brains blown out after eating veal in a restaurant. Anyway, I got an eye for detail and I never forget. For example, I notice that Cammy Loomis has got this thing for you." This ting.

I fold my hands and stiffen my lips. "Look. If you think I'm moving in on…"

Frank waves dismissively. "Hey. Not to worry. I didn't ask you here to tell you I'll cut your balls off if you don't stop seeing Cammy. Go ahead. See her."

I unfold my hands and raise my eyebrows. What gives?

"Cammy wants you for two reasons. First." He points an index finger at me like a gun. "She's attracted to you. I can see it. Hell, everybody can. Cammy never grew up. Loves exotic men, like spies. You're a spy, right? Second, you're useful to her. And that's more important to her."

"I'm listening." I may be dead tired and mushy brained, but the gray matter has suddenly come to life. The wheels shake their rust and are spinning. I'm struggling to figure out what this guy wants from me. I'm struggling to figure out who he is exactly, where he fits into the picture.

We've munched our way through the bib lettuce and tomato salad. On comes the stracciatella soup. The clientele appears to be a mix of out-of-towners on tour and locals, the latter heavily leaning toward the self-made man with a paunch and a cadillac married to the mousy heavily permed local girl set. The air is filled with garlic and oregano. No fusion cuisine here. No teriyaki jalapeño wraps. No mango lassis.

"Anyway, it's like this. Cammy appears hard, or at least strong. But I can tell you that she's very vulnerable and very insecure. That's why I lined her up with Jared Loomis years back. To give her security. I just never counted on the cocksucker living so long." He takes a big gulp of his martini.

"I better stop drinking this shit. I'll end up spilling my guts. Guys like me. We can't afford to be careless. Know what I mean?"

"No."

Frank jabs four fingers into his sternum. "You don't know who I am? I mean my background?"

"Nope."

"Hey. I like that. No prejudices. We start from scratch." He orders a third martini – for himself. I resolutely abstain. "What the hell. Might as well let my hair down. After all, it's not like I'm talking to the fuckin' FBI, is it? CIA. You guys couldn't care less, right? Not your turf."

I laugh.

"No, seriously. I made my bones in Jersey, even though I'm from New York. Made it the hard way."

"How's that?" I ask.

"By grinding the balls of my adversaries," he says with dead seriousness. "I came up from nothing." Nutting. "My father drove a bread truck. Then, nights, he tended bar. Worked the docks. Anything. He wasn't too proud. He had six mouths to feed. My mother cleaned apartments. They both died young. I was left to take care of the rest of us. To make a long story short, I got into construction, then diversified. Had to break some rules along the way, which hasn't endeared me to the federal government. But, never done any time. Seen my share of grand juries, though."

This guy has me riveted. He's a born story-teller; emanates humor and warmth. At the very least, I find him entertaining.

"Then what's a bad guy like you doing with a good girl like Cammy Loomis?" I ask tongue in cheek.

"Let me tell you about Cammy." He leans on one elbow, points a finger straight at me. "But you got to promise me not to breathe a word to anybody else."

I nod.

"I rescued Cammy. Poor white trash from West Virginia."

I register surprise.

"Oh, yeah. Cammy-Lou McGuthrey was her name. Daughter of a coal miner and a seamstress. Married when she was eighteen. That's when I met her. Passing through on my way to Louisville on some labor deal. Working in a diner. This girl comes over. She's striking. You should've seen her. It wasn't just her beauty; she looked like Miss America, blonde, built, radiant. She had this quality, this charisma. I couldn't take my eyes off 'n' her. I'll never forget, I asked her what the specialty of the house was. She answers, 'Despair on toast and poverty à la mode, mister.' Smart, this kid was." Frank taps his temple. "And sassy."

The main courses arrive. Wafts of garlic and oregano.

"So, you fell for her," I say.

"No, nothing like that. Honest." He raises his right hand in a scout salute. "So, I tell her, I says, 'That bad, huh?' And she looks me straight in the eye, those diamond blues of her drill right into me, and she says, 'Not for long.' I says, 'Win the lottery?' She answers, 'Yep. And I'm lookin' right at the winnin' ticket.'" Frank says this with a mock hillbilly accent, more like a guy from Brooklyn with a speech defect. "Next thing you know, she has her bag packed and hops in my car."

"Camilla Harrington Loomis, society doyenne, was a runaway? A teeny-bopper diner denizen with a hillbilly-hubby?" I ask. "McGuthrey? Where did Harrington come from?"

"Her maiden name was McGuthrey. Her husband, apparently he was a kid himself, worked in a garage. I never met him. Name was...Romano, Romagna, something like that. Italian miner family. A bunch settled in those parts long ago. Good people, but not too swift. So, she kept McGuthrey. Those hill people do funny things. Not stuck on formalities. Frankly, I'm not sure they were even married. Harrington. She made it up. Sounded classier than McGuthrey or Romano. And, of course, the 'Lou' went the way of McGuthrey. Cammy-Lou became Camilla, which I bet you won't find on her birth certificate, if she has one."

My head is spinning, and not just from the martinis. "Cammy-Lou McGuthrey Romano. Go on, Frank. I'm all ears."

"Yeah, so, I take her to New York, put her on the payroll as a filing clerk. I wouldn't let her answer the phone. Who could understand her? But she was a very quick study. On her own, she starts reading all the trade journals, *Construction Today, Equipment Leasing Digest, Contracting News*, stuff like that. Makes your eyes water just looking at the cover. But this gal gobbles it all up. At the same time, she smoothes out the accent, sounds less like a hick. Before you know it, on her own initiative, she's answering phones, greeting clients, talking business with them using the lingo of the trade."

"Eliza Dolittle," I say.

"What?"

"*My Fair Lady*. The lead character who was transformed from a common working class girl into a refined woman."

Frank points his fork at me. "You got it. Same time I recognize her potential, she's on to me to get her a diction coach, give her a clothing allowance *and* a dress advisor at one of those posh ladies stores, introduce her around. Meanwhile, with her fantastic looks and sparky personality, she's got people – men – coming at her from all different directions, guys who want to do business with me. She boosted sales through the roof. The kid was some kind of phenomenon, I tell you. So, I go for it, the whole nine yards. I pay for the speech lessons, clothes, some private tutoring, take her out to the best restaurants. And she transforms herself like this magnificent butterfly. And in a very short space of time. After a year and a half, you don't detect a trace of her Ellie May Clampett accent. She's the toast of society and her origins go from a blur into total darkness."

"Just like that," I say.

"Just like that."

"And then what?"

"Like I said, I introduce her around. Of course, every guy wants to get into her pants. Their wives hate her or envy her, or both. Biggest cocktease in the Western World, Cammy. She uses these guys – married or not was not important to her – to gain further entrée into the good life: expensive vacations, diamonds, fancy little cars, more lah-dee-dah clothes. You name it. She uses them, then drops them. And the poor dumb fucks keep coming back for more. The married guys, they were the most pathetic."

The waiter removes the dishes of the main course. He runs down a short-list of heart-busting desserts ranging from chocolate cheesecake tortoni to cherry tiramisu flambé. Frank looks down at his paunch. "I'd have shit for brains to eat one of those." Instead he sends the young man scrambling around the neighborhood for anisette *biscotti* to munch with a double espresso. I follow suit.

"Okay. When does Cinderella meet her Prince Charming?" I ask.

"Having tied the knot once before, once burnt, twice shy. She's smart. She goes for the sixty-four million dollar prize. I introduce her to Jared Loomis, worth at least twice that amount. We hooked up on some oil deals way back. Very lucrative for us both. So, the guy's seventy-four and has the sex drive of an alley cat. They turn out to be very compatible: he's got tons of dough, she's got…well, she's got it. An irresistible combination. Love at first sight." Frank slaps his hands.

"And?"

"And the rest is history."

"I don't get it, Frank. What do you get out of all this?"

"I'll be very frank with you. Cammy came into her own real quick. She entered circles of politicians and business people that were pretty much off limits to me. Before you knew it, she was introducing *me* to the right folks. Did wonders not only for my business, but also my reputation. Though, I must add, I'm still not seen as one-hundred percent legit. And, probably for good reason." Frank emits a loud guffaw which momentarily disrupts the dinner conversations around us.

"So, she remains loyal to you. I saw you at her Issues Night with Senator Dodge. But I could see you were keeping a low profile."

"To say the least. She takes a risk associating with Frank DeFalco, but she does. I'm the only male of the species she remains loyal to no matter what. And there's two reasons why: I rescued her from Shit Central *and* sex has never entered our relationship. You should also know this – and consider it top secret. Cammy had a kid back there. Little girl. Left her with relatives."

"Ohh."

"Yeah. I've never discussed it with her. And neither should you," Frank says.

"So. You invited me here to tell me all this?" I ask.

"Yeah. By way of two things. First, you should know that Cammy is hungry. Yes, she's a passionate woman. But, ultimately, she sees you like every other man: a stepping stone on the way further up."

"And second?"

"And second, I'll cut off your balls if you get in the way of the biggest oil deal since Alaska."

I stare stonily at Frank. He reciprocates.

He leans back and wipes his mouth with his napkin, still unblinking.

"And if you're smart and you help me, get me that insider information you CIA guys have, I can make it worth your while."

Frank slurps down his espresso with a flourish and wipes his lips.

CHAPTER SEVENTEEN

Washington between November and March is simply rotten. Damp cold seals the city like a sarcophagus. Advancing winter makes its bitter presence felt by wreaking ice and snow squalls on a city JFK described as combining southern efficiency and northern charm. Snow removal isn't contained in the local DNA. The self-absorbed citizens barrel down the metropolis's unplowed thoroughfares like kamikaze pilots. Leaving the office nights at nine, therefore, doesn't irk me so much in this dismal time of the year. The days stink and I shiver, not of cold, but at the mere thought of demolition derby rush-hour in a vast urban skating rink.

But once home, I shut the world out, at least to the extent the bank of official phones in my house will permit me. This Monday evening, I just want to crash, watch some escapist fare on television while eating my take-home Cantonese dinner, and then turn in.

Half-way into the egg drop soup, my regular home phone rings. I want to be annoyed but find I'm too exhausted to find the energy. Besides, it could be Laurie. And it is.

We chat. And we chat some more. About her classes, her professors, her friends; about my work, or what little I can say about it. I sense my daughter is dancing around something, something's on her mind, but she needs to get up the nerve to tell me.

"How's the guy scene?" I ask bluntly.

"Guy scene?"

"Yeah. You know, those big hairy creatures who sometimes walk on two legs, but who otherwise have been seen hibernating on their asses in front of Monday Night Football hugging a six pack of Bud?"

Laurie lets out a nervous laugh. "Yeah. Guy scene."

I let silence force the issue.

"Yeah. Well." Deep breath. "Um, now that you mention it, um, gee, I've met this really nice guy."

"Met and fell for him."

"Uh…Yeah. Dad, I need advice. And Mom, well Mom is, you know–"

"Busy."

"'Fraid so. Between her business and Mel the geek."

"Is he good to you, Laurie?"

"His name is Ryan. That's his first name. Last name's Kirkpatrick."

"Nice name."

"We met at a debate. He's against the 'Star Wars' missile shield. I'm sort of for it. He's a man with causes. Passionate. We argue politics a lot, but he's so…dreamy. Oh, Dad. I feel so funny talking to you about this. I'm sorry."

I reassure her and ask her to go on.

"He's tall, has dark hair, sort of shy at first. The girls are all crazy over him. Dad. I don't know how to ask you this. So, I'll just say it. He's asked me to join him during spring break."

"Join? How?"

"He's fascinated with the Middle East. Wants me to go with him to see ancient sites."

"Laurie. The Middle East?! Don't you realize—"

"And I want your permission."

"Oh, Laurie," I say. Visions of a pixie-like five-year old flash through my head. Then, a ten-year old girl in straw bonnet and frilly dress picking wildflowers. Images of my child. My child. A sensation runs through me, into my groin, dizzying, like that of falling suddenly.

A pause comes between my daughter and me. Setting our intelligence objectives for the Sudan and arguing with the Joint Chiefs of Staff over how to nab Bosnian war criminals are a cinch compared with what my daughter is laying on me. I wrestle with my heart. But my vision on this matter is clear.

"Laurie. You're nineteen."

"Almost twenty."

"Yeah. Twenty."

"What were you doing at twenty, Dad?"

"I led a squad at the DMZ."

"And got shot for your efforts. Very grown-up things."

"Let's stick to the subject, Laurie."

"My point is…at twenty, we're more or less grown up. At forty, fifty, people look back and think twenty-year olds are kids."

"Laurie, you ask my permission to travel with a man you just met. I think it's not a good idea."

"You don't approve, then?" she asks sharply.

"No, I can't, babes."

A deep breath at the other end.

"Dad. I…I don't know…I—. It's late. I gotta go. Bye." She hangs up.

Nothing in my work, save losing agents to a firing squad, approaches the way I think of my only child at this moment. I abandon my eggrolls and mu goo gai pan, sit back and ponder. Am I overprotective? Can I conceive of Laurie as anything but 'my little girl'? Am I a hypocrite? Who can I consult? When would I find the time?

The miracles of fiber optic technology, however, keep me from completing my contemplation. The same phone rings again. I jump at it and pick up the receiver.

"Look, Laurie, I want to make it clear that—"

"Mr. Brennan? Oh. Maybe I dialed wrong," says an accented male voice at the other end.

I set him straight.

"This is Sergei Maximovich Nemsky."

My fatigued and taxed brain can't shift gears quickly enough. My mouth moves, but no words come out.

"Mr. Brennan." *Mister Braynahn.* "Is it you?"

I clear my throat. "Yes. Harry Brennan."

"Ah. Good. You remember me, don't you?" I half envision the tongue in cheek.

"Yes, of course."

"I do not like phones. Can we meet?"

"Sure." I try not to sound too enthusiastic.

"Good. Tomorrow then. Dinner. Eight o'clock. Corner of Wilson Boulevard and George Mason. There's someone who wants to see you." *Click.*

Spooks prefer late rendezvous. Most people don't realize this fact. It's one of the infinite number of fine details of tradecraft the 007 fans never get exposed to, but Smiley's people do. Espionage pros make optimum use of the oblique, of simplicity, of practicality. Anything to make them invisible. James Bond is a walking bull's eye. George Smiley blends into the wallpaper. After-sundown encounters, simply, provide cover of darkness. Also, the good spy must give himself, at minimum, an hour to do an SDR – a surveillance detection run: the intricate backtracking, meandering, double tracks, sleights and feints required to be reasonably sure that one is not being followed. Eight pm is the perfect time. You can run your SDR after the debilitating rush-hour traffic eases up, but in time, in this case, to have dinner before fatigued by hunger; and do your business with clandestine contacts with enough time left over to return home and turn in at a decent hour.

My first reaction was that Nemsky chose eight o'clock out of habit. After all, he's meeting with what the old KGB used to call, "the main adversary" – me, the CIA. But I know enough about Nemsky to realize he's too good a spy to allow himself to be a creature of habit. He still ran his SDR, under cover of darkness, to shake somebody. A third country intelligence service? Or, his own.

I arrive at the corner of Wilson Boulevard and George Mason promptly at eight. The neighborhood is an older, scruffier version of America's oncological suburban sprawl. Formerly the preserve of laboring class crackers, it is now a rainbow amalgam of Africans, Asians and Latin Americans; refugees, immigrants, opportunists. To my right is a Korean shoe repair shop. To my left, a Vietnamese bakery. Across the street, an Ethiopian eatery. Behind me, an Afghan restaurant. The aromas from these establishments waft into the air to combine and clash like angels and devils in a cultural *Götterdämmerung*.

I've often thought that the association of the secret agent with trenchcoats has to do with the fact that they too often find themselves standing in dreary weather in marginal neighborhoods, as I am doing now. Ever see 007 in a trenchcoat? Frigid rain, with the ambition to become sleet, has been drizzling for the better part of a week. The slate sky is low and suffocating. And I am not a happy camper. I look again at my watch. Nemsky's late by ten minutes.

"Sorry I'm late, Mr. Brennan." Nemsky appears out of nowhere. "But a little countersurveillance is in order to ensure you are indeed alone." Nemsky had hidden behind some bush or storefront window and cased me and the area to see if I had arrived with back-up. Again, the good intel field officer.

With a sly smile, he gestures me toward the door of *Paktia*, the Afghan restaurant. Typical of the ethnic hole-in-the-wall joints in the neighborhood, it sports formica-topped tables, linoleum floor, kitschy regional decor and delicious home-cooked food at bargain prices. A framed photo of Kabul's Masjid-e-Pul-e-Khishti mosque graces an otherwise barren wall. In one of the more insane acts of the self-destructive fratricidal war that engulfed Afghanistan after the end of Soviet occupation, this beautiful mosque, a symbol of Afghan pride, was demolished by rocket fire.

Warmth and the pungent aromas of kabobs, nan, saffron, grilled onions, fennel embrace my cold body and kick in the salivary glands.

Nemsky leads me to a small table in a far corner, naturally. There sits a man with a familiar face. He removes his *pakol* and with a big smile, bows his head and covers his heart with his right hand, the Afghan salutation.

"Hello, my commander." It's Haji Rakhman.

Mental overload steals my voice. I strain to process this scene. My on-again-off-again quarry, Nemsky seeks me out, I suspect, on his own, covering his tracks from his own service; and delivers an Afghan *mujahid* with whom I had once collaborated to bloody Russian troops; an old friend who, the last time I'd seen him, had saved my life from still unidentified attackers.

Rakhman and I embrace.

"Did you bring my M9 sidearm?" I ask.

Rakhman tilts his head in a left-right-left motion. "I am sorry, my commander. But the airports, you know."

I slap his shoulder. We sit. The cross resemblance of the teenage waiter and waitress with the woman in the kitchen and gentleman tending to money and paperwork behind the counter clearly marks this as a family enterprise. We order.

"You are surprised, are you not?" Nemsky remarks.

"In more ways than one," I reply.

He makes a lame joke about having abandoned a load of groceries at the Georgetown Safeway, the only tangible outcome of our last conversation, my desperate effort to recruit him.

"First, I should explain my acquaintance with Mr. Haji Rakhman here, I suppose," Nemsky says.

"Good start," I respond.

"It is actually fairly obvious. Would you like to guess?"

I take this challenge, do some quick mental analysis and say, "Hmm. When the Taliban took over, the Northern Alliance accepted covert aid – barely covert – from Moscow. Heavy stuff. Artillery, heavy mortars, tons of ammunition, as well as food and other materiel support. Your government fears the spread of militant Islam into your former Central Asian republics and worse – more Chechnyas. Ahmad Shah Masood, the so-called Lion of the Panjshir, and Engineer Bashir Khalili were the only *mujahidin* commanders from the days of *jihad* against the Soviets who still packed any punch. Use the Northern Alliance to keep the Taliban off balance. Then the latter's friend, bin Laden, made a knock-out blow by assassinating Masood. Nonetheless, the Alliance remained potent."

Nemsky says nothing, but his trademark thin, foxy grin gives him away.

"The enemy of my enemy is my friend,'" I say. "It goes for both of you, Russians and the Afghans."

Nemsky sips his yogurt lassi. "I was political liaison to them. Haji Rakhman and I are pretty good friends. Would you say so, Haji?"

Rakhman lifts his own lassi toward Nemsky and drinks.

"Ironic," I say.

Nemsky arches his eyebrows inquisitively.

"Rakhman, his superiors, and I at one time conspired against you. Masood and Bashir were your worst nightmare. And now you're allies. Where does that leave me? The U.S?"

"Precisely," Nemsky says cryptically as he tears off a

piece of flatbread and dunks it into spinach *sabzi* and eats. "As for ironies, history is replete with them. Let bygones be bygones. Otherwise, we end up like the Balkans, or Northern Ireland. Such are the shifting sands of geopolitics."

"Yeah, yeah. Let's save history for another time."

Nemsky smiles again. "How do you say? Let's get down to brass tacks." Nemsky wipes his mouth. "We wish to make a deal."

I nod for him to continue.

"At our last encounter, by the lettuce bin, I told you that your leadership has concocted a scheme, a grand and stupid scheme, to make inroads in Central Asia, at my government's expense. I said that perhaps, at another time, we could discuss this as well as other possibilities between you and me."

I nod again.

"First, I shall show you evidence of the grand and stupid scheme." Nemsky reaches into his coat and pulls out an envelope. He removes a document and hands it over to me. I study it.

It's on White House stationery. Classified TOP SECRET, it is a National Security Presidential Directive – NSPD for short among us bureaucrats. It bears the President's signature at the bottom of the second page. Having seen many of these formal presidential decisions over the years, with only the actual title changing depending upon the whim of the incumbent in the Oval Office – National Security Directive, Presidential Decision Directive, and so on – this one looks like the genuine article, or it's an exceptionally good forgery.

I look up into the expressionless face of Nemsky. He tells me to read on.

Central Asia Policy

For the first time in their modern histories,
the ex-Soviet republics of Central Asia

*enjoy true independence. They are also
presented for the first time with an
opportunity to pluralize politically as they
pursue free market reforms. It shall be the
policy of the United States government to
support these CIS nations in these goals.
The relevant agencies will submit to me a
comprehensive policy framework, including
concrete actions and programs, in furtherance
of the objectives set forth in this Directive.*

So far, so good. Ho-hum.

A little analysis follows. It rehashes the facts of oil around the Caspian Sea, how it poses a "counterweight" to the Middle East, an "alternative" source from OPEC, how it needs to be exploited – the faster the better, and how the United States must be the leader.

I look at Nemsky and shrug. He signals for me to read on.

*Historical circumstances now offer the
United States a unique opportunity
to optimize its strategic interests in the
region with the objective of establishing a
long-term presence. It is recognized that
Russian and Iranian sensibilities will be
affected and that this potentially could lead
to tensions with the U.S. Nonetheless, it
must also be recalled that it was Russian
hegemonism that stifled national and societal
development in the Central Asian republics,
and Iranian meddling that has inflamed
ethnic and religious animosities. The U.S.
is now in a position to offer a third option:
stability with democracy. It is therefore the*

guidance of this Directive that United States political and economic interests shall be pursued irrespective of Russian or Iranian objections and that disruptive or hegemonistic designs on the part of Moscow or Tehran shall be countered.

Finally, to ensure regional stability and to optimize access to petroleum, peace in Afghanistan is essential. Parallel oil and gas pipelines from Turkmenistan to Karachi through Afghanistan will make this possible. It would augment the main pipeline to the Turkish coast and it would prevent Moscow from realizing its goal to dominate energy resources in Central Asia. All incentives therefore must be given to the concerned Afghan parties, including the Taliban, to accept this plan. Furthermore, the Taliban must forsake terrorism and enter into a coalition government. As a confidence-building measure, secret feelers will be extended to Taliban leaders to begin discussions.

I look up at Nemsky. "How did you get this?"

He shrugs. "I am a spy, after all."

"Why are you showing it to me?"

"As I said, I thought you should know what schemes your government is up to."

Though I try to hide it, I am dumbfounded that he is showing me this. Thieves, after all, don't go to the cops to show them what they stole. Nemsky's revealing the goods would enable our security types to walk the cat back, follow the evidence trail to the document's last owner and arrest him, or her, on espionage charges. Nemsky's gambit just does not follow SVR practice.

Nemsky doesn't meet my eyes, but simply stares ahead stone-faced.

"You have an insider, a mole," I say.

"Now you are questioning sources and methods," he says with a dollop of sarcasm. He wags a cautionary finger. "Off limits."

I lean forward on both elbows and lock onto the Russian. "Okay. No games. What am I supposed to do? What if I told you that I find nothing shocking in this directive? That it strikes me as a sound notion blocking Russian and Iranian influence in the Central Asian republics that you Russians sat on with your fat asses for a hundred years? That diversifying the West's supply of oil is also right on mark?"

"And making peace with the Taliban?" he asks. Nemsky raises his voice. A sternness sets on his face. "You should see the reason behind the treachery. Against *your* operation. TALISMAN. Why were you not told, but instead betrayed, and framed? Ask yourself with this new knowledge: was the slaughter of hundreds, perhaps thousands, of innocents worth it? Not to mention the utter immorality of it. Moral policy is a special hang-up of you Americans, after all."

I sit back, arms folded. I look at Rakhman. "So, Haji. What's your role? What do the Odd Couple have in store for me?"

Haji shifts in his seat, looks at Nemsky, then back at me. "Engineer Bashir sent me."

"And?"

"He says he wants your help. To reverse our fortunes. To bring vengeance upon our enemies who betrayed us. To avenge the deaths of our comrades and loved ones. To defeat Taliban."

"Is that all?" I ask.

Haji looks perplexed.

I turn back to Nemsky. "So, is the SVR attempting to recruit me?"

"Such foolishness, no," he says and shakes his head dismissively. "At Safeway, when you made that clumsy effort to recruit me, I laughed inside. I laughed because I knew that you knew it was futile. A desperate lunge by a dedicated professional in response to the undue pressures of dimwitted superiors. No. No. I knew this was an intelligent man. A strong-willed man. As much as the Center would love for me to dangle some offers to try to entice you, I am not so stupid as to try."

"You seem to know a lot about me," I say.

The foxy smile reappears. "Sources and methods," he responds again cryptically.

I have no doubt that the Russian service has a dossier on me. Probably going back years. I can imagine Nemsky went to lengths to update it after our first, yes, clumsy, encounter at the Pakistani embassy when Cammy spilled the beans on who I really worked for. Nemsky would have started out by requesting SVR headquarters' bio database on me, gleaned from agent reports from various Soviet KGB *Rezidenturas* in the capitals I'd served in as well as from its agents among the Afghan *mujahidin* during my time at Islamabad station in the '80's. Next, he would have the Russian embassy's electronic listening post, strategically situated high on Mount Alto, tap into my phone conversations from home and probably work as well, having obtained or stolen the latter number from any number of acquaintances, such as Haji himself. His staff would have gleaned the newspapers for any mention or photos of me once I'd entered the stratospheric social circles of Cammy's world. Given the way he skulked up on me this evening, I can assume he's had me tailed off and on for months. Knowing already I was a CIA officer, tracking my daily movements to CI-60's front organization in the suburbs, he would have easily deduced Allied Services Group was a façade for an espionage or counterespionage operation against his embassy. Only the effectiveness of Ray Frasini's counterintelligence security measures would determine how much Nemsky has been able to learn about it. Any inroads Frasini's operation may have made should now be considered questionable and discarded because of double agents. One thing is for sure, though. CI-60 is now compromised and will need to be shut down. Finally, he may have run any number of agents by me to pick up tidbits to be pieced together later. I'll be racking my brain for months over who these might be. Foreign diplomats at receptions. SVR-bought journalists, or bureaucrats of any stripe. My cleaning lady. Salesmen. Roni. Sources and methods.

But the thing that nags at me like a mangy pitbull is the notion of a mole inside the USG, perhaps inside the Agency. It wouldn't be the first time. And the only thing more remarkable than his having a top secret NSPD in his possession is his revealing it to me.

"Okay. Let's cut the bullshit. Bottom line. I now know you know one of our most close-hold policy decisions. Let's say, for argument sake, that I'm really, truly pissed off. That extending America's influence into Russia's backyard isn't worth the price in blood and betrayal. Am I supposed to try to stop it? Blow the whistle to the world? What?"

Nemsky shakes his head impatiently. "No. No. You don't get it, *Braynahn*. All of this…this noble verbiage…" He smacks the document with his hand. "…is fiction."

I shake my own head uncomprehendingly.

"'Democracy,' 'free markets,' 'independence.' *"Eto sovsem govno!* It's all bullshit! It's greed, Brennan. Greed."

"Oo-kay. I look at my watch. I've had a long day—"

"Brennan," Nemsky says calmly. He extends an arm urging me to stay seated. "I know what you think. Warmed over old Soviet propaganda. No." He shakes his head firmly. He leans closer to ensure the confidentiality of what he's about to say.

"Listen carefully to me, Brennan. The oil. Yes, the oil is vitally important. With this, I agree. And my government needs to acknowledge this fact. But this…" Again he slaps the paper. "It is merely a pretty curtain concealing a deal. A business deal. The deal is this. American oil companies are extremely eager to play the Caspian oil game. Like a gold rush. Now flip the other side of the coin: your political parties wish to have their chosen candidates elected president. So, Big Oil gives to Dodge. Dodge places high priority toward opening up Central Asia for American oil companies. America has a new source to feed its oil addiction. The people are satisfied and vote again for Dodge. This 'tapestry of shared interests' is nonsense. There are people who stand either to become very rich or to attain power by this deal. Believe me, nobody strategized what is good for America. Only, what is good for themselves. Money runs politics and politics runs on money. The American way!" Nemsky shrugs and extends his arms – not his fault.

I mull this over. "And the Kremlin, which uses energy resources like a billy club against any consumer nation who crosses it, isn't about to roll over on this deal."

Nemsky pulls a face.

"So, who's the Darth Vader of this master plot?"

Nemsky doesn't get it.

"Who's pulling the strings?"

"Blair Evans," he replies.

"He's an old fart. And he's already rich and powerful," I say.

"Such people are never satisfied. We have them in Russia too. Only worse. In my country, there are no rules."

"Who else?" I ask.

"Norfolk. For him, it is the power and prestige. Mr. Frank DeFalco. He stands to gain the most money, I believe."

"What's his greater role? He must have one."

Nemsky shrugs again. "I do not know this yet."

I stare at Nemsky for a long moment. "Camilla Loomis?"

He purses his lips. Looks at his feet, then back at me. "As far as I can tell, she is an innocent. A dupe."

"And what's that make me?" I mutter to myself.

"I beg your pardon?"

"Uh, never mind."

"I'm aware of your relationship with her," Nemsky says matter-of-factly. He switches gears. "So, you see. When all this was concocted, the decision was made to end TALISMAN, to sell out Bashir to make a deal with the Taliban: access to oil – and the riches it will also bring to them. This also helps Dodge politically. It will enable the new president to withdraw all American troops from Afghanistan. You see? New source of oil. Troop withdrawal. Dodge will then be re-elected. But crippling the Taliban's only credible adversary inside Afghanistan – Bashir and his people – is the price."

"And, so, people like me. What?"

"To speak frankly, Brennan, you, and your fellow civil servants, are nothing. Meaningless. To be swept under the rug." He makes a sweeping motion with the back of his hand.

"Except that Norfolk wants me around, says he likes my style in getting things done."

Nemsky frowns. "This I do not know. Perhaps he does."

I contemplate Nemsky. He has the face of a professional poker player: walled off, indecipherable, unreadable. An entire adulthood of guarding secrets and building emotional moats to ward off the barbarians of hostile intelligence services makes one that way. The good ones, anyway. We coast through life like men-o'-war, hatches battened, cannons loaded, silent, yet ominous.

"You're free-lancing this," I say.

My volley cracks the hard façade like a direct hit into the hold. He jerks his face forward, registering shock and surprise. But the words are aborted before they can reach his lips.

I launch a pre-emptive strike before he can get his thoughts, and a line, together.

"You took the time to case me out after I'd arrived. Given the rendezvous time, and your agency's SOP, standard operating procedure, you did a countersurveillance run. But against whom? Not us, "cause you're meeting with 'us'. No secret there. That means you're either countering a third country service, or your own."

I eye Nemsky carefully. The poker face fades. The flexing jaw muscles and hard eyes indicate he doesn't like this. The espionage game is very much a game of chess. The Russians pride themselves as masters of that game and simply hate to be foiled at it.

I drum my fingers on the hard table surface. "I'd have to guess it's the latter. So, *Colonel* Nemsky, why the Lone Ranger bit? What's your game?"

The cool Russian is now perspiring. His jugulars throb. His hands fidget. He's the lie detector technician's model victim right now. He fixes his eyes on the linoleum floor. Then looks up, glances at Haji, then back at me. In a barely audible voice, he says, "Now about the 'other possibilities.' I have a proposal."

CHAPTER EIGHTEEN

In November 2006, surgeons in Oregon injected cells derived from aborted and miscarried fetuses into the brain of a six-year old child suffering from Batten disease. It was a first. Ten million fetal cells emplaced two-and-a-half inches into the basilia ganglia, where movement is controlled. The jury is still out.

Fats and proteins collect in brain tissue of this genetic disease starting at about age five. Clumsiness and stumbling, the first telltale signs, lead to ever worsening brain seizures, loss of eyesight and motor skills. Eventually, afflicted children become blind, bedridden and demented. Batten disease usually kills its victims by late teens.

Thirteen-year old Anya Nemsky's seizures are worsening.

SIGINT reports, from the bugs we've placed in the apartment, phones and car of the Nemsky family, land on my desk like stink bombs. They document the steady deterioration of the girl's health, and her parents' relationship, as the stress takes its toll.

The intercepted faxed medical reports describe increasing mental impairment, worsening seizures, and progressive loss of sight and motor skills. She is now nearly blind. Topiramate, the powerful anti-epileptic drug used to control her seizures, is having less impact. Her doctors, in fact, are scaling the dosage back from 60ml; side effects include possible further vision and movement loss.

At thirteen years, Anya may be coming to life's end game. The Nemsky's have been advised to "shift emphasis to providing comfort over interventionist treatment." Batten disease has no cure.

More faxes from two neurological treatment centers in the U.S. which have experimental programs to transplant the stem cells into the brains of Batten patients convey "regret" at not being able to accept Anya, citing "limited slots" and "constrained resources." Without explanation, one neural surgeon helpfully attaches a copy of a news magazine article titled, "Stem Cell Research Further Crimped by White House." No explanation is necessary.

As with all Russian diplomats, the Nemsky family's medical insurance is covered by the Foreign Ministry. Life's usual afflictions – heart disease, cancer, broken limbs, routine childhood illnesses, trauma – are covered. Non-emergency treatment is almost always to be done in Russian hospitals where, according to the State Department, "the quality of service ranges from unacceptable to merely uncomfortable." Extraordinary treatment for exotic diseases, requiring massive cash outlays, is not covered. The fact that most Russian men drop dead in their 50's and women are lucky to see 70 speaks volumes about the state of health care in that country.

At the bottom of the unclassified SIGINT fax pile is one from the Neurosurgery Department of the Navy General Hospital, People's Liberation Army in Beijing. Deputy Superintendent, Dr. Huanqing Fu, "is pleased to accept your daughter, Anya, into our experimental stem cell implantation program, which has shown promising results in early testing for Batten disease patients." Treatment would be at the hospital's expense. Travel and lodging costs would be the responsibility of the family.

I re-read this fax. A hot flash crosses my skin, leaving goose bumps in its wake. I instinctively rub my forearms with each hand to try to smooth them out. Funny how a stranger, one you've never met, can enter your heart. The photo of the sepulchral Anya pops into my mind. Maybe being a father is the cause. Maybe it's because Nemsky now seems almost a friend rather than an intel target. Conflicted emotions set in.

The rest of the SIGINT take, marked TOP SECRET, describes husband-wife tensions; arguments and bickering within the walls of their home, walls festooned with state-of-the-art listening devices. I've always been struck by the work of NSA's intel processors. No Such Agency, as the hyper-secret eavesdropping organization is known colloquially, recruits twenty-two year olds straight out of unprestigious hinterland colleges and universities, packs them off for training in languages ranging from Portuguese to Nepalese, then parks them in warrens of office cubicles to translate and interpret reams of messages intercepted from the four corners of the globe via a stunning array of satellites, listening stations, ships at sea, wired-up aircraft and microphones which, programmed with keywords, vacuum-clean the ether for useful information. Whether translators or mathematically gifted codebreakers, these anonymous foot soldiers of America's vast intel empire always struck me as quasi-autistic: singularly focused on their one task at which they excel, but otherwise socially challenged geeks devoid of personality, and dates. At times, I've mused that NSA Nazi doctors zap their brains and install computer chips in their place, creating legions of Manchurian candidates faithful to Big Brother to the end.

These minions boil conversations between people down to pasteurized, executive summary–style reports. Rarely do we consumers of this "product" view verbatim transcripts. Too often, the reports read like the ingredients on a breakfast cereal box.

I concentrate on the description of the Nemskys' marital difficulties. "On Sept. 16, Mr. Nemsky and Mrs. Nemsky had a contentious exchange concerning Mr. Nemsky's employment. Mrs. Nemsky felt the embassy was not doing enough to help the family and urged Mr. Nemsky to seek alternative employment. Mr. Nemsky held firm in his view that he should continue to stay in his chosen career."

Reinsert the passion and I can imagine the raw exchange went something like:

"Sergei. I can't keep going on like this. You're gone every night and you can't tell me where."

"You know my work! How many times do I need to explain it to you?"

"I'm not stupid!"

"But you are thick!"

"Chort tzdbya biri! The devil with you! Mne nasrat', chto ty dumaesh' I don't care what you think!"

"When have you ever?"

"Poshyel k chyertu, Sergei! Go to hell, Sergei!"

"All right. Enough. What's this all about anyway?"

She sobs. "Anya. It's about our daughter. Are we to sit idly by and let her die? The embassy doesn't care. Moscow doesn't care. They are heartless. They tell us to return to Moscow 'to make arrangements.' That means to dig her grave. And you work for them as if everything is just fine. How can you? How can you, Sergei?"

"It's my job. I must work."

"Za dereviannie rubli. For wooden rubles, useless money. Without money, lots of it, we can do nothing for her. And, as long as you work for them, we can do nothing."

He collapses into a chair. Silence ensues.

Reading on, I find the apparent catalyst for the blow-up. Citing security grounds, Moscow has rejected the Nemskys' request to take up the offer of the Chinese hospital, a foreign military institution, to treat Anya. To the SVR, permitting one of its spooks to accept a favor from the likes of the wily Chinese would be like Red Riding Hood falling for the wolf's line. The risk for compromise is too high.

If the tenth circle of hell is helplessly watching your child die, the Nemskys are smack in the bulls eye.

With Moscow reasserting its political and economic power, the pressure to recruit Russian agents builds. Under pressure from the White House's National Security Council, the Director of National Intelligence is barraging the CIA with demands that it step up efforts to recruit spies inside the Russian leadership and intelligence apparatus. Leaks to the media that the Agency is a gun-shy outfit manned by supercautious, careerist bureaucrats enslaved to the lawyers is clearly the work of NSC hotshots in pursuit of an agenda.

Truth be told, the Agency still has not recovered from the devastating betrayals of FBI turncoat Robert Hanssen and CIA traitor Aldrich Ames. Hanssen alone was responsible for the deaths or imprisonment of an astonishing fifty, or more, Russian agents or prospective agents. It takes many years, even decades, to acquire a network of human assets, especially in a hard target like Russia. The shift to fighting terrorism in the Muslim world has also diverted attention and resources.

But Russia is back. Big, bad and bold. From knocking around little Georgia to cutting off the energy spigot to Ukraine, we are compelled to take her seriously again.

And Eddy Frechette was chosen to bag Sergei Maximovich Nemsky. By whatever means it took. Money. Sex. Blackmail. Any combination thereof.

Eddy acquired the nickname "Mike" as a young field officer in Latin America. After "The Baddest Man on the Planet," heavy weight champ Mike Tyson, whose career at that time was at its peak. Eddy has a knack for homing in on a target's greatest vulnerability, then delivering a knockout punch in that spot, just like the boxer. What Eddy lacks in discretion, he makes up for in results. He is legendary in the Agency for the sheer number of "scalps," i.e., recruited agents, he has taken in service to his country. Born and raised in Catahoula Parish, Louisiana, he is the grandson of sharecroppers, great-great grandson of slaves. To say that Eddy does not fit the classic mold of East Coast, Ivy League spawn of professional parents is an understatement. He could double as a Dallas Cowboys linebacker – not exactly a face in the crowd, especially not the gray world of stoop-shouldered government functionaries. In fact, many foreigners find Eddy downright scary. Eddy didn't need to waterboard al-Qaeda prisoners to get answers from them. Reportedly, all he needed to do was to haul all 250 pounds and six-foot-four of himself into a prisoner's small cell, take a deep breath, cross his thick arms and scowl directly into an insurgent's face to get him to think twice about clamming up.

When courting potential agents overseas, Eddy used a different tack. He would lay on his creole charm, thicken it with a rich roué of southern storytelling and simply not take no for an answer. This combination of likability, exoticism and menace has proven to be a winning formula.

I see Eddy in an unused conference room in the six-story new headquarters building. Having just returned from Afghanistan, he is in between assignments. Like maneuvering a heavy artillery piece, one target-aims Eddy Frechette with deliberation. HR is taking its time. So, Eddy is temporarily assigned to my old slot in CI-60 under Ray Frasini.

Eddy sizes me up with his intense midnight eyes. His handshake is uncompromising. Never having previously met, we know each other by reputation only.

"So, this is Fighting Irish Harry Brennan. At last we meet," he says in a low boom.

"Hiya Mike. Likewise."

He forms a hand with index finger out, gun-like, and points to me. "'Mike.' Yeah. Good intel."

I laugh. "No. Just your reputation getting around."

He cuts to the chase. "What's up?"

"The Nemsky file."

"You worked it before. I know that," he says.

"It's a delicate case. Nemsky's actually not a bad guy. I've developed a relationship with him. I'd call it constructive. I'm convinced it'll lead to something. But it'll take time."

"Time's run out," Eddy says with finality. He again balls his fist up like a gun, points it at a file photo of Nemsky and says, "And I'm gonna nail him. Like a possum. I'm gonna nail his ass high up on a tree for all to see."

"This isn't a hunt for a bayou rodent," I interject.

Eddy looks at me quizzically. "What? You gettin' soft in your old age?" A bayou drawl stretches this out. "Orders from on high. 'Highest Priority.' The guys at the top want this guy's ass. And like yesterday." He taps Nemsky's folder with his hand. "Shit. He's beyond the developmental stage. You did good work, Harry. But too much is happenin' now. On lotsa shit. And this guy, Nemsky, holds the keys to the kingdom. At least some of them."

"If you try to bulldoze him, he'll run," I say.

"Two barrels of twelve-gauge shot trumps a rabbit on the run." This time he extends his arms out as if shooting a long gun.

I take a deep breath. Arguing with Eddy Frechette is like taking on Mount Rushmore in a debate. "OK. Can I ask what's your hook?"

"Since this was your case, why not?" He fumbles through the file until a eureka grin unfolds across his large face and pulls out a photo. It's that of the failing Anya with the empty eyes. He points to it triumphantly. "Here's my hook, man."

My heart sinks. I slowly shake my head. I think back to my own, fumbled attempt to drag Anya into the recruitment equation. And the shame I'll never live down. "The girl's thirteen years old. She's a civilian, for chrissakes."

"Are you kidding me? 'Civilian'?!" He guffaws. "In this business, it's always open season. Nobody who's not an Amcit is off limits. You know that! Gimme a break."

"Oh yeah? So what're you going to do? Say, 'Work for us, or your girl dies?'

"Yeah. Somethin' like that," Eddy says without missing a beat. He riffles through the papers some more and holds up the SIGINT traffic. "Says here, the kid's been turned down by American hospitals. No room. Her disease is too advanced. According to our medical guys, this girl's probably got a year. Max. Shit, she's almost blind now. Any kind of treatment is strictly experimental. Stem cell stuff. So, guess what? We can grease the skids with the best place there is for this kind of treatment. Out in Oregon. And we'll pay for everything. No expense spared. We'll even boost their entire research program if they take the kid. We'll use DoD as the cut-out. 'Humanitarian case.' Makes it go down better for the nice docs who might recoil at having any dealings with us puke-faced CIA types." He grimaces and wiggles his fingers like a Halloween ghost. Then he shrugs and adds almost as an afterthought, "Hey, dad does the right thing, turns out good for his kid too."

"Eddy. I already pitched him on that. He wouldn't bite. But I think he will eventually. I just need more time."

"Oh, didn't you know? You're off the case. As in, Bye-bye. Nice try. Thanks for the memories. Now go away!"

"OK smartass. Go pitch him with that. He turns you down too. Then what?"

For the first time, Eddy hesitates. He's not sure he wants to waste any more time with me. He's mulling it over in his mind. Then, reluctantly, he slowly pulls out another sheaf of intel reports.

"This is on the missus."

I reach for it, but Eddy pulls away. "I'll give you the Reader's Digest abridged version," he says. "Mrs. Nemsky's been dealing with a guy in the Chinese embassy. A Mr. Wu. She's been hammering out modalities for whisking the kid over to the PRC for treatment."

"Let me guess. The Navy General Hospital in Beijing."

Eddy nods. "Good. She's been doing this behind her hubby's back and, of course, their embassy's. Totally freelancing it. We've got photos. The whole nine yards."

"So, you blackmail Nemsky with this," I say.

"Such terms. Tsk-tsk."

"And if he still doesn't bite?"

"Oh, didn't I tell you? Shoot." He snaps his finger and thumb in mock surprise. "Mr. Wu is a spy. Or should I say, *spy-der* – spinning a web to nab an asset from the neighbor to the north. Seems like Mr. Nemsky is in high demand. So, you get it now? We're in a race. If we don't nab him, the Chinks will. Sure as shootin'."

I feel like an avalanche has just hit me.

"And Eddy Frechette acquires another scalp."

"Not bad for a black man from Bumfuck, Louisiana," he says proudly. "And I'll be the first African-American to be awarded the Distinguished Intelligence Medal for agent recruitment."

Of course. The Beltway Ambition Sweepstakes. I should've known. Eddy's like all the rest of them. Like some hoary barbarian, climbing a mountain of skulls to glory. I look down and just shake my head.

"And then the sky's the limit," I say.

Eddy tilts his head side to side in a gesture of 'anything's possible.'

CHAPTER NINETEEN

The *Post's* revelation in its Sunday edition that a consortium of America's leading oil companies are in talks that would have them tap the world's second largest petroleum reserve in the Caspian Sea basin captures my undivided attention, especially a proposed agreement with Kabul to build a pipeline that would carry crude from Turkmenistan across the Pushtun plain, across Pakistan to the port of Karachi. This would supplement the principal pipeline which extends a thousand miles from Baku through Azerbaijan and Georgia to the Turkish port of Ceyhan, on the Mediterranean. A petrol conduit highly vulnerable to Moscow's machinations. It is a grand strategic concept, in nineteenth century style; one aimed at feeding the West's enormous thirst for oil, enhancing its economic security while excluding two potential troublemakers and strategic rivals to us – Russia and Iran.

This news is followed quickly by a reception at the posh Park Hyatt, near Embassy Row. I manage to weasel an invitation. I scan the attendees. It's the predictable hodge-podge of crisp business executives, unctuous lobbyists, burnished diplomats and hungry reporters mixed in with stolid Uzbeks, Kazakhs, Turkmens and westernized Afghans. I see familiar faces. Some of the same CEOs of big oil companies I had seen at Cammy's mega-fundraiser are there. They stand quietly, smug expressions on their otherwise non-descript faces. One cannot escape the image of the whirring of cash registers behind the impassive, beneficent expressions. If these companies get their way, the Caspian oil stage will be largely an American production. The massive fields in the various 'Stans would be awarded to and divvied up by these men, whose persistence and aggressiveness in cultivating the new nations' leaders seem to be paying off largely at the expense of the bribe-paying, yet clutzier French, the stodgier British, the starchy Dutch and the hated Russians. These new countries hold a fascination with the once forbidden fruit of America, driven by our hyper-power status, razzle-dazzle technological prowess, big spending ways and, oddly, their utter fascination with our pop culture, especially Hollywood. Bruce Willis is on a par with Tamerlane, while Scarlett Johansson has conquered more Central Asian men with a flash of her thigh than had Genghiz Khan and Josef Stalin together with their terror.

First Eagle Petroleum is also there, first in line in the planned consortium of oil and gas companies leading the way. Collectively, they are to buy the Taliban off. I call Frank DeFalco to congratulate him.

He asks me to meet him at Mezzaluna, a family-run Sicilian restaurant in a generic strip mall in Vienna, Virginia, two days hence when he's back in the Washington area on business.

We sit opposite each other in tall, red vinyl booths. Frank's favorite aroma in the whole world suffuses the air – garlic in oil and tomatoes and oregano. He closes his eyes as he breathes this ambrosia in deeply. The expression on his rugged face is oddly like that of a school girl after her first kiss from a boy.

"This is a terrific place," he says. "Best sausage outside of New York. They make it themselves. They got sweet, hot, and very hot. I eat the very hot, but watch out. It'll burn a hole right through you. Try it. Also the gnocchi. Takes real art to make gnocchi right. This family has got that art. You know, the guy that owns this place, Mico Bucarelli, was born in a village just five miles from the one my old man came from. We're probably related! *Salut'!* He raises a glass of deep red Sicilian wine at me. I return the toast.

We order. I ask for the gnocchi and sausage special. I make more small talk, about what a tough go it is in the restaurant business. But Frank looks distracted. Finally, his head slung low, he looks to the right, then to the left. Then he looks me straight in the eye. Without flinching, he reaches inside his double-breasted jacket and pulls out an envelope. It's thick. He pushes it at me, taps the top of my hand with his and gives a reassuring look on his face. Like, *It's okay. Just fine. No worries.*

"What's this?" I ask.

"I'd advise you to stick it in your pocket. Outta sight. And don't ask questions," he says.

I ignore this and rip a top edge off. Inside is a wad of crisp one-hundred dollar bills. There must be at least a hundred, probably more. I look at him. He looks at me. The blood drains from my head.

"Frank. What are you trying to do? Bribe a U.S. official?"

"Perish the thought," he replies. He looks right, he looks left. He drums his fingers nervously on the table.

"Then what's it for?" I demand.

Frank leans forward. Before he can spout a syllable, the teenage waitress brings antipasto and bread. Frank waits till she's gone.

"You remember the last time we met? I said don't do anything to block this huge oil deal and that I'd appreciate any insider information. My company is about to land the deal of the century and this here is just a token of my appreciation."

"For what?"

"For not getting in the way, goddammit!" Frank's face is flush. His eyes are like daggers. "Whaddya, born yesterday?"

I push the envelope back to him.

"You're serious, aren't you? You aren't going to take it."

"You got it," I say.

One elbow on the table, Frank points at my face. "There's lots more where this came from, my friend. A lot. A few nuggets of inside commercial information now and then. That's all I'm asking. I'm not some fucking enemy agent here. We're working for the same cause, you and me."

My imagination tries to stretch to meet this bold claim, but comes up dry. I shake my head. I don't get it.

"A strong America. Whaddya think I mean? A smoke-free work place?"

"Keep your money, Frank. You should know better."

With a show of resignation and a shake of his head, Frank reluctantly puts the envelope back into his inside breast pocket.

"Lemme ask you this, Brennan. Why'd you call me anyways? Must've been something on your mind."

"Yeah," I say. "I just want to let you know that I know about The Deal."

Frank does an upward pinching gesture with the thumb and forefinger of both hands. "But what deal?"

"*Frank!*"

"No. I mean it. What deal?"

"The one that's turning you into a billionaire."

"Maybe it will. Maybe it won't. What's it to you?"

"My operation was betrayed because of it!" I go on to tell him more or less what Nemsky related to me.

"That's bullshit," he retorts.

"Convenient bullshit, if you ask me. It fits together just too well. A perfect circle of money feeding power generating more money, and so on."

Frank is shaking his head vigorously, but holds what he's about to say as the girl returns with our main courses, of which the homemade sausage occupies center stage.

"You don't know what the fuck you're talking about. What you describe is normal. It's the way politics is run in this country. Maybe you've been outside the United States too long. Me and other CEOs give to our favorite candidates. We, in turn, expect favors. Don't always get 'em. But we try. Everybody scratches everybody else's back. Everybody wins in the end. This operation you say was betrayed, I don't know nothing about that."

I study this man. In some ways, he's an open book. His candor in giving me the low-down on Cammy, for example. In other ways, however, he's an enigma. By his own admission, he has a shady past, compelling him to keep a low public profile. Yet he's well connected to the power broker set. A man in search of respectability, but who crudely attempts to bribe an official. A man for whom the truth is a whore – to be used at his pleasure and discarded when no longer useful. Why should I believe him? Then again, he's been square with me up till now. I think.

"How do you like the sausage?" He digs in.

CHAPTER TWENTY

The Oracle of the Fudge Factory, Vince, as always, is my guide to wading through the murky swamp water of this agency. I need his twisted mind to help me sort through the layers of confusion that blind me from the truth. I figure the sooner the better, since he's now in the oncology ward at Fairfax Hospital.

I enter his ward. It smells of medicine and industrial soap. There is an absence of color, white barely offset by beige. I observe him sleeping and tread silently to the only guest chair. Tubes run from Vince's nose. An IV drip feeds into his arm. Gray stubble and diminishing hair give him the aura of an old man in decline. His breathing, however, is strong and even.

Helen, Vince's wife, called me to let me know he'd been admitted to undergo intensive chemo. Out of shame, pride or insecurity, he didn't want any of his friends to know, she explained. But she felt it was important that his closest friends knew, that they visit him and undergird his spirit, lend some cheer, get his mind off his sickness. The doctors thought they saw signs of early remission, Helen said, but only time will tell.

I lean forward in the chair and contemplate Vince's face and our friendship. Flashbacks of Mogadishu, of Kuwait run through my brain in fast forward speed. Being in the line of fire, facing the barbarian hordes, having the technological might of a superpower at our fingertips, ultimately relying on our animal instincts and wits to survive.

I'm wakened from my reverie by a loud snort from Vince, who is stirring from his sleep. He appears to have sensed my presence and turns toward me. Sad, puffy eyes blink open and focus on my face. They remain that way and it makes me nervous.

"Hey, how ya doin'?" I say with a wan smile.

Vince takes a breath and opens his mouth, only to collapse into a coughing fit. I give him a handful of tissues. He clears his lungs and wipes his mouth of sputum. He loudly clears his throat and says, "A little under the weather. Something going around."

"Yeah, gotta watch that," I reply, not missing a beat.

Vince reaches over and we shake hands. His grip is firm.

We exchange some guy talk about the NBA. The Sixers don't have a chance this season having made so many trades, I say. Hah! The Knicks will clean everybody's clocks, Vince scoffs. Blood returns briefly to his sallow face. He clearly enjoys this element of male bonding.

"So how's it going?" I ask, nodding at the tangle of tubes and wheeled serving table topped with bottles of pills and other medical paraphernalia.

"Not so great. I'll be dead within a half year, year at the most."

"Doctors seem to be holding out hope; say a remission could be happening."

"They're all fulla shit," Vince scoffs. "When you get it in your bones, like I've got, all they can do is prepare you for death; reduce the pain as you waste away in agony."

"Don't give up, Vince. You never were a quitter."

He takes a deep breath. "Yeah, well."

Vince turns to me again and looks me in the eye. "So, how's work?"

I bob my head shoulder to shoulder and give out a simple, "Eh."

Vince launches into a soliloquy of what's wrong with the agency, of congressional meddling, etc. Before he can get to 'What they've got to do is…," I pull a paper out of my jacket pocket and unfold it. I hand it over to him. Vince reaches over for his reading glasses and studies the document. After thirty seconds, he looks back up at me. "Where did you get this?"

"Where do you think?"

"How the hell would I know?"

"How much distribution would a Presidential directive normally get?"

Vince shrugs. "Depends. Could go to half a dozen agencies. Then the xerox machines take over. Before you know it, GS-7 analysts and junior desk officers have it. It's part of the game of 'need to know.' As long as it stays within official channels—"

"This one didn't."

"How do you mean?"

"I mean I got it from an outside source."

Vince registers surprise, but looks unconvincing. "Your buddy Wilder. At the *Post*. The leaks hit that paper like Niagara Fall—"

I shake my head. "Try again."

"Bah! What am I? Nostradamus? Give me a break, Harry."

I pause and catch my thoughts in silence. Vince's remaining days are likely few and knowing that he'll be gone tears at me. Funny. We both came so close to becoming fatality statistics in our crazy youthful days, yet we must have felt indestructible for I can recall no deep sense of mortality then. I guess it's like us all. All human beings. We have an abstract sense we will die one day, but we act and think like we'll be here forever. Vince, in his current state, drives home that this is not the case. It drives home as well my own mortality. It tells me the loss of a good friend is one of the cruelest plays on life.

Vince asks me to hand him a sipping cup from the table. He takes a deep draft of what appears to be Gatorade, then coughs.

"Vince. When did you first meet Sergei Nemsky?"

He jerks his head in an act of surprise, but his eyes betray him. "Who're you talking about?" he asks.

"You know, the "S&T officer" in the Russian station here."

Vince looks away, focusing on nothing particular out the window.

"Your respective careers have followed a remarkably similar course. Vienna, Delhi, Phnom Penh, Tehran, Washington."

"You don't say," Vince responds flatly, eyes still on the window.

"Nemsky knows a lot about TALISMAN. In fact, he seems to know everything, not to mention a hell of a lot about our decision-making, political shenanigans involving the White House, a whole host of characters who pull the strings in this city."

"He must be good. Then again, if he reads the *Post* regularly, not to mention all the books 'investigative journalists' and others write about us, he can tell Moscow all kinds of good shit."

"True. But, to my knowledge, the *Post* hasn't published any NSPDs of late."

Vince shrugs.

"Should be a matter for CI, don't you think?

Vince shifts in his raised hospital bed, then shifts again. He still makes no eye contact with me.

"So, what's the deal between you and Nemsky, Vince? Who's on whose payroll?"

He turns and looks at me warily. "What if I told you neither?"

I arch my eyebrows.

Vince takes his time, analyzing me with his still intense gaze. He's running some quick risk analysis through his brain. Will I betray him? Will I understand? Does it matter at this point?

"Aw shit. What've I got to lose anyway? No. I'm not a Russian agent. And, no. Nemsky is not in our pay. We met as eager-beaver young officers in Vienna back when that place was a playground for cold war intelligence agencies. For over a year, we circled and watched and tested each other. It got to be farcical. Here we were, sending breathless dispatches to our respective headquarters about a 'potential,' loaded down, of course, with bio information. The good thing was that we each had a sense of humor and healthy disrespect for the more ludicrous aspects of our métier. Finally, it was at the Kunstmuseum, I think, we called a ceasefire and retreated to one of those marvelous Viennese cafes that serves gut-busting *Sachertorten* and rich coffees *mit Schlag*. We had a long philosophical discussion, found we had a lot in common when the pretenses were shed."

A nurse enters the room with a plastic tray of cellophane-covered rubber chicken, pureed potatoes, cold carrots, lime jello and a packet of instant Nescafe. She reminds us that visitors hours will be over in twenty minutes.

Vince turns his nose up at the food and shoves it aside. I tell him preemptively that I will not act as procurer of unauthorized goodies. He harrumphs.

"We made a deal right then and there that we'd keep each other informed on things of mutual interest. Did it on a handshake. So, there you have it," Vince says with finality.

"Whoa. Wait a minute. That's it? There's got to be more," I say.

"Like what?"

"Like, what was the deal exactly? 'Keep each other informed.' On what exactly? And on what terms?"

"Simple. Enough gems of information to keep our respective superiors happy and asking for more. Enough to embellish our careers, make us look good, get us promoted. Huh. Sorta like…an inside joke." Vince wags an index finger. "But we drew a line. We would not betray our countries. Also, no deceptions. Just one betrayal of trust by one of us and the relationship would end cold." We shook on it.

"And so you coordinated your tours of duty to try to be in the same place at the same time."

"Right. Which wasn't so difficult, since the CIA and KGB were more than accommodating. They each thought they were close to snagging a 'main adversary,' a 'hard asset.' The main problem Sergei and I had to deal with was fending off the repeated attempts to get us to feed elaborately doctored disinformation to the other side. Sometimes we had no choice but to take the disinformation. But then we'd shit-can it. Then lie about it."

"Vince. How can you go after a potential asset without offering cash?"

"We fudged it. I told headquarters Nemsky was a Russian patriot disillusioned with communism and wanted to bring about change in his own way. Too proud to sell himself out for cash. Sergei told the Center that I was a big-mouthed, independently wealthy Yank with a fragile ego. Didn't need the dough. Something like that."

I pause to digest all of this. "You two guys carried out a deception against your home agencies."

"Ahh! Semantics," Vince grunts with a dismissive wave of a hand.

"Semantics?!'" I yelp. "Vince. How in the world did you pass the lie detector?"

"Oh, easy. Sergei taught me the techniques. Hold your breath, think about screwing a woman. Stuff like that. Besides, remember, I never betrayed, never revealed a source, never sold out. I almost didn't have to lie."

I look at him incredulously. Then I begin to laugh. It gets out of control and I can't stop.

"What's so funny?" he asks.

"You 'almost didn't have to lie'?"

Vince ponders this, then chuckles. He, too, breaks out into uncontrolled laughter.

The lights blink off and on. Time for the visitors to vacate.

My time is up. I glance at my watch, then back to Vince.

"Vince. Top secret White House documents isn't kids' stuff. That's more than touching base in a café to shoot the bull. It *was* you, wasn't it?"

"I plead the fifth," he answers.

"This isn't a court of law, Vince."

The nurse returns. I signal I'm about to leave.

"Sir, time really is up," says the nurse as she points to her watch.

I get up, but my eyes bore into Vince, demanding an answer. He resumes his mute vigil out the window.

I'm just out the door when I hear, "Hey, Harry."

I stick my head back in. "Yeah."

Vince has a wry smile on his face. "That cute Spanish girl you were seeing."

"You mean Roni?"

"Yeah. That one. Stick with her. They don't come better. Don't let her get away. That society broad. Dump her. Bad news. I know the type. She's a preying mantis."

"I don't get it," I say.

"After making love, they devour their mate."

CHAPTER TWENTY-ONE

January in Washington is no fun. The weather is miserable and the residents see the slightest bit of ice and snowfall as an invitation to engage in demolition derby on the roads. It may be a reason why they scheduled the presidential primary season kickoff in January – to give the political set an excuse to escape. Trouble is they chose balmy New Hampshire as the first primary state.

Norfolk has pretty much dropped everything else and is spending all his time up there acting as Dodge's foreign policy advisor. With two debates by the party's candidates scheduled just before the primary, Dodge can't afford to slip up, even, or perhaps especially, in an area where he is strong, like foreign policy.

Norfolk peppers me with long distance taskings. A policy paper on Latin America, data on the Russian economy, Chinese missile development, refugee updates in Africa, the Arab-Israeli peace process, and on it goes. It doesn't hit till I watch the first debate that Norfolk has been using me to draw on official government papers in order to support one candidate, Dodge. The Hatch Act strictly prohibits federal workers from engaging in partisan politics. Otherwise, what Norfolk has been having me do is downright unethical. I stop it.

Jason Mariner shows up suddenly. "I'm here to pick up some stuff on U.S.-E.U. trade relations," he says matter-of-factly.

"The Library of Congress is that a way. Just take the orange line due east," I say.

He looks puzzled.

"I can't be assisting the Dodge campaign," I say.

"Why not?" Mariner's face is all ingenuousness. He doesn't get it.

"Or any campaign, for that matter. I'm a federal employee. We're *prohibited*."

"Oh." Mariner shrugs. "Technicalities. Besides, it's an archaic rule."

"Wrong. What's the opposite of face time?"

He shrugs again. "Beats me."

"Jail time."

"Does that mean you really won't help?" Mariner is either the planet's thickest human being, or he has the singlemindedness of a barracuda.

"For a political campaign? Read my lips, 'No new help.' I'm a public servant not a campaign worker."

"Then how does Norfolk get away with it?"

"Political appointees seem to have a special dispensation from God."

"Ah." Mariner nods in mock seriousness.

"I suppose Mrs. Loomis is also up there?"

"Cammy. Cammy has been wooing the less antediluvian of them, holding dinners, that sort of thing. The New Hampshere*ois* are a breed apart. More guns. No taxes, by God. Just the right ingredients by which to Live Free or Die, don't you think?"

Mariner always instills a chuckle and I laugh.

"She knows you're here, seeing me, I assume," I say.

"She's my boss."

"Okay. And?"

Mariner offers a wan grin. "Well, she says she apologizes, for whatever it was that came between you two." He makes a quick disingenuous glance at me and diverts his eyes again as he leans against a doorjamb, arms crossed. "Would like, no, would *love* to get together again. *Also sprach Cammathustra.*" Another sideways glance and crooked grin.

I ponder this cryptic invitation, obviously programmed into the clever Jason Mariner with decided calculus by Cammy.

"Tell her I'm spoken for, or at least attached," I say.

He purses his lips. "Oh, she doesn't care." No further explanation or clarification.

Camilla Harrington Loomis aka Cammy-Lou McGuthrey Romano is a much more interesting person to me now that I know her secret. What makes it more tantalizing is that she doesn't know I know. This type of inverse knowledge comes with the territory in the spy trade. You know a secret about another person who doesn't realize that you know it. They act in a certain way which makes them vulnerable. The emperor with no clothes. The fool in a glass house. The leverage gained by an ops officer in such a situation vis-a-vis a target can be tremendous. Cammy as intelligence target. Hmm. Why not?

"You know. I like Cammy," I say, trying to conceal a hollow ring. "That such a distinguished woman takes an interest in a nobody like me is flattering. You can tell her that I'm available to see her whenever it's suitable. And," I add, "with all due respect to Mr. Loomis, whom I hold in the utmost regard."

Mariner frowns. "Bullshit. Anyway, she, or I'll, be in touch." He turns to leave, then stops in his tracks. He's again facing me. "Are you sure you won't help Norfolk?"

"Not with election stuff."

"He'll fire you."

"Correction: he can remove me from my White House job, but he can't fire me. After all, everyone knows you can't fire a government lifer." I wink. Mariner winks back and is gone.

The Dodge campaign has picked up steam. The candidate rolled through the primaries vanquishing the other Democratic contenders using his brilliant mind, command of the issues, charm, savvy, aides and growing war chest. The media lap up opportunities to film and interview the candidate with his wife Cathy, one of those maturing ex-beauty queen-cum-college valedictorians with a high-profile job in a non-controversial do-gooder organization, and their three trophy children.

The Democratic Establishment has circled its wagons around Dodge. There are the Wisemen Who Advise the Candidate, elder statesmen of administrations of yore who can never let go and secretly hope to be asked to come back into the fold to run things like federal departments or high councils of the White House, or the World Bank. There are the loyalist thinkers who for years have cooled their heels in the gulag archipelago for politicized intellectuals – think tanks, foundations and universities – biding their time until The Restoration. Then there are the political junkies, wonks and hangers-on who, like brain-fried rock groupies, simply thrive on the adrenaline-fed drama and glamour of an election. The latter organize, raise money and get out the vote. I conclude that Cammy is of the last category. Norfolk is part wonk and part prince-in-waiting, who plays both sides of the fence under the guise of "bipartisanship." Politics' version of a high-class call girl. Evans, however, clearly falls into the first grouping – an elder of the party with a long résumé of prestigious past jobs who relishes his role as Advisor to the Candidate/Future President. What is less clear is what he wants in return after the restoration.

Like Orwellian perpetual war, the U.S. presidential campaign season has no beginning and no end. The mobilizing of the masses and fundraising are always in overdrive. Cammy has organized the biggest most elaborate fundraiser in years: a dual event at the Loomis country estate near Leesburg, Virginia. Aimed at raising over $1 million in hard and soft funds for the Dodge campaign, the attendance of the high and mighty from politics, big business and Hollywood will put Cammy's gala just behind Oscar night in attracting media interest.

Cammy calls me and somehow manages to persuade me to attend this bash of the titans as part of a weekend of hashing out foreign policy issues with other administration professionals and academic and business types. She assures me there will be no Hatch Act conflicts of interest. "Besides," she said, "Everybody who's anybody on the federal bench is my *dear* friend and wouldn't lay a judicial finger on you if I objected."

I remember not so many years ago how pleasant the drive up Route 7 along the Potomac used to be. Now slob-burban sprawl has devoured the rolling green countryside and hamlets like a metastasizing tumor. The traffic-without-end on widened roads has strangled what life remained in the erstwhile stomping grounds of Stonewall Jackson. As I negotiate my way along this automotive calvary, my mind goes back to the "Farm" not so long ago, to the slow pace and reward of the classroom and to rolling in the grass with a gorgeous young Latina named Roni. I've neglected Roni. Fourteen-hour days of pressure-cooker labor at the White House hasn't helped any, not to mention overseas travels. But since our last encounter at my place and Roni's catching on to what I do and her hard questions about Cammy, subconsciously, I've felt ashamed, too cowed to see her again, though two phone calls between us since that time have kept intact at least a thread of our relationship.

Past Route 15 and onto country roads, I find myself in horse country. The sprawl has yet to gobble up the manors and riding grounds that blanket this rolling landscape. The fresh spring air is a very welcome change from stale office atmosphere. This is Cammy country. Actually, no. Cammy's old sod lies further west, in the coal communities and small farmholdings of the upper Appalachians. A pastoral place that no doubt resides in Cammy-Lou McGuthrey's soul like a piece of old shrapnel, a hidden presence with painful connotations. No, this is Loomis country, Cammy's adopted homeland.

I ask myself as I wend my way closer toward the Loomis estate why I am going back to her again. And I come up with no answers. I just go.

Finally, a rustic sign on a plank of wood hanging by two chains from an ancient oak announces "Colchester Wood." A long stone-covered drive takes me into the Loomis' home away from home, sixty acres of manicured, white-fenced equestrian territory crowned with a noble graystone manor house atop a hill flanked by a guesthouse, barns and horse stables. An enclosed swimming pool lies discreetly to the rear of the house, itself swathed by elms and dogwoods. Horses graze in the distance amid small willow-lined streams, woodlands and meadow gardens.

As I pull up to the house, Cammy appears on the porch, all done up in riding pants, jodhpurs, an ascot around the collar of her tailored khaki shirt. Her bright hair is tied up in the back with a black velvet band. Country beauty to perfection. She skips down the steps and wraps her arms around my torso as I step out of my car. Then a peck on the cheek.

"It's so good to see you, hero-man," she gushes. "Come." Cammy takes me by the hand and pulls me with gusto up to the house. My car door remains open, my luggage sits in the back.

"But…" I mumble and point to the car.

"The staff will take care of it."

Indeed, a young man emerges to take my car keys and haul my bags.

"Not the guesthouse, Peter. Take them into the Willow Room in the house," instructs Cammy.

A gray-black liveried butler oversees this while a white-skirted maid delivers ice-cold lemonade on a silver tray.

"I'm so glad you could come, Harry. The place is ours till tomorrow evening. That's the Big Bash. I'm on pins and needles, but Jason tells me not to worry. He's riding herd on everything. But just in case…" She pulls out a tiny cell phone from her waistband and holds it prominently. It rings. "Oh dear. Just a moment, Harry." She's now all business.

"Yes, Jason. Of course I want Horton at the same table with Dodge and myself. He's the Veep-to-be, after all. No, Mrs. Horton will sit with the oil people. You know…" She waves a loose hand impatiently. "Those balding bores with the big bucks…I don't care, Jason. Wives are a drag on things. They can spread some of the glory like the good little girls they are. Besides, they're used to it."

She folds the phone and carries an expression of annoyance. "I'm afraid the little bugger will only jangle my pants more as the day goes on. The phone, that is." She throws her head back and giggles in her trademark fashion.

"Come." Again, she takes my hand and pulls me into her refuge from Washington. "I'll give you the grand tour."

There's the Hunt Room, featuring dark, oak-paneled walls adorned with assorted stag antlers and heads of beasts who met a tragic end. Ancient musketry and antique shotguns lend an air of aloof menace. And the sun-room, more modern and open, leading to the pool. The living room is large, with a looming old fire-place topped with a coarse mantelpiece and various copper and wooden farm implements. A small "leisure room" to one side contains a flatscreen TV along with casual leather furniture strewn carelessly with magazines. Yes, *Town and Country* and *Southern Living* are among them. A floor-to-ceiling library with the musty aroma of old books and polished furniture takes one back to another, genteel era. Finally, Cammy leads me into the Lady's Sitting Room, one of those throw-away accoutrements of pretend aristocracy at turn-of-the-last-century America. It is a cozy, sun-filled room with the trappings of muted femininity: a mirror, a tea table, a small bright-colored overstuffed chair and ottoman, a cabinet with antique figurines. A few paintings adorn the walls.

"I call this the Belle Boyd Room," she says with a glint of mischief in her eyes.

I register a blank.

Cammy points to an old gilt-framed oil painting. It is of an elegant, willowy woman dressed in white chiffon, posed with one elbow slung daringly over a day bed chair. A saucy, challenging look emanates from an ivory face, the timeless beauty of a Greek goddess.

"Harry Brennan, meet Belle Boyd," Cammy says.

"My pleasure," I mock.

"Ah. Time for a history lesson. Belle is a heroine for the folk in these parts – and I don't mean the juggernaut of transient carpetbaggers responsible for all that...that suburban blight out there." She gestures dismissively in no direction in particular. "Belle Boyd was a Confederate spy who charmed military secrets out of her Union suitors."

"Is that why you admire her?" I ask.

Cammy looks me in the eye and bites her lower lip teasingly. "Among other things."

"I'll keep that 'charming secrets' bit in mind."

"You should." Without missing a beat, she continues. "On May 15, 1862, she overheard plans that northern troops were vacating Front Royal, leaving behind a token force. Belle passed this piece of 'intel,' as you would say, on to General Stonewall Jackson and a week later guided his troops into town. The Battle of Front Royal ended with the capture of almost all of the thousand bluebellies remaining in the fort." Her face reflects pride in relating this.

"A real charmer," say I.

"The best."

"Is that a southern soul I sense stirring inside that proud breast?" I ask.

Cammy blushes and, for the first time, I see her lower her eyes demurely.

"Ah. Well. That's another story." She links her arm inside mine and leads me onward. "Let's go, kemosabe. There's more."

The question of Cammy's origins remains buried.

We stroll in the rose garden, to one side of a courtyard behind the house.

"You say we have the place to ourselves till tomorrow night," I say.

"Yes."

"So, where's Mr. Loomis."

"Ah. Jared," Cammy says, as if an afterthought. "He's off at some family reunion, his kids and grandkids. That sort of thing. Up at the cottage in White Fish."

"As in Montana?"

"Uh-huh. Jared – we – have a nice place there, in ski country. Actually, with six bedrooms, it's hardly a 'cottage.' It's nonetheless very cozy. I'm flying him back here tomorrow with the Avanti in time for the event."

"What's an Avanti?"

"Our plane, silly. A Piaggio P-180 Avanti II, if you must know."

"Ah, yes. 'Our plane.'"

She elbows me in the side. "Jared is much too old and too respectable to be experiencing the indignities of airport processing and lost luggage. And, besides, it saves me lots of time as well. I had to talk the old coot into buying it. Jared still has his first dollar, hates to part with a dime. But I've eased his life in his old age and I know he appreciates it."

We stop at a clump of white rose bushes. The blossoms are big and fleshy. The aroma is sweet. I close my eyes and take a deep breath of one high blossom.

Cammy issues a stifled laugh.

"What's so funny?" I ask.

"Oh, sorry. It's just that you don't seem like the flower-loving type."

"Why not?"

She takes me in with a studied eye from head to toe and back again.

"Let's face it. You're more like…the Marlboro Man. Scent of boot leather, whisky-eyed, ram-rod straight. Yep. Nope. Giddyap. Not 'Ooh la la, these flowers are s-o-o heavenly.'"

We both laugh.

"My ex-wife loved roses. Our gardens always had them. And, if the circumstances were right, she'd grow white roses."

"Garden*s*?"

"We never spent more than two-to-three years in any one place. Because of my job. As soon as we'd arrive in a new home, Kate would run outside and scout the yard to plan her garden."

"What happened? I mean with your marriage?"

"Too many gardens to have to abandon. And too many lies to live. Kate was not cut out for the life, the clandestineness. Each move sliced into our relationship. One notch at a time till it was gone too far by the time we paid the proper attention to it."

"You loved her though?"

I stare at my feet and shuffle the dirt around. "Oh, yes. Very much. We met in college. She was this...how to describe her? This viking goddess. Freya, Norse Goddess of the Family and Home, I would call her. She was from South Dakota. Had this flaming red hair she'd tie into a single braid that went down her back. She had a temper to match. A spirited woman. But strong. She kept me in line – in a positive sense. My anchor."

"Sounds like you still hold a flame for your old flame," Cammy says.

I look at her and smile. "Hm. It's finished. Been so for years. We should've seen it from the start. I'll never forget, our relationship – the day I proposed to her and she accepted –almost came to an abrupt end. I told her who I really worked for. She cried. She couldn't stop crying. I hadn't expected that. I suppose it was the beginning of the end."

"And what about you?"

"You certainly learn about yourself. I'm still learning from that experience. We share Laurie, the enduring thing from us."

We leave the rose garden and proceed down a path leading to the horse pastures. Four young Saddlebreds graze lazily in the lush green carpet of grass before us.

"Now you," I say.

Cammy shakes her head, a stiff grin on her face.

"No. It's all checkered. I'd sooner not get into it."

"Sorry. But you have no choice. I spill my guts. Now it's your turn."

Cammy has her arms crossed and contemplates the ground as we stroll.

"I live the present and look forward to the future. The past is history and that's where I prefer to leave it. Let's just say that I had a rough youth and climbed my way out of it. And to answer your other question, yes, Ah'm a lady of the South and durn proud of it, suh!"

We both laugh, then continue in silence, comfortable in each other's company. A soundless, invisible bond connects us now. She has much she is not ready to reveal about herself. I decide not to push the envelope, but ask, "How long have you been with Jared Loomis?"

Cammy stops and looks up at me with a serious face. "Why do you want to know?"

I shrug. "Just asking."

She resumes her stride. Before us lies a wooded area. Beyond it, the sky is turning dark with rain clouds.

"The original Colchester Wood," she says. "Lord Colchester, the original owner of this property – after he stole it from the Indians, that is – kept the woods, original primal forest, and the subsequent owners have left it intact through the centuries. No Department of the Interior, no World Wildlife Fund, no Greenies, no EPA were ever involved. How's that?"

"Environmental *noblesse oblige*," I say. She throws her head back and giggles her giggle. "Don't change the subject," I add.

"Okay." In measured words, she says, "I met Jared seven years ago. We were introduced at some Washington function. There was an immediate magnetism between us, despite our age difference. Believe me. I'm not a golddigger. I know what people say. In a way, it's what they think but don't say that gets to me more. You can see it in their faces, the way they observe discreetly at a distance, their smarmy grins when introduced to me in Jared's presence. 'Oh, yes. The young social climber, the bimbo marrying Mr. Big Bucks.' Well, damn it. I was determined to show them otherwise, and I have." Cammy looks up and searches my face. "Do you see?"

I nod. "Do you love him?"

"I knew you'd ask that. I knew because you're the only

person I know who has the guts to ask me." She stops again and stares at my face intently. "No. I don't."

I say nothing. I may have hit the button I was aiming to avoid. Best to let her steer our discourse at this point.

"Jared and I need each other. There is something there, a magnetism, as I said. But one helps the other. Trite as it sounds, I crave the security and relish everything beyond that. Jared is at the end of his life. He wants to feel young one more time. And he can't bear being alone, without a woman. He lost his first wife, Chiara, years before we met. He was devoted to her. But Jared saw – sees – in me, funny as it sounds, an extension of himself. He sees me as someone specially in tune with himself, a person who captures that which he wishes to achieve beyond his own life.

"And that is?"

"Greatness."

"Oh, is that all?"

"Sorry. I'm sounding like Marie Antoinette, aren't I?"

"Eva Peron?"

"Ha. Ha. Funny."

A storm cloud barrels down on Colchester Wood. A warm current collides with a cool one in the changeable spring sky. Drops begin to fall. We run for cover in the green-black woods. The rain intensifies as we reach the edge. We scamper among the tall trees like a pair of fairy tale waifs. Grand old oaks and straight pines sway majestically above. White birch shimmer in the powerful breeze. Dead leaves jump in the air like woodland banshies. A downpour hits us and within seconds we are drenched.

"There!" Cammy shouts, pointing to a ravine.

"We'll drown down there," I shout back.

Cammy shakes her head. "There's a small cave. Come." She grabs my hand and pulls. We reach the edge of the ravine. A small rock path tamped, no doubt, by generations of adventurous children, leads into it. We rush down it and, behold, a cavern. The ashes of countless camping fires mark its entrance. We duck and, plomp, we're inside, on a cushion of musty old leaves, out of the rain.

"Whoo! It's wetter out there than a fat cow pissing on a flat rock in April!" Cammy shouts in an accent I'm not accustomed to hearing from her. Her blond curls hang soggily over her eyes and the nape of her neck. The natural blush of her face is more intense, magnified by the beads of rain on her skin. She's wringing her skirt and flailing her arms. It's all futile and she realizes it. She looks up and smiles.

Here we are. In the earth. Soaking wet. Nowhere to go. Alone. Cold.

Between that moment when our eyes locked and that when she is in my embrace, lips hungrily on mine, bodies pressed hard, a rush of heated passion engulfing us, I cannot say what transpired. All I can say is that it is as natural as the rain, as the clouds that drove us here, as the earth and rock that surround us.

CHAPTER TWENTY-TWO

I am startled from deep sleep at dawn. Metal against metal. Trucks gunning their engines. The bang-bang-bang of hammers against wood. I am momentarily disoriented. Strange room. Unfamiliar surroundings. I had been dreaming of Mogadishu again, of running around like a madman shredding documents, loading my Browning semiautomatic, preparing to bug out by chopper with the ambassador. It is a recurrent dream. I sit upright and shake my head to throw the whole scene, the fears, the panic from my brain. The bed I'm in is a big old four-poster with one of those silly canopies that always reminds me of a funeral bier. Ah. Yes. Cammy's house. Cammy. I pat the covers. I am relieved. No woman therein.

I leap from the bed and go to a window, part the curtain. Below is a cavalcade of workers, vehicles, implements. On the lawn, they are erecting large tents, a stage, serving tables. From my vantage point looking down it is a Lilliputian scene, people smaller than life scurrying around with rope, tools and assorted paraphernalia – to tie down giants.

I throw on slacks and a shirt and go downstairs. Cammy is seated at the table in the breakfast nook, coffee cup before her. Her face is all seriousness as she pores over a stack of paperwork. The grave expression gives way briefly to a sunny smile as she looks up at me. She gives a simple "Hi," then returns to her documents.

I take a seat. The day maid appears with a glass of orange juice and takes my breakfast order – blueberry pancakes with bacon and a cup of *latte*. Yes, they have that. An Italian espresso machine that looks all the world like an antique locomotive takes a place next to Sub Zero refrigerators, an institutional range-oven, cuisinarts, juicers and the whole range of modern kitchen gear necessary to sustain masses of the world's elite.

I take a sip of my juice. "Big day, eh?"

"Mmm," Cammy rumbles, eyes remained fixed on the papers.

"Anything I can do to help?"

"Mm-mm," she murmurs, turning a page.

"Well, if I can, just holler."

"Mm-hhm," she acknowledges.

The pancakes are delicious, as is the steaming *latte*. I sit in silence wondering what the hell I'm doing here.

I meander around the premises, observing all the activity. Cammy is in the house now taking calls on her cell phone as well as the house line. At eleven, an old, rusting Saab pulls in. Out steps Jason Mariner. He's holding a stack of folders. I run up and offer to help.

"Thanks old boy."

"You look like hell," I say. Mariner's face is drawn and pale, his eyes have dark circles, he's stooped and appears as if he has the weight of the world on his shoulders.

"I feel worse," he says with a wan smile.

"You need a break."

"Ah, but the show must go on."

He drags himself up the porch steps and into the house. I follow, folders piled in my arms. Cammy comes to the door.

"Now, Jason, the invitation lists. I'm really worried. And all these people." She makes a sweeping motion with her arms, in the direction of the workmen. "Are you sure they'll complete it all in time? What's the weather report for tonight? My God. We should've had them start days ago. Oh, the contributions. Are we taking checks here tonight, or only the pledges? If pledges, how do we ensure they follow through? You know, we're billing this as Million Dollar Night. Is my dress ready? And what do I say for opening remarks? I assume I'm giving them?"

Mariner sets down his folders with a loud thud on an eighteenth century credenza in the foyer.

"Jared's scheduled to arrive at eleven," he says with a tired voice.

Cammy looks momentarily distracted. "What?"

Mariner repeats himself. "I've arranged for him to be picked up at Dulles at that time. You should also go," he says.

"Yeah. Jared. Right. Um. We have the briefing/luncheon on at noon at the Doubletree Inn. The DNC's got it all set up. They just called."

"Shall we take Jared directly from the airport then? Not sure he can handle that," Mariner says.

"Oh. I don't know. Figure something out, Jason." Cammy runs in to answer the incessantly ringing phone.

"Jesus," Mariner says. He slumps into an overstuffed chair in the living room. He crosses his hands over his stomach and closes his eyes. Immediately, his breathing becomes deep and regular.

"*Jason!*" Cammy shouts. She's standing before us, legs apart, hands on hips, simmering.

Mariner's eyes open, but he otherwise remains still. Exhaustion has taxed his body to its limits.

"Jason, are you crazy? My remarks, I assume you have them? I need them now, I need to hone them and practice for tonight."

"Yes'm," he says and drags himself out of the chair. He digs into the pile of folders and presents her one. "'A New

Agenda for a New Millennium.' Robert wrote it – no thanks to present company, I might add." He throws me a sideward glance. "Says you'll love it."

"Wonderful." Cammy takes the folder and glances inside. "And the invitations? Seating arrangements?"

"Well, pretty good."

"What in blazes do you mean by 'pretty good'?" she hisses.

"Everybody who's supposed to get an invitation has gotten it, and the rsvp's are streaming in fine."

"So?"

"So, it's like we're getting *lots* of rsvp's. More than on our invitation list."

Cammy looks perplexed.

"Cammy. You're the hottest ticket in town. Every *arriviste*, climber, office-seeker, wonk, *poseur*, king-maker, aspiring king-maker, social register listee and de-listee, totem, icon, idol, hero, born-again-cross-dressing-lost-and-found democrat, socialite, acolyte, parasite and luddite with a cause wants in."

"Cut the humor, Jason. What are you saying?"

"What I'm saying is we can expect several hundred more guests than we originally invited."

"Say what?!" Cammy snarls.

"Yeah. This is better than a Stones concert. Gate crashing left and right. I kid you not. My ear is red and sore from holding the phone receiver to my head. See?"

"Aaaaahhh!!" Cammy storms past Jason and out the door. The clickety-clack of her heels follows as Cammy paces across the broad porch, arms crossed, head down, deep in thought. We follow.

"How could you let this happen, Jason? We didn't plan for this. We'll need more food, drinks, tables, chairs. My God. These tents won't manage—"

"I called the caterer already. They'll take care of everything. The DNC's paying for it all. Local vintners are providing the wine. Look, this isn't Colchester Wood. It's The Winners' Bandwagon, and everyone wants on. So, we've got the high rollers – those who are giving ten grand and up – joining Dodge, Horton and the rest of us elite types for an exclusive dinner reception here in the house. The hoi-polloi – those cheapies who think they can buy in by forking over a thousand measly bucks – will be outside in the tents. Mort Blikstein's big bash last month in Hollywood netted $1.2 million. This is the chance to show those west coast phonies who is the real power behind the throne – those empty suits or us uptight preppies."

"Shut up, Jason," Cammy says. She mulls this over and her eyes light up. Jason knows this woman's vanities better than her husband. Watching him working on her is like observing Haifetz with a Stradivarius, a master deftly producing magic from a beautiful thing.

Magic does not happen at American chain hotels. *Hotelica generica*, subgenus, *suburbia identica omnia*. The usual conventioneer crowds hover outside plastic and brass banquet rooms murmuring about "proactive sales strategies," "genome patents and government policy," "changes in pedagogic prioritizing." The crowd I am thrust into is distinctly a breed apart. The movable type sign outside our wassail hall reads, "Foreign Policy Choices in the Post-Post Cold War Era." These burnished professionals' fashion, heavy on buttoned-down Oxfords and blue or gray pinstripe suits, is less spiffy than that of the extroverted sales crowd, less interesting than that of the dressed down science lot, but definitely classier than the J.C. Pennied teachers clan.

This get-together of foreign policy eggheads is allegedly non-partisan and its convening on the same day as and within spitting distance of coronation night for the Dodge-Horton duo, a mere coincidence. Coincidence is to politics what an alibi is to a crime. Or in the parlance of my trade, the disingenuous organizers gave themselves "plausible deniability" simply by denying any connection.

The discussion panel consists of a blue ribbon collection of the once great and powerful, the super stars of Ivy League academia and a sprinkling of business high-flyers who are actually capable of thinking beyond the bottom line. Nick Kollar, former National Security Advisor and Secretary of State, is the dean of this illustrious menagerie. He is seated in the center of a semi-circular table. Around each side sit the others, like apostles, in reflecting distance of the glow of Kollar's halo.

Kollar kicks off the proceedings with the obligatory dollop of humor, segueing then into the first sub-topic of discussion: "Globalization: Benevolent Wave or Tsunami of Destruction?" – one of those typically ungainly mashed metaphor titles that self-important academics and other self-styled "thinkers" love to wrap themselves around.

Kollar is in his element. One of those 1956 Hungarians who made the transition to being an American only halfway, Kollar is a complicated mix of Hapsburg and Horatio Alger. A self-made man of the New World with the superior airs of the Old. He is in total control of a collection of fawners who willingly turn themselves over to him like moonies to their prophet.

He lays out the "agenda for discussion." In 5,000 words of tortured overanalysis, Kollar basically says it comes down to whether one thinks globalization is good or bad.

All of these grayheads are on first-name terms. Having been to countless such skull sessions since my college days, I've never been able to determine whether the first-name thing is part of the aggressive informality of our culture or a sign that our nation's most important affairs of state actually are hatched by a cabal of conspirators in a star chamber somewhere.

Bernard Kirschner, professor emeritus at Yale, rises from his seat and launches into a dissertation of the wave theory of the futurologist Tofflers. Five minutes into an ornate theory that posits that a fourth wave of sociological change can be foreseen called the "post-information age morality-based society" it becomes as clear as crystal that Kirschner has no point, or that it's buried so deep in his convoluted, ego-dripping speechlet that we mere mortals are incapable of fathoming it. But everyone politely ponders what this aged scion of political science textbooks has to say, a few nodding in mock comprehension.

The thread is quickly picked up by R. Claiborne Luce, a cold war CIA director, a fixture at these events. Luce is a dapper 83-year old who has been on a twenty-eight year stations of the cross political atonement of his sins for all the governments he corrupted, the progressive grass-roots movements he stifled, the lies he told Congress – all immaculately recorded by the *Washington Post* and a parade of authorial exposeurs of the spy agency. Luce, gratefully, speaks in blunt, concrete terms that we can all understand, but don't care about – trivialities and truisms wrapped in a pretty package of the much abused "American ideals."

The ball gets rolling and serious insights are offered from the perspectives of businessmen who see firsthand a global marketplace taking shape, of non-governmental organizations who witness plagues like AIDS transcending borders swiftly, of journalists who liken the free flow of information to, yes, a tsunami.

An hour into the debate, Kollar imposes a pause to sum up common themes and to hammer down a rhetorical signpost for the next turn in the discussion. "We've talked about how globalization affects the industrialized world and a bit about its impact on the developing world. But what about those thus far excluded from the winds of change – what about the failed states? And, centrally, what should the United States' role be in this process? What policy choices face the next administration?"

Whether out of a subconscious burst of interest or an instinctual need to do something to keep myself from nodding off, I find myself standing with my hand raised. I give my name and identify my line of work only as "government analyst." I then proceed to unload my thoughts, criticisms and frustrations, based on a lifetime of dealing almost exclusively with broken societies, dysfunctional governments, massive human catastrophes and indifferent or self-serving U.S. policies as well as occasionally enlightened ones. I talk about those countries that have some hope of reaping some of the benefits – not to mention the blights – of globalization, like Cambodia, and those so consumed by anarchy and retrogression as to be light years away – like Somalia and Afghanistan. Strangely for me, I find my heart competing with my brain; I can't get the words out fast enough. Inside, I sense an emotional dam has broken open releasing a torrent of pent-up obsessions and regrets over my country's failures to stave numerous human disasters, of the "globalized" world's neglect of those world members who have fallen off the edge, but also of the real limitations of being able to save ruined populations from themselves, their nations from imploding.

As I catch my wind, I see a diorama of eyes riveted upon me, of people taking notes, of heads nodding.

"Finally, I say, "If one is to talk about policy, one must talk about commitment. Too often, we walk away from problems and turn inward as a government and as a people. Sometimes, we go further than that and we…betray."

Ears prick, bodies lean forward, eyebrows scrunch.

I feel I've reached a line beyond which it makes no sense to go before such a group. I quickly do a mental systems check and ask myself, is it catharsis I'm leaning into? But, ultimately, the brain vanquishes the heart.

"But that's another topic for another discussion another day." And I sit down.

There's a pause. Then a pair of hands clap, followed by others, then a cacophony of applause.

My God. They're applauding me. My head goes into a spin. What the hell is going on? What the hell am I doing here in the first place? Not only is my life out of control, being swept into some swift stream where I don't belong pushing me God knows where, but I...I am out of control. The wheels are spinning so fast, they're flying off. This crowd, this woman. I'm a rebel without a cause on a fast track without direction. I ask a waiter to bring me a double vodka.

During the break, I find myself the subject of curious attention by many people whom I don't know, and some whom I do, at least by reputation. They approach me to explore further my views on American policy over the past three decades, or its future direction, to challenge my assertions, but gently. They give me their cards. They want to follow up sometime. Give me a call. Drop me a line. Stay in touch.

The Lion in Winter, Blair Evans, saunters up with his silver-handled cane. He has a large, square head topped by a mane of hair with the sheen of ivory soap; watery eyes set in a perpetually furrowed brow and an octogenarian's smile that displays surprisingly good teeth. He extends an arthritic hand.

"My boy, we've met before," he says.

"Yes sir, at the Pak ambassador's reception."

"So. Kinneard's let you out of the closet!"

"Actually, that's my fault. In fact, I'd better get right back in."

"Nonsense!" Evans places a firm grip on my elbow and pulls me aside. "Listen, Brennan. It is Brennan, isn't it? I never forget a name."

"Yes. Brennan's my name."

"Brennan, I like your gutsy style. How come we haven't seen you before?"

"Actually, I can't figure out why you're seeing me at all."

Evans lets out with a deep hoarse laugh. "Damn!" He bangs the floor with the cane. "I like you, Brennan. You've got pluck.

"Yes. You're not any old bureaucrat. Listen, Brennan, Cammy tells me good things about you. Stick by us. Once *President* Dodge is in the saddle, this country is going to move in brave new directions. A rejuvenation. We're going to need good people. People with brains *and* balls. People to make things happen. People who know the system from the inside. Your kind of guy."

I thank him for the compliments.

"And, uh, one other thing, Harry. I can call you Harry, can't I? Well, just one piece of advice, Harry. There's a lot riding on the future of Caspian oil. Geopolitical stuff *and* business. Above your pay grade."

He wags a finger and locks a steely eye on me.

"A smart guy like you would be wise to go along, not stand in the way."

Evans winks at me, pats me on the shoulder, then wades in to work the rest of the crowd.

Cammy's Big Bash takes on the trappings less of a grand political gala than of a Roman spectacle. These affairs are

milk and honey for the Washington power set. They thrive
on them as life-giving events, as if their subconsciences are
telling them: Life indeed is short. Truck with the gods, or
perish. They crown their new emperor-to-be with the gold
tribute of political donations, thus empowering him, and
themselves, before going off to battle their mortal enemy.
Morituri te salutamus.

And like the coliseum, there is a central arena where
all the action takes place and where the emperor and his
entourage are situated, and the surrounding stands where
the multitudes of unwashed citizens observe and cheer,
having paid their day's wages for the privilege. Ten-thousand
dollars got you a seat in the inner circle, those who would
dine on rack of lamb with the candidates, their spouses and
a scattering of shadow cabinet contenders and distinguished
party stalwarts inside Colchester Manor's small colonial
ballroom, this evening graced with a baker's dozen of white-
linen-and-orchid-bedecked large round tables. All the rest,
stinkards and groundlings who forked over one-thousand
dollars, are consigned to the tents outside, where mediocre
wine and skimpy hors d'oeuvres are served. Mariner fixed
it so I could cross into both worlds freely. The two would
converge after coffee when the speeches would be made.

I choose first to rub elbows with the high rollers.
Tuxedoed waiters serve smoked eel and trout paté canapés,
along with crystal flutes of Moët et Chandon. A string
quartet fills the air gently with Vivaldi. Faint aromas of crisp
brut and understated scents of expensive colognes punctuate
the atmosphere, clearly identifying the people and place, like
incense in a church.

A very distinguished crowd of elegant women and
self-assured men stand in clusters. Drinks in hand, they are
engaged in the forced conviviality that marks such mass
events.

I stand amid this gathering, taking it all in, wondering what Eammon Brennan, foundry foreman, immigrant, father of five, never having once taken even a sip of champagne or a lick of pâté in his short, hard 59 years, would think. The past again tugs at me. It reminds me that my throat will always feel like it's in a noose when garroted in a necktie, it tells me that honest sweat trumps cosmetics, that truth is to be found among men and women who toil and struggle for a living. Eammon, what would you say to a son who finds himself in this rarefied world?

An arm hooks into mine and I feel myself being swept away, as if on rollerblades, across the ballroom floor. Cammy has me by the hand and is yanking me toward one of the power clusters.

"Harry, come. I want you to meet some people. Carry on where you left off at lunch. What was it, globalization?"

Cammy's face has the impish grin of a young girl up to no good. But she looks like anything but a little girl. Her hair is pulled up, fastened with a black velvet band again, and a diamond pin. Unpretentious diamond earrings. A black and white silk dress that lets her body speak for itself.

She introduces me to the first cluster: CEO's, mostly. This is Harlon so-and-so, of Hydra Oil Services; and Marty dah-dah-dah, Icon Technology; Wilmer-----, from San Antone, AP-Temoco; Josh hum-hum, founder and CEO of Dynamic Power, Inc. And so it goes.

The second cluster as well as the others are similarly populated. In true fashion, Cammy is given to her trademark hyperbole. She introduces me as "the man to watch at the CIA" and "a key policy advisor to John (Dodge)." Alternately, she whispers in my ear, "Wilmer's angling for ambassador to Italy"; "You *must* get to know him, they say Josh is going to be next Energy Secretary"; a banking guy with a big paunch and squirrelly wife gave $100,000. "I think they're awarding him Nebraska, or something," giggle, giggle. Cammy, the consummate insider.

I study the men's faces as Cammy veers into their orbit. They're too refined to leer, but the salivary glands are at full throttle. The wives, on the other hand, with their guarded smiles, act as if a reputed thief had entered their domain.

The clusters begin to spin and deconstruct, attracted individual-by-individual toward a new galaxy forming near the entrance of the ballroom. The straight-and-tall figure of John Dodge is clearly visible, the lode-star of this event. He is smiling and pumping hands. Quips fly. The charm is laid on thick. In his wake is Senator Horton, the reputed V.P.-to-be. No slouch himself, Horton picks up those who Dodge missed as he cruised in at full steam.

Cammy cuts me loose. Outside this inner sanctum, hordes of well-turned-out people are converging on Colchester Manor, like Visigoths, only with manners. They're milling about without direction. The diesel-roar of buses accompanies this human deluge. Cammy peers out the window. The buses are disgorging yet more guests. Police are attempting to untangle a honking, dusty traffic snarl on the country lane outside Colchester's front gate. Cops are shouting orders at drivers.

Cammy turns heel. She's pale, her face the picture of angst. I read her lips: "Jason."

She runs out the door into the mad rush of humanity. She ignores greetings and extended hands. Her radar is targeted against one object – Jason Mariner. I follow her into the garden.

She has lock-on and charges in a straight trajectory for Jason, who is no more successful than the cops in directing people to their pre-designated seats. Like hunter-gatherer nomads, the dapper guests mill around searching for strategic territory, the best location to view the podium, a place near food and drink. From the dynamics of it all, however, a driving force appears to me to be a pecking order instinct whereby those highest on the food chain naturally converge and stake out turf at front and central locations, leaving the hoi-polloi to pick over the left-overs – tables at the outer reaches where marauding mosquitoes, dim lighting and the risk of not being seen are greatest.

Cammy is waving her arms furiously at a hounded Jason. He keeps opening his eyes wide, then shutting them as if having difficulty focusing. As I come near, I hear the full fury of hurricane Cammy. "…can't happen, Jason! You told me it was all planned out. It looks like a fucking rock concert! Fix it! Fix it, goddamn it!"

At my peril, I wade in. "All right. I see the problem. Let me help. I know something about crowd control."

Cammy diverts the flame in her eyes from Jason to me. "Crowd control?! This is fucking Armageddon! And dickhead here is the Lord of freaking Hell!"

"Jason, where's the caterer?" I ask.

With a vacant stare, he points mechanically at the rear of the main tent where a bar has been set up.

"Let's go. Cammy, I'll handle this. Go back to being hostess," I say.

Her face a mask of doubt, Cammy trudges back to the house, twice looking back at us, as if making sure we don't simply abscond and leave the whole mess with her.

With my hand on Jason's back, I gently but quickly steer us toward a beefy, bald, mustachioed man, who garrulously introduces himself as Rick Santizo, of Santizo Catering and Supply. He presents his card.

"Rick, do you do these things regularly?" I ask.

"Our specialization. We cater Hill events, campaign parties all the time, in addition to the big weddings, stuff like that."

I point to the swirling masses, now trampling Cammy's beloved rose bushes and manicured shrubbery. "Rick. What do you see?"

"A crowd out of control," he says matter-of-factly.

"Rick. What can you do about it?"

A bulb goes off. Rick smiles and points an index finger upward. "Gotcha. Can do. We call ourselves the 'Can-do Caterer.' Watch." Rick grabs a flunky, orders him to ride herd on drinks and food. He then glides across the area and, one-by-one, enlists servers and preparers. He convenes them on the lawn nearby, and barks out orders like General Patton. The staff fan out in a 360-degree direction. Soon, human corridors form, foot traffic takes linear direction, tables and chairs are re-formed, people's heads are nodding in welcome comprehension about what to do. Santizo's people are there to greet guests decamping from the big buses, which have been ferrying them from the race track several miles away, by accounts now coming in, an even worse mess than here, a situation only somewhat less dire than Iraq before America struck.

As order takes shape, I turn to Jason and pepper him with questions about the rest of the evening's activities. He looks at me and slowly blinks his fatigue-circled eyes.

"Jason. Jason, are you listening to me?" I shake him by the shoulders.

"Everything is all right. Everything is all right. Everything..." he says robotically.

"Jason. You okay, pal?"

The light is not on inside Jason Mariner's head. He begins to tremble. His right arm goes limp, then his right leg, and he buckles to the ground. I call for a doctor.

Eventually, an elderly tuxedoed guest appears and does a quick appraisal: shock from exhaustion. House staff bring a blanket to cover Jason as the doctor repositions him and an ambulance is called.

I bend down. "Jason. Can you hear me?"

He gives a slow nod.

"You'll be okay, buddy. You've been working too hard. It got to you. You need to lay low."

The ambulance arrives. The paramedics rush over and begin to position Jason on a stretcher.

Jason moves his head back and forth frantically.

"Wait. Wait. What are they doing?" he says.

"You're not well, Jason. They're taking you to the hospital."

The paramedics strap his legs. Before they can get his arms, however, Jason is waving them agitatedly. He grabs a table leg.

"No. No. This is my show. You can't take me. You can't take me!"

I help pin him down while the medics strap him in.

"Jason. Calm down," I say.

"Cammy! Stop them! Don't let them do this!" he yells full force.

I accompany him to the ambulance and watch them put him in. As they close the doors, "C-a-m-m-y!!" reverberates from inside. The ambulance, red dome light twirling, eases its way off the lawn and out to Colchester Lane. Jason's impresario aspirations go with it.

Whatever the dear departed soul of Eammon Brennan may think, here I am amid chandeliered splendor, a far cry indeed from the wrong side of the tracks, Kansas City, and the fast track to the pen, or worse. I am put at the second most prestigious table in the ballroom. Cammy and a bunch of the flushest business tycoons (minus wives) occupy the holy see with Dodge at its head. The lead character at table no. 2 is none other than Blair Evans. Joining us is Cleo Derwood, the presidential team's reputed selection for Secretary of Education (and, by the way, a high-profile black female to round out the ranks of political equity); a prominent academic, Kurt Reitzling, a physicist of great renown, apparently here to add cachet, along with a sprinkling of Hollywood types; and several more CEO's: a computer magnate and three from the power and petrol complex.

Evans holds forth about what sad shape the country is in, how he hasn't seen it this bad since the Carter years. The best President was FDR. Evans was a newspaper delivery boy then who loved reading the articles between drop-offs. That's when he got hooked on politics. He leads in to how the Dodge administration will provide a much-needed shot of adrenaline into the economy and the national spirit. Yadda, yadda. My mind wanders.

"Beware the phonies and sharpies, lad. They'll eat ya for breakfast and spit out yer bones." It's my old man. "It's yer family what counts, followed by kin and clan. Don't believe the rest. It's all a game to them. And it's called, 'I Win.'" Funny, how the mind can conjure up memories from distant childhood. I can see him, seated before the fireplace, in denim pants and workman's cotton shirt, lighting his pipe with his thick, permanently grimed fingers. Deep lines on his wary face, passing on the wisdom of a lifetime to the tikes.

"Don't you think so, Brennan? I say, Brennan." I snap out of my reverie. My tablemates are staring at me. Did I fart? Did I snore? What?

"I said, Brennan, you have interesting insights into that part of the world. Give us your opinion." Evans says.

"Central Asia? Ah. What in particular?" I ask.

"How about a quick and dirty political risk analysis?" says one petrol plutocrat. "With so many opportunities opening up economically, what are the political downsides? Share with us the CIA's *special* insight."

Chuckles all around. I emit a wan smile. Funny how Hollywood has managed to turn a government agency, one as hobbled by its own internal contradictions, bloat and mismanagement, with at least as many incompetents and nincompoops as any other government entity, into the Super Oracle of the Planet, all-knowing, ubiquitous, unnerved and brilliant.

I take my time to ponder the question. I look at the faces of my fellow diners, all expectant. These are the faces of success and self-contentment. They bear no visible emotional scars of fear or failure, much less of hunger or panic, which I've come to know only too well in the countries where I have served. These are faces of the people who call the shots, not those who take them.

I smile slightly. "The Afghans have a saying, 'Forget your enemies, but never your friends.'"

The expressions of expectancy change to puzzlement, followed by disinterest.

"Meaning," I continue, "if we, as a nation, don't stand by our friends, nobody else will either, and we'll pay in the end in the form of greater instability, or worse. Central Asia offers opportunities, yes, but it also offers up dangers. The peoples in that region have long historical memories and they're not of a forgiving nature. The Russians know that too well. Anytime you cross an Afghan, an Uzbek, a Kazakh, a Georgian, an Azeri, they'll never forget and they'll get back at you."

The piercing sound of an over oscillated microphone screeches in the air, causing everyone to wince. A spotlight goes on and radiates the figure of Cammy at the head of the ballroom. Her beauty positively sparkles in the bright light, which glints off her pearly whites almost as powerfully as her diamonds.

"Ladies and gentlemen, fellow Democrats. I know what you're thinking: The Queen of Spleen, that walking infomercial, is going to give it to us again."

The hall erupts in laughter.

"Well, there's going to be plenty of time for that!"

More laughter.

"But this evening is a particularly special one. We have the great honor of joining together to show our support for and faith in a great man, a man who embodies the spirit of justice, progress and compassion that is the Democratic Party. The man the American people are about to choose as their next president...John Patrick *Dodge!*"

A riot of applause breaks out as the dashing senator rises from his table and waves.

"But as we bless the future, we must also pay homage to the past and those among us whose brilliant work and ardent sacrifices got us to where we are today -- on the cusp of a great new victory."

She gestures toward Evans, referring to him as the "Elder Statesman" of the Party.

Evans pulls himself up on his cane and waves an unsteady hand as he does a 180-degree turn to acknowledge his admirers.

Cammy then recalls the days of McCarthyism when the "radical right held this country in its grip of terror," "the Camelot days of John Kennedy which lifted our nation from darkness and showed the people that anything was possible if you were the strongest nation in the world," and "the crumbling of decrepit communism when hundreds of millions of people could finally breathe free." At every major turn in America's history over the past half-century, a great man stood side-by-side with the Party's leaders, in the White House and out. A man whose advice and whose prestigious posts in the area of national security helped protect America and keep it free. That man, of course, is "my husband, Jared."

Cammy claps and then extends an arm out show-biz style as a fill-in for Jason wheels out the old titan himself. The wasted, slumped shell of Jared Loomis is contained in a spiffy new suit, starched shirt and tie. Somehow, vigorous apparel on ancient men is a study in deception. As incongruous as fresh paint on driftwood.

The crowd rises to give Loomis a standing ovation. Cammy bends down and embraces him, kisses him on one cheek. She beams before all of these people, the makers and shakers of politics, captains of industry, intellectual giants. Jared is the lightning rod for public adulation, whose energy Cammy sucks in like an aluminum smelter. I mark in my mind the contrast of tonight's loving and devoted wife with the consumed, couldn't-be-bothered apparatchik of yesterday.

Cammy stands and resumes her oration as Loomis is wheeled off the center-spot. Another prop in Cammy's repertoire of slick tricks. He is rolled within a few feet of my seat. His alert eyes fix on me. Deep within the stony face and limp body, through those living eyes, a spirit stirs still. Those dark eyes, turning to stay fixed on mine, seem to be telegraphing outrage. I nod my head in acknowledgement. His lids slowly close and reopen a second later as if to indicate that he is pleased to have gotten his message to me.

After they tear through several carcasses of lamb, washed down with a small river of fine wines, followed by an infarction-inducing Belgian dessert and coffee, the attendees begin to get up and schmooze.

This is the point when the commissars of the Party, led by Evans and Cammy, followed by the shadow cabinet and a bevy of prettified young agitprops pounce on their willing invitees to deliver the Party line and to talk more contributions out of them. As they fan out among the faithful and turn on the charm machine, I shake my head in amused admiration over Jason's organizational skills. If Jason were at Corregidor, things might have turned out differently.

While Cammy is irresistible, Evans is clearly the master of this black art. He softens up his targets with scintillating tales of yore, insider stories of his days as an aide to JFK, about his one-on-one chats in the Oval Office with Lyndon Johnson over civil rights, and his personally handing in his resignation as Army Secretary over the direction of the Vietnam War – "I could see what was coming – a catastrophe." He recounts his friendships with Sadat, the Shah, Mao, Willy Brandt, Gorbachev from his various diplomatic and special envoy assignments.

Once he has his listeners' undivided attention, Evans then launches into a debate of where the country is going and where it needs to be steered.

"Bill, you're in the oil business. I don't have to tell you that diversification of our energy sources is the name of the game or we'll find ourselves right back waiting in gas lines just like in '73.

"Tyler, I know you'd be the first to say that investment in our information technology education sector is essential if we're to keep this economy plunging ahead and remain the world's leader.

"Carl. How many times have you said we have the tax system of a banana republic? We've got to fix it."

And so it goes. The punch line, of course, is, "John Dodge is the man to fix it all and he needs the resources to pull it off. And he needs your help. The new administration will not forget its friends."

Evans treats me like a favorite nephew, good-naturedly pulling me into these lectures as "our guy in the CIA." He prods me into saying a few things, obviously to add weight to his own postulations. I feel increasingly uncomfortable, yet another prop on the set.

I am struck by the interaction of the two wizards of this particular political magic, Evans and Cammy. They clearly have their roles down pat and make optimum use of their talents by working in parallel yet separately. On the occasions their orbits link, however, Cammy looks up wide-eyed at the old man, listens and nods. Sometimes, she holds one extended arm by the elbow with the other hand. The conversations don't last more than a minute or two, then Cammy scampers off. They are the body language of a little girl, I can't help but think.

I make a point of joining one of these convergences. It's Cammy, Evans, a couple of the guests and Norfolk, of all people, who arrived late. From his flush complexion and wet hair, I can imagine what kept him.

Evans is jabbering on about the business cycle or some such fish food the rich and quasi-famous thrive on. Norfolk offers his fifteen cents whenever Evans will let him, the latter evidently knowing how to keep the motor on this particular mouth down to a fast idle. Cammy is close by Evans's side, her arm linked in his. It's a grandpa scene. Cammy's natural assertiveness is tucked away somewhere.

To emphasize "democratic" in the Party's name, they finally remove the partitions that separate the inner crowd from the outer. A stage is set up which faces both. Now it is the candidate's turn for speechifying. And he does it with aplomb, emotion and humor. Big hit with the by-now sloshed Party faithful. A band follows. The emphasis is on salsa and meringue. The Democrats were always a funner ilk than their compatriots across the aisle. Everybody gets into the swing of things. Cammy calls Dodge back up to the stage with his wife and they all join in a conga-style line, hips swaying more or less in unison. A cap to a very successful evening, the unplanned hordes notwithstanding. Vindication for Jason.

I observe all this from the shadows, again privately wallowing in the incessant struggle over my workingman's soul. Cammy spots me, but doesn't beckon me to join them, as I feared. Instead she slithers free of the conga line, clapping; then slowly backs away from the rhythmic swell of dancers, smiling and clapping all the way. All eyes are trained on the next president. Evans is off at a table holding forth some more on weighty issues of the day.

The bum-bum-bum of the Cuban drums combined with the orgasmic-paced strums of the guitars are seductive, rather out of place in such a setting, a colonial English manor, graying money-bags, politics. But this sensuous music transcends all that, if one averts one's gaze. One feels genuinely human, devoid for the moment of the artifices of the everyday world, or this charmed one. A warm breeze flows through effortlessly and caresses the skin.

I savor the music with my eyes closed, and smile.

A warm hand presses against my chest, then another. I turn. It's Cammy behind me.

She grasps my hand. "Come."

She pulls me into the darker shadows away from the festivities. She pulls harder until we're in a trot toward the edge of the woods. Cammy is giggling wildly, again like a little girl.

"W-o-o-o-o-o," she screams and brings us crashing down on the soft wildflower bedding of a meadow. Ha-ha-ha-ha-ha."

We're both on our backs, out of breath.

"How much did that dress cost?" I ask.

"What if I said $2,300?" she answers.

I choke.

"There you go again. Mr. Practicality." She tickles my ribs. We laugh some more, then settle down.

Cammy points to the sky, a deep pitch sprayed with a frothy sea of stars. "Look. What do you see?"

"Lots of stars," I answer lamely.

"Uggh! You're hopeless, Harry. You know what I see? I see eternity. And my place in it."

"I may be hopeless, but you're positively narcissistic."

"No. Let me finish. You look at such a sky and you realize just how meaningless you are; just a passing speck of dust on some directionless terminal breeze. That's what we all are. And that's why I revert to being a girl at moments like this. And why we all need to be silly sometimes. But also why if we don't grab that breeze that is our life and make *something* out of it, we just become…somebody's allergy. See what I mean?"

"Somebody's allergy. In other words, a piece of snot?"

"You can put it that way. Or this." Cammy leans on one elbow, bends over and puts her lips on mine. Strands of her hair that have been released from all the dancing and running float tantalizingly on my skin. We kiss hungrily. Cammy moves her body on top of mine. Our outstretched hands lock above our heads. The evening dew's dampness presses through my clothing. Alternately warm and cool breezes lap against our skin. Cammy presses harder against me, her firm breasts rub up and down across my chest. I feel her thigh pressing into my groin. A low groan emanates from deep inside her. This lets loose an energy surge from within myself and the lovemaking grows in intensity.

Cammy deftly unzips my fly and pushes my trousers down with her thighs. My hands are now inside her dress. I release the slip of a black bra and caress her breasts.

Cammy wiggles off her panties. She's in complete control of the situation. She raises herself, leaning forward with both hands pinning down mine. As she presses herself hard against me, Cammy lets out a cat-like screech, which sends her into a passionate fury. The lovemaking is aggressive and fast. We reach a crescendo in amazing synch and collapse in a tumble of thrashed-out exhaustion.

In the afterglow of lovemaking, something flashes in my brain. It jolts me like an involuntary spasm.

Cammy lifts her head. "What's wrong?"

The memory of Roni with me in the Tidewater meadow had hit me like an electric shock.

"Nothing."

Cammy throws an arm over me and kisses me sweetly.

Time to get back. We preen and pat as best we can in the darkness in an effort to reconstruct our appearances. We laugh in the recognition of the near futility, like two kids on prom night just before returning home.

"We can sneak into the guesthouse and clean up," she says.

On the path back, hand-in-hand, I ask, "How long have you known Evans?"

"Blair? Oh, as long as I've known Jared. They go back, uh, at least a century or two."

"You seem to be close to him."

She looks up with an arched eyebrow.

"I mean...just *close*. You know."

"What you're saying is that Blair and I are intimate in a platonic way. After all, he's a whisker's breadth from eternity."

"Uh-huh."

"Blair's been such a good friend. He's been at Jared's side since the time of the pyramids. And since Jared had his stroke, why, Blair has helped me in every way. Like a favorite uncle." She looks up and searches my face to see if I understand. "It's all so complicated." She lets out a deep breath.

"What is?" I ask.

"Oh, all of this." She takes in Colchester Manor with a broad sweep of her arms. "Jared's affairs are *so* involved. Stock options, debentures, convertible securities, not to mention all the properties. And the staffs to run them! It makes my head spin. I can't deal with it. I simply can't. And I'm busy enough as it is with all this Party work. It's important."

"So, Evans helps you out?"

"I've signed over to Blair management of Jared's investment empire. 'Just keep the money coming, Blair,' is my only instruction to him. It works out so well this way."

The lights from the house and tents glow on us now. We release our hand-hold.

"What are debentures anyway, do you suppose? Something they put in your mouth?" she asks.

Another peel of giggles flows from this girl-woman.

As we approach the guesthouse, Cammy looks at me thoughtfully and says, "Harry?"

"Yeah?"

"You've got a great future."

CHAPTER TWENTY-THREE

NEW YORK, NY

It's debatable whether Jared's death detracted from the sterling success of the Americans for the New Millennium fundraiser or acted as a multiplier effect. In any case, Cammy wasted no effort in pulling out all the stops to focus the nation's attention squarely on the passing into history of one its human monuments to the twentieth century, a man whose name was linked with Churchill, de Gaulle, the Kennedys, Gorbachev, popes, famous royals, financiers and intellectuals.

He passed in his sleep just two nights after the big bash. Cammy was in Austin supervising the first presidential campaign debate. Upon receiving Jason's call, she rushed back to Virginia in the Piaggio Avanti, the family jet. Jason, still recovering from his exhaustion from the fundraiser, was thrown into the thick of it again, exercising his organizing and PR magic to translate Cammy's visions into reality.

Actually, his was merely to put into action one of the three options plans devised for just this occasion. True to form, Cammy had been busy planning for her husband's demise months in advance, down to the minutest detail. Jason explained it to me. One option involved holding the funeral in New York, with a memorial service in Washington. The second entailed the reverse, and the third burial at sea off a U.S. war ship with full military honors. Cammy favored the third option for its pomp and pageantry and for its mobility;

it could be performed off the Virginia coast, or in New York Harbor. Trouble is, the United States Navy would have none of it. Old Man Loomis's only claim to America at sea was his membership in the Chesapeake Yacht Club.

All of Cammy's pull – she even enlisted Evans, as former Navy Secretary – couldn't trump the hard and fast rules and procedures of a two centuries old naval establishment. That made choosing between the remaining two options fairly easy. The United Nations General Assembly convenes every September and continues in session for several months. The opening always attracts world leaders. Should Jared die during this fairly small window of time, Cammy would see to it that attendance at his funeral would rival that for royals and heads of state. On the other hand, in the event Jared died in, say, February or July, the next best option would be to eulogize him in Washington while Congress was in session, thereby capturing that august crowd as well as everybody who's somebody in the administration, not to mention big-time CEO's headquartered near the nation's capital. Jason and a small team had phoned the offices of every major personage to ascertain their whereabouts during given timeframes. They fed this information to Cammy in the form of situation reports. So as not to be too macabre about it, however, Jason gave the project the anodyne title, "Crossing." The plans were collected into three thick color-coded binders, complete with annexes covering everything from seating arrangements to caterers to carefully selected eulogies. Cammy and Evans chose the latter from dozens solicited from English lit professors and speech writers from defunct White House administrations.

As the doctors' prognoses made it increasingly clear that the ninety-one year old financier was selling all his positions short and soon to be permanently excised from the D.C. *Social Register,* Crossing preparations went into overdrive and the core team was doubled in size. With a presidential election looming, Cammy made New York target zero for the funeral of the decade. Plan A was put into condition red alert status. And with the uncanny timing of a super arbitrageur, Jared obliged, closing out all accounts, leaving a healthy bottom line going forward for his widow.

The religious service at the cavernous St. John the Divine Cathedral, overlooking Morningside Park, is marked by somber majesty. The New York Philharmonic plays lugubrious pieces by Bach, Albinoni, Williams, filling the century-old church with ethereal strains which tug at the mortal soul with the powerful pull of a cold ocean undertow.

The pews are filled with statesmen from every continent, enough ambassadors to constitute an ex officio session of the General Assembly, old money scions and new money upstarts, the governor, the mayor, an ecumenical panoply of the Establishment's chosen high churchmen and the de facto politburo of New York's rigid arts hierarchy.

I sit next to Jason well to the back. In between his monitoring of the choreography of events, the irrepressible Jason wisecracks that funerals and fundraisers have much in common. They both start with "f", they bring together the living and the dead – with lots of money about to be transferred from the latter to the former; and they're both aimed at burying someone following a long, hard fight. He reveals that the Crossing staff had carefully researched the funerals of J.P. Morgan, Andrew Carnegie, Henry Ford and several other rapacious moneybags in preparation for this one.

John Dodge delivers the main eulogy, a touching encomium replete with references from Walt Whitman, Shakespeare and, yes, JFK. "O Captain! My Captain! our fearful trip is done; The ship has weather'd every rack, the prize we sought is won." Cammy and Evans had commissioned the eulogy months before to an aging speech writer from Kennedy's time; it was annex three of Plan A. With his Harvard-trained intellect, Dodge delivers it with just the right balance of articulateness and pathos. Barely an eye is dry. But it is a two-way street, as such bargains tend to be among the powerful. The glow of reflected greatness, combined with the heightened – and free – media attention, has won for Dodge the posthumous public endorsement of the late Jared Loomis.

Cammy is lost in a cascade of black mantilla specially designed by Balenciaga. This mourning outfit had been strategically stowed at the ready in the Loomis's Park Avenue penthouse like a nuclear missile in a silo waiting to be launched. Now in it, Cammy is the picture of the grief-stricken widow, moving slowly with noble grace, head high, bosom full, occasionally dabbing an eye with a silk lace handkerchief.

Episcopal Bishop Kenneth Hornblow, another "dear friend," came from Boston to conduct the service. Jared's only grandson, five grandnephews and Norfolk serve as pallbearers

After the service, there is time for some post-funereal schmoozing in the aisles, down the nave, onto the stairs and cathedral entrance. Press and media cover the event, cameras clicking away like a nocturnal swampful of crickets and beetles, per annex five. Cammy graciously and with sad refinement accepts condolences from scores of mourners.

The weather cooperates. Low, gray clouds, a cold chill with a slight drizzle on park blossoms and city asphalt lend just the right aura of gloom. Hollywood could not have done better.

A small coterie of family and close friends proceeds north to the Loomis estate of Den Bosch near Croton-on-Hudson overlooking the Hudson River. Originally the estate of a governor in Dutch colonial times, the thousand acres of placid rolling landscape feature an eighteenth century gabled manor house, a guest house added in Victorian times, stables, riding grounds and woodlands.

The mourners gather under the shade of old oaks in the Loomis family cemetery. Jared's coffin is set beside a freshly dug grave situated between those of his mother and his first wife, Chiara.

As Bishop Hornblow carries on with the final liturgical rites, my mind wanders. I ponder the simple gray headstone of Chiara Angelica degli Strozzi Loomis. Beneath the dates of her birth and death, is a simple epitaph: *Amor che a nullo amato amar perdona.*

"Can you read Italian?" Jason whispers to me.

"No."

"'Love, which insists that love shall mutual be.'"

"Ah."

Hornblow tosses a handful of sand on the coffin as it is lowered into the grave. "Amen," say all in unison, some crossing themselves at the end of the benediction. The mourners slowly leave the site and return to the motorcade, onward to Den Bosch Manor for food and refreshments and reminiscing.

Jason and I linger.

"Chiara was an amazing woman," he says. "She stemmed from an old Venetian aristocratic family who opposed Mussolini. The Fascists made the family destitute. They jailed and then killed Chiara's father, a prominent banker and royalist, but also a proponent of democracy. Jared met Chiara on one of his diplomatic shuttles to Rome immediately after it was liberated. Talk about a mismatch. Here's this dour, moneyed Yankee bachelor with no sense of humor taking up with a stunningly beautiful and spirited young Italian woman, made poor as a church mouse. But somehow it worked. I think she provided the spark his life lacked. He provided the anchor her life needed. After marrying, he took her back to New York where she became an instant hit with the postwar high society. She was a magnet for artists and writers and the stage crowd. Their parties were *the* place to be."

I nod toward Chiara's grave. "Then what happened?"

"She wanted children desperately. In ten years of marriage, they remained childless. She went back to Italy to consult with a leading fertility specialist in those days. All the doctors in New York had told her it was impossible. But this guy in Italy said they were experimenting with new techniques, but it was risky. If she became pregnant, she'd have to stay in bed all nine months. In bed. Period. Well, bam, she gets pregnant and follows the doctor's orders to a 'T'."

"And?"

"Jared sets her up in a classy old villa, with servants. In her seventh month, she suddenly hemorrhages. In the middle of the night. Before medical help can reach her, she, and the fetus, are dead."

"Jesus."

A cold breeze blows from the slow-moving Hudson. We pull the collars of our long coats tighter as we stroll in the direction of the house.

"Yeah. Shitty. Jared was devastated. He subsequently remarried, they say out of a sense of duty and not love. She was this dreary WASP ice princess, straight out of central casting for a Henry James story. After three children in quick succession, they grew slowly apart, separate bedrooms, that sort of thing. Typical for that class. They had an amicable divorce seven years later. Jared stuck to discreet affairs after that until he met Cammy."

"You think the old guy saw in Cammy another Chiara?" I ask.

"What do you think?" Jason shoots back.

"Dumb question. And, so, what's with the epitaph? I don't get it."

"'Love, which insists that love shall mutual be.' It's from Dante. As best I can piece it together, it was something she had repeated often when she was alive to rein in Jared's wandering eye. But—"

Jason stares at the damp earth as we trudge down a muddy winding path. He makes one shake of his head and crooks the side of his mouth.

"But what?" I prompt.

He looks at me dead serious and holds it. "It's a call from the grave. She wanted his love always. Even unto death."

"Holy shit."

"Yeah. You can say that again. You think that's something. Cammy is green-eyed jealous of that woman."

I look at Jason with a start.

"You heard me right. Jealous. It's like Eva Peron. The cult continues from the crypt. Vibes. Something. I don't know. But you mention anything about Chiara and Cammy gets sullen and hyperventilated all of a sudden. She's gone way out of her way to obliterate the memory of Chiara, even removing her artwork, totally remodeling Chiara's rooms in all the Loomis holdings. She got Jared, in his doddering last months to sign documents renaming the Chiara Loomis Foundation for the Arts to the Camilla Loomis Arts Foundation. Gives even me the willies."

We walk on deep in thought. Then it hits me. I halt. I point my thumb back in the direction of the little cemetery. "Wait a minute. We just planted Jared smack dab next to Eva ...I mean...Chiara."

"So we did," says Jason with no further comment.

The memorial service at Washington's National Cathedral is equally as moving, and well staged. Like an actress flitting from performance to performance of the same play, Cammy again dons the Balenciaga mourning dress, holds herself proud and dabs an eye now and again.

This performance, of course, is for the Washington crowd. Much of the Hill, the top layers of the State Department and other elite agencies of government, famous talking heads of the news apparat, yet more ambassadors and CEO's of big corporations which have increasingly relocated to or sprung up in the D.C. suburbs in recent years take their place in pre-designated sections of the church as carefully delineated as any assortment of bantustans under apartheid. Such is the meticulousness, again, of Cammy's planning.

I ask Jason what the bill for all of these events will come to. He gives a quick shake of his head and screws his mouth up in consternation. "Let's just say *beaucoup* bucks. Cammy...Cammy acts like she's the House of Windsor. There's a flood of cash outflow and it's only getting bigger. I'm out of it, but I hear things. Evans and his gang take care of it all now. Maybe that's what pushed old Jared over the edge. There's got to be a limit."

Things settle down. A month later, I'm back in my rut. D.C. is now white-hot politically as the elections bear upon us. I scan the *Post* over my usual pre-dawn breakfast. I can't escape that woman. Cammy is featured in the Style section: "Camilla Loomis: Life of the Party," reads the headline. Beneath it is a photograph of Cammy in her Georgetown home, fully at ease, one arm cocked on her hip and her head tossed back rakishly, her mouth emitting her trademark laugh. The feature is a gushing one which paints Cammy as practically the Joan of Arc of the Democratic Party. Certainly, her having raised $3.5 million at Colchester boosted her clout into stratospheric proportions.

I devour the article. Gushing it may be. So is it true. It accurately paints a picture of a young woman who comes out of left field to seize skiesful of thunder for herself. Her marriage to Jared is portrayed in neutral terms, but leaves the lay reader with little doubt what constituted the rocket fuel that launched an obscure girl from somewhere south of Mason-Dixon to national and international fame. But it also gives her credit. A single-minded, strongwilled charmer, some say courtesan, who has used her beauty to full advantage. She's now a powerhouse within the Democratic camp, a rainmaker of Neptunian proportions. It can be assumed, of course, that she will be able to name her reward in a Dodge administration. In any case, she is a much-needed spark of life in a fairly lifeless town, a welcome successor to such legendary socialites of yore as Pearl Mesta and Pamela Harriman.

As I finish the article, I can't help but think that the Life of the Party has certainly jumpstarted some life into me as well. I think I must be losing my mind. What did Frank DeFalco say? She's a passionate woman. But she uses men as stepping stones on the way up. How can Harry Brennan, GS-15, be that? I shake my head. I also feel a surge of shame. I made love to a married woman and under circumstances somewhat less than dignified. Then I remind myself that it was she who made love to me, albeit a willing partner. I think this, as if it detracts from the immorality of it all. No, Brennan, you're a shit. And, you may not realize it yet, but you may be a whore too.

I return to the national section of the paper for a quick glance at headlines before brushing my teeth and departing for the office.

"Human Remains Shellgame – Body of Dead Financier Never Buried" jumps the headline on page six at me like some gag trick at a magic show.

It is clear from the article's sourcing to "disgruntled family members," that Loomis's children tipped off the *Post* after somehow stumbling onto the fact that Jared's corpse remains above ground. In fact, the man eulogized in the country's two principal power hubs just weeks before is now stored in the basement of the Alfred R. Munderhouse Funeral Home in Croton awaiting further disposition. It states that the Potemkin gravesite where the interment ceremony took place was immediately filled in upon departure of the mourners and the coffin shuttled off to the Munderhouse establishment "at the explicit direction of Loomis's widow" pending final instructions.

It goes on to quote a lawyer with the law firm of Cairns, Blumenthal & Evans lamely claiming something about "pending final paperwork authorizing final remains disposition" as the reason for non-burial. Loomis's progeny, however, refute this, asserting Cammy's animus against their father's first wife. Past examples are cited of Cammy's petty attempts to expunge the memory of Chiara, including the remodeling of her rooms and the renaming of the arts foundation. It is unclear what motivates these now middle-aged patrician offspring of Jared, whether it's a respect and affection for a woman they never knew, or, as one suspects, a driving antipathy toward the young parvenu who placed their father under her spell – and his wealth, and their inheritance, further from their grasp.

When I arrive at the office, I detect tension in the air. Shareen, Norfolk's latest secretary, has the look of a forest creature who senses the pre-tremors of an oncoming earthquake. Wide-eyed, alert, subdued. By the way, Shareen is a blonde. She doesn't respond to my "good morning."

I approach Norfolk's office. The door is open. He's doing the AT&T marching step – phone at his ear as he paces back and forth like a caged animal, gesticulating with his free arm while almost shouting at the individual at the other end. He catches me passing by and signals me to enter and have a seat.

"...but Ned, you gain nothing by printing this story...

Whah? What's this bullshit about freedom of the press? Since when did the *Post* give a rat's ass about freedom of the press? This story just makes you guys look mean. Picking on a distraught widow in her time of grieving...Come again? Even-handed? Oh, yeah? I haven't yet seen the story of the corpse of some Republican big shot rotting in somebody's basement rec room. Ned. Ned! Don't hang up. We're all Democrats, after all. Ned! I'm calling Don Graham, Ned! Hello? Hello? FUCK!!" Norfolk slams the receiver down with all his might. A plastic part goes flying and ricochets off the wall.

"Fuck. Fuck. Fuck!!" He's red-faced and orbiting past Pluto by the look of the fire in his eyes. "Frigging press! All they wanna do is tear you down. Especially that shit-rag *Washington Post*. Been on a glory ride ever since Watergate." Norfolk has his arms crossed. The fat around his stocky frame bulges against his suit jacket. With his lower lip jutted out, he looks to the left, then abruptly to the right, as if desperately seeking a new idea to use as a weapon.

The fiery eyes then bore in on me. With his arms still crossed, Norfolk points his right index finger at me.

"Brennan. I want you to round up some disinformation specialists at your agency. I want them to work immediately on spreading the word that the *Washington Post* has a vendetta out against Camilla Loomis. Those nosebleeding Eastern snobs have it out against a southern girl who did well for herself in the D.C. shark pool."

I chuckle.

"What? I say something funny here, Brennan?" Norfolk is clearly not amused.

"No. It's just that what you ask is not possible."

"'Not possible,' Brennan? May I ask why it's 'not possible'?" He mocks me. "This is not the time for some candy-assed equivocating by some born-again, socially responsible spook, Brennan."

"One. We don't do that sort of thing anymore. Seldom, anyway. Not since the demise of the Soviet bloc. Two. Anyone stupid enough to try a stunt like that can expect an all-expense-paid extended stay at a federal penitentiary of their judge's choosing," I answer.

Norfolk plops down into his chair, deflated. He gazes out the window. "Shit, Brennan." He turns back toward me. "It's Cammy, for chrissake. She's the greatest thing to come along since Betsy Ross and the pooh-bahs want to tear her down. She's a laughing stock over this burial thing. She's beside herself, Brennan. I left her in tears just an hour ago. Thought you could do something. Let's face it, Brennan. It's an open secret – you two, I mean." He grimaces and turns his palms up.

He gets no response out of me. I'm shocked, but have no right to be. Our cavorting has been less than a covert operation, after all. And, in D.C., if you're anybody, you have no claim to a private life. As soon as your profile rises above a blip on the screen, you can be sure the wags will be wagging and intern trainees have started a bio file on you at the news bureaus.

"Face it, Brennan. You're a rising star." He stifles my instant protest with a downward wave of one hand and a look of serious impatience. I draw back into my shell of inscrutability, or, better yet, resignation. "It's okay. It's okay. But don't kid yourself. You may be sharp, but so are a zillion other terminal civil servants out there. In this town, it's who you know that makes or breaks you. And the unwritten code is, you help those who help you."

CHAPTER TWENTY-FOUR
LANGLEY, VIRGINIA

Jared finally got laid to rest. In the ground. Deep in the ground. Presumably permanently. And when he did, the titters and chuckles at Cammy's expense of America's Empowered Class subsided and passed into the distance like a spring storm.

Cammy chose as her late husband's final resting place an idyllic spot next to a large pond on Den Bosch Estate, some two-thousand yards away from Chiara. The new burial ground features two plots. In a couple of carefully chosen interviews with soft-pitch journalists, Cammy revealed solemnly that the second plot was hers, as if millions of readers are going to buy the line that a rich, knock-out 35-year old social climber is going to save herself like some high-caste Hindu widow for five or six decades till mortality joins her with her long-gone pre-millennial mate.

The landslide victory of the Dodge-Horton team dissipated the widow Loomis's grief with surprising speed and propelled her out of her mourning faster than you can say inheritance.

She is there at all the key events. The inauguration. The balls. The press conferences. So are Norfolk and Evans, mostly. And so am I, mostly. People I hardly know, or even not at all, suck up to me. They want to "do lunch," "compare notes," "drop by." Small klatsches gather around to chat me up. Suddenly, I'm somebody. Dr. Jekyll has become Mr. Hyde. I've metamorphosed from a face in the crowd to an up-and-comer. The capital crowd have a sixth sense for such things and act like bees to honey. This all happened without my even trying. Hell, I was oblivious to it.

What's happened to me? I had a quest – to get to the bottom of the treachery or incompetence that resulted in my covert operation being blown and the lives of hundreds of people being snuffed out. I wake up one morning to find that I've been co-opted. I'm one of them now. Or, am I? I set out to vanquish the evildoers. Where did they go? Instead, inexorably, like a leaf on the edge of a stream, I am swept by the flow and carried along, to this place.

I'm in the expansive, seventh-floor office of the DCI. Behind the desk sits Norfolk. I, alone, face him in a modest chair.

Norfolk is leaning forward on his elbows in his trademark fashion. He's blathering away, but I'm not listening. I'm wondering what I'm doing here and where I got off course.

"So, how about it, Brennan? Deal?"

I make a slight shake of my head to force my brain to pay attention. "Deal?"

"You all right, Brennan? You getting any, Brennan? Nothing focuses a man's mind like a woman, you know. Take my word for it." He sits back in his chair, a huge, overstuffed black leather job with gear shifts at knee-level that look like they came off a Maserati. "I said, will you be my executive director?"

Norfolk was sworn in as Director of Central Intelligence the previous day. Becoming DCI was his payoff for the political support he gave to the Dodge team. He'd been angling to be named Secretary of State, but that went to Dorothy Pittock, a Dodge loyalist from way back; an ambitious academician who also happened to help round out a cabinet line-up as carefully selected for its ethnic and gender make-up as for qualifications and connections to the President. Now Norfolk was offering me a job, in some ways more powerful than that of Deputy DCI. The Executive Director is in charge of the paper flow and the people flow to the DCI. This equates to information flow, which translates into power in Washington. An intelligence agency is an information agency and he who triages that essential commodity sits in the nexus of power.

Without any real forethought, I say, "Yes."

"Good. Keep me informed, but don't inundate me. In the human flow to my office, to the extent possible, screen out the assholes. Pass them off to Deputy Hanks or some other senior person. I want the inside line on the personal dynamics within this agency as well as the issues. If someone is fucking up, I don't want to read about it in the newspapers first. Finally, by all means, keep the Old Boys at bay. I have no patience for the Hindu caste system which no Director of this agency has yet been able to crack. I'm a realist, Brennan. I've long learned not to mess with ancient, ingrained tribal customs and rituals. It makes the natives restless, then they go after you. Just keep them busy and out of my hair, like you did for me at the White House."

"Can I ask you a question?" I say.

"Shoot."

"Why me?"

"'Why me' what?"

"Why me for this job? I mean, you don't know me so well."

Norfolk opens a wooden box on his desk and pulls out a six-inch Monte Cristo No. 9. The Mexican ambassador is his procurer of Cuban contraband. Such are the extents of networking among the power set. He runs the cigar under his nose to embrace its full aroma. "Not to worry, Brennan.

I'll savor this God's creation after lunch on the terrace. If only Castro knew where some of his stuff was ending up. Think he'd try to poison me, like the CIA tried to poison him with his cigars?" Norfolk lets out with a hearty laugh.

"I like you, Brennan. Took to you immediately. You're a trustworthy guy, not easy to find in this town. And you're very good."

"I have to ask this. Did Cammy influence you in any way?"

Norfolk's eyes narrow. He frowns. "No. I want you on your merits. I love and respect Cammy. What's going on between you two is your business. You're both of age and free."

I ponder this. I want to pursue the Cammy angle, but something deep inside tells me to drop it. "Remember that old Disney movie with Jerry Lewis starring as 'Cinderfella'?"

Norfolk looks puzzled. "Uh. Never was strong on Disney. David Lean pictures. Now that's a different story."

"It's about a klutz who finds himself suddenly thrust into a charmed existence, but hasn't a clue why and then screws everything up. I'm Cinderfella."

Norfolk laughs.

The perks of power are many in my new job. And seductive. Even if I wanted to be apathetic or passive or cynically removed, I couldn't. The demands are many. To ignore the many left curves and fast balls that come fast and furious in the direction of the Seventh Floor of CIA headquarters would be to court lethal professional injury, a fate I have no interest in courting. In the Director's name, I snap orders, dictate responses to new crises and hold accountable those riding herd on a host of projects from the mundane to the critical – ensuring our self-contained power plant is upgraded on deadline to seeing that a top Chinese nuclear scientist who's been on our payroll for years, on a tip from a double agent, is quietly exfiltrated a step before arrest, trial and execution by firing squad by the People's Procuracy. I sit on umpteen task forces and inter-agency groups on issues ranging from budgeting for more spy satellites to reorganizing personnel recruitment practices to responding to threats to American lives in disintegrating West African nations. The Counterterrorism Center commands high attention both for the hair-trigger threat alerts against American interests posed by a seemingly endless array of terrorist groups and for some of the hare-brained proposals for responding to those threats dreamed up by the brilliant misfits of the CTC.

I head a small team of some of the Agency's most promising officers in the Executive Directorate in triaging the veritable Niagara of information that flows to the DCI. And I often travel with Norfolk on his missions abroad, in style in CIA aircraft, with bodyguards, to sumptuous dinners with other countries' elites to discuss the grand events making history and how to respond to them. I control what is told to the media via the Agency's spokesman. And on it goes, down to the five specialized telephones installed in my house, including a secure dedicated line directly to the DCI, one to the DNI, one to the National Security Agency and yet another to the National Security Council at the White House.

The five Deputy Directors and numerous Division Chiefs, all senior to me in grade, show deference, bow and scrape, behavior I thoroughly enjoy. The tables are turned on Croswell now and he avoids me as much as he can. But I turn on the heat and go out of my way to make life as miserable for him as I possibly can. This is easy. Our people's recruiting successes against meaningful Russian targets continue to be pitiful and the KGB's successor spy agencies prove themselves surprisingly effective in foiling our attempts to penetrate them. Croswell, of course, also doesn't help himself by being the Agency's most disliked officer, a smug, coldhearted ego-tripper whose patriotism extends no further than Croswell Land. I eagerly await his tripping over the many hurdles and traps I throw in his way to provide an excuse to shift him over to some bureaucratic Siberia.

As one of my first acts upon coming into the job, I placed a document under Norfolk's nose and, with the stroke of a pen, got CI-60 transferred immediately out of Croswell's bailiwick. It was my first shot across his bow. I take a proprietary interest in the operation and call Ray Frasini regularly for updates.

And, naturally, I am drawn to events in Central Asia. I stay on top of the latest intel. I see it all: signals intercepts, human reporting, satellite imagery, assessments and analyses. Norfolk's efforts in his previous job pay off. We weave a "tapestry of shared interests" with all the states from the Caucasus to the southern Siberian steppes – except Russia, of course. This makes Moscow jittery and Tehran resentful as both countries view American encroachment into their backyard as part of some nefarious plot by Washington aimed at encircling and containing them.

Afghanistan, meanwhile, remains a cauldron of confusion. What is interesting are noises the Taliban is making toward rapprochement with Washington. But the violence continues, the central government's writ extends to Kabul city limits only and opium is king.

"Braveheart. You are Braveheart," Cammy says with conviction.

I laugh. She jabs me in the side with her elbow. I wrestle her on the Queen Anne bed in the master bedroom of the Loomis Georgetown house. She puts up a fierce resistance with surprising strength. The disciplined workouts with her private trainer have paid off. Beneath her smooth pale skin taut muscles bulge with cable-like hardness. I pin her shoulders down. She sways her head back and forth futilely. She finally relaxes but glares at me with flames in blue irises. I love a spirited woman. This gorgeous tigress pressed against my body generates an energy I cannot describe. I lower myself and devour her soft neck and shoulder. I press myself against her.

"Whoa, whoa. Stop," Cammy says breathlessly. She crosses her hands in the sports signal for half-time. "Break time."

I pull back. "What's wrong?"

"Absolutely nothing. This is the greatest sex I've had in a long, long time. I need to enjoy the glow a bit before we begin the fifteenth round. Do you mind?"

I dismount and lean on my elbow. With an index finger I gently draw circles around her lips and cheeks. She closes her eyes to savor the sensation of this touch.

In a barely audible voice, Cammy says, "You're not Cinderfella, you fool. You're Braveheart."

I kiss her lips.

"Mmm. Jerry Lewis never kissed like that."

"Funny. Ha. Ha."

"No, you're definitely Braveheart. Strong, courageous, a leader. But—" Her eyes are still closed.

"But what?" I don't let her answer. I press myself against her willing body, we lose ourselves in a lingering passionate embrace and kiss hungrily.

"Oh, Harry. I love you."

The embers of our passion modulate to a gentle glow. Cammy opens her eyes and takes me in with great seriousness.

"But remember how Braveheart met his end," she says.

I grimace. My erection collapses. "They tore his guts out."

Cammy nods. She caresses my ear and cheek. "Can I offer some advice?"

I shrug my shoulders and gesture palm up for her to continue.

"These people here, in 'Our Nation's Capital,'" she says mockingly, "are the Redcoats. They'll trample you and tear your guts out. Come with me, join me in London."

I furrow my brow. "As what, the American ambassadress's kept man?"

"No. As station chief. You could head up all intelligence functions there. Plum assignment. It would be perfect for both of us.

I study her face. So many conflicting thoughts race through my head. How we got here. Where I thought I should be. What lies ahead.

"That easy, huh?"

Cammy says nothing. She looks at me searchingly, a demi-smile on her lips. She raises her brow and gives a barely detectable nod, as if afraid of the answer.

I shake my head. "I can't." I lower my head. Our lips touch, the kiss as delicate as the moment.

CHAPTER TWENTY-FIVE

Since Cammy went off to London, my sex life has been on hold. Roni and I have drifted apart. No break-up, just a lack of communication. And a middle-aged bachelor is a pathetic being. Totally out of synch with nature, not to mention his contemporaries.

I divorced when I was 39. In the ensuing eight years, I've been consumed with my work and supporting Laurie. I've seen a handful of women, but no one who held my interest for long. I've been blessedly free of mid-life crisis manifestations and feel no compulsion to 'prove my manhood' by being a serial lover. But there is an ache for passion, for companionship, for validation that I won't enter old age alone or face mortality with a naked heart. At nights, sleepless in my bed, I ponder the parallel universe of womanhood, its mysteries and boundless capacity for love and I desperately want back in. These are the secrets of companionless men, secrets that none will admit, for the blunt armor of manhood won't permit it.

The heartfelt advice from a dying man needs to be taken seriously and Vince's parting words stay with me like the waves of a receding tide. I drive out to Great Falls where the Potomac narrows to a boulder-strewn, forging torrent. Just in time to watch the sun set in a brilliant orange-blue sky. I wish I had done this more, retreating to a quiet spot of nature to reflect. A cool breeze picks up, barrels through the gorge, lifts dead leaves from the ground, hits me smack in the face, tousles my hair. It takes me by surprise; at the same time, it's refreshing. The dead air of sterile offices leaves my senses, the cobwebs of urban entanglement blow away. I close my eyes, take a deep breath and savor the moment. At this moment, I feel liberated, though I am not.

The chains that bind my soul are twofold. One is a career in which my heart is no longer invested. The other is my heart, in which no womanly love is truly invested. Vince's gaunt face confronts me and I see death. I see my own death, as we all must from time to time anticipate the end of our lives. This space of life is for rent only, to be taken by a succeeding generation in due time. The only question is how long the space is ours. In Vince's case, it's abbreviated. And Harry Brennan's? Your own? The only sure thing is that it will be short in the grand scheme of things; the only question is how short. Make it count. Fill it with goodness and love.

I open my eyes. In the fading light a devil wind kicks up. A whirling dervish of dust and leaves, it blows my way. My instinct is to escape its path. But I freeze. Two figures take shape. Female figures. One fair, one dark, both beautiful. The long blond hair of the first swirls with the circular motion of the devil wind in a beguiling way that alternately covers and reveals the pallid face of the woman in the sheer white lace gown. Cammy beckons. The devil-may-care eyes and mischievous smile tell me to hurry. Hurry. Hurry. Before it's too late. Before you're too old. Before you're dead. Take a chance. Life is full of risks. Grab on for the ride. Come what may. She throws her head back in her trademark laugh. Ha! Come lover boy! What have you got to lose but your manhood!

But the other figure catches up, arms and open palms outward. Straight black hair falls to her strong bronzed shoulders and full breasts. A simple leather frock covers this woman's rich compact body. Gold bands on her upper arms, a gold and turquoise demi-crown on her head. A Mayan princess. Roni. She emits a direct, no-nonsense gaze that says, "Believe not in illusions. Believe in me." Love. Family. Eternal truths. Simplicity. These will get you through life. With me. With me.

I shut my eyes once more as the miniature tornado sweeps into me, taking my breath away. The force yanks my clothing. Twigs, dust and debris hit and sting my face. I squint tighter and hold my breath. Then, as suddenly as it came, the devil wind is gone, leaving me with my thoughts.

I drive and drive, something inside prevents me from executing the turns that will take me home. An internal divining rod takes over and I allow its force to direct me. Suburban la-la land spreads out in all directions. Cancerous conformity metastasizing out of control. Chain stores and fast food drive-ins, malls, stupefyingly bland condo towers. On it goes, the aimless consumer soul of post-modern America.

Somewhere between Arlington and Falls Church I make a turn into a small strip mall. Ah, yes. Blake's. Where I met Roni. I hanker after a jalapeño burger and a beer. I park and enter the place, unchanged right down to the dingy carpet, fluorescent-lit snack machine at the entrance and liquor and grease-laden air. The forlorn bartender remains at his post like some ancient Chinese funereal statue. He nods a curt hello. I take my old seat next to the blue-and-red neon-festooned window. I wait.

A honey-skinned young woman comes to take my order. "Con I halp jew?" she asks, order pad at the ready.

"Uh, yes. I'd like a jalapeño burger, please."

She expresses surprise, this stand-in for Roni. "Hime sorry, sir, but this is not on the menu. Khhow about our California platter? Eet's kind of Tex-Mex."

"Any jalapeños on it?" I ask.

The young woman smiles. "No. But I con harrange it. No problem."

"And a beer."

She turns for the kitchen, casting a mischievous and appreciative eye at me.

Two software salesmen, 30s, love handles bulging through their J.C Penney dress shirts, faces from any crowd, perch on bar stools over draft Bud Lite, carrying on loudly about "The Game" as the forlorn bartender pretends to be interested. Outside there is the roar of tractor trailers gunning their powerful engines as the intersection light changes to green. Everything is the same, except for Roni not being here.

The young woman brings my food and pauses expectantly with her hands clasped. I give her an amused look. "Let me guess. You want to see if my sissy tongue can actually handle this."

She laughs. "Oh, no! I only want to see if it is to your liking. That is all."

"Okay. Here goes." I chomp down. I grin with a full mouth and cast a thumbs up. After several more mastications, I feel it coming on, a Central American volcanic assault on my defenseless Celtic tongue, blood rushing to my head, beads of sweat forming on my brow. I valiantly succumb, lurch for the cold beer and down it as if I were a just rescued shipwreck castaway.

The woman puts her hand to her mouth, unable to disguise her amusement. We laugh together as I quell the fire.

"It's really very good," I tell her. "It's just that...that I was caught by surprise." More laughter.

"Say. Maybe you can help me," I say after the mirth subsides. "There was a young lady who worked here before, name of Roni."

"Ah, *sí!*"

"She still work here?"

"No. She quit several months ago."

I frown.

"You know her?"

"Yes. I'm her seester." She extends a hand. "My name is Dolores."

At first awkward, our coming back together soon finds the comfort groove of before. Roni has landed a job as assistant auditor at a well known accounting firm. The company is clearly grooming her for advancement and she is happy. We both ascertain the other is unattached. She doesn't ask about Cammy, though I know this will come later. Good thing too, because I haven't yet sorted it out in my own mind. Cammy has "dropped a line" from time to time in the form of a short letter, email and phone call, but passion doesn't carry long distance.

Roni and I pick up where we left off, rekindling the coals in a measured yet accelerating pace. We lose ourselves in frenzied lovemaking, whole weekends behind closed curtains, not answering any of my phones, official or otherwise; lost in heat, as if to make up for lost time.

The afterglow of lovemaking is when our souls knit together, in our hushed talks, gentle stroking and tender embraces. We learn about each other's past, our dreams, passions, frustrations, wants and needs. On the third such love marathon, we lie on my sofa, with a sheet around our naked bodies, listening to Andrea Bocelli and sipping herbal tea. Roni lies with her back against me. I envelope her in my arms.

"Harry, what do you fear the most?" she asks.

"Hah! Why do you want to know?"

"Just answer. Please."

I think this one over. "I guess...dying alone."

She looks at me with a start. "You want somebody to die with you?"

"No, *querida!* I don't want to finish my life a lonely old man, or lonely middle-aged one either for that matter. And I don't want a grave stone that says, *Harry Brennan – Loyal Bureaucrat.*"

Roni mulls this over. "I don't suppose they would allow you to have, *Harry Brennan – Great Spy?* Must your identity be kept secret even into death?" She giggles at this provocation.

"I'll check with Human Resources and let you know."

"Do you still enjoy your career?" she asks.

I think this one over. Roni looks up at me for an answer. She strokes the back of my neck with one hand. "Do you?"

"It gets back to a sense of being alone. These days, I feel very much that I stand by myself at that place. Especially with Vince not working. The Agency always instilled a sense of purpose, of direction in me."

"And now?"

"And now…I feel like I'm being manipulated, used."

"Then quit, Harry. Quit. Make a fresh start."

"Naw. I can't. I've got unfinished business. And a score or two to settle."

I squeeze her tight. "And you. Now your turn. Your greatest fear?"

"That you'll leave me again," she says solemnly. "And that woman. The rich one, will take you from me again."

I shake my head. Before I can reply, she raises a hand.

"Shhh," she goes.

"What?" I ask.

"I have something important to tell you."

"Like?"

"Like I am joining the Army. I, too, want to serve. Like you."

A concussion grenade just went off in my head. I try to grasp what she's telling me. I struggle for words, but they don't come.

"I report for duty tomorrow. I love you, Harry."

CHAPTER TWENTY-SIX

The soulless archipelago of star chambers that constitutes the Central Intelligence Agency comes to life and unites when power sweeps in. And like some preternatural force, the power of the presidency makes people sit up and pay attention. Division chiefs call me to confirm if it's true that President Dodge will visit the Agency and, if so, what for. They, of course, want to contribute anyway they can – say, prepare briefing papers, make presentations and such. The great suck-up at work. How can these morons hitch their wagon to the biggest star in the universe, make themselves look and feel important? The worst are the deputy directors who, unable get hold of the DCI directly, try to twist my arm to weasel their way into the Big Meeting. The pathetic thing about all this petty maneuvering is that the actual reason for the President's visit is of secondary importance to these people.

I'm in on the preparations from the start, of course, being at the vector of Agency happenings – usually anyway. The NSC Executive Director had phoned me earlier in the week to say that Dodge was to bestow the Presidential Medal of Freedom on Norfolk for a lifetime of achievement in the service of his country.

Norfolk, of course, is on cloud nine and, insufferably, at his worst. An ego the size of time has transmogrified itself into an otherworldly force, one of those celestial black holes, heavier than gravity, that devour everything that should come within its orbit.

The first to fall in is Shareen. Norfolk brought her over to the Agency in his move from the White House. As DCI, Norfolk has been saddled with a true executive secretary, one of those burnished super-efficient matrons who hasn't slept with a man since her girlhood, if ever, and whose sense of duty approximates that of Carrie Nation. But Norfolk managed to keep Shareen on the public roles as a "scheduler," such are the special skills this dedicated young woman possesses. Apparently, CIA security had some serious problems in granting her a top secret clearance, however, with all of the esoteric compartments that come with it as a DCI staffer. Something about work at topless bars in her long-ago wayward youth. But Shareen has been bored at the CIA. The lockdown environs and stiff work culture have left her cold. I've also sensed that her expectations of her relationship with Norfolk had withered. Even sex objects have dreams and aspirations. I'm not sure with Shareen whether hers are to nest and raise babies or to return to her former life of titillating men onstage. I make a mental note to ask. She'll tell me anything under God's sun, if I should ask, because she likes me.

Norfolk is in London for a couple of days to help fine-tune the Anglo-Saxon intelligence conspiracy vis-a-vis the rest of the world. At the beginning of the cold war, the white English-speaking nations decided to pool their intelligence resources in a secret arrangement called Echelon. This ethnocentric cabal is the world's most exclusive club. When its existence became known in the 1990s, it annoyed the other NATO allies greatly, but sent the vain Anglophobic French into a self-righteous fury. Unperturbed, the Anglo-Saxons continue to carefully tend their garden of shared secrets, confident that it is God's work to save the world by proxy.

On a dreary Monday morning, I find Shareen forlornly cleaning out her desk, piling a small hoard of cosmetics, mirrors, pantyhose, jewelry and tabloid magazines from her desk in a side cubicle where she sort of worked over the past six months.

I ask her what she's doing.

"What's it look like I'm doing? I'm leaving this…place," she spits out, machine-gunning the executive suite with contemptuous eyes.

"Can I ask why?" I ask.

Shareen starts to say something, but her words are drowned out in a stream of tears and blubbering. I take her hand. She sits down, wiping the tears with a Victoria's Secret lace hanky. "I'm leaving, outta here, after today. I'm getting as far from this town as I can. Back to Chickasha, Oklahoma. With my mom. With normal people. Away from these… these sharks." She attempts to neaten wayward toe blond strands with shaky fingers.

I shake my head. "Just like that," I say. "He ditched you."

Shareen raises her head and locks her big blues on me with a hardened gaze. "No. Actually, I'm doing the ditching," she snaps.

"I see," I say. My mind attempts to make a quick count of Norfolk's ex-girlfriends – the ones I know about – since I've worked for him. Now, let's see, the next bimbo will be number…

"No you don't see!" she says with a harshness having the impact of a flying brick. "I'm pregnant. I'm going to have his baby! But he doesn't want it. Says it'll wreck his career. Know what he wants me to do? He wants me to get an abortion!" This last sentence sets off a renewed torrent of tears.

There is nothing I can say at this delicate point. I study this broken woman. Used, abused, discarded. No doubt, the latest episode in a life of hard knocks and crushed dreams.

She sniffs back the tears, juts her chin out with a determined dignity. "But I'm not. I want this baby. I've always dreamed of having a baby. Nobody can stop me. Nobody. Finally, I'm going to have a normal life. Yes. Normal." She ponders her last statement with the unpersuasive conviction of the hesitant convert.

"Norfolk knows this?" I ask.

"I told him."

"And?"

"And first he threatened me. Says he'd see to it I'd never get a job, make sure the IRS picked over my puny taxes with a fine-tooth comb. But I don't care. Told him so."

"Are you going public then?" I ask.

Shareen bends her head and stares at her hands which are locked in a nervous grip. "No," she says weakly. She shakes her head in confirmation.

"You've been through enough. I can understand why you just want to get out of here and get on with your life," I say.

She doesn't stop shaking her head, then looks up with a steely expression on her pretty face. "You don't know. You're a good man. You have no idea."

I furrow my brow.

"A girl like me. I get around. I've been passed around. Now it's the end of the line. Used and tossed like last night's leftovers."

"Before Norfolk?"

"Yes. And would you like to know where?" she says challengingly.

I suppress the prurient voyeur that lurks inside every healthy male like a flesh-eating beast lying in wait in the brush. I tell myself to stay on track. Strictly business.

"How about the White House?" she says. "The very top."

"Dodge."

"Mm-hm. Shock you?"

"Not in Washington. It's happened before. And will again."

"But I know things," she adds. "Like how Dodge is in Blair Evans's hip pocket. Johnny is an empty suit in the end. He likes the glory and prestige, but the power is elsewhere. They talk about it all the time. Johnny relies on that old man like a kiddie does to his daddy. Daddy gives junior all the allowance he needs and daddy takes care of the rest."

"What else?" I ask.

"Croswell. He's one of Evans's evil little wizards. An insider, like a spider who inhabits a corner, then weaves his web wider and wider. Norfolk's afraid of him. That man Croswell made a pact with the devil a long time ago. I'm convinced. I know these things. My grandmama taught me."

"Where does daddy get the allowance for Dodge"

"I don't really know, but all these big shot businessmen have to have something to do with it, if you ask me."

"If you go public, you can bring them all down. Payback time," I say.

Again she shakes her head.

"Why not?"

"Two reasons. One, I have no desire to be another Judith Exner or Monica Lewinsky. He says he'll make sure that's how I'm portrayed if I don't keep my mouth shut. Two, he's paying me off."

"How?"

"Twenty thousand a year."

"Dollars?"

"Yeah." She shrugs and pulls a face of resignation. "I gotta live somehow. No skills. No savings. A child to support. I asked him for child support too, but he insists I get an abortion. I'm not though. Twenty thousand is okay for Oklahoma. It'll supplement whatever I can earn from a regular job."

She places a hand gently on my cheek, then leans over and kisses the other. "Goodbye, Harry Brennan. Stay a good man."

John W. Dodge comes out of central casting for the post-modern president – youthful, urbane, witty, intellectual. The traits that in Kennedy's era were not quite ready for prime time. Perhaps a little dangerous in this anti-intellectual era. Nevertheless, the magnetism of the man is palpable. As the word spread through the corridors of Langley that the President was coming, one could detect a not-so-subtle flurry among the females as they primmed and chatted with each other visibly more animatedly than usual.

Dodge is coming to lionize and heap laurels on Norfolk. To hear Norfolk talk, the Good Lord was descending upon us to make him His first apostle. If anything, Norfolk has become even more insufferable, like a spoiled child used to getting his way all the time who insists on yet more. He's got me in his office. I'm aware he's laying on all kinds of taskings, but I'm not paying attention. Instead Shareen preoccupies my thoughts. I think how this man devours people and spits out their bones like some mythical monster in constant need of feeding its limitless appetite. Admittedly, Shareen has fashioned her life into her being every lecher's tasty morsel. But the starkness of her humanity as she sat and cried and asserted her right to motherhood has planted itself in my brain. I see Norfolk as a killer, and a selfish, self-centered pig of a man. And I see myself as an abettor of his appetites, the Renfield to his Dracula.

"Are you listening to me, Brennan?" he snaps. "Because if you aren't up to this, I'll get somebody else to take it on. It's the President, goddamn it! Not some pea-brained politico from some fleabag country. It's not every day the President comes to visit. I want all senior staff turned out in that auditorium. You hear me?"

I nod.

"And get those protocol biddies to do their job right for a change. Remind them this is the Central Intelligence Agency, not the Cunard Lines shuffleboard club. Try to get security not to turn this place into the Alamo. After Fort Knox, we're the most fortified installation in the whole frigging country. Christ. And if the press can't be here, then line up some in-house photographers. And no, no slouches from our 'sister' intel agencies may attend. This is our show…"

Dodge glides in like a Renaissance prince into one of his palazzos. Handsome, self- confident, on top of things. I think back to Cammy's Issues Night and to her big pre-election bash at Colchester Manor. Dodge seemed so much his own man. Not some empty suit, some tool of an aging Fu Man Chu of the Washington power scene like Evans.

Norfolk's fear of his already security-obsessed agency being taken over by demonic minions of *Recht und Ordnung* turns out to be unfounded as a small phalanx of Secret Service agents discreetly fans out on the margins of the agency's main auditorium. A handful of White House aides joins the President, led by the Director of National Intelligence and the National Security Advisor. Norfolk's fear of there being no press, however, is well-founded. The President visiting the CIA for in-house purposes is what the White House communications people term a "non-media event," meaning no news coverage. This is a no-brainer for all except a self-absorbed egomaniac such as Norfolk. Two agency photographers record the proceedings for posterity and the CIA's classified in-house employees journal.

Norfolk has done all the right things to ingratiate himself with the President's inner circle, doling out juicy secrets like gum drops to small children. Private briefings on Iran and North Korea and al-Qaeda custom-tailored to the recipient's

interests and ego. This impresario of human vanities has made
the world's foremost intelligence agency his personal stage on
which to parade his ambitions to a gullible audience, not least,
the equally gargantuan egos of Capitol Hill. Along with the
adulation comes power and this at the expense of the State
Department, whose clout in this administration approaches
that of the Bureau of Mines. And what goes around comes
around. No less than the President of the United States is
coming to crown Prince Robert of Norfolk.

Dodge jauntily steps to the podium with a movie star's
smile on his finely sculpted face. He opens by praising the
bravery and dedication of the agency's people, "those who
serve their country courageously, but in the shadows; who
seek the truth in the defense of freedom; whose victories go
unsung, but not unappreciated."

He hits a chord among a crowd that feels too often
shunned and dumped upon, made the scapegoats of all the
haywire schemes of the "National Command Authority"
– yet another bureaucratic catchall term used to describe
an amorphous leadership encompassing everybody from
the president on down to the department secretaries with
responsibility over national security. It always occurred to me
that these all-encompassing, impersonal labels were concocted
to keep the buck passing, with no one taking blame whenever
any of their decisions resulted in blunder. Like a "Pass Go.
Do not go to Jail" card for the cover-your-ass set in face of
congressional investigation. The other self-insulating CYA
contrivance favored by this ilk of teflon-coated "decision-
makers" is the passive voice, as in, "mistakes were made."

But today is a love-fest between President Dodge and
his shadow-hugging spook corps. Dodge thanks them for
"helping to hold the line with Iran," for "making it only
a matter of time before al-Qaeda is finished," for "seeing
through the opaque screen that cloaks North Korea," and

for "defending American interests and American lives with little or no public recognition."

The applause is frequent and hearty. Norfolk basks in the glow from this mega-star. Sitting front and center before Dodge, he resembles a bloated, self-satisfied Mandarin, gleeful and mocking at the same time. This is his moment. King for a Day. All light comes laser-like to him. The hundreds of CIA rank-and-file who fill the auditorium are mere extras in this production. The President may heap praise upon them with orotund empty paeans to their valor, sacrifice and the like, but the truth is nobody really cares. The American public despise all civil servants as lazy bloodsuckers; and spies are just downright un-American. And the big power set are so wrapped up in their ego games, they come and go and really couldn't be bothered with the troops. Mere valets, footmen, concierges and lapdogs to the rich and powerful on a lark. In the case of poor Shareen, chief camp follower to the rich and powerful.

And so he sits, smug, puffed up with self-pride, having been fed countless bodies before Shareen like a serial vampire. The NSC aides he canned, the bimbo secretaries he boffed, the fools like me who did his bidding and are discarded, or, in my case, soon will be.

After ending with a "hearty thanks" for a job well done and award presentation, Dodge and Norfolk exchange a bear hug that would do an old Soviet premier proud. The crowd breaks into applause. I turn to see. One set of hands remains still, arms folded defiantly across a bony chest in a now baggy suit. Pale, mostly bald now, a spectral Vince glowers. A fire burns within his spent body. We don't make eye contact. I turn back to see Dodge taking leave. We all rise, applauding. Dodge is out the door, with Norfolk on his heels. I look backward again for Vince. I want to catch him before the big exodus from the auditorium begins. But he's gone.

CHAPTER TWENTY-SEVEN

PAKTIKA PROVINCE, AFGHANISTAN

Bashir takes the binoculars from his aide and carefully focuses the lens on the encampment below. He sees a group of Westerners, maybe eight or nine, sitting on the ground opposite black-turbaned Taliban fighters. These number about a dozen. Bodyguards standing close to two of the Afghans indicate to Bashir that the guarded men are senior Taliban cadre. A campfire is going. A goat is turned on a spit. The Afghans are hosting the foreigners to a wilderness feast.

The sun is setting over the denuded hills of Afghanistan's Paktika province, just across the border from Pakistan's South Waziristan. Soon, Bashir will make his move.

His sources within the Taliban had tipped him off that this meeting would be taking place. It is an important meeting. A follow-on to the earlier meeting between the fat American, Norfolk, and Omar, the Taliban chieftain. Bashir observed that confab too, but left it alone when he saw his old friend, Harry, there.

Bashir learned so much from his mentor, Ahmad Shah Masood, Lion of the Panjshir, nemesis of the Soviet Red Army occupiers, a legend to his people. His assassination by al-Qaeda operatives two days before 9/11 struck a devastating blow to the anti-Taliban forces. But Masood the legend lives on in the hearts of Afghans. Just before launching combat, Bashir kisses the amulet he wears around his neck, a gift

from *Amer Sahib e Shaheed* – "Our Martyred Commander," as
Masood is referred to posthumously.

"Select the tactic of seeming to come from the east
and attack from the west; avoid the solid, attack the hollow;
deliver a lightning blow," Masood used to tell him, quoting
from Mao Tse-tung, whose writings on guerrilla warfare he
had studied closely.

As the sun's last rays succumb to Paktika's rolling terrain,
Bashir kisses his amulet. He issues a command by walkie-
talkie to his men on the eastern slope opposite. A fireworks
rocket screams skyward from that slope and bursts into a
panoramic pyrotechnic display of red, green and white
against a black sky – the colors of the Afghan flag. Whistles
sound. Sub-explosions boom. White whirligigs twist and
turn. Fire streams soar. The night sky is brilliant.

As the Taliban and their guests are temporarily
mesmerized by the sudden and inexplicable fireworks display
to their east, Bashir makes his move, with a surgical strike by
a squad of his best men concealed in the landscape a few
meters west of the camp.

They rush the spot from three directions, machine-
gunning the Taliban hosts, most armed with slabs of meat
and flat bread in their fists. Sentries have already been
garroted. The foreigners hit the dirt. In minutes, it's over.
Bashir now has eight prisoners. All Americans.

The chirping phone interrupts my brief attempt at
escapism by watching the Broncos and Packers.

"Hi. This Jeff Wilder."

"The *Post* guy," I say.

"One and only."

I turn off the TV.

"I haven't got a lot of time, Harry. I'm going off to jail."

"What?!"

"Yeah. For contempt of court for refusing to divulge my sources for the series I've been writing on government corruption."

"Geez! What is this country coming to?" I drop the receiver on the hardwood floor. Something flies out of the mouthpiece. I pick it up. It's a listening device.

"Harry. You there?"

"Yeah, yeah. sure."

"I'm gonna do one more story before they send me to the slammer. It's on the oil-White House connection. Caspian Sea deals. What can you tell me?"

I pause. Take a deep breath.

"Let me call you back from somewhere else," I say.

CHAPTER TWENTY-EIGHT

I find myself in the eerily familiar and uncomfortable position of standing across the oversized desk of William Hanscom Croswell. It's Monday morning, one of those dreary early autumn days that holds desperately to summer in face of the dreary winter soon to come. Croswell has that cat-who-swallowed-the-canary look on his cold, calculating face. The DCI has instituted a restructuring of the agency. It's one of those pre-emptive strikes against the bureaucracy where one shows up to work only to find a pink slip on one's desk. In this case, Norfolk has foisted a "RIF," a reduction-in-force in tandem with a reorganization. It's the bureaucratic equivalent of the Great Cultural Revolution, whereby thousands of people are driven into the paddy fields of re-revised flow charts, indoctrinated in the dogma of redundancy and then summarily liquidated by social class. Knowing the man as I do, I can see Norfolk, a kindred spirit of Chairman Mao, sitting back and delighting in the deviltry he has hatched on the masses. There is no true objective other than to wreak havoc, the purpose being to keep the masses off balance and in line.

Croswell peremptorily tosses the morning's newspaper across his desk for me to see. On the front page is a photo of eight American men inside a large donkey-pulled cage on wheels. They are clutching the chicken wire, looking nothing if not like primates on their way to the zoo. The headline reads, "American Oil Men Seized in Afghanistan." The story goes on to state that a renegade commander of the Afghan government, Bashir Khalili, took the First Eagle Petroleum representatives prisoner during a lightning strike on a Taliban encampment and delivered them unharmed to the Canadian Provincial Reconstruction Team headquarters in the southern Afghan city of Kandahar. In an interview with the Reuters reporter, a swaggering Bashir presented him with a gallon of motor oil, stating, "If America needs petrol so badly, I give her this with a promise of much more. But only when the Americans deal with true Afghans, not Taliban traitors!"

"You have anything to do with this?" a red-faced Croswell demands.

I look up from the paper, speechless. I begin to laugh involuntarily.

"Think it's funny, do you?" demands an unamused Croswell, now DDCI, Deputy Director of Central Intelligence – the number two slot, right under Norfolk. For a career spook, it's nirvana. It ensures that the incumbent will be remembered, for better or worse, for maybe seven years after he leaves the office – immortality by Washington standards.

"It looks like a goddamn medieval circus, how these men were treated. America's image is sullied!"

"American oil reps hobnobbing with Taliban leaders. Hmm. The American public will surely understand this," I retort.

"This, on top of Wilder's story on Norfolk's secret meeting with the Taliban previously. You're the one, Brennan. You leaked it."

I reach in my pocket, pull out the listening device I retrieved from my phone and toss it on the desk.

Croswell looks at it. He says nothing. He knows exactly what it is.

He leans back in his black leather swivel chair, fingertips held steeple-like in front of his thin lips, his bony Ichabod Crane frame all sharp angles. Malice radiates through the frameless glasses.

"As you know, Brennan, we are instituting Total Quality Management measures at this agency, putting into place leadership enhancement processes and multidirectional validation systems that will leave us a leaner, meaner organization going forward."

"Which is MBA mumbo-jumbo to say that I'm being reassigned," I interject.

"You might say that," says Croswell with the smugness of a cardsharp with all the aces up his sleeve. "You are being reassigned all right. But not because of the reorganization." He picks up a folder from his desk and opens it. Boyhood scenes of detested teachers smirking and lecturing me over bad report cards flash through my brain.

Croswell leans over, hunched on his elbows, just like Mr. Simmons, my fifth grade teacher and a terminal misanthrope, not to mention a world-class shit. "You're under security investigation, Brennan."

I bolt upright. "I'm what?!"

He drops the file on the end of the desk. "See for yourself."

I take the folder and scan through it. On top is a copy of *National Security Presidential Directive 37 – Central Asia*. It's marked "Exhibit A." Below it is a packet of grainy black and white photos. They are of me meeting with Nemsky at the Safeway in Georgetown and at the Afghan restaurant in Arlington. I look up. "What's this?" I ask.

"I don't have time for games, Brennan. I won't show you the surveillance reports nor, of course, the wire taps. I suggest you consult a lawyer. Your SAO, SI and other top secret clearances are hereby suspended pending further investigation. And, oh. By the way, you have been replaced as Executive Director, effective immediately. You will report to Human Resources, retirement division, pending the outcome of the investigation."

I shake my head. "'Human Resources'?! HR is for losers!"

"Then you should feel at home, Brennan." Croswell looks impatiently at his watch.

"What's going on here?"

"'What's going on here' is that you, one very aggrieved and angry officer under tremendous strain since you bungled your operation in Afghanistan, became a turncoat against your own agency, not to mention your country."

"Bullshit. It's all about oil," I say.

"I don't know what you're talk–"

"Yeah. Make peace with the Taliban by selling out Bashir and pulling the rug out on TALISMAN. Force Karzai into a shotgun wedding – a 'coalition government' – with the Taliban. Get our forces out. Then lay pipes across Afghanistan and get the oil gushing all the way into our SUV's. Lot a money in that too. Good for business. Great for your career."

"Like I said, I don't have time for this, Brennan." Croswell rises, puts some documents in his brief case and snaps it shut. He takes it in hand and starts for the door.

I place one hand against his chest. "Just one more question, Croswell. Why does it take the Deputy Director of Central Intelligence to tell me this information? Seems like some slug in a bad suit in Security should get the honors."

A smirk forms on Croswell's stone face. "You may turn out to be the biggest sell-out since Aldrich Ames and Robert Hanssen. Especially if we find any dead agents turning up. And, by the way, the U.S. Attorney in Alexandria is preparing the case against you. In the meantime, you are what the lawyers call, a "person of interest." I wouldn't be planning any, er, vacations. You won't get far should you try to escape the Beltway's orbit. And I want to make sure I'm right front and center when you're nailed."

"Wrong, Heinrich. Too much is riding on this scandal and the fabricated case against me must be airtight. Or billions of dollars and some serious power positions are in jeopardy. You were behind my being ambushed; tried to have me killed. I see right through the whole stinking mess and I'm going to bring you down. You and Evans and Norfolk and everybody else involved."

"See you in court, Brennan. Now get out of here." Croswell points to the door.

Almost as shocking as Croswell's rolling out his elaborate frame-up against me is my being allowed to walk out of his office and out of headquarters without being placed under arrest, or at least escorted out by security. Is it a gross oversight, or am I the bait set in some elaborate trap to ensnare say, Nemsky? But then again, I'm a "person of interest," the twenty-first century equivalent of the Scarlet Letter. In any case, I'm too numbed and shellshocked to think about it clearly. As I walk the colorless corridors of the old building, people appear to steer clear of me, cast sideward glances, hold that wary stare a moment too long. Or so my rattled brain perceives it.

I'm being steered by autopilot now, unthinking and without conscious purpose, except to get to my car and to drive out, to any place, away from this place.

For the first time in my life I don't know where I'm going. No office to go to. No mission laid before me. No purpose, except self-preservation. This thought sinks in. I'm not fleeing General Aideed, nor steeling myself against an onslaught of Saddam's army. I'm the target of the very government I work for. I need answers and I need a strategy. I also need loving. Roni. In the army. Jesus.

Right now, Vince is the one I need. My Clausewitz, Nostradamus and Coach Lombardi all rolled into one. I need Vince to walk me through this thicket of confusion and betrayal, to lend his sarcastic insight and insider's knowledge to make sense of things; and, most of all, I need him to help me out of it.

Vince is home now. Helen, a close friend of my ex-wife, is a warm and stoic woman. She kisses me on the cheek as I enter the two-story brick home in a quiet cul-de-sac in McLean. Vince is watching football. A smile crosses his face as I walk in. He's filled back out a bit, there's color in his face, some hair coming back in. But his weakness shows in the tremulous hands, tentative gait and shortness of breath. Vince's mind, however, remains sharp and he's glad to see me.

We trade some uneasy chit-chat, superficialities about politics, my daughter, the weather. Neither of us broaches the Mt. Everest issue which looms in our midst: Vince's mortality.

The Dallas Cowboys score a touchdown, the crowd of tens of thousands erupts in a miasma of raucous cheers through the TV speaker, punctuated by the inflated howls of two jock sportscasters.

I remember when Vince would jump out of his chair in such moments, drawing a clenched fist down and whooping, "Yes!!" Now, however, a weak smile forms across his pallid face. The spark, the energy are gone. He turns to me.

"They're in sudden death now. Can you fuckin' believe that? Best game since the L.A. Express and Michigan Panthers went to three sudden death overtimes in '84. Geez. Remember that one?"

I shake my head. "'84. Hmm. I was in Peshawar then. Keeping the AK's and B-40's flowing to the muj."

"Oh yeah. Talk about sudden death. Those poor Red Army slobs met with a lot of it. Heh, heh." Vince turns back to the game. "Tony Romo. Just lookit that guy. 'Mr. Completion' himself. Sent here by God. I swear."

My mind is light years from this game, but I bide my time. I fidget.

Finally, it's over. The Broncos score. Cowboys lose. End of game. I turn off the TV.

"Last time I saw you, you had tubes up your nose," I say. "Makin' progress."

"Progress my ass," he scoffs. "Cancer's spread all over now. I'm on more pain killers than a rock star. They sent me home to die. No 'sudden death' for me, I'm afraid. Though, I'd welcome it. This is no way to go."

I place my hand on his forearm. I have no words.

Vince coughs, then spits into a cup. "Yeah, well. As my old man used to say, 'Whaddya gonna do?' I've lived five lifetimes compared to most people. It's been good.

"You're in trouble," he says, switching gears.

I nod.

There's a long silence. The grandfather clock in the next room ticks with the indifferent, relentless predictability of mortality. A jet roars 10,000 feet overhead. Rambunctious boys returning from school liven up the neighborhood with raucous laughter and taunts. Chirping birds gorge gleefully at Vince's backyard feeders.

"Those birds out there." He nods at the yard. "They can't be bought, they can't be blackmailed and they can't be framed. And you know why?"

I shrug.

"'Cause they're free. We...we *public servants* are anything but. We're chained to the oars. To think otherwise is delusional. Anything goes wrong, we get thrown overboard. Things haven't changed a bit since the royal courts of Europe. Look at the intrigue and backstabbing in Elizabethan England or the House of Borgia. Washington's as putrid as any of those old courts. In the long run, we're all dead. So, what's the point? What's that line in *Julius Caesar*?

Glory is like a circle in the water,
Which never ceaseth to enlarge itself,
Till by broad spreading it disperses to naught.

I nod slowly in response to this pearl of wisdom and conclude that, in his last weeks of life, Vince is losing it.

"I know. I know. You think I'm crazy. Or, well on my way. Not yet, my friend. You'll know I've lost it when I'm talking to those birds out there. Look. What you're facing is an avalanche of Everestian proportions. They've not only got you by the balls, but they've nailed them to a plank with number twelve spikes. Jesus Christ. What'd you do anyway? Screw the President's daughter?"

"Worse."

"I'm all ears."

"I'm standing in the way of money and power. Big money and power."

'Shit. You might as well take away their oxygen and water. This is the Caspian deal. Am I correct?"

"Yup."

"And you're now a 'person of interest.'"

I start. "How do you know?"

"Oh, a little birdie told me. And he's not in my back yard." Vince hands me the *Washington Post*. On page three is my face, my work I.D. photo, to be precise. Next to it , the headline reads, "CIA Officer Under Investigation for Espionage – Named a 'Person of Interest.'"

I quickly read the article. "Unnamed senior officials" have confirmed that CIA operations officer Harry Brennan is under investigation for "allegedly" being a paid agent of Russian intelligence. While little is known of the damage to national security at this point, the officials believe that Brennan potentially passed thousands of pages of highly classified documents to Moscow. "The agency is assessing whether foreign spies working for the U.S. may have been compromised or killed."

I look up at Vince not believing what I've read.

"And that little birdie over there." He points out through a front window.

I peer past the curtains to see a dark colored Buick parked across the street. Inside are two men looking in our direction.

"And that birdie right under your nose." He points to the phone.

I silently mouth, *"Bugged?"*

Vince nods. He turns the TV back on and jacks the volume way up in order to neutralize the effectiveness of wire taps and leans forward to within inches of my face.

"I'm being outed," I say.

"Not only that. Remember Brian Kelley? The mole-hunters zeroed in on him when it was really Hanssen who was giving away the farm. Kelley was a good guy. I knew him. They suspended him for two years. After they caught Hanssen, Kelley was 'exonerated,' but his career was in ruins, his life turned upside down. Same thing happened with Richard Jewell, the Centennial Park security guard, and Steven Hatfill, the military scientist suspected of anthrax-through-the-mail attacks. All these guys were tarred and feathered by the media. Their reputations turned into shit. What did they all have in common? They were named "persons of interest" by the government. When you lack evidence, just call people "persons of interest." Great means of character assassination. Hell, Stalin wiped out whole classes of people with terms like that."

"Now it's my turn."

"You got it, compadre."

"So, what do I do?"

Vince washes down a handful of pills with a glass of water. He stares blankly out the window, uncharacteristically silent. "I dunno. I can't even help myself. I'm dying." He turns and studies my face. "Hit back. What else can you do? Hit 'em hard."

CHAPTER TWENTY-NINE

MARIB, YEMEN

The German bond trader from Frankfurt was the first one shot. In the back of the head as he knelt, hands tied behind his back before his executioner. The second one was beheaded while being videotaped. Just a kid from Lyons, on a Middle East lark with some friends. But his eighteen-year old killer botched the effort using a short-bladed *jambiya*. As the slashed Frenchman gagged and screamed pathetically, the group's commander delivered the coup de grace, a bullet in the head, then kicked his victim over. Blood gushed from the corpse's neck in torrents, wetting the dry, stony sand.

Allahu Akhbar!" they all shouted in unison. A scene to make Genghiz Khan proud. Exacting blood for blood's sake.

The eight remaining hostages huddled terrified against a wall in the cave, each wondering if he or she would be next. There were three Germans, two Italians, a Japanese woman and two Americans. They ranged in age from 20 to 81; they were students, tradesmen, an educator and retired; one was gay. But they all had one thing in common: fear that violent death would be imminent.

But the commander ordered his men to take the bodies away. He glowered at his captives, his bloodshot eyes the picture of rage. This man, not yet thirty, rained down death with the ease of a barbarian god. It was not new to him. He then stomped off, leaving his victims to ponder their fate at the mercy of two younger men, each armed with an AK-47 and a dagger, left to stand guard.

"Oh, Ryan, hold me. Please hold me," sobbed Laurie.

They held each other tightly, hearts beating loudly, each palpitation a countdown to who knew what.

Again I'm there. Laid out on a platform, arms and legs tied down. The big, ugly man standing above me, razor-sharp knife held tightly in both hands, preparing to lunge into my guts, to tear me to pieces. I want to scream, but cannot. The more I try, the more my throat seizes up. The knife, glinting in the sun's rays, comes down, cutting into my abdomen. I want to scream, but no sound comes. He raises the knife only to plunge it back into my body and the big, ugly man yanks the blade with all his might, tearing flesh and organs; blood gushes, but I cannot scream. The pain. Oh God. Help.

My recurrent *Braveheart* nightmare abruptly ends with the phone beeping. I bolt upright, soaked in sweat. I shake my head to cast off the terrible dream, a dream that invades my brain every night now. *Beep. Beep. Beep.* The alarm clock next to the phone reads 3:15 am. *Beep.*

I grab the phone with my left hand and mop my drenched brow with the pajama sleeve of the other. "Yeah. Hello."

"Mr. Harry Brennan?" The connection is scratchy, the voice barely audible.

"Yes, I'm Harry Brennan."

"Mr. Brennan, I'm Paul Buriak, consular officer at Embassy Sanaa. I'm sorry to inform you that we have a hostage situation here. Al-Qaeda, we think. They're holding two Americans, and your daughter, Laurie, is one of them. She was taken, along with seven other tourists earlier today at Marib…"

I strain to process this into my tormented brain. "Say what? Laurie's been what?"

"Kidnapped," says Buriak.

"Kidnapped?! When? By whom?"

"Earlier today, Mr. Brennan. We think al-Qaeda. We're still seeking details. The Yemeni police informed us. Laurie was seized along with seven others at the tourist site of Marib. It's an ancient city, a popular tourist destination – for the few intrepid tourists who come here these days."

"Who...what other Americans are involved?" I ask.

"Uh. A man by the name of Ryan Kirkpatrick."

"Holy shit. She did it," I mumble to myself.

"I beg your pardon?"

"Nothing. Ryan's her boyfriend," I answer.

"I see. Mr. Brennan, I have to tell you that the hostages' lives are threatened. We just received an unconfirmed report that two have been killed. Europeans, I believe. We are in contact with the police and..."

I tune Buriak out as my mind races to figure this all out in the dead of night. She actually did it. Laurie skipped off to the Middle East with that kid, Ryan. Without telling me and against my instruction not to. Jesus Christ. I rub my eyes with my free hand.

"...the Bureau for Consular Affairs will be your principal point of contact..."

The adrenaline has kicked in. My heart is racing. My head is clearing up. My mind is organizing actions, next steps, logistics at lightning speed. I now have a purpose, a mission. All the years as an operative, the training, the real-life hardening and instincts-honing come to bear. I know what I must do. And there is no time to waste.

"...do you have any questions Mr. Brennan?"

"Huh? Oh, yeah. Where exactly are they being held, the exact coordinates?"

"Um. Let me check with my colleagues," Buriak says. He's stumped at my first and only question. America's finest. Right on top of things.

Half a minute passes. I'm already changing out of my pajamas, headed toward the bathroom. I need to make plane reservations. A thousand drop-dead actions flood my mind and this bureaucrat obviously couldn't find an hors d'ouevre at an embassy reception if his life depended on it.

"Well, all we have at this point is it's near Marib, in the center-west of the country…"

"Thanks. Bye." I hang up.

I throw clothes and essentials into a duffle bag. Anticipating that my name is on various watch lists, I retrieve the passport of the fictitious Nelson R. O'Meara, confected for me by the nerd cover officer Kaiser months ago. I run downstairs, grab a quart of orange juice and guzzle it. In the dark, I peek through the curtains at the street. No obvious surveillance. Nonetheless, I silently descend to the basement, open a window and slither through, then sprint across my backyard, scale the short wooden fence and race down a residential alleyway. *Smack.* I fall down on the pavement. I find myself on top of another body, face-to-face with another stubbled male. I pull myself off. I lunge at his throat with both hands.

"No, my Commander! It's me! Here to help you. Me, Haji Rakhman!"

The commotion has alerted neighbors. Lights go on in nearby houses. Shades part.

"For God's sake! You almost gave me a heart attack." I pull him up by the arm and yank him into a high hedge. "Quiet. Be still, before the neighbors call 911."

"I heard about Laurie," Rakhman whispers. "I am here to serve. To help."

"You 'heard'? Already? Embassy Sanaa just called me five minutes ago. The media don't even have it yet."

"Our contacts inside al-Qaeda," Rakhman responds. "They work for us. Our agents. Part of my *haji* network of pilgrims to Mecca. The network your CIA scoffs at because they think they are smarter than us and think we are unreliable, like Curveball. Come, my Commander. I have made preparations."

A long ago Arab poet said, "When God created the sun in the heavenly crucible, some spilt out and became the Yemen." The sun is blinding and the 114 degree heat mocks the growling and clearly overwhelmed a/c on the white Toyota landcruiser as it negotiates the ribbon of rough road ascending an ever-rising mountain. I swear we are going to go flying off the edge any second into a thousand-foot death spiral onto the boulders below. A jet-lag-induced headache and nausea complete a picture of a perfect hell for me. Whatever His intentions, God did not drop a piece of heaven down when he inadvertently created Yemen.

The squirrelly driver unwisely looks back and, without explanation, offers a branch with leaves. His smile is distorted by a big bulge in his left cheek and stained, misshapen teeth.

"Hal tukhazin?" he asks.

"What?" I say. "Could you tell him to keep his eyes on the so-called road? My life insurance isn't paid up and becoming a one-way Flying Walenda was never in my life's plans."

"Do you chew, he asks you," answers Mubarak, our Yemeni cohort, one of Rakhman's *haj* alumns. "The leaves, they are *qat*."

"Hell no!" I say.

"Bukrah insha'allah," Mubarak politely responds to the driver. "Tomorrow God willing."

We hit a rut. The vehicle lurches down, then rockets upward and lands hard. I upchuck. Stuff goes flying all over the vehicle, including this driver's beat-up Kalashnikov which narrowly misses my head on its way to the rear cargo area. We come to an abrupt halt. After a human and vehicular systems check, we resume travel.

The driver returns to his increasingly erratic driving, alternatingly ripping off more *qat* leaves to stuff into the side of his mouth and swigging another can of Pepsi from the case sitting on the front seat. A pile of empty Pepsi cans clangs around the front floorboard. The caffeine of the cola acts as a multiplier effect on the mild narcotic in the *qat* leaf to induce a buzz Janis Joplin would return from the grave for. The driver jacks up the CD player. He's switched from Lebanese pop hits to George Michael's *Careless Whisper*, an inexplicable mega-hit from the Maghreb to the Levant. The driver's eyes are bloodshot and glazed. In a move he undoubtedly learned from *kamikaze* pilots, he steps on the gas, nose just millimeters from the windshield.

"Tell him to slow down damn it! Where the hell...I'll talk to him. What's his name?"

"Mohammad *al-Majnoon*," says Mubarak.

"Is that his last name, *al-Majnoon*?" I ask.

"Oh no!" answers Mubarak, guffawing. It is his nickname. He is called, "Mohammad The Crazy." He twirls a finger near his ear in the universal sign indicating "insane."

I slump back. "And I left my rosary beads back home." I resign to leave my fate, and physical well-being, in the hands of Allah. I look out. The Yemeni countryside is striking. Stark, somber mountains jut into the crystal blue sky, tall mud houses on the foothills overlook deep green valleys lush with vegetation. *Qat* farms, perhaps? Irrigation channels encircle terraced stonewalls built when Europeans were living hand-to-mouth in forests and caves. This was the land of Balquis, the legendary Queen of Sheba, who ruled three thousand years ago.

I shut my eyes. I think back to my ill-fated sojourn into Afghanistan to forge ahead with Operation Talisman against orders not to. How stupid I was. It was not worth risking my life over. To potentially leave my child fatherless over such a thing. That mission used up the last of my nine lives, I'm convinced. The chambers are now empty. Out of life's ammo.

This, very personal, mission, however, is worth everything. My daughter's life is at stake. To save hers, I must safeguard my own – at least until she is rendered into safekeeping. A careless move, being in the wrong place at the wrong time, or just bad luck could scotch everything, potentially breaking this branch of the family tree off at the trunkline. So, I start with Crazy Mo'. I tell Mubarak to order him to stop, which he does just as a bus comes careening around the bend, no doubt driven by Crazy's twin brother. The ramshackle vehicle is barreling right at us, kicking up rocks and clouds of dust. It is crammed with people. Baggage is piled on the roof. The road can't be more than ten feet across.

The bus driver slams on the brakes. The junk bucket shakes, shudders and skids left and right. The passengers are screaming. We run from our landcruiser in holy terror. A second later, *Crunch!*

I'm flat on my belly in the middle of the road. I see Mubarak ahead of me, on his butt, his face expressing excruciating pain as he holds an injured ankle in both hands. Crazy Mo' is running like an Olympic athlete down the road, albeit one inspired more by performance-enhancing substances than sheer physical strength.

My hands are badly scratched from the hard landing. My trousers are torn at the kneecaps. Blood trickles from somewhere on my face onto the sand. I crane my head back and see the bus's front fender planted firmly into the tail section of our Toyota. Baggage is strewn all over the place. The bus's passengers are streaming out wailing, flailing arms, yelling. The besieged bus driver is gesticulating wildly in our direction.

I carefully raise myself. Except for some scratches, I'm ok. No broken bones, sprained limbs, or concussion. Just an

injured ego and wounded pride. I brush the dust from my
clothes and nurse my facial cuts with a hanky. This appears
to act as a red cape to the mob from the bus. They're coming
for me.

Quickly, I'm surrounded by twenty irate Arabs screaming
at me.

"Whoa! Whoa! I don't speak Arabic," I say.

This only angers them more and the decibel level of their
collective tirade increases.

"I *do NOT* understand!" I shout back.

Finally, a pot-bellied, middle-aged man steps forward.
"They say, you almost kill them," he says in halting English.

"What do you mean, *me*? I wasn't even driving. Besides,
your bus was going too fast. Your driver is reckless." He
stands nearby, spitting green gunk onto the ground. "And
he's obviously high on *qat*. Look at him!"

As the pot-bellied one translates this, the mob gets even
more stirred up. I look around frantically. Mubarak is of no
use as he continues to wrestle with his pain. And Crazy Mo'
is nowhere to be seen, clearly AWOL and probably halfway
to Mecca by now.

Now I know how Jim Bowie and Davy Crockett felt like
at the Alamo.

"He say you must pay two-hundred thousand riyal," the
bus driver announces through the good offices of the pot-
bellied man.

"Pay what?! Tell him he ran into *us*." I do a quick
mental arithmetic. That amount in the local currency equates
to $1,000. Yemen is no different from most other poor
countries around the world. In such situations, fault takes a
back seat to wealth. All Westerners are considered to be rich.
Ergo, they pay up no matter who is at fault. And the amount
demanded typically meets or exceeds the average annual per
capita income.

A dust cloud rises up the road, followed by the roar of engines. All heads turn.

Two dark landcruisers come booming toward us from the ascending road before us. Each one screeches to a halt on our flanks. Men jump out and level AK-47s at all of us, a true show-stopper. An Omar Sharif doppelganger saunters forth. As with the others, he wears khaki, but sports a traditional red checkered *keffiyeh* on his head. He comes directly up to me, pistol drawn. I'm a dead man. He signals one of his men to frisk me.

"And who are you?" he asks in slightly accented British English.

"My name is Jason," I lie.

"You are American."

'American' in the Middle East these days too often equates to 'dead meat.'

"I'm out of Toronto. I'm Canadian," I lie again.

"No you are not. If you were, you would say, 'oot' of Toronto, not 'out'. And, whatever your real name is, you will come with me." He gestures to the lead jeep. "Get in."

I hesitate. His men raise their weapons. I climb in.

The jeeps roar off, leaving the irate bus passengers, the injured Mubarak and my urgent plans to rescue my daughter in billows of dust.

An hour-and-a-half later, we pull into a dusty compound on an elevation at the far end of a fertile *wadi*, or valley. Just beyond the compound, colorfully painted houses stand precariously on the side of arid, brown-rock cliffs. Women and children mix with armed men in a laid-back setting except for sentries in strategically situated watch towers along the compound perimeter. The Omar Sharif character clambers out of the front passenger seat, extends his arm in a welcoming gesture.

"Please," he says. "Come. Take some refreshment. Welcome."

I was fully expecting to be greeted by executioners. Instead, a flunky appears out of nowhere with a jug of cold lemonade and glasses. My captor takes a filled glass and offers it to me with a nod. I accept and wait for him to follow suit. We salute each other and quench deep thirsts.

He places his right forearm across his heart in classic Muslim greeting and then offers it for a handshake. I reciprocate.

"My name is Hassan Mabkhout al-Zaidi. I am in charge here."

"I am Harry," I reply.

"Ah! So, this is indeed your true name then? Harry?"

I nod.

"You must wish to bathe and to rest, Harry. Please, follow this man. He will take you to your quarters." The lemonade man smiles and gestures me to follow.

"Yes. Well. Can I ask what's going on? Am I your prisoner, or what?"

"You are my special guest. We will discuss this over *iftar* in an hour's time."

Rather than being tied, gagged and thrown into a dark dungeon, I am escorted to a spacious room with stuffed furniture, a double bed and a table and cabinets with snacks, juices and tea. A large, filled fruit basket greets me on a low, rosewood table. A white-tiled bathroom with shower and western – sit-down – toilet is off to the side. There is, however, no reading material, radio, television, nor telephone. I test the door. It's locked.

The shower's spray is like a blessing on my parched, sweat-and-dust-caked skin. It seems the atmosphere of the entire Muslim world from Casablanca to Karachi is permeated with a blanket of fine dust which finds its way into every pore, up the nostrils, through the hair and in clothing. I linger under the stream, grateful for its cleansing effect.

As I shut my eyes to let the water flow across my face, I ponder my fate in this strange place as a captive of Hassan, undoubtedly the most gracious kidnapper who ever lived. But it's Laurie who occupies my thoughts above all. Every minute I'm delayed, the greater the risk she'll die. I think the unthinkable, that it already may be too late. If I lose my child, I will have nothing to live for. Nothing.

On the bed, a freshly pressed *thoub*, a white cotton, long-sleeved dress for men, has taken the place of my filthy clothes. Sandals have been placed neatly at the foot of the bed. Lemonade Man strikes again. I don the airy costume and view myself in the wall mirror. Like Peter O'Toole in *Lawrence of Arabia*, I primp boylike with a flourish. There are two knocks on the door. It opens a crack and there peaking in is the friendly visage of Lemonade Man. "*Iftar*," he says and beckons me with his hand. Dinner time.

He leads me to a second floor *mafraj*, the room for socializing and relaxing. Hassan, a big smile from ear to ear, greets me like a long lost friend.

"You look better in the *thoub*, Harry. See how much more comfortable it feels? Please." He motions me to have a seat on a floor cushion. The large room is decked out in a cavalcade of patterned Persian carpets, puffy cushions and dishes of dates and pistachios. A flat screen TV sits in a far corner.

Lemonade Man pours spiced black tea into two small glasses. Hassan raises his to me. I reciprocate and we drink.

"Uh, Hassan, I thank you for your, er, hospitality, but I must…"

Hassan raises his hand to signal me to stop.

"Harry, let me explain to you why you are here."

I look at him expectantly.

"You are my special guest."

Three servers enter the room with trays and proceed to lay out a feast before us.

"But first, let us eat. Now here we have *saltah*." He removes the top off a large crock with a steaming meat stew. A divine aroma of chilies, tomatoes, garlic and spices embraces me in a culinary act of seduction. My empty stomach growls. The other platters bear eggs, vegetables, saffron rice and flat bread.

"I hope you like our *malooga*," he says, gesturing at a plate piled high with warm flat bread. "Our Yemeni *malooga* is the best in the Middle East." Hassan brings his fingers and thumb to his lips to punctuate his statement.

Hassan passes the bread and then tears off a piece for himself and commences to eat heartily in true Arab style, *sans* utensils, right hand only. I, too, dig in, savoring the rich, piping hot *saltah*. While a nice cold beer would be the perfect top-off, so would my personal freedom.

"So, Hassan. Can I now have an explanation?"

"Ah, yes." He wipes his mouth. "Forgive me. To give you the long and the short of it, Harry, you will stay here until the leadership delivers on their promise of a power plant to our region and also releases six of my men who were arrested months ago on trumped up charges of smuggling."

I take this in. "In other words, I'm your hostage."

"Bah! Such a word. I prefer to call you my special guest."

"Guests aren't held against their will," I shoot back.

Hassan smiles indulgently. "Oh, but you must understand the politics of our country. Many promises are made, but few are delivered by our leaders."

"Sounds familiar," I say.

"Yes, but in America it is, how do you say? 'All for one and one for all.' Or, better yet, *E Pluribus Unum* – from many, one. I know this. I studied engineering at Queens University in Canada. I visited America many times as a student. In Yemen, everyone belongs to a *biradari*. What you might call 'tribe' or 'clan.' I am an *al-Zaidi* belonging to the *bakil* tribe. Those who have controlled Yemen are of the *sanhan* of the *hashid* tribe. The great-grandfather of my great-grandfather fought the *hashid*." At this point, Hassan's jugulars throb, his dark eyes widen. "They are brigands and scoundrels, which is why Yemen is so poor today. *Hashid* only respect strength."

"So, why me? I'm a target of opportunity, I suppose? And what if the government refuses your demands, or attacks this place with force? Am I then a dead man?"

"This they will not do, Harry. Do not worry."

"Hassan. I am a mere school teacher…"

"Oh no you are not." Hassan signals one of his flunkies to activate the TV. He puts a tape into the VCR. A news program flickers on the screen. It is none other than *Al-Jazeera*, English language broadcast. *Listening Post* is the program. A female announcer reads the headlines. Number three on the list:

> *From Washington, the Justice Department announced it is investigating CIA officer Harry Brennan in connection with spying for Russia. Mr. Brennan has escaped custody and is thought to be out of the country.*

My unflattering work ID photo appears onscreen.

> *It is feared that Mr. Brennan, whom officials say is armed and dangerous, also has ties with jihadi groups overseas and that he has been supporting them with inside intelligence on U.S. government facilities and personnel. According to sources, Mr. Brennan served previously in Afghanistan where he befriended anti-*

*American elements and may have converted to Islam
years ago. He is described as a 'rogue agent.' He
is now believed to be in Yemen. In 2000, al-Qaida
bombed the USS Cole, killing seventeen sailors…*

"Croswell. Son of a bitch. He did it! They want me
dead."

Hassan places his hand reassuringly on my forearm. "No
one can kill you here my friend."

I turn to him. "You knew my true identity all along."

"Only after I took you. How much will your CIA give me
to get you back alive?"

"That's it. Don't you get it? They want me dead."

"Why do they want you dead? Did you kill somebody?"

"No. I know too much."

"I see. Well, do not worry, Harry. We are not *jihadi*. You
are safe here…as my special guest."

"Then I'm just a target of opportunity to you. But do you
know what you're involved in now?" I nod at the television.
"Your holding me helps you not at all. Once they know
I'm here, Washington will put the pressure on to send your
country's army after me. And you. Do you understand?"

Hassan mulls this over. He studies me closely with
intense eyes.

"What they said, about me being a traitor is all fabrication.
Lies. Just an excuse to go after me."

"Then why are you here?" he asks.

"My daughter. She's a hostage in Hadhramaut. Listen to
me Hassan. Do you have children?"

"Nine. Five sons and four daughters."

"Well, I have only one and I love her more than anything.
She is held by the Islamic Army of Aden."

"*Ya Allah!*" Hassan's brow furrows. "She is prisoner of
the *Jaish Adan al Islami*? This is bad. Very bad. You know
they have already killed two hostages. They believe that in the

last days an army will arise from here, led by them, to fight
for victory in God's name, and that God will grant them
success. They are fanatics, mostly Saudis and Egyptians. They
want only blood. We kidnap foreigners only to embarrass the
government to grant us what they have promised. We treat
them as honored guests and then release them, with gifts.
No harm done!" Hassan accentuates this with an outward
flourish of his hands.

I place my face close to his. "Listen, Hassan. Listen
close. I am worthless to you. On the contrary, I'd say I'm
about as valuable to you as a *wadi*ful of live explosives. You
don't want me. I can guarantee that your government and
mine will come after you with hellfire and damnation once
they learn you're holding me. *Let me go!* I need to save my girl.
Do you understand?! Do you?"

Hassan studies me closely. His handsome features mirror
calculation and concern.

"Harry, this I will do. Let you go. But you must grant me
one wish."

"And that is?" I reply.

"That you will allow me to help you rescue your girl. And
to kill the *Jaish Adan al Islami.*"

"This I do grant you."

CHAPTER THIRTY

Allah u Akbar
Allah u Akbar
Allah u Akbar
Allah u Akbar
Ash-hadu allā ilāha illallāh
Ash-hadu allā ilāha illallāh
Ash-hadu anna Muhammadan rasūlullāh…

The lilting, haunting strains of *al-Adhan*, the Muslim call to prayer, transport one to another dimension and time, especially when accentuated by the vast, star-strewn Yemeni night sky.

> *God is The Greatest*
> *I bear witness that there is no lord but God…*

The first weak rays of sunrise pierce the dark horizon. Within the hour, the world will be ablaze with the unremitting Arabian sun. I stand on a balcony wondering how one can believe in an all-powerful God who encompasses goodness and salvation, yet countenances the beheading of innocent tourists. But these cosmic musings take a back seat to the more down-to-earth plotting of force to save my daughter's life.

There are four principles essential for hostage rescue mission success: surprise, intelligence, operators' skill, and deception. If any one of these four principles is overlooked, the operation is doomed. But the principles also are the most critical factors that change as a hostage crisis develops.

On the intel side of the equation, Hassan has already dispatched three of his best men to Hadhramaut to scout and reconnoiter the area where the hostages are held and to discreetly collect as many details they can on the hostage-takers themselves. Also, on the intel side, are items brought to me by the wayward Haji Rakhman, who had failed to link up with me earlier because he and another Afghan cohort had been taken into custody for interrogation by the Yemeni Political Security Organization, the country's feared internal security service. The Afghans were released after they had convinced their interrogators they were on a side-*haj* to visit Yemen's beautiful mosques.

How Rakhman had managed to conceal the treasure he brought with him, however, is a mystery to me. Large envelopes containing satellite photography – not the commercial stuff available to anyone today, but very high resolution overhead that could've been taken only by the super-sophisticated assets of a great nation. Digital and radar imaging displaying fine geographical relief, heat imaging of urban areas. Cars whose license plate numbers are readable. Pedestrians going about their daily business.

A second envelope contains signals intelligence. Intercepts of voice communications, signals traffic analysis with rough translations from Arabic to English. On one document, my eye gloms onto somebody's half-assed attempt to white out a classification designator in the top right corner: СОВЄРШЦЕННО СЕКРЕТНО -- *sovershchenno sekretno*: TOP SECRET in Russian.

I look at Rakhman. "Where'd you get this?" I ask.

He shrugs. "A little bird, let us just say," he responds.

"But…but…I mean, look at this stuff! This is highly

sensitive intelligence and you're...you're walking around with it as if it were just...a...a bunch of store coupons."

Rakhman looks at me sheepishly.

I study his face a moment. "It's got Russian written on it."

"Oh?" says Rakhman disingenuously.

"Nemsky. It was Nemsky, wasn't it?"

Rakhman shakes a finger admonishingly. "Sources and methods, sources and methods, my commander. You taught me. Never reveal one's sources and methods."

"Hm. Let's see how we can use this stuff."

Rakhman smiles.

Marib is a scruffy outpost in Yemen's Wild East. The discovery of oil two decades ago has added flesh to the skeletal economy without, however, the threat of boomtown corpulence. Commercial sprawl here takes the form of shops brimming with machine guns and munitions. And the typical suburban arriviste sports an AK-47 slung around his chest. Downtown is less lethal in nature with auto parts and colorful housewares spilling into the street. Juxtaposed against this incongruous scene are Southern Arabia's foremost archeological sites just outside of town. There, can be found ruins of the kingdom of Sheba, or Saba, which began a thousand years before Christ and thrived for more than a millennium.

Hassan leads us to the Old City, which exudes a kind of beat-up beauty with its precariously constructed buildings of clay, straw and thick logs. Flanked by two of Hassan's burliest guards, we head into *souq a-silah*, the gun market. Uneasy side glances from its denizens betray nervousness and hostility despite my sporting a beard, a *mowez*, a kind of a male skirt, and a cheek full of *qat*. In-your-face young boys sidle up to me. *Qallam, qallam!!* they shout with hands held out.

"What?" I ask Hassan. "What do they want?"

Hassan holds up a hand and makes a clicking gesture with his thumb. "Pen. They want from you ballpoint pens. Ignore them and keep moving. We must make this quick. No complications."

Hordes of mangy homeless cats dart among the market stalls, competing with the throngs of unschooled kids and beggars for the bottom rungs of Yemeni life. Green *qat* spit stains blotch passageways. The tantalizing aroma of bakery bread mingles with the stench of uncollected rotting garbage and cat urine. This competition for the five human senses reflects the larger contradictions of timeless Yemen, a country anchored in the past as it grapples with a fast-globalizing present and future.

A blue-and-white police car, its roof lights pulsing, screeches to a halt on a side alley. Hassan ducks behind a partition and signals us to do the same. Two cops exit from the car and accost the driver of a smoke-belching Toyota pick-up. Some kind of driving infraction – or shakedown. Not our problem.

We wend our way through the *souq-a-silah* in the wake of Hassan, a man who clearly knows this lethal market well. This is the *Whole Foods* of weapons bazaars. The best arms an indifferent world has to offer Third World miscreants who are unable to govern their societies according to the rule of civilized law are on display here, as neatly laid out as Coho salmon and imported asiago cheeses, all for the taking for the right price. But in place of deli items, one encounters in this *souq* countless Kalashnikov rifles in infinite variations and states of repair, a dizzying array of handguns democratically reflecting all countries who produce them, assorted hand grenades and even Russian Dushka medium machine guns which can double for anti-aircraft weapons.

We finally arrive at a stall in the rear of the market. It displays a few AK's, pistols and ammo cartridges and little else. This would seem to be the *souq's Dollar Store*, where the bargain shoppers drop by to grab a few bullets on the way to a clan feud. A bored-looking middle-aged man with a bald pate and a paunch stands idly taking in the routine commotion of market activity. His face lights up when he sees Hassan. The two embrace and plant kisses on each other's cheeks. They hold hands as they exchange greetings.

Hassan turns to me. In English, he says, "And this is my good friend from America, Harry. He is my honored guest.

"Harry, meet my very, very beloved cousin, Bakr al-Attas."

We shake.

After the formalities and the obligatory serving of green tea, the cousins get down to business, negotiating in good faith deals on God-knows-what.

After ten minutes of good natured haggling, Hassan abruptly turns to me.

"Harry, which would you recommend, the PK machine gun with 7.62mm bullets or the PP-19 with 9mm rounds?"

"Huh? Uh, well. It all depends."

"On what?" Hassan asks.

"On whether you're planning stand-off or close-quarters ops."

"Ah! Yes, indeed! Maybe both then." Hassan turns back to Bakr, who's keeping a grocery list on an order pad.

After a few more minutes, Hassan turns back to me.

"Harry. "You know anything about incendiary grenades? Are the ones made in China any good? Or just crap like their DVD players?"

"Well, can't help you there." I shrug.

And on it goes.

Business done, the cousins kiss again. No money

exchanges hands. We depart. Back in our Landcruiser, I ask Hassan what he bought.

"A dozen *Misrs* – AK's made in Egypt, cheaper than Russian ones but very good quality. RPK light machine guns and also PK and PP-19s – following your suggestion. And some of those Chinese grenades, including some Sixty-niners – the incendiary high-explosive kind. And, for good measure, a few M67 fragmentation and MP-84 stun grenades – made in America! Smuggled from Iraq!"

"You're kidding me," I say. Appearances aside, Bakr is not the *Dollar Store* after all; he is rather *Sam's Club*.

"Why kidding? This is no joke. We will go rescue your kid. Got to do it right. This I do as your special friend."

"How much did this cost? I didn't see you pay him."

"Cost? Oh, a lot. Not to worry. I pay Bakr myself, later. C.O.D. We are beloved cousins. Everything on a handshake. It's ok."

"Hassan. From what I saw of your holdings, you are not the House of Saud. Those weapons must set you back at least fifty grand."

"Grand?" This is one American slang term Hassan hasn't learned.

"Thousand. It must cost you at least fifty-thousand dollars."

"Not to worry, Harry. I have family in Saudi who pay. They give me whatever I want. They are proud of me."

"Oh yeah? What do they do there?"

"Oh, many things. Mainly construction and banking."

"Maybe I've heard of them. They're also named al-Zaidi?"

"No. Bakr's aunt Hamida was from Syria. She married a man named Mohammad, who moved from Yemen many years ago to Saudi to make his fortune. And he became very wealthy. Good family. They help us poor cousins in Yemen."

"And their family name?"

"Bin-Laden," Hassan answers without missing a beat.

Hassan's scouts radio in that, after a long lull, the Islamic Army of Aden is again threatening to behead one of their hostages. The scouts report that the new threat apparently is in response to a growing Yemeni army presence in the valley. The central government has long become exasperated with Yemen becoming a playground for terrorists, indigenous and otherwise. Stuck between a rock and a hard place, they alternate between negotiating hostages' release and storming the perpetrators' strongholds. The latter tack, unfortunately, has too often resulted in foreigners being killed, which, in turn, puts a damper on tourism and foreign investment. It could be they're alternating use of force as well as negotiation to effect a release. In any case, the situation is now getting dicier, especially given Yemen's political turmoil.

I ask Hassan to ask his scouts if they can spot the hostages. Hassan relays that his men catch glimpses now and then of the captives, often as they relieve themselves outside the cave entrance. They report the red-haired girl is alive and appears to be physically ok.

My long and meandering journey through life has taken me far afield from my forefathers' Roman Catholic faith. Not from some rejectionist attitude on my part. Rather, my focus on career and my immersion in alien cultures have de-emphasized the spiritual, or, at least, diluted it. But now, faced with mortal danger to my child, I pray. I pray hard. I try to recall the prayers from long, long ago. The Hail Mary, the Apostles Creed. I stumble through the recitation, ashamed at how much I'd forgotten. I'm conscious that I am a Rainy Day Christian, like so many others, seeking God's intervention only when trouble visits me and mine. But I do it. I pray. I know guns and intel are not our ultimate salvation. Following the prayers, however, the latter will also be invoked.

I contemplate my own personal situation. Hassan seems genuinely trustworthy. But this is the Middle East where treachery is an art form and trust is a luxury of fools. It's so-far-so-good with Hassan. I need exactly his help. Alone, I am little more than a kamikaze pilot without a plane. I anticipate what the Agency is up to now that I am officially a "traitor" and dangerous renegade. Croswell undoubtedly has trained the full range of force the USG can muster to go after me. And, knowing what I know, it is definitely not in the interests of him and his cohorts to have me captured alive. Too much is at stake. Dead men don't talk. They also make convenient scapegoats for the nefariousness of others.

The CIA station in our embassy in Sanaa would be under orders to devote all human resources toward finding out where I am. They would be on the Yemeni government's back to muster their intelligence, law enforcement and military forces to come after me. So, every cop, spy and soldier in the country is after me, no doubt with the prize of a fat bounty on my head as an incentive. CIA case officers are paying informants to ascertain my whereabouts, which makes me wonder about the reliability and loyalty of Hassan's men.

The intelligence community's awesome technical resources are certainly also aimed in my direction, ranging from NSA's listening outposts and satellites which vacuum clean the ether for radio and telephone transmissions which contain keywords such as my name and Laurie's, to overhead satellite imagery scouring Yemen's parched surface for any sign of Harry Brennan's presence.

An army of analysts in Washington is collecting this incoming tide of data to parse things out, look for patterns, piece together puzzles. Their combined brainpower is enough energy to rival Hoover Dam's annual output.

Finally, there's our military. CENTCOM – Central Command – headquartered in Tampa, with a forward operational base in Qatar, is responsible for U.S. defense activities in the Middle East. I could expect an Apache helicopter, an AC-130 gunship, an F-18 Hornet, a Maverick air-to-surface missile or a wily drone suddenly swooping from the sky with a ton of high explosive munitions with my name on them ending my tenure on this planet as well as that of anybody within at least a couple hundred yards of me.

But this is the same U.S. government which, for a decade hunted for Osama bin-Laden and his sidekick in evil, Ayman al-Zawahiri, with the full force of a superpower and at a cost of tens of millions. Taking a page from al-Qaeda's playbook, I immediately tell Hassan to ensure he and his people never use my name or Laurie's in any of their communications, or even to refer to "American." I provide codenames: "Merchant" for myself; "Flower" for my daughter. I ask that they keep the radio traffic down to a bare minimum, that they use couriers for any extensive communications and that they report contact with any strangers. I ask that Hassan make his compound's activities appear as normal as possible during the day so as to thwart overhead scrutiny. Also, no more convoys. We travel singly in our vehicles and link up after sundown. Do not provoke the Yemeni government any more, I plead. Do nothing to call attention from the authorities. Finally, I ask Hassan if he can get his rich Saudi cousins to make a substantial financial outlay with which to provide hefty salary increases and bonuses to his men to make them less vulnerable to co-optation. All of these measures constitute what is known in the national security trade as OPSEC, or operational security.

We travel at night with headlights dimmed, taking remote routes, to the extent possible, to avoid detection. Hassan has put together a force of a dozen of his best trained men, most of whom have been battle tested in Chechnya and Afghanistan. I don't ask what these *jihadi* think of me, an American, a CIA official. What I do know is that they're fiercely loyal to their chief, Hassan.

Hadhramaut is like the dark side of the moon without the craters. Dry, barren, rough and remote. It is a place ideally suited to puncturing tires and breaking axles, where vultures and snakes feel right at home. Guys like Moses and John the Baptist might even have felt at home here if they got wigged out enough stuck in the wilderness.

Before we set out, I made an effort to impart some operational art training on the fighters, who appeared to be fairly familiar and comfortable with their new-bought weapons, but ragged on the finer techniques of assault. I had Hassan break them up into three elements: two rifle squads and a support squad with the heavy machine guns and grenade launchers. My experience with Muslim guerrilla fighters showed a tendency for uncoordinated mass attack, driven by poor training and a misguided enthusiasm to become *shaheed*, or martyrs. The result inevitably was high casualties.

After a day-and-a-half of bone-rattling, teeth-cracking travel, we link up with two of Hassan's scouts. It is dawn. We cover the Landcruisers with camouflage tarps and hunker down for a briefing and rest. The scouts report that the cave where the hostages are held is two kilometers away, on a steep hill overlooking a valley. They've counted a dozen Islamic Army of Aden fighters in and around the holdout. They have wide visual coverage of at least nine kilometers and a commanding fire zone against attackers. Surprisingly, there are no government troops nearby, the nearest being at a road checkpoint much further east.

The scouts have compiled a careful log of the enemy's sleeping patterns, eating habits, and sentry relief times. They use radio commo sparingly, relying heavily on young boys as couriers.

I take out Haji Rakhman's treasure trove of SI – sensitive intelligence – and lay it all out in a shady spot of the grove. The overhead provides an extremely detailed bird's eye view of the target area and surrounding terrain for at least thirty klicks. I note two paths and a ridgeline ascending to the cave. The paths likely are guarded, leaving the ridgeline as likely the best line of approach. The established paths should be used to lull and channel the enemy into easy kill zones. Bright red spots in the thermal imagery reveal the insurgents almost certainly have a generator. They also reveal the warm motors of two vehicles concealed at the foot of the hill.

The intercept traffic in the SI is sparse, testimony to the enemy's good COMSEC, communications security. But they do uncover one area of sloppiness. The hostage-takers refer to each other by name in their radio communications. The leader's name is Yunus. I ask Hassan if he knows of this man.

He searches his brain. "Yes. Now I know. He is not Yemeni. He is Chechen. He was one of the leaders who took over that school in Russia some years ago. Do you remember?"

"Yeah. The Beslan school massacre. Almost two-hundred school kids were killed."

"Yunus Matsiyev. We know of him. A thug. He is truly evil, a child-killer." Hassan spits to express his disgust. "He fights now with al-Qaeda in Iraq and here.

"Look, Hassan. We need to plan. We need to act quickly. I want your forward observers to report immediately any commotion in and around that cave, any indication they're threatening the hostages. We need to act rapidly, to neutralize the Islamic Army guys without harming their captives."

"We will have victory, Harry. *Mashallah!*"

With intelligence and operators' skill (*Inshallah!*) in place, we now need to work on surprise and deception. First, however, we must ensure that we ourselves are not surprised by an ambush. In the moonless dark, at the bottom of the two paths, we carefully attach M-69 fragmentation grenades to small trees and brush, run tripwires across the paths, connect wires to the straightened pull rings of the grenades and remove the secondary safety pins. A person coming down either path will trip the grenades and hear his last sound on earth, a loud kaboom that will also alert us to action.

We slowly move two two-man teams with Russian-made RPK light machine guns and grenade launchers a hundred meters on either flank of the cave opening. One of the scouts remains in his concealed overwatch position on the next hill, some thousand meters away, closely monitoring the situation in the cave through the powerful scope on his Dragunov sniper rifle.

Finally, the assault team of five men, fanned out, crawls into place in the low brush directly below the cave opening, three armed with AK's and two with PP-19 submachine guns.

The sun comes up on the eastern horizon like some ancient apocalyptic god. And we are embedded in the natural surroundings as if to escape its death rays. Hassan and I, along with Haji Rakhman and a couple of base support fighters, are to the rear. Two Islamic Army sentries at the cave's mouth scan the terrain with binoculars. They take their time, scan and re-scan. Any of us in the brush who needed to scratch, cough or fart could give up the ghost instantly and we'd have one bloody mess on our hands. But Hassan's men are disciplined, hardened guerrilla fighters. They are as still as dirt.

Hassan's forward team leaders and sniper each carry small burst transmission walkie-talkies with single earphone and mike. Hassan ensures each follows his orders closely and carefully.

The sun's heat quickly envelopes us. How long can a man sweat without pulling his canteen for a drink? The sun is in charge now. It will tell us how long we can lie in wait, when we will need to strike.

Several of the Islamic Army men emerge from the cave. All are armed, except for one with a videocam and another who has the bearing and strut of a leader. This man gives orders, punctuating them with sharp arm gestures. The wind carries on it the snippet of a command. *Yel-lah! Yel-lah!*' Hurry! Hurry!

The men take up a formation as drilled into them as that of any conventionally trained soldiers. An outward-facing U-shape with the commander at the crux, his armed cohorts flanking and the cameraman facing from the opening. Another insurgent emerges with a scabbard. The leader pulls a huge gleaming blade from it and nods.

Through my field glasses, I see emerge from the dark recess of the cave two burly men. Between them there is a slight figure with a white top and the sun reflecting brilliantly off her red hair. It's Laurie.

Hassan flinches. He issues orders through his mike. He turns to me. "This is she, isn't it? Your girl."

"Yes," I answer hoarsely.

Her hands are tied behind her back, the two burly men hold her firmly by the upper arms. I can see her face clearly through the glasses. She's neither crying nor crestfallen. She holds her posture ramrod straight. She looks up at the sun and then shuts her eyes tightly as if to enjoy its warmth for the last time.

Hassan listens intently through an earphone. "I told the sniper to shoot the leader. He reports he does not have a clear shot." Hassan looks again through his field glasses. "They are too close to the cave walls. His line of sight is blocked." He muffles more instructions into the mike and listens to the replies. "The assault team is ready, but look!"

The leader nods. The men holding Laurie roughly bend her down on her knees. The video man is recording the scene. The leader commences to make a fiery speech into the videocam.

"We must move fast!" Hassan spits. "But, Harry, I'm afraid they'll shoot her as soon as we act. We have no choice. No choice!" He begins to alert the assault team to move. I stop him.

"No," I say.

Hassan looks at me confused. "*What?* They're going to do it! Behead her. We must…"

"Now it's time for deception. Stay still."

I rise from the brush, and wave a white handkerchief. "Hey! Hey!"

Hassan hugs the ground. "Are you insane?!" he spits through clenched teeth.

"Stay put!" I hiss without looking down.

The terrorists raise their weapons and point them at me. Commander Yunus lifts an arm to signal them not to shoot.

With arms high, I slowly walk toward them. Yunus trains binoculars on me.

"Don't shoot! I'm unarmed and alone," I shout.

Yunus gestures for two of his men to go fetch me. They head down the left path. The others, weapons at the ready, step forward away from the cave entrance to get a better look at me. Laurie is on her feet again, still in the grip of one terrorist. She spots me walking. Her expression is one of disbelief.

I continue my slow, deliberate approach. At least six guns are fixed on me. All it would take is one well-aimed shot and I'm a dead man.

Yunus then signals for two additional men to descend the other path, no doubt to check for any other intruders.

The first M-69 grenade explodes seconds later on the left

path. Then a second. Yunus's men on that path are chopped meat.

I hit the ground. I see Hassan rushing forward with his two other men, he brandishing his sidearm, they with AK's.

The head of the man holding Laurie bursts into a red spray and flying skull fragments and brain tissue, the consequence of a dead-on shot by Hassan's sniper. Laurie falls to the ground.

Grenades on the right path explode, taking care of the second pair dispatched by Yunus.

Then all hell breaks loose. The RPK machine guns open up from the left and right flanks. The five-man assault team, letting loose with a blood-curdling battle cry, storm the cave entrance from below with AK's and submachine guns blazing. As several of the Islamic Army men jump down to counterattack the assault team, the latter toss the type sixty-nine Chinese incendiary grenades at them. Upon detonating, the grenades send up a sun-burst of light, followed by flames which engulf the terrorists.

Hassan's two-man flanking teams rush from the sides. As they reach the cave entrance, one tosses an MP-84 stun grenade into the cave itself. A deafening explosion goes off, followed by an intense smoke cloud from the mouth of the cave. The stun grenades are meant to do just that, to temporarily incapacitate, not kill. Hostages and hostage-holders alike will be stunned and prostrate. The assault force quickly overpowers three not killed, including commander Yunus.

The fighting ends abruptly.

I run to the cave. Rakhman follows. There is Laurie, sword firmly in both hands plungerlike, its tip drawing blood from the back of a prostrate Yunus's neck. One quick, easy shove and Yunus will join his fallen companions in paradise, or rather, hell.

"Laurie!" I shout.

But she seems not to see or hear me. Her face is beet red, strands of her flaming red hair fall over her eyes. She's hyperventilating. Every muscle taut. She casts a slow glance at me with bloodshot blues, then redirects them to the task at hand. I don't know if this is my daughter or some vengeance-wreaking she-god from mythology.

"Laurie!! No!!"

CHAPTER THIRTY-ONE

We're pushing our vehicles as hard as we can through the hardscrabble Hadhramaut terrain back toward Marib in a mad dash to leave the area before al-Qaeda or Yemeni armed forces catch wind of what happened at the cave and come after us. All security is thrown to the billowing, dust-filled winds as our small convoy pushes through the desert in broad daylight.

Hassan is in the lead Landcruiser, half a kilometer ahead of us, already launching into what can be delicately described as a vigorous interrogation of my daughter's kidnapper, hog-tied in the rear. The ex-hostages and handful of surviving terrorists are in the vehicles behind us. Laurie has her arms tightly around me, as if holding on for dear life, her head on my chest. We say nothing, the strong, silent bonds of father and child as strong and as durable as granite.

Our bodies are tossed this way and that by the jarring ride. Haji Rakhman is in the front passenger seat. Ever the professional, his eyes rake the sun-drenched horizon for any sign of trouble.

"Daddy?" Laurie murmurs. She looks up at me. "Can you forgive me?"

"For what?" I respond.

"You know. Disobeying your instructions. Coming here with Ryan."

"Not now, Laurie. We'll have plenty of time to talk when we're back home."

"Can I ask you one thing, though?"

"OK. Shoot."

"Were you a little bit proud of me? I mean, the way I snatched the sword and held it right on that bad guy's neck?"

I look into her eyes. "My god. How did you do it?"

"I was thinking of you. How I want to be just like you. Brave and coolheaded. Doing the right thing. For something bigger than any one of us."

"I'm prouder that you didn't kill him."

"I would've though. I swear I would've." She says this with a hardbitten tone I've never heard from her before.

"Justice must be served, Laurie. He'll be dealt with by those whose citizens he killed. According to the law. Could be us. Could be the Russians. We'll see. That is, after Hassan is done with him. Come to think of it. Haji, get Hassan on the radio. I need to talk to him. Make sure he doesn't make minced *saltah* of Yunus."

Haji raises Hassan on the radio and hands me the mike.

It seems like the sun enveloped the earth in a wrathful embrace. Brilliant light flashes in all directions. Rocks blast the windows. We are upside down, rolling, tumbling, our bodies thrown from side to side. I instinctively cover Laurie with my body, bracing myself with all my strength against the sides of the Landcruiser. Through a window, I see the world twirling as if on spin cycle. But, strangely, I hear nothing. Silence amid a storm. My mind tells me violence has visited us, yet I am detached from it, hearing nothing, feeling nothing. Until the vehicle crash lands on its side.

A maelstrom of emotions hits hard. Pain, fear, panic, confusion. My ears ring loudly as if someone has clapped them. I yell, but I can't hear myself. I look around. The Landcruiser is tipped onto its right side. There's blood on the cracked windshield where the head of the now motionless driver rammed forward. Haji is slumped down on the floor.

"Laurie! Laurie!" I shout. But I don't hear myself. I feel like I am separated from my body. I shake my head, hoping to bring my physical and mental selves back together. I look down. There's Laurie, squatting in front of me, blood running down her forehead, saying something, but I don't hear her. Like a silent movie, the scene plays out, but I'm missing all but the visual.

I reach up to the left door and open it. I raise myself out, then extend an arm to Laurie. We jump to the ground. I shake my head repeatedly, but the numbed detachment and loud ringing remain. I look around. The sun's rays hurt my eyes. I squint in all directions. Ahead of us I see billowing black smoke. It's the lead vehicle, with Hassan, obliterated, twisted shards of smoking charred metal. I look at the sky. In the distance I see a dark speck hovering, slowly, like a vulture. I may be numbed and deaf, but the brain is still working.

"Predator! Let's go!" I shout. I grab my daughter by the arm and run like hell to boulders at a cliff bottom fifty meters away. I see Haji limping in our wake. We jump into a deep ravine, getting cut and bruised as we tumble down.

"Down! Hit the dirt! Cover your ears, close your eyes!" I command.

Another brilliant flash of light. The earth shakes. Rocks and dirt fly. A wave of heat passes over.

"Goddamn you, Croswell! Damn you to hell!!" I scream.

The video images flickering across the screen are grainy but clearly show the targeted vehicles and the impact of the two Hellfire missiles.

William Hanscom Croswell leans over, peering over the shoulder of Air Force Maj. Brett Clarendon, the pilot of the MQ-1A Predator drone aircraft hovering in the cloudless skies over Yemen. Clarendon gently nudges the joystick to get the drone to circle again over the smoking carnage ten-thousand feet below. MQ-1A personnel call the detailed video a "God's-eye view" of a targeted area, no doubt reflecting the sense of godlike power they have in the Predator.

Croswell squints through his rimless glasses and purses his lips. "Hmmmm. Direct hit on the lead vehicle. Any survivors?"

One of the two sensor operators focuses the aircraft's electro-optic/infrared zoom lens onto the site.

"A bulls-eye hit with two twenty-pound high-explosive anti-tank warheads?" he says in a southern drawl. "Any living, breathing creature within fifty meters is now part of the ozone layer."

A close-up comes into view. A ground crater with smoking debris around its perimeter. The sensor operator flicks a couple of switches to change over to thermal imagery. The impact site and smoldering wreckage appear bright red. Outlying pieces are orange and yellow. The sergeant studies the scene.

"It's all burning metal and such. No sign of a living human in that quadrant," he says. He switches back to photographic imagery.

More ground is revealed as the drone flies slowly over.

"And those then?" asks Croswell in his even, nasally voice. "Those figures. Who are they?"

"HUMINT through JDISS identifies them as the hostages. This SCI just came in through JWICS via Trojan Spirit II channels." He holds up intel reports stamped TOP SECRET.

"Can you tell me in English?" Croswell demands in a deliberate tone as if he were talking to a child.

"Uh, yeah. Battlefield intel coming to us through real-time secure channels. Ground assets report they're the hostages," he answers.

"Hmmmm." Croswell again squints at the screen, elbow

on knee, thumb and forefinger supporting his chin. He appears amused. "They look like ants scurrying away from some kid's magnifying glass burning them with the sun's light," he smirks.

The Ground Control Station staff look at him in puzzlement.

"Ah, yeah. Uh, get me O'Connor on the STE line."

A commo specialist inserts a crypto card into the secure phone. Two minutes later, Larry O'Connor is on the line from MQ-1A Forward Operating Station, Camp LeMonier Naval Base, Djibouti, in the Horn of Africa.

The contrast between Nellis Air Force Base, home of the 11th Reconnaissance Squadron, outside Las Vegas and Camp LeMonier, Djibouti, nine-thousand miles away, couldn't be more stark. The Predator Ground Control Station, where Croswell is ensconced, is situated in non-descript low-rise buildings among vivid green lawns in a setting suggesting a country club rather than a military base. Security in the immediate area is unobtrusive to the point of near-invisibility. The drones are piloted from here.

Camp LeMonier, by contrast, once a base of the French Foreign Legion, is five-hundred acres of transplanted American military infrastructure manned by two thousand Yanks in an impoverished former French colony whose year-round weather is so hot and humid that the poor souls assigned there refer to Djibouti as "the Devil's Belly Button." LeMonier is home to Combined Joint Task Force - Horn of Africa, or CJTF-HOA, in the vanguard of America's war against terror. Predators are launched from here. Command and control are relayed through the Predator Forward Operating Station.

Assigned to Djibouti as punishment for disobeying Handley's orders and joining me to launch Talisman, Larry O'Connor is drenched with perspiration. Outside the air conditioned 30' x 8' x 8' trailer, it's 110 degrees. And it's only 10:00 am. The blast of cool air stems the energy drain from his body exacted by the unrelenting East African heat.

"Good work, O'Connor. This'll get you a promotion," says Croswell through the secure phone.

"I just read the incoming traffic. Mr. Croswell, I was led to believe this was a senior al-Qaeda asset we were after. The intel refers to an Amcit. What gives, sir?"

"Well, O'Connor, he's actually a renegade. A turncoat. In al-Qaeda's hip pocket. Had to be neutralized. Like Ahmed Hijazi."

Croswell is referring to a dual U.S.-Yemeni national killed by the CIA in 2002 with a Hellfire missile fired from a Predator in Yemen. Also killed were Hijazi's five traveling companions, all al-Qaeda operatives.

"What's his name?" O'Connor demands.

Silence.

"I said, what's his name, sir?

"I think you know, Larry. He had to be neutralized. To save American lives..."

"Harry Brennan. Isn't it?"

"Yes."

"We have no legal right to target Amcits, sir. And he's Agency. One of us for chrissake. I know Brennan. He's no turncoat." O'Connor's voice is strained.

"O'Connor, do I have to remind you there's a presidential finding that permits covert action against any American citizen deemed a justifiable military target for associating with al-Qaeda?"

"Bullshit, sir."

"I beg your pardon. Listen O'Connor, I'll have your ass..."

"I've got good news and bad news. The bad news for you is Harry Brennan's alive. The lead vehicle you took out contained a Yemeni chieftain – an enemy of al-Qaeda at that. Yet more collateral damage, *sir!* Brennan was in the second. He walked away. The good news is: I quit. This isn't what I signed up for!"

The line goes dead.

O'Connor steps out of the cool cocoon back into the great outdoor oven. With a deliberate stride, he goes to the back-up generator for the trailer and fires it up. He switches the setting from 120 volts to 240, then engages the current. Four million dollars of state-of-the-art advanced weapons circuitry fries, sending sparks and smoke in all directions. One Predator satellite-link station down. One armed American Unmanned Aerial Vehicle hovering over Yemen flying blind. And Larry O'Connor walks away, to start a new life.

CHAPTER THIRTY-TWO
WASHINGTON, DC

Eddy Frechette isn't feeling up to par today. Maybe it was the crawdad étoufée he had at Mama Louisa's for lunch, or the spat he had with his girlfriend the evening before. Or it could be his angling for a promotion to the senior service and a supervisory job, causing him to lose sleep. Maybe it's all of these.

Or, maybe, for the first time since he was a junior case officer he's nervous over a recruitment pitch. An intercepted phone conversation from the night before galvanized him into action. The Nemsky's called 911 for an ambulance to take Anya to the hospital. The girl had gone into multiple seizures. It was time to strike. Eddy would nail down all the details to arrange stem cell treatment in Oregon. His superiors had given him the green light to proceed. An Agency front organization would make the arrangements with the hospital, keeping the CIA's involvement opaque. And, as far as the Russian embassy was concerned, it would be simply a pro bono humanitarian offer directly from the medical center, no USG involvement at all, no strings attached. No CIA fingerprints.

A six-foot-four, 250-pound, very dark African-American is likely to attract more notice lumbering down this hospital corridor than most people. So, a bouquet of flowers in hand might deflect some of that notice, reassuring all that he was just another visitor paying his respects to an ill loved one.

He had rehearsed his pitch dozens of times. His bosses in the National Clandestine Service had chopped off on it. Yet, yet he felt an unease. Using a kid as a hook. It was new to him. Eddy, aka "Mike" Baddest Man on the Planet, Frechette was about to add to his collection of scalps, in service to his country. And get himself promoted. And yet...

As he ambles down the corridors, disinfectant penetrates his nostrils, ailing people, young and old are wheeled through. Anguished relatives sit or stand, waiting. Waiting for the news. Did he come out of it ok? What's the prognosis? When can we see her? Many had been there for hours by the looks of their sleep-deprived faces and rumpled clothes.

Eddy zeroes in on his target, in the children's unit. Room A-303. He clenches the flowers too hard. The stems bend in his hand. A familiar face down the corridor, a man walking slowly toward him. Nemsky.

Eddy takes a deep breath, stands erect and plants himself directly in front of Nemsky. The latter's blue eyes fix on him, but betray neither surprise nor offense at the big black man blocking his way.

Eddy stares him down. "I'd like to have a word with you," he says simply.

Nemsky closes his eyelids, reflecting impatience. "What?" he says sharply.

Eddy pulls the Russian into a side corridor leading to a janitor's closet. No introductions needed.

"I'll make this quick and to the point, Nemsky. We can help you and you can help us. Agree to work with us and we'll pull out all the stops to save your daughter."

"And if I don't?" asks Nemsky.

"You'll be PNGed. Kicked out, sent back home. What does that bode for Anya? Not good news, I'd say, given the state of Russia's medical establishment. And we're prepared to pay that price as well. We kick you out and we know

Moscow will retaliate by making *persona non grata* one of ours in our Moscow embassy. Maybe more." Eddy shrugs his huge shoulders.

Nemsky simply stares at Eddy, an indecipherable Mona Lisa expression on his haggard face. He takes a deep breath. Shakes his head.

"What? I say somethin' funny?" Eddy asks.

"I don't know your name. What is your name?"

"Huh? Uh, it's Eddy. Let's just leave it there."

"I would guess that you, Eddy, are what? A great-great grandson of slaves. Am I correct?"

This throws Eddy off. Makes him at a loss for words. "Somethin' like that. So what?"

"So what, you say? To buy and sell children. You, of all people. How can you?"

Eddy has no answer.

"Come." Nemsky signals Eddy to follow him. Nemsky's head is low and he shuffles his feet as if they were weighed down with chains.

They proceed up the corridor to room A-303. Nemsky pauses, hesitates, then gestures with a listless wave of his hand for Eddy to look inside. He pokes his head in and sees Nemsky's wife, Irina, making the Orthodox sign of the cross as she kneels by the lifeless body of her daughter.

"I have lost everything I have today. I have no child to sell you. Now go away."

A wave of heat rushes from Eddy's head to his legs and back. His skin breaks out in goose bumps. He feels lightheaded.

"Oh, man. Oh man. I'm...I'm so...sorry. I'm so sorry." Eddy's eyes well up, tears flow down his cheeks. "I didn't know. I didn't..." He drops the flowers on the floor, turns and walks away.

CHAPTER THIRTY-THREE
AL-HAZM, YEMEN

Having made it safely back to Hassan's compound near al-Hazm, northwest of the capital of Sanaa, there is no time to mourn. And there is no burial. The Hellfire missiles did their job in transforming the mortals in the lead vehicle into the ozone layer. No bodies.

Rafi, Hassan's eldest son, is in charge now. His bearing and cool, confident demeanor belie his twenty-one years of age. He is comfortable issuing orders to men much older than he and displays an organizational bent that must run in the genes. Also handsome like his father, young Rafi is now *sheikh* of his al-Zaidi clan. He sports his grandfather's *jambiya* on his belt, a sign of inherited power.

Rafi's first act upon reaching the first town of any size is to turn the rattled hostages over to the nonplussed local police. They would be turned over to their embassies which would make the travel arrangements home. This does not, however, include Laurie, whom I want out of this place as soon as possible. I can't risk Croswell grabbing her to get at me. Instead, I entrust her to the al-Zaidi clan network which will escort her safely to Abu Dhabi, where she will catch a flight to Switzerland to stay with friends. Our parting is emotional. I tell her to stay put in Zurich and await my call once I was through here.

"But Dad. You don't need to stay here. Come home! Please!!"

"Laurie, if I go back now, I'll be arrested on phony charges. Croswell and his cohorts will produce the best 'solid evidence' the CIA can concoct to get me convicted in Federal court as a traitor."

"They won't believe him! They won't!" Laurie says between sobs.

"No, baby. I can't take the chance. And I owe it to Rafi here. His dad paid for our lives with his own. The least I can do now is to help the son."

Laurie cries and doesn't want to let me go. With a nod, I signal Rafi's men to pull her away. Getting back in the Landcruiser and seeing my child wailing and waving goodbye as we pull away tears into me big time. Predators, renegade CIA bosses and terrorists, I can deal with. But leaving my daughter like this is something else entirely. No amount of training prepared me for it.

Our stay at the al-Zaidi compound ends abruptly. Rafi's men are picking up radio messages between Yemeni army units and reports from villagers that government forces are racing toward the remote outpost. Any minute, no doubt, Yemeni Air Force MiGs will be roaring over the compound. We have no wish to join Hassan in the ozone sphere, so we load up and hightail it out of there toward the Haraz mountains where, Rafi assures me, we can hide out for days, if not weeks, without being detected.

Forty-five minutes into the open desert, we spot in the distance at ten and two o'clock two formations kicking up dust. Yemeni army columns headed straight for us. From our rear, out of nowhere, two MiG-29's roar above us. One swoops around in a circle and buzzes our four-vehicle convoy at a thousand feet. The blast of the fightercraft's turbofan engines assaults our ears, shakes our innards. The pilot is reconnoitering us and fixing our small, moving column as a target. The next pass could be deadly.

Rafi, in the front passenger seat of the lead vehicle, turns to me, finger pointed straight ahead.

"Haraz! Look! We are close now," he shouts.

I lean forward and see through the windshield dark-blue mountains looming ahead.

Rafi barks at the sweat-drenched driver to step on it. The small man, scrunched forward, face near the windshield, is visibly scared. He nods and floors the accelerator. The Landcruiser is rocking and swerving. All it would take is one large rock or rut to break an axle, puncture a tire, or send us flying onto our side.

The two convoys heading toward us are more visible. I look through binoculars. The one on our right consists of assorted Russian-made BTR armored personnel carriers and Gaz jeeps. That on our left is smaller, comprising civilian four-wheel drive vehicles led by a Gaz with a rear-mounted manned machine gun. As the convoys close in pincerlike, they'll start firing at us.

In a series of precise booms, thirty millimeter cannon rounds rake close to us as the MiG swoops back down in an earsplitting roar, firing away.

Rafi instructs the driver to swerve and zigzag, then shouts the same order into the Landcruiser's transceiver to the other three vehicles in our group.

The MiG passes over us and soars vertically to make the circle for a return strafing run. The second MiG will certainly fall into place to double the trouble.

Haji, next to me, has a walkie-talkie pressed hard against his ear. In halting Arabic, he shouts for the person at the other end to repeat what he said.

"Oooohh!" he croons, eyes wide.

Rafi points to the approaching Haraz mountains.

"Soon we will be there, *inshallah!*" he says.

"Or in heaven as martyrs," I reply.

Haji grabs my forearm. "My commander. My haji network moles tell me…" The Landcruiser flies across a small ravine and lands with a teeth-cracking bump. "…tell me one convoy is Yemen army. The other is…is American."

"What?!" I say.

"Yes, American. Their leader is Handley. His name is Handley."

The MiGs come in for the kill from the rear, firing their cannons. On orders from Rafi, our vehicles have broken formation and are now fanned out.

A large explosion. The last Landcruiser, containing four of Rafi's fighters is hit and turns into a fireball.

"*Ya Allah!*" Rafi shouts with hands bracing his head, hardly believing what he's seeing.

The Yemen army convoy is a thousand meters from us and is now breaking into a flanking formation to intercept us. Soldiers scramble out and set up mortars and aim RPG launchers at us.

Haji has his ear pressed to the walkie-talkie, then shouts to me, "They say Handley has come here to personally take control of the operation to kill you, my commander!"

Rafi has the three remaining vehicles make a sharp leftward turn away from the Yemen army column, then another adjustment to press a mad dash toward the mountains now looming before us.

Mortar rounds blast around us. An RPG round whooshes feet away, a near miss exploding the desert floor.

I open a window and look at the sky for the MiGs. As they again move to complete another attack circle, I see a smaller object against the pure blue desert sky.

"Holy, holy shit!" I yell.

Rafi looks up through the windshield. "What?! What?!"

"A drone! Another goddamn Predator!"

The convoy of civilian vehicles is also closing in. Men

with machine guns extend out the sides and commence firing at us.

The windshield in our vehicle bursts into a million pieces. The driver covers his eyes with both hands and lets out a scream. Rafi, covered in tiny cubes of automotive glass, quickly grabs the wheel to keep the vehicle under control.

"My commander! My haji friends can give intel to the Americans…false intel to make the Predator target Handley! My double agents. They need to know right now! So?"

Hell is sometimes described as eternal chaos. If that is so, I'm in hell's crucible. I must decide on the spot, immediately whether to take out a senior CIA officer, or to risk having him take me out. A no-win scenario.

"They need to know *now!*" Haji exclaims.

"Do it! Do it!" shouts Rafi. "Or we will surely die!"

I open my mouth but no words come out.

Without taking his eyes off of me, Haji speaks into the walkie-talkie.

An eternal minute later, divine fire blasts down from the sky. Two Hellfire missiles slam into the civilian column, taking out the first three vehicles. The decapitated column comes to a sudden halt and men exit, running in all directions.

Heading northwest, we pass it and witness the twisted flaming remains of the vehicles and men on the ground firing blindly at us.

We are also gaining distance away from the army convoy.

Haji and I look at each other in silence. He then calmly turns forward, pulls the safety on his pistol. He opens the window and fires back at the men shooting at us.

We reach the abrupt beginning of the Haraz Mountains, a narrow pass, our womb of safety.

The MiGs swoop down. *Boom! Boom! Boom! Boom! Boom! Boom!* The cannon rounds blast the sides of the pass at the rate of 1500 per minute, causing rock debris to rain down upon us. Their crunching impact rips open the hood and roof of our Landcruiser. Rafi keeps it under control despite wind and sand blowing in through the now nonexistent windshield.

Yemeni army jeeps race out of nowhere on our right flank, gaining on us in an effort to cut us off.

"Jesus! Where'd they come from?!" I yell.

One of the Gaz jeeps swerves to ram us in the side. We clash, then separate. Soldiers in the vehicle are blasting away at us. Haji and I fire back. The bouncing and swerving of our vehicles prevent a sure aim.

Again the Gaz swerves into us. I fire at its tires, but miss. Their rounds slam into the rear side of our Landcruiser. Again we separate.

Another Gaz races up to our left. I see a soldier standing taking aim with a machine gun right at my face.

As we enter the pass, the Gaz on the left turns into a fireball, jumping skyward like an inflamed beast and crashes hard onto the earth. An RPG round slams into the engine of the other Gaz, sending it and its occupants rolling across the ground in a zillion burning pieces.

Deeper in, our two Landcruisers and pickup encounter no more attacks. We look back to see armed fighters from the rock formations above shooting and tossing grenades down at the pursuing soldiers.

"*Hashemi! Hashemi!*" Rafi shouts, waving a fist and smiling.

"What?" I yell back.

"They are *banu hashemi!* he exalts. "Hashemite tribe rebels! They are Shia. My friends! They save us! Hah-hah!!"

Rafi brings the battered Landcruiser to a slow halt below a low precipice. The other two shot-up vehicles pull up alongside, brakes squeaking, engines smoking. The men get out and embrace each other, hardly believing they are alive.

Rafi pulls a small prayer rug from inside the cab, lays it on the ground, prostrates himself with his head facing north and proceeds to recite the *asr*, or afternoon prayer. The others do the same.

Hashemite shia fighters arrive. Rafi embraces their leader, Abdelmalik.

I prop myself on a promontory and scan the horizon with binoculars. The MiGs are gone. No sign of the Predator. The two columns are heading east, back toward Sanaa.

Haji again has been in contact with his cohorts, those who fed the wrong coordinates to the CIA, who, in turn, used that information to direct their drone unknowingly to kill Handley.

Haji's eyes are wide, a big smile emerges. "My agents say, Yemenis are calling off the assault. The American boss is dead. So, they order troops to go back, MiGs return to base. End of operation!"

I put the binoculars down and stand looking out on the jagged massifs of the Haraz Mountains. So beautiful.

CHAPTER THIRTY-FOUR
ARLINGTON, VIRGINIA

As the six stout percherons draw the caisson slowly to the burial place, the Navy escort platoon presents arms. The six enlisted-man casket team bears the flag-draped coffin to the gravesite, sets it down gently and carefully secures Old Glory. A military chaplain performs the service and pays homage to "the noble sacrifices of his generation, the 'Greatest Generation', in protecting our country from dictators and hateful ideologies." The brilliant picture-perfect autumn day is punctured by the *crack* of rifle volleys from seven sailors, three in quick and precision-drilled succession. Startled birds scatter skyward in all directions. A moment later, a bugler plays taps. The NCO-in-charge oversees the ritualistic folding of the flag, then presents it to an ancient and frail woman seated at graveside.

"This flag is presented on behalf of a grateful nation as a token of our appreciation for the honorable and faithful service rendered by your loved one," he says as the old woman accepts his offering.

The escort platoon snaps to attention, turns and marches away, leaving a lone seaman to hold vigil over the dead veteran until he is interred.

Blair Evans had followed his old friend Jared Loomis's example and departed this earth quietly in his sleep. Service as a WWII combat Navy lieutenant entitled him to burial at Arlington National Cemetery with military honors.

The trial and Congressional inquiries had to have broken the old man, quickening his slide into the grave.

David Rosenstern, District Attorney for Manhattan, used an already high-profile case to make maximum political hay and raise his own profile in a naked quest to become Attorney General. He convened a grand jury to investigate Evans's and DeFalco's ties to politicians and organized crime. Additional indictments were drawn up for multiple violations of campaign finance laws.

"Mr. Evans. The Federal Bureau of Investigation finds that you made $15 million in profits from bank stock you purchased with an unsecured loan from First Eagle Petroleum's financial arm while you served as board chairman of that company, which grew to become the tenth largest diversified oil company in the United States. How do you explain this?" Rosenstern demanded.

"Uhm. I-I-I…I-I-I…Yes, er, I mean no. Ahh." Evans shakes his head as if trying to cast off a net caught around his brain. Under the glare of courtroon lights, he stares up at the stern DA. "It was a difficult situation…they said it was alright. They…they…" The old man cannot hold his train of thought. He gives up, lowering and slowly shaking his head.

The grand jury issued indictments against Evans, DeFalco and a host of other players from the current as well as the previous administration. The U.S. Justice Department opened its own investigation. Evans's assets in New York, where he kept the bulk of his investments, were frozen.

The "Report to the Judiciary Committee of the United States Senate" stated that a key strategy of "First Eagle's secret pursuit of oil resources in the Caspian Basin was its aggressive use of a series of prominent Americans," Evans among them. Evans, who prided himself on a lifetime of selfless public service and meticulously ethical conduct, summed up his predicament when he glumly told a reporter from the *New York Times*, "In the eyes of the nation, I appear either to be stupid or venal." In fact, it became clear during his appearances before Congress and federal court that the old man had early signs of dementia or Alzheimer's as he stammered, went blank or sat silently in the face of vigorous questioning.

Dupe or puppeteer? We'll never know.

Middle East peace cannot be secured without the active and willing commitment of both the Israelis and Palestinians... the commentator drones on.

I wince and grab for the peto bismol every time I see Croswell's smug face on Fox, CNN and MSNBC lending his learned opinion as a Talking Head on the foreign policy issues of the day. Taking his cue straight from Watergate players, Croswell found God, devoted time to charitable endeavors, wrote an autobiography, then a novel and, finally, sold himself to a host of business security consultancies, which have made him a wealthy man. The icing on his cake is his successful launch of a career as a TV pundit.

His TV adventures, however, didn't start off auspiciously. At the height of the inquiries and trials, each day, TV news showed a slight variation on the same ritual: William Croswell and his defense team doing the *Alphonse and Gaston* routine at the mammoth doors of the E. Barrett Prettyman United States Courthouse on Constitution Avenue, a stone's throw from the Capitol. Their plastic grins while juggling take-out cups of designer coffee belied the depth and breadth of Croswell's crimes.

"CIA KILLS AGENT OUT TO KILL OTHER AGENT," "CIA AGENTS EXPOSE ABUSES, CORRUPTION," "CIA INVESTIGATION REVEALS OIL MONEY FOR CAMPAIGN SCANDAL." The headlines became richer by the day, implicating Evans, DeFalco, Norfolk, members of Congress as well as administration officials and oil industry executives and lobbyists.

Larry O'Connor and I spent hours on the Hill testifying about TALISMAN's betrayal, the subterfuge to get a U.S.-financed trans-Central Asian oil pipeline to the Arabian Sea built through Afghanistan and Pakistan. This scenario would bring Croesus-like wealth for the oil companies, back-channel cash to politicians and American political and economic supremacy in Central Asia at Russia's expense. It would also force our Afghan allies to share power with the Taliban so pipelines could be built and our troops finally withdrawn. Machiavelli, Metternich and other past practitioners of cynical power diplomacy would be awed.

Following a grand jury investigation, Special Counsel Edmund Mulcahey indicted Croswell on six counts: one count of manslaughter, one count of violating the Intelligence Identities Protection Act, one count of obstruction of justice, two counts of making false statements to agents of the FBI, and two counts of perjury in his testimony before the grand jury.

I was called to testify at his trial. During the entire proceedings, day after day, week after week, Croswell sat composed, always exhibiting an enigmatic buddha-like smile on his face. He answered questions from the prosecutor crisply, matter-of-factly, with no emotion. He made no eye contact with me nor with anyone else who didn't directly question him. I couldn't help but admire the man for his self-control, his discipline.

His high-powered defense team, fueled with an outsized defense fund fed by magnanimous political contributors and armed with reams of declassified documents, state-of-the-art presentation technology and a bevy of the best private sector intelligence expert witnesses money could buy, pushed the line of "friendly fire" to account for Handley's death. The late Kyle Handley, of course, was a "rogue officer" acting out of misguided or mentally unbalanced motives.

I, on the other hand, was painted as a congenitally rebellious officer, incapable of sticking to orders, a loner with a drinking problem, a self-styled misogynist with a string of broken relationships, one of the CIA's worst, who should have been fired long ago.

In the end, Croswell was found guilty on three of the six counts. Mulcahey stated, "The jury was clearly convinced beyond a reasonable doubt that the defendant had lied and obstructed justice in a significant manner ... I do not expect to file any further charges." Croswell was acquitted of manslaughter and divulging the identity (to al-Jazeera) of an American intelligence officer, i.e., me. For the guilty counts, he was sentenced to thirty months in prison and fined $250,000. In addition, he was ordered to perform four-hundred hours of community service.

I decided Croswell wasn't evil. He was simply typical. Yet another ambitious Beltway mediocrity out to grab all the glory he could at whatever the cost. But the question is begged: To whom did Croswell answer? Who put him up to it? Sanctioned his vile acts? Or, in the end, protected him? Mulcahey had also stated that "a cloud hangs over the White House."

Perhaps a clue can be found in a trail of White House documents obtained through the Freedom of Information Act in connection with the President's commutation of Croswell's prison sentence. All of the reports to the President on the case, including memos of the White House Counsel recommending commutation, bear the signature of Special Assistant to the President for Political Affairs, Jason Mariner.

Scandal, even an inherited one, is to be avoided at all

costs lest a President be stained or side-tracked from his ambitious agenda for the country.

So, the Dodge administration survives. The wagons circled to protect the President. And a hefty popularity-laden teflon coating on John Dodge combined with deft spinmeistering limited the damage, albeit at the inevitable cost of majorities in both houses of Congress after the next general election with the guarantee of years of political gridlock.

Another axiom of Washington politics is "shit rolls downhill" when truth runs for the exits. And there's nothing like a dead man to take all the blame. Hence, Kyle Handley's's cold corpse, or what was left of it, became a lightning rod of culpability. The finger-pointing toward his grave channeled much of the guilt to that "rogue CIA agent." The Ultimate Fall Guy. The Congressional hearings, rich in posturing and sanctimony, petered out as the war drums for the next gathering crisis beat louder. The country needed strong leadership for the latest clear and present danger.

Aonde o vento é brisa
Onde não haja quem possa
Com a nossa felicidade
Vamos brindar a vida meu bem...

The care-free, sensuous lyrics of Vanessa da Mata flow through the phone as freely as the waves crashing on Copacabana Beach.

"Frank? DeFalco?" I shout into the receiver.

"Yeah. It's me. Frank. Your eating buddy."

"Where are you?" I shout.

The music and party noise drown out the voice at the other end.

"Frank. Can you find a quieter spot?" I yell.

A moment later, Vanessa is history and I hear the throaty, Brooklyn-accented voice of Frank DeFalco.

"Listen. I want you to have dinner with me. The food here is outta this world! And so are the babes!! I know this great place where they cook seafood right at your table…"

"Whoa! Frank! Where the hell are you anyway?"

"Rio. You can catch a flight that'll get you here in…"

"Slow down, Frank. You're in Brazil?"

"Yeah."

"What's going on, Frank?"

"I've had it with all the bullshit."

Frank DeFalco's First Eagle Petroleum was found by American and British regulators to be engaged in money laundering, bribery, arms trafficking, tax evasion, smuggling and illicit financial and real estate transactions. The conglomerate was also found to have at least $100 million unaccounted for.

"So, I says, shove it and took the next plane down here before the Feds could get me."

"Frank. They'll get you anyway. Come back."

"The hell they will. I'm Brazilian and it's against their law to extradite their own citizens."

"What do you mean you're Brazilian, Frank? You were born in New York."

"My old lady was born down here. Folks emigrated from Italy after the war. Married my father. Moved to New York. Came back when I was a kid. I went to school here. Then we moved back to Brooklyn. Long story. Yeah. I'm *Brasileiro*, all right. Now, back to this restaurant…"

I can't stifle a chuckle, nor the uncontrollable laughter that erupts from within. I can't stop myself.

He skirts around the dance floor with a nimbleness seldom seen in a male crowding sixty. In his bright red barber shop quartet outfit, the man is in perfect musical synch with the muscle-toned, scantily-clad bombshell who is his dance partner. Hips undulating to the seductive rhythms of the samba, Robert Norfolk, now twenty pounds lighter, is a happy man, reborn into a dimension about as opposite as one can get from the stiff, conforming culture of the nation's capital: *Dancing with the Stars.*

"I'm either insane or stupid," Norfolk says on *Jimmy Kimmel Live*, "But I'm having the time of my life!"

Not since the Monica Lewinsky scandal had the tabloids had such a field day exposing the sexual shenanigans of a senior government official. The mainstream press joined in. Blitzer and Olbermann joined Grace and van Susteren in devoting countless hours to Shareen McCahill's lurid accounts as a mistress to the powerful, specifically CIA Director Robert S. Norfolk. Yes, Shareen decided to spill the beans after all, reluctantly agreeing to come forward and, ahem, bare all after *Penthouse*, aggressively pursuing its first amendment rights, made a munificent, yet undisclosed, monetary offer in exchange for an exclusive in-depth interview accompanied by a multipage photo spread of the ex-CIA secretary in all her glory. The cover featured Shareen clad only in an unbuttoned trench coat, Versace sunglasses, fedora and blood-red lipstick. *Femme fatale par extraordinaire.*

Norfolk, at first, denied Shareen's allegations of being his sexual plaything, having his baby and being paid by him to keep silent. Then a Krakatoa-scale series of blonde bimbo eruptions brought out more salacious tales from other women. Shari, Shareen's immediate predecessor, was the next to break her silence. Others followed, each making her own separate deals with assorted publications and TV shows, ranging from the gossipy to the pornographic.

This tidal wave of revelation and embarrassment, abetted by demands for a DNA paternity test and congressional hearings, sent the nation's number one spook into immediate political exile after he issued a terse two-sentence resignation letter to the President. The investigations actually exonerated Norfolk, who was revealed to be a clueless, hands-off, vainglorious and incompetent DCI who cut Croswell all the slack he wanted. And, of course, Norfolk fell for Taliban chief Omar's ruse about al-Zawahiri being dead. The fingerprints of the severed hands were not those of al-Qaeda's master, leaving Norfolk with multiple layers of egg on his fat face. It's hard to figure what's the worse fate in America's post-Watergate political culture: the martyred, but redeemable, criminal, or the terminal national laughing stock.

But that's all in the past. A regular on the talk and quiz show circuits, and a public speaker much in demand, even at twenty grand a pop, Norfolk indeed is having the time of his life.

CHAPTER THIRTY-FIVE

Nemsky signals that he wants to meet me at the Whole Foods in Georgetown. We're not to rub shoulders among the hoi-polloi of mid-market Safeway, as in the past, but with the upwardly mobile tempeh-and-endamame bean set. Perhaps the Nemsky's now have an enhanced grocery budget. Hmm. The intel analyst's mind overlooks no detail.

I find Nemsky focused intently on a pile of machengo cheese, an empty wire-mesh shopping basket slung on one elbow. He greets me with a slight grin and a handshake. He invites me for a coffee at the small store café. No stealthful tradecraft techniques. He clearly doesn't care who sees us; Whole Foods is just three blocks from the Russian Embassy.

He orders a soy milk cappuccino for himself and a whole milk one for me.

"The Russian diet is atrocious, as you know," he says. "I am learning to change." He raises his cup to me. I reciprocate. An awkward minute of silence follows.

"Sergei. I'm so sorry about Anya…" I begin.

He raises a hand. "Please. Thank you for your help."

"I did what I could, but it was too late. Croswell upset the apple cart sending in that oaf Eddy Frechette to pitch you. I had just finalized arrangements independently for Anya to be treated when they barged in."

"Thank you for tipping me off beforehand about Mr. Frechette. I was ready for him. Haji is very discreet in passing highly sensitive messages back and forth," Sergei says.

"Funny thing about this country. To get help for another human being in dire straits, all you need to do is to ask. I asked the hospital directly, gave them the paperwork and they said yes immediately. Anya would've been treated. And at no cost to you."

Nemsky nods his head. "I know. I know. Please. Anya…" He clears his throat and takes a deep breath. "Anya had an incurable disease. Any treatment would have merely given her a little more time. That's all. My wife is a believer. She says our daughter is now in a better place, in heaven.

"I get through this terrible thing by knowing I could help save another person's daughter. Your daughter. It is very meaningful to me," Nemsky continues. He lifts his downcast eyes to mine. "Cherish her. Keep her safe."

"I owe her life to you, Sergei. Without the intel you fed to Haji and your behind-the-scenes interventions with Yemenis, Laurie wouldn't be here. And likely neither would I. You risked much in doing that. If caught, you'd be in a dungeon now."

"I hold to my promises," he says. "To you just as I had to Vince. Our children transcend politics. We helped each other and betrayed no one."

"As it always should be," I say.

"As it always should be," he repeats.

Another minute passes without a word said.

"But let me ask you this, Sergei. I know that you had made alternative arrangements for Anya. In China. What was that all about?"

Nemsky takes a long sip of his coffee. "You know, cappuccino with soy milk is like vegetarian 'sausage.' Just not the real thing." He puts his cup down. He purses his lips and carefully ponders what he is about to say. He directs his blue eyes intently on me.

"Irina. She initiated that. She met a very nice gentleman from the Chinese embassy at one of those countless diplomatic functions we must attend. He knew about Anya and offered to help. The military hospital in Beijing has been doing some wonderful things with stem cell replacement. They treat kids like Anya at no cost. They are exceptional."

"And?"

"And by the time I had learned of Irina's actions and involvement with Mr. Wu, that is, *Colonel* Wu, we were in deep. Too deep. To protect my wife, and to save my Anya, I decided to go ahead even at the risk of being caught, using my special professional skills, shall we say, to cover our tracks, keep it secret from my own people. Colonel Wu, a true and discreet professional himself, assisted me in this. But, of course, there was a price."

I cock my head and furrow my brow. "Are you telling me...?"

"That I sold out to the Chinese?" he replies.

"Yeah."

"First, let me ask you, Harry, what is your situation with your own agency now?"

"Oh, well. When I returned, my name was cleared. I'm exonerated of all the made-up charges Croswell had tried to frame me with. But, in true Washington fashion, I'm washed up. The stain of accusation will never go away. All their assurances of 'restoring' my reputation are hollow. I'm back teaching tradecraft to junior officers. Way out in left field, out of sight and permanently sidelined until I get the hint and retire of my own accord."

"What will you do?"

I shrug. "Spend more time with Laurie. You know what she wants to be after finishing college?"

"What?"

"A spook. Like her dad."

Nemsky smiles and shakes his head. "You would think she'd have learned something. Had she lived, I would have counseled my Anya to help other people. Medicine. Social work. Anything but...but this." He spreads his hands to include the both of us.

"And you?" I ask. "You meet me here, out in the wide open, three blocks from your office."

Nemsky frowns. "I no longer care. I also don't know what I will do. We each must find our own way. The light of my life is now gone and is irreplaceable. Irina tells me God will guide me. Who knows?" he says with a shrug.

"So?" I say.

"Ah, yes. The Chinese. Since we both are, as you Americans say, 'trying to find ourselves,' I will make a confession." Nemsky frowns at his coffee, makes a long reach to the counter, grabs a decanter of half-and-half and, with a mischievous smile, pours it into his cappuccino. "Yes, I have been selling secrets to Beijing. But I have not betrayed Russia."

I shake my head, puzzled. "I don't get it."

Nemsky leans forward, looks to the right, then to the left. Still sporting the mischievous smile, he says in almost a whisper, "I've been selling *your* country's secrets to them... in return for their helping us with Anya. That was the price I paid."

"What?"

"All of those classified U.S. documents about Caspian Sea oil I showed you. About how your government and oil companies were colluding to take over that area at our expense. I gave them to Wu. Who, by the way, was most grateful."

"The Chinese are signing contracts left and right out there. Moscow and Washington are in fits. They're being aced out in this twenty-first century version of the Great

Game. China is going to dominate that region. New game. And it was you…you who facilitated it."

"No. I played only a small part. The Chinese dragon is emerging. She will surpass all of us. Her time in the sun has come. It is inevitable."

"And you got away with it."

"My Anya is dead. My interest in the bargain failed. But Moscow did award me the *Medal Za Otlichye v Sluzhbe*, Distinguished Service Medal, for performing so well in Washington. Ironic, isn't it?"

I laugh. "'Ironic' indeed. Life is full of ironies."

We rise and shake hands.

"Good luck, Sergei."

"Good luck, Harry."

CHAPTER THIRTY-SIX

I sleep fitfully, left each night to struggle alone with my thoughts and demons. A goal-free life of loneliness confronts me. I drift like a nomad. What to do?

On this night, I manage to fall into slumber, at least for a while. Two figures take shape. Female figures. One fair, one dark, both beautiful. The long blond hair of the first swirls with the circular motion of the devil wind in a beguiling way that alternately covers and reveals the pallid face of the woman in the sheer white lace gown. Cammy beckons. The devil-may-care eyes and mischievous smile tell me to hurry. Hurry. Hurry. Before it's too late. Before you're too old. Before you're dead. Take a chance. Life is full of risks. Grab on for the ride. Come what may. She throws her head back in her trademark laugh. Ha! Come lover boy! What have you got to lose but your manhood!

But the other figure catches up, arms and open palms outward. Straight black hair falls to her strong bronzed shoulders and full breasts. A simple leather frock covers this woman's rich compact body. Gold bands on her upper arms, a gold and turquoise demi-crown on her head. A Mayan princess. Roni. She emits a direct, no-nonsense gaze that says, "Believe not in illusions. Believe in me." Love. Family. Eternal truths. Simplicity. These will get you through life. With me. With me.

I bolt upright, shake my head to clear it. What is real? What isn't?

I jump out of bed. I know what I must do. It's 3:00 am. I'll have to wait. I dress, go downstairs and sit on my back patio, staring at the trees, wondering what I've been doing all my life.

The sun comes up, the world comes alive. Birds chirp. The roar of traffic begins at the onset of rush hour. I'm out the door and join the automotive fray, heading out into the Virginia suburbs. It's slow, stop-and-go, pushing through the concrete atherosclerosis that constitutes the capital's road system.

Past Arlington, toward Falls Church. Sterile sprawl. Host to utilitarian people who value convenience over charm. America's essence.

I pull into the parking lot. Blake's is open for business. It hasn't changed, right down to the same sad sack bartender getting ready for the day. The same stale, over-air conditioned atmosphere. The same dated decor. The same everyman-everywoman clientele.

I take a seat. A young black man comes to take my order. "My name is Nadif. What can I get for you?" he says in Somali-accented English.

"Hi. Uh. Actually, I was wondering if...uh, Dolores was still working here," I say.

"Who?"

"Dolores. Latina gal. About this tall. Nice figure."

"Hey, Al!" the waiter shouts to the bartender. "You know a Dolores working here?"

"Yeah, sure. Why? Who wants to know?"

"This customer. Sorry, I don't know your name, sir."

"Brennan. Harry Brennan."

Al looks at me a moment, then recognizes me. He comes over and gestures to the young waiter that he may go.

"Yeah. Hi. You knew Dolores, huh?"

"Well, sort of. Actually, I was a...friend of her sister's."

"Yeah, Roni. Great gal." He shakes his head sadly. "I remember you used to date her. Am I right?"

"Right."

Al seats himself across from me. His dark features display concern.

"Dolores. She moved away, right after…"

"After what?"

Al's eyes are sad. "After she got the news. Roni. She got hit in Iraq. One of those roadside bomb deals. Young girl like that. Had so much to live for. Happened about three weeks ago. Shitty war."

"Wha'?"

"Yeah. I'm sorry. Real sorry." Al rises, places a consoling hand on my shoulder and returns to the bar.

I stumble out of Blake's. I drive with no destination in mind. The suburbs turn into the exurbs. Things open up. McMansions give way to horse farms. A half-hour later, a rustic sign hanging by two chains from an old oak announces, "Colchester Wood."

My God. Is this coincidence? Or did my subconscious mind take me here? I pull into the stone driveway. I drive up the meandering way until I see a man running toward me from the right side. I stop. The man is wearing the basic green uniform of a caretaker.

"Can I help you?" he says challengingly.

"I'm looking for the owner," I reply.

"Sorry, buddy. The owner is in Falls Church. Corner of Lee Highway and North Westmoreland. Virginia Commerce Bank."

"What?"

"You heard me. Virginia Commerce Bank. You need to see anybody, or wanna buy this place, you go there. Number's in the phone book."

"But wait. This place belongs to the Loomis family," I reply.

"Not no more. Bank foreclosed on it last week. Now, I gotta ask ya'll to leave…"

"Yeah. Sure, sure." I turn around and get back on the road.

At a stop light, I shut my eyes tight, trying to make sense of what I've heard today. My world has turned upside down.

Honk! Honk! Honk! The light is green. Those behind me aren't interested in joining in my contemplation. I step on the gas, back to the city.

"There are no masterminds," she says. "They're all stupid." Cammy has lost weight, her face is gaunt. She has a nervous tick around her left eye. The oversized designer sunglasses don't conceal it. A plain housemaid's kerchief covers her limp hair, the radiant sheen gone from it as well as her face. She appears nervous, jumpy, sitting opposite me in the French bistro on Wisconsin Ave., Georgetown's main drag. It's a piebald sky, dark clouds against bright blue.

"Funny how the world perceives every pratfall and dumb-ass action coming out of this city as part of some clever, elaborate conspiracy hatched by evil wizards in the chambers of power. If they only knew. If they only knew." Her voice is laced with bitterness and remorse. She takes a sip of her ginger ale.

Cammy came to me in my darkest moment. I'd been getting so little sleep that I'd begun to hallucinate. Visions of the Hindu Kush, desert sky, limbless children, drone aircraft, Pushtun warriors, *qat*-chewing Yemeni beggars, Heinrich Croswell Himmler, my old man, the White House on fire, my high school sweetheart all tumbled in my brain fighting for attention. Jameson's did nothing but exacerbate the condition and escaping my house, going to work did nothing to alleviate the torment.

Cammy turned up on my doorstep this morning. Now we're here together. Two zombies catching up on old times.

I'm glad she showed up though. I'd read she'd summarily quit her post as ambassador in London a couple of weeks ago. I knew she'd come back to me. Hoped for it. Dreamt of it. But it's different now. Two survivors holding onto each other, more out of necessity than devotion.

"The true masterminds are money and power. It's as simple as that. They drive everything in this place. Tempted with either, people will do anything, *anything*," she continues.

"Are you talking about yourself?" I ask.

"All of us. And I was one of the worst." She looks away at the traffic and goes silent.

I take a gulp of my double espresso. I found caffeine to be a less destructive vice than Irish whisky. I place my hand on hers. She turns her face back to me. The old mischievous smile returns fleetingly. A flash of the old incandescent beauty.

"Oh, Harry. How I missed you. I thought of you every day."

I lean forward, kiss her on the cheek. "We can start over. Make it work."

She shakes her head. "You know, I used to think I was happy, what with Jared's money, the power, prestige, connections, attention." She smiles again. "But, you know, I think I'm feeling happier being broke. Blair Evans actually did me a favor by mismanaging my money. Brings me right back to my roots."

"Ah, yes. Cammy-Lou," I say.

She looks at me with a start. "How...how did you know?"

"I'm CIA, remember? We know all," I say theatrically.

She smiles again. The sun breaks through the clouds and brightens her face.

"Bull," she retorts.

"So, what will you do now?" I ask.

"I..." She pauses, looks down at her hands, catches

her thoughts. She takes off the shades and the kerchief and shakes her hair free, then looks back at me. Her face is serene and vulnerable. Gone are the pride and sass. "I had...have a little girl. Um, gee, she's not so little any more. Nineteen last April. I left her in West Virginia a long, long time ago. I'm going back to find her. Whatever it takes. I'm going to find her. My...my daughter." She dabs tears with the kerchief.

I nod with understanding and place my hand back onto hers. She grasps it tightly.

"Be good, Harry. Be good."

EPILOGUE

As CIA director, Robert Gates is reputed to have said, "When an intelligence officer smells flowers, he looks around for a coffin." A follow-up would be, "It is in a cemetery that an intelligence officer feels most at home." The solitude, anonymity and security of a graveyard are what a...spook... craves most.

For the first time in a long time I feel all three sentiments amid the acres of granite headstones set in a blanket of serene green. The brilliant sun and gentle breeze lull me further into a sense of comfort and ease.

I ponder life as I walk among the dead. I wonder about the lives they led. Were they meaningful? Were they squandered? Were they with purpose? Or thrown away? My own?

I ponder whether there is a God. If there is, would God really foreordain people who spend their adult lives ferreting out the secrets of others with the aim of damaging or destroying them? How perverse we are. We create saints, scientists, artists, philosophers. And, as if as antidote, we also create murderers, harlots, thieves and spies. And the latter sometimes encompass the former three. I try to make meaning of it and shake my head.

But I am determined to make up for a questionable past, one devoted to chasing nightmares and turning them onto others. I've found a measure of serenity since leaving the CIA. My devotion to my daughter, and her to me, accounts for much of it. But also being free of the old hypocrisies, the treadmill existence, the narcissistic ambitions of others makes me feel alive for the first time in a very long time. Especially here, among the nonliving.

I lose track of time as I linger at Vince's grave. He claimed we could never wean ourselves off the "juice" – the excitement of intel work. If anybody could reconcile the kind of work we did with life's meaning, it was Vince. I wonder if he felt that way in the end. I'll never know.

A kaleidoscope of memories streams through my brain like a movie. Adventure, history, mission. Vince and I shared these. Escaping rampaging Somali warlords, plotting the Soviet Union's demise, enduring Saddam's imprisonment. Were these meaningless?   Did we actually accomplish something?   Did we, in our wilderness of mirrors, make things better for others?   Perhaps I'll have more time than Vince did to reflect on it.

The wind picks up and ruffles the fresh flowers lying against the headstone. Ah, Vince.

VINCENT A. COLLETTA
"OUR TRIBE LOST"

*   *   *

CENTRAL INTELLIGENCE AGENCY
TOP S E C R E T 221305Z JUL 11 STAFF
CITE DIRECTOR 827101
TO: IMMEDIATE ALL NESA STATIONS
WNINTEL RYBAT CATOMIC
SUBJECT: CONTAINING IRAN: "OPERATION
   KEYSTONE"
REF: DIRECTOR 727899 (NOTAL)

1. PER PRESIDENTIAL FINDING DTD

07/12/2008, HQS INFORMS ALL NESA CHIEFS OF STATION OF CREATION OF "OPERATION KEYSTONE." PER REF, HIGHEST PRIORITY WILL BE GIVEN TO COUNTERING ISLAMIC REPUBLIC OF IRAN'S EFFORTS TO ACQUIRE AND BUILD A NUCLEAR ARMS PROGRAM, TO INCLUDE THE FOLLOWING:

A.) AGGRESSIVE ACQUISITION OF INTEL ON IRI'S NUCLEAR PROGRAM

B.) INTERDICTION OF NUCLEAR MATERIALS AND KNOWLEDGE FROM ILLICIT SUPPLIERS

C.) DISINFORMATION COUNTERMEASURES AGAINST IRI'S PROPAGANDA THROUGH A VARIETY OF CHANNELS

D.) COVERT MEASURES TO DESTABILIZE IRI'S CURRENT LEADERSHIP

E.) COVERT AID TO ANTI-REGIME IRANIAN EXILE GROUPS

F.) INTEL AND COUNTERMEASURES SUPPORT TO DOD FOR OPERATION PYTHON GOLD CLOSE-IN WAR GAMES IN ARABIAN SEA AND PERSIAN GULF

2. INSTRUCTIONS TO INDIVIDUAL STATIONS TO FOLLOW SEPTEL.

3. NO FILE. ALL TOP SECRET.